MORE PRAISE FOR 31 PARADISO

"Rhoda Huffey writes like an angel who saw what happened in the garden and still remained an optimist. On each page of Francine Didwell's story there is an original joy, many times rescued from the powers of her religious family and many from Francine's amazed view of the world. At times her empathy feels like X-ray glasses and all the ordinary things in her teeming cosmos of Venice Beach glow. She can hear her dog's thoughts and her cat is her AA sponsor. This is a special book. With all its signs and wonders, there is tap dancing too." — Ron Carlson, author of *Five Skies*

"Huffey's third person is pure and flexible in a way that gives us access to Francine with vivid, large directness, but also to the animals and people around her. Everyone, and even objects have their own soul and subjectivity. Every single one of Huffey's characters is terrific. The family dinners are as fun as they are treacherous. There is something very 'now' about this novel, despite it being set in the early '90s. Maybe the world is finally ready for this book." — Varley O'Connor, author of *The Welsh Fasting Girl*

"Rhoda Huffey writes with an unforgettable voice—astringent, funny, ironic and whimsical. This voice is perfect for 31 Paradiso. Her subject is the crazy quilt of humans in Venice, California, and the human condition as seen through the lens of overpriced real estate and middle-aged passion. Jesus, of course, is never far from the action. Reading 31 Paradiso is like hearing a great story from an old friend." — Mark Childress, author of *Crazy in Alabama* and *Georgia Bottoms*

ALSO BY RHODA HUFFEY

The Hallelujah Side

31 PARADISO

A NOVEL BY

RHODA HUFFEY

DELPHINIUM BOOKS

31 PARADISO

Printed in the United States of America

For information, address DELPHINIUM BOOKS, INC.,
16350 Ventura Boulevard, Suite D
PO Box 803
Encino, CA 91436

Library of Congress Cataloguing-in-Publication Data is available on request.

ISBN 978-1-953002-35-8

23 24 25 26 27 LBC 5 4 3 2 1

First Paperback Edition: October 2023

Jacket and interior design by Colin Dockrill

FOR BILL McDONALD

1
SIR DUCK

The Great Duck Massacre of 1993 occurred the day Francine Ephesians Didwell moved to Venice Beach from Orange County. This was Venice, California, the famous beach, not Venice, Italy. Abbot Kinney, a tall man and real estate developer, had in 1905 conceived of Venice of America as a kind of snob amusement park: a city by the beach with lectures and symphonies and gondolas floating everywhere. It was to be a tiny Venice, Italy. Perhaps it was the light or the electromagnetic vibrations in the air, but in this Venice, people felt good even doing nothing.

The snob amusement park had briefly caught fire. Real estate lots were sold, and the wealthy built their houses on the sand in the first block from the boardwalk. Fat (not skinny) sidewalks cut the beach at right angles. It was extremely thrilling. They were called walk streets—no cars allowed, only people on foot—so people could congregate and not be lonely. They had names like Park, Plume, Breeze, Paradiso. The help of color had little houses several blocks inland. These were modest, and the black people who lived in them could walk to work beside the ocean. This was the Venice on the west edge of America, the amusement park with flair, the one that offered breeding (see symphonies and lectures); the one that was known for its crazy people and gang warfare by the time Francine arrived eighty-plus years later. Many blue-collar workers lived here too, especially those who liked to surf, but they kept a low profile and stayed out of the news and went about their business and kept their boards where they could grab them at a moment's notice. They could be seen each early morning before work, heading for the ocean, and again before dinner, moving down the walk streets with their wet suits half on. In the summer, tourists flocked here from all over the world—but a travel destination, like a prophet, has no honor in its own country.

Where the debris meets the sea, said the better-dressed types in Los Angeles.

Rent control, exploded Mr. Didwell in a flash of moral outrage, and hit the table.

Francine stood on the twelve-foot-wide sidewalk named Paradiso Avenue in her moving clothes, shorts and a T-shirt, with no makeup except red lipstick and medium-long blond hair. She was of medium height. Her valuables, the cat and dog and a sturdy plastic bag with kibble and three plastic bowls, were close at hand. The cat was small and delicate, with bones like matchsticks, and wore a red collar. The dog was a Lhasa Apso. It was a sound location. The cat and dog and she stood staring, reluctant to go inside the new house and leave the slightly balmy air that made you feel like you could float, one of several physical properties of Venice, the others being a constant slight breeze and a certain quality of light along the beach.

The house itself was plain, but the yard had two trees. The first was a large Italian stone pine with a flattop haircut, its bare lower limbs spiraling off in all directions and covering the front yard, property line to property line. The second tree stood at the corner of the house on the side by the ocean, a Sierra juniper whose top limbs rose beyond the height of the house and looked like flames against the sky, but green with powder-blue berries. At the bottom, it completely obscured the front side window. Behind the house was a building with four small rental units. Francine stood looking at the square brick box, circa 1905, one of the original Venice properties. The whole front of the house could be flung open because there were two sets of French doors with two corresponding sets of art deco security screens you could swing wide so you lived for all intents and purposes like Rima, Child of the Jungle. Francine felt goose bumps of new beginnings. Someone had left an empty flight cage in the yard, and on top of this Francine planned to place her exquisite lavender geranium, which often had babies. But she was no gardener.

Escrow had closed at 10:05 this morning.

From the gate where Francine stood at number 31, you could see the ocean, a dark blue band so close you could hit the water in two minutes running. The cat and dog and woman didn't move. The slight breeze ruffled their hair/fur. The street was oddly marked by a meandering red line of paint from top to bottom, and this was a happy accident. The story went that a house painter had started home after a long day and had failed to see that his gallon can was leaking until the top of the first block, when he looked back and said, "Fuck it." He was exhausted.

The sky was blue, the red line was a dark red, blue and pink flowers stuck out over fences and shone against the water, and Francine stood there with her cat and dog and plastic bag of food and three bowls with broad bases. She had the essentials.

"Here I plant my flag," said Francine.

She had just lifted the gate latch, the cat against her chest and the dog beside her, a ceremonial moment, when a well-kept man with glasses hurried down fat Paradiso Avenue and practically bumped into her. In his hands he held a brown paper bag, and in the brown paper bag something was panicked.

Quack quack, the bag said.

"Oh dear," Francine answered. "What's happening?"

The man told her that the State of California, possibly in cahoots with the United States government, had picked this day to eliminate all the ducks in the canals of Venice. *Quack quack!* said an ordinary cardboard box in passing, carried by a wild-eyed woman. The ducks had lived in Venice Beach since 1905, and now their offspring owned the Venice canals just blocks away, ducks floating on the pretty water, ducks waddling along the narrow sidewalks that bordered the water, ducks naturally not moving so that you had to go around them if you weren't a duck. This made sense, as the ducks had right-of-way due to seniority. Even the Hells Angels who had lived here in the 1960s—now there were only stragglers—stepped aside with their big boots in order not to interrupt the ducks with their duck families, little ducklings trailing behind, everybody quacking. Now four ducks on a red wagon quacked as they went past, a laundry basket over them.

Quack, one added.

Apparently the State of California, in dark congress with the dark forces, had decided to exterminate the ducks because they carried a disease, or might carry one and might infect other birds. Or perhaps it was just stupidity. Perhaps it was a germophobic city employee, or perhaps it was a business scheme to fill in the canals with high-rise apartments. Under rent control, you couldn't evict tenants to tear down the old houses. Perhaps getting rid of the ducks would break the Venetians' spirits, and they would leave to make room for normal people.

But the whole community was in full revolt on the morning Francine's escrow closed in Venice. Ducks quacked from duffle bags and out car windows on Pacific Avenue. Ducks quacked from sinks. Ducks quacked from bathtubs.

Quack quack, said a guitar case, jogging.

Francine hesitated. The ducks weren't her family. They were strangers outside her purview. This was a sacred moment, if a house and a woman and a cat and dog were like a marriage. It wasn't her problem. When she went in through the yard and up three stairs and turned the key and put the kibble down and drew the water, she relaxed. She smiled. Tonight, she and the cat and dog would sleep on blankets on the floor—the furniture was coming in the morning—with actual Venice all around them. Finally they weren't in Kansas!

She was opening all four front doors to let in the balmy air when she heard the first scream from a pedestrian. She dropped the cat and locked the art deco security screen doors and flew back out to Paradiso. Animal Control Truck #54 rolled silently along Pacific Avenue, no warning siren. The ducks and ducklings had no idea what was coming. Short blocks away they strolled through the canals. The ducks out for their morning sun were going to be murdered.

"Call Greenpeace," said someone.

At the top of Paradiso more trucks were rolling down Pacific Avenue, then turning left on Venice Boulevard to the canals. People ran down Paradiso, ducks flapping in their arms or duck heads sticking out of their backpacks. Undoubtedly the ducks in the canals kept walking, unperturbed (but perhaps faster), unaware of the threat. *These are seeds we eat, these we don't*, said duck parents to their children.

Across Pacific Avenue at the top of the red line a truck had stopped. Two men holding nets were running after ducks people had dropped, the open back of the truck revealing captured ducks, who felt extremely confused. *What are these four walls, no flowers?* Now more ducks ran, the nets chasing them.

Quack! the ducks said.

"Help!" screamed Francine.

Out of nowhere a duck waddled past her, and she lunged to get it, lunged so hard her hand swung out and her fingers ruffled the duck's feathers. But the duck, although he seemed slow, was just out of reach.

She lunged again.

He waddled forward.

"Duck? I'm trying to help you." She tried to sound like a duck mother.

He ran up Paradiso and she ran after him. At Pacific, he waddled right around a stunned pedestrian. How could he move so fast? Again she lunged. But the duck had powers beyond the powers of imagining. Although Francine was an athlete, each time she sprinted, the duck feet accelerated in a surge of speed that put him slightly out of reach. Was the duck Jesus? He waddled around a corner and past a homeless woman who had three ducks in a shopping cart.

"Sir!" Francine commanded.

The duck catcher's net came out of nowhere and landed over him with such a lightness it seemed incapable of holding him. The duck tried to lift his wings. His eyes darted toward Francine. In the truck, he stood on both feet with the net around him, elegant.

"That's my duck, your honor," she said, improvising fast. Everybody had a heart. "He's a family pet. His name is Eduardo."

The man threw one door closed, and for a moment the duck looked out, eyes alert. The other door slammed shut, but just before it did, Francine put her right hand to her forehead in a salute, one soldier to another.

She needed to find Cyrus's ghost. She got in her blue Miata and shot fifty miles south to Costa Mesa to the house she had sold just this morning. It was Cyrus's favorite spot on earth, and he would probably be there. Her animals were locked into the square brick house in Venice, and had food and water and a view out all four art deco security screen doors.

In the fast lane of the 405 freeway she pressed on the accelerator, top down, hair blowing. Speed was of the essence. The wrecking ball might come at any moment. A developer had bought the property to build six of his condominiums that resembled packets of Saltine crackers. When a fucking SUV cut right in front of her and made her hit the brakes, she smashed the dash with her hand and gave the tinted windows a piece of her mind.

Quack! she shouted.

The Miata surged forward.

On the night of her first date with Cyrus, she had simply stepped out of the Didwell family, a cult of two parents and three siblings. There are quantum leaps. Because Cyrus was some kind of wizard, so that she could relax with him and be herself. Cyrus was medicine. One week after she met him, they left for Alaska, and they stayed gone for good until his stomach forced him to come home and see a Doctor Milhouse, who explained he was dying.

In Costa Mesa, Francine of Venice sped down side streets, and when she screeched around the corner, no wrecking ball had smashed the house to smithereens. It stood thinking the world was normal. The sun shone on the paint, white white, if you knew colors.

She got out and leaned against her car. Her breathing deepened.

This house looked like a farmhouse in Iowa, where she had been happy in childhood, except this house was plopped down in the middle of suburbia. The bright clapboard cascaded down the walls, and there were big windows, and grass on four sides. You half expected to see cows grazing, Angus or Herefords.

Francine pushed forward off the blue Miata and walked across the street and up onto the green grass. When she first met Cyrus, he had scared her, he was so unlike the world she grew up in. She had considered he might be from Mars. For one thing, his nose was gigantic.

"Would you like to have dinner?" Cyrus looked up at her in the restaurant where she was waiting tables, including his. He was a man who made a cardigan look dangerous. He had just said, "Never trust a Christian," and his eyes were ice blue, like a devil's.

His giant eyebrows made her every cell shrink.

"Certainly!" she said. "I would love to!"

Hopeful, Francine halted on the front lawn in Costa Mesa and looked for anything strange, a flash of light or the sound of a stick breaking. Cars passed. A fly buzzed. Cyrus had been quiet since the day after he died, when he broke dishes at a genius rate in their old kitchen. Was Cyrus busy?

"They're killing ducks in Venice!" she cried out in hopes he was listening. "I can't live there! I can't live anywhere."

It was quiet.

On their many trips home from Hoag Hospital, driving slowly to avoid bumps, Francine and Cyrus always stopped to see the white house they would someday buy and live in to their ripe old age. Because he was too weak to drive, she always pulled his half-ton Ford truck up and parked across the street and turned the engine off.

"This place is neat and clean," he liked to say of it.

If it was after dark, light spilled out the open front door where four people sometimes sat at a table playing cards and laughing. Two ceiling fixtures with protruding bulbs shed light on the gamblers. If Cyrus felt strong, the two got out and leaned against the truck and Cyrus crossed his arms.

"I hope I'm here this time next year," Cyrus said.

"Of course you'll be here," Francine said. "You're getting better by the minute."

Not dead yet, his pale eyes looked out at her. "Thank you."

In the fresh air, they stood planning how to get the money.

How do you call a ghost? Cyrus liked to travel, and might be on Pluto, or touring hell. To Cyrus, all phenomena were interesting. On the lawn, no spaceship landed. She sat down on the third front stair of her lost home, keeping her knees together like a lady. In the sun, her face was burning, but she was still. After two hours, she stood up.

You had to pick the mountain you would die on. In the nine years between the time she moved out of the Didwell house and the time she ran away with Cyrus, she had lived in twenty-seven places: the small slum where Cyrus picked her up for dinner, and before that Truxton in Fullerton, and before that the rich Sapphire house on Balboa Island, and before that the cute apartment over the surfers, and before that the Spanish stucco on Lacy Street, and before that the party palace, and before that Queen Anne Hill in Seattle, and before that the air-conditioned duplex in Coral Gables, and before that El Monte, ad nauseam. Each empty space was hopeful when she signed the month-to-month agreement, but by the time she moved the last of her cute clothes in, the air had grown dark in every room, including the bathroom. The Venice house was her last chance to be happy, because she had not one more single solitary change-of-address with the PO in her.

Her key still worked.

A felon, she entered the white house that no longer belonged to her. In the ceiling overhead were the two light fixtures, and Francine decided to steal them. No wrecking ball showed out the windows. She had first seen these two lights with Cyrus, leaning on the truck out in the dark, Francine against his yellow cardigan. The fixtures were antique, porcelain, with painted flowers around the three bulbs that stuck out to impress the neighbors of the time when they were brand-new. Behold! Electricity!

Cal next door had a ladder, and her erstwhile neighbor wouldn't care or notice if she borrowed it. It was leaning on the wall outside his one-room converted garage apartment, from which came snoring. He had a black Labrador who shat on her lawn, but the one time she had marched next door to complain, he nodded in sympathy.

"I know. He shits on my lawn too."

She carried the ladder back to the white house she had sold just this morning, steadied it and pulled out the little platform, then unscrewed the lightbulbs by twisting them—in 1900 life was simpler. She wished she had lived then but realized in the next moment that she would be dead now. *Cyrus*, she hissed for good measure, but no one answered. She had tried to save him: pulling on his toes, macrobiotics, laughter, prayer. When she got the fixtures safely on the platform without electrocuting herself, she climbed down, walked with criminal panache to the Miata, and placed the stolen items on the car floor. Back inside, she told the Spirit of the House to get in the car and ride shotgun. The wrecking ball could be here any minute! Quickly admiring the two holes in the ceiling, very satisfying, she folded up the ladder, locked the door behind her, and leaned the ladder by Cal's open door without disturbing him.

As usual, her stoner neighbor was adrift on the couch, eyes closed, mouth open. Once, before her time, he had given a marijuana plant to Ethel, the woman from whom Francine had bought the house six months ago. Ethel had the greenest thumb in Costa Mesa, but here was one plant she didn't recognize. When it did well, she replanted it all over the half-acre, in sunken bathtubs and next to the nasturtiums and as a border along certain walls, until the night the helicopters came with flashing lights.

Ethel found the raid confusing.

The police were loath to book a woman who looked nearly eighty and refused to be booked anyway. She couldn't or wouldn't remember where she got it. People dropped plants off at this address all the time, she explained. The police gave up, and Ethel and her husband went off to bed. The next day a city crew came and dug up the marijuana plants—a veritable plantation—with Ethel supervising to make sure no gladiola bulbs went missing. They were the beautiful old-fashioned colors. You couldn't replace them.

It would be nice to say goodbye to someone.

"Cal!" Francine shouted through the open doorway.

Cal turned his body away on the couch, which served as both bed and table.

"I'm moving to Venice," said Francine in a loud voice, but he snored soundly on. A bomb wouldn't rattle him. She considered. To make a reverberating clap, you had to cup your hands exactly the right amount. She did it, and the dog's ears came up.

"Say what?" Cal looked out from the dream world where he lived. He sat up a little and lit a doobie.

"I borrowed your ladder. I sold my house and I'm about to take off."

"What?" said Cal.

"I bought a house and four tiny apartments. Bread-and-butter units in Venice Beach."

Cal shot up straight as if struck by lightning. His hair stuck out.

"Bread-and-butter units in hell," he cried out, stone cold sober, and fell down on the couch asleep.

In Venice, after forty-five minutes, Francine found parking. No ducks quacked from bushes. She walked with an antique light fixture under each armpit, hands free for whatever new thing might happen. Venice assaulted your senses if you came from Costa Mesa. For one thing, she had no idea in which part of Venice she had parked. She walked blindly and was careful not to squash the six bulbs, total. Where was home? The streets were circular, or on diagonals, or went every which way. She listened for the sound of traffic, like you listen for a river in Alaska. Beside the Spirit of the House she walked this way and that. In Venice Beach, the streets were laid out like the spokes of a wheel, but not exactly, at angles where the pattern changed to some other pattern, like the unconscious part of your mind when you had no idea what was going on.

At the sound of gunfire she increased her speed. Soon it would be dark. In which direction were Kitty and the dog?

Finally she heard traffic. Over a slight rise, she saw Paradiso Avenue across four lanes of whizzing automobiles.

All Venetians jaywalked, and she ran like hell between the cars, her shoulders stiff from holding the lights in her armpits without breaking them. She stepped up the far curb in one piece.

The moment you stepped out of crazy traffic at one end of Paradiso Avenue or off the crazy boardwalk at the other end, you entered a peace bubble. As always, the walk street was weirdly quiet, and people's doors stood open. She put one foot on the red line and followed it, because why not? A painter had leaked it out of his can at the end of a long day and said, "Fuck it."

She squiggled left.

There was the dark blue band of ocean at the bottom of the street. There were the bougainvillea-laden fences and the puffy 1950s hibiscus. After five more houses, she could give the animals their kibble. She had just retrieved her keys from her right pocket when something came into focus. Three men were outside the gate of the new old square brick house that had just closed escrow.

She continued walking, careful not to show she was from Costa Mesa. Black men dressed in black hoodies, they were gang members, Crips or Bloods, and one hang-loose body leaned against her front gate itself, the elbow elegantly draped.

The either Crips or Bloods waited.

There were two options: (1) Go in, or (2) Pretend she didn't live here. She slowed her pace to a snail's crawl. Different gangs fought to claim different streets, or so she had heard passing the tattoo parlor on the corner, straining to hear conversations not intended for her. Her key was out but hidden in her palm in case it seemed the better part of wisdom to keep moving. Who owned 31 Paradiso? was a good question. From their sweatshirt hoods three sets of eyes flicked over her with radical indifference. What would she do? she and the three men all wondered. When she reached the point of no return, she turned in toward them.

One brown hand rested on the latch itself, and no one moved. Surf broke every seven seconds. Three sets of eyes seemed not to see her, and the dog and cat were far too quiet beyond the gate across the yard behind the doors to which she had the keys.

"Excuse me." Francine's voice came out a weird soprano.

Slowly, slowly, the hand slid. When the gate was clear she opened it, lightbulbs still unbroken beneath her arms, the three hooded figures planted where they were in attitudes of total relaxation, a philosophy of cool, of pause, of not a thing to hurry for. She walked across the yard, not shot in the back yet. Through the double art deco security screen doors, Hank the dog had started jumping up and down, and Kitty had begun one of the mayhem operas that would soon make her a Venice icon. She changed octaves.

"That cat is *bad*," said one of the dudes behind her.

2
CYRUS

Before the new old house in Venice, there had been the old old house in Costa Mesa, fifty miles south, the one Francine had sold to buy 31 Paradiso.

Cyrus had driven her by the old old house after dinner at Mi Casa. They liked the chips. They liked the salsa.

"I like this property." He pointed.

This was when he was still driving. They had been headed home with their full tummies—Mi Casa had big booths, the waitress knew them—and he slowed the truck down to a stop. The house had space around it, and gravel for parking. Swedish, Cyrus was interested in functionality and not gargoyles. The two of them leaned back against the truck seats, breathing deep at the expanse of what looked like a pasture with fruit trees, a large parcel out of a time warp. They came back at many times of day, and the peace was different in between these two lines of survey. They parked and strolled by in the evenings when that was still possible. When Cyrus could no longer go for walks, they drove by to and from Emergency, and it appeared each time, the nasturtiums, the white house, a wonder of tidiness. Cyrus got sicker. In their large empty apartment they had one used couch and one stuffed chair where Cyrus sat up straight to breathe while he watched *Sharks!* on TV. His eyes on fire, his muscles moved on his long bones as his shark brothers sliced through the water. Alaska with its Northern Lights and grizzly bears was distant. Then Cyrus died, which was impossible, and she no longer went to see the house, but sat staring out at the blank walls of the apartment and drinking all the cans of Ensure (a complete meal) that were left over. After she sat on the couch for who knows how long, she took a walk again one day and stood staring at a sign on the front lawn of the antique property: FOR SALE BY OWNER. A shiver traveled up her bones. How she knew the house would take care of her, she had no idea.

She had no money.

"Hello?" called Francine.

The green grass went back as far as she could see, and now she saw that there were two more structures: a duplex in the middle, and a house by the back fence. Three more front doors signified three more units. To be sure, she checked the electric meters. There were poinsettias, and gladiolas in old-fashioned colors. There were nasturtiums in the many thousands. A man with white hair stood at the side of the pristine house, hands on hips, looking up at a rain spout and shaking his head. The rain spout couldn't see him! Some wild daring inhabited her. There was utter darkness except at this address.

"Hello," called Francine again.

"Who is it?" said the man, turning slowly, not like a young person.

"I want to buy this house." Francine heard her own voice.

"Do you," said the man, whose joints were hurting. Obviously.

"I don't have any money," she added.

"Ma!" he yelled. The front screen door opened, and his wife peered out. "Some kid is here and she wants to buy the house. She doesn't have any money."

"This is my house," Francine said, like it was.

She hadn't been called a kid in years, and it felt oddly

nurturing, as if these people and the house itself were her parents. Mrs. House stepped out from behind the screen door that hid her.

"I put on this roof myself," she said, pointing up. "A ladder and a brush for tar, and roofing paper. That's all you need."

Francine marked every word exactly. "A ladder and a brush for tar, and roofing paper."

"There were mustard flowers around here forty years ago." Mrs. House's finger pointed. "As far as the eye could see."

Francine imagined them beyond the woman's finger.

"We need money, though," the man said. "No fancy carry-backs, due and payable. No six percent to any real estate lady."

It was just money, and there was lots of it in the world. Bankers had lots. Anyone could get some.

"We don't want any strings," the man said. "We're clearing out."

Each day, when she went back, the man yelled, "Ma! The kid is here." Then one day it turned out the house was sold. A man had bought it and given them a good-faith check, twelve thousand dollars. The three stood in the long driveway, exactly three hundred feet of orange flower heads moving. It was already her house. Besides nasturtiums there were hydrangeas and daffodils.

"That check is going to bounce," said Francine. Which surprised them all.

"I've planted every single thing that's here," said Mrs. House. "Bulbs, shrubs, whatnot. I know where every single pipe is underground and I have a map to prove it." She pointed at the buildings. "I hauled the other two houses in from Santa Ana once when Jack got drunk and went to Mexico."

"We have this fellow's check," said Jack. "In any case."

"Well, I don't care who gets this place or what they

do to it," said Mrs. House, whose name was Ethel, old-fashioned, like her flowers. They were retiring to be near their children in Wisconsin. "They can smash it to smithereens for all I care."

Three months later, when Francine ran into Jack in produce in the grocery store, they chatted by the apple bin. Francine was tossing apples in the air—she preferred constant movement—and catching them. She no longer walked by the house. At the moment she stood holding one green apple and one red apple, unable to decide. She never knew what she wanted in the world, but she wanted this. She put both apples down exactly where they came from.

"The check for the twelve thousand dollars bounced," Jack mentioned.

Francine called her estranged father that very night, a chance to forgive him, but he wasn't interested. He was interested, but he was busy. Besides his actual job, preaching, he was building an apartment complex, luxury units, and anyway her parents were leaving the next day for the World Pentecostal Convention in Switzerland. A real experience with God was sweeping the world, more proof that Christ was returning in time for Mrs. Didwell to escape death by ascending in the Rapture, and to this end Mrs. Didwell ate wheat germ. Even on the day he died, neither Francine nor her parents mentioned Cyrus, whose existence was not acknowledged. On the phone, her father promised that he would get down when he could to look at the white house, but they went to the World Pentecostal Convention, and returned, and that stretched into three more weeks. Every day she walked down to stare at the house Cyrus had found. She called her parents in Monrovia and asked again and again until one night she screamed.

"You never do anything for me!"

Her mother spoke up where she had been listening on the other telephone.

"Daddy sliced his finger off up on the scaffolding of the apartment. It was hanging by a thread, and your daddy had to climb down holding it against his chest and using one arm. He was alone and he drove himself to the hospital. It's a miracle they saved it and he didn't break his neck. He doesn't want to complain."

"I don't care!" Francine screamed into the telephone. "He has to do something!" Her voice went into splinters. "He has to come and see!"

He came to take a look the following Saturday, the first time they had seen each other in the nine years since she ran away to Alaska with Cyrus. If you can run away at twenty-seven years of age, which you can if you are a Didwell. Francine, waiting for the doorbell, worked the numbers again and again, this mortgage, those rents, writing on a napkin, this many units on a half-acre of land, two one-bedrooms, two three-bedrooms. Francine was her father's daughter. She paced the large apartment like a cat, past the fireplace and back by the sliding door to the patio and past the couch. When the doorbell rang, she flung the door open.

"God wants us to buy this house," said Mr. Didwell, who hadn't seen it. He knew God was real.

He had a beard, but of course she still recognized him. His hair was thinner. Also, his neck bent forward at an angle to support his head, which was not quite upright. On his right hand was a kind of cast where the doctor had saved the digit. Despite his thinning hair, the usual weird power inhabited him. The Didwells were God's favorite earthly family.

"I was halfway here," Mr. Didwell said as if he were preaching: drunk on God although he didn't drink, dreaming although he was awake. He looked like Moses seeing the burning bush. Francine Ephesians didn't invite him in. "I was driving, but driving is a good time for reflection. I happened to look down, and do you know what the dashboard showed?"

"No," said Francine.

"Seven sevens if you count both the mileage and speedometer. Seven number sevens. *Seven. Seven. Seven. Seven. Seven. Seven. Seven.*"

Francine didn't say *Praise God!* Like her father, she was stubborn.

"Do you have any idea what those odds are?" His birthday was the seventh day of the seventh month. "That I would look down at my speedometer *at that exact moment?*"

"No," said Francine.

"Let's go see what God has for us."

They drove down the street to see the house and units, and the Didwells shook hands with Jack and Ethel. It was a great property, but Mr. Didwell wasn't surprised. God always led him. Their euphoria was without bounds as they drove back to the apartment, where Mr. Didwell wrote a check for the down payment to his daughter, who would own the house: Didwell Revocable Living Trust. Francine's hand reached out to receive the check, but he pulled it back. The door to the room where Cyrus died had just swung open from the outdoor breeze, and Mr. Didwell was staring at the mattress, which had begun to glow, like neon. He hated Cyrus. His eyes narrowed. *Possession is nine-tenths of the law* was a Didwell family saying.

"I believe you and your friend purchased a little house out in the desert." Mr. Didwell wouldn't utter Cyrus's name, because his own lips were holy. The deed to that house was the only legal contract she had ever signed with Cyrus, proof of their marriage, Francine Ephesians Didwell and Cyrus Shaver Gustafsson, tenants-in-common. It was precious.

"To make this deal work," said Reverend Didwell, "I think it only fair that you sell that house."

"No." Her heart stopped.

"Yes," the man continued. "As a sign of good faith."

"Dad? There's hardly any money in it."

Mr. Didwell loved the *Reader's Digest* column "It Pays to Increase Your Word Power," and besides verses from the King James Version of the Bible and farm terms from growing up, esoteric words popped out in conversation. His eyes looked like a killer. You could see he had another personality. They both watched the mattress.

"It would be a caveat," said Mr. Didwell.

In the bed, when he was dying, Cyrus needed many pillows. He had to sit up to breathe. On his last night, he threw the pillows on the floor, one after another, and lay down flat, and his breathing deepened.

"I rested!" he said when he woke up.

She ran around to get his pillows but he waved her off.

"Things change," he explained.

"Well?" said Mr. Didwell, Cyrus gone, Mr. Didwell leaning back with his arms crossed and staring at his daughter.

"I'll sell the house out in the desert," she said, surrendering. She needed the money.

Six months after she bought it, Francine sold the old old house in Costa Mesa and bought the new old house in Venice, an unstable real estate decision. During her six months in the old old house, no ghost of Cyrus had appeared in any of the Costa Mesa hot spots they used to frequent, Mother's Market for the health food or Der Wienerschnitzel for the kraut dogs, extra relish. Which was puzzling. There was nothing whatsoever after the day Cyrus broke dishes and made her giggle.

Six months and fifty-three days later, Francine stood on the sidewalk outside the new old house, looking at the ocean.

She was failing as a Venice landlord.

One rent short, her hubris had destroyed her. Six weeks after the close of escrow, Apartment 2 had not paid the first rent. It was eight days late, with the new bank mortgage due tomorrow, the last day of the extended grace period. Francine, landlord, had left messages by telephone, left notes, done everything except pound on the door. In Orange County, where the landlord was king, tenants answered; but Venetians were monsters. *Rent control is the gateway drug to Communism*, Francine's father, Mr. Didwell, was fond of saying. *It is of Satan.*

Where was Cyrus?

Inside the brick house, Francine walked in circles, checking each of seven mirrors to make sure she existed. She could stay until the sheriff came to lock her out, the bank having foreclosed, after which she supposed she would join the homeless, with Hank and Kitty. There was no furniture except the massage table made up for tonight's first new client, plus a small chair and her five-foot-by-seven-foot Persian rug, plus the seven mirrors, not large ones. Through the adjoining arch, the dining room contained a small pine table and many boxes clearly marked MISCELLANEOUS. She had packed in a dither of excitement. Which box had the gladiola bulbs? Where were the pliers? Where were her black Chinese Laundry high heels that made the calves look like panthers? Where were the salt and pepper? The saving grace was in the corner: unpacked first and sitting on a bookshelf were all the books that raised her. They had information, like if you had a clubfoot and dreamed of being a dancer, don't let an idiot slice your Achilles tendon in two, *Madame Bovary*. There was a wealth of information not covered by the Assembly of God Church she grew up in. On the top shelf were her best friends: *On the Beach*, *Auntie Mame*, *The Fountainhead*, *Collected Poems of T. S. Eliot*, *Don Quixote*. In each book a lively person lived in secret. She crossed the floor to touch the spine of *The Day of the Jackal.*

On the pine table where she ate and paid the bills, the

rental contracts stuck out from beneath a pile of to-go menus. There it was, the single sheet Apartment 2 had signed, passed on to her on the day she took ownership. Frankie Frank, Occupation: Wrestler. Two citizens passed outside on the sidewalk.

"Tonight Ima kill that bastard knifed me," said one voice now.

"Man! Fritos," responded the other. Something crunched.

"Ima get him when—"

The men passed by before she could find out the ending.

Babe Light, the Venice realtor, had explained that when the tenants paid their rent at this particular parcel number, 4226-004-012, each individual stuck their individual check (tucked in a white envelope) into the green thicket of bamboo trees lining the front yard on the side nearest to the Pacific Ocean. It was the landlord's job to pluck them out. In Venice, Babe Light assured her, rent in trees was normal. Then Babe Light, pretty and tough, like Venice, leaned back against the wall next door—the houses were close, this was the beach—and looked at Francine to see what stuff she was made of. And indeed, as promised, on the first day of the month Apartment 3 rent had appeared in the green leaves, and on the second day Apartment 1, and on the third day Apartment 4. Francine looked out the door again, but no white envelope protruded.

She stepped out.

Francine turned right along the house, past the impenetrable Sierra juniper that formed a natural cave where yesterday she had seen a tennis shoe pull itself in quietly. The opening was so low you could only climb in on your stomach. She continued down the little side path past her house, and launched herself across the ten feet of concrete that separated her from Apartment 2.

Just short of the stoop she brought herself up short to gather her resources. *Mortgage, late fee, foreclosure,* she chanted to herself. She ascended the single step and knocked three times.

She had not yet met the gentleman inside, who was inarguably home. Heavy metal music blasted through the atoms in the walls, and a shadow moved behind the curtain. Francine bit her lips to make them red and positive.

Mortgage, periodic interest, overdraft, she incanted.

Neighbors looked out the windows. Did no one go off to work in Venice?

Francine knocked again, five polite cracklets of sound. Straight above, the sky was brilliant blue in the narrow corridors between the buildings. The air was quiet. *Mortgage, tax, gross multiplier,* Francine spat out. She was a Venice businesswoman. *Cap rate.* Inside Apartment 2, there was a small crash. She didn't budge. She wiped sweat from her face onto her palms onto her jeans, an old pair of Cyrus's 501s rolled up at the bottom and under at the top. She looked down at her exposed abdomen, the seat of power and her favorite body part.

"Pow!" said Francine out loud. "Pow. Pow. Pow!"

She was just about to say *pow* again when the door opened and music hit her in the face so hard her cheeks stung. The woman, not man, facing her had enormous thighs and biceps, and enormous long pink fingernails, the best of both worlds. Tenants were looking out the windows of the buildings on either side, which were impossibly close together, as if this were a college dormitory.

"I'm the new owner," Francine said, her voice cracking almost at once. "I'm the owner!" she screeched over the awful music. They called it heavy metal for a reason. The sound was damaging her ears.

It ended, suddenly.

Her torso retracted, but when she tried to pull her tank top down, it was a tank top. She lifted one flat hand, like an Indian. "Francine Ephesians Didwell." Why had she said *Ephesians*? "I need your rent to pay the mortgage."

Behind the woman body builder looming in the doorway was a poster that said *The First Woman to Make a Fist*, showing a woman much like the one standing here. The faces were different, but both women were gorgeous: long blond country hair and thick expertly applied makeup. When the real woman moved, Francine jumped, and then tried to pretend she had not. The real woman had leaned back against the small refrigerator, property of owner, as per contract, and the appliance tilted and hit the wall. The wall! The coils! It was a small kitchen. A snake tattoo traveled up one arm and across the woman's pectorals and down the other arm so that the snake seemed to be slithering with each movement.

"*I need your rent to pay the mortgage*," the tenant mimicked, staring at Francine as if she were a double-headed chicken.

Francine felt her shape diminishing, *The Shrinking Man*, one of the books that raised her, third shelf from bottom. A spider had chased him.

"The bank will foreclose," Francine said, or thought she said. The sky was reeling. Francine backed up, a bubblehead from Orange County, careful not to fall off the small concrete door stoop. In Venice, the amount of open space was tiny, and all the neighbors were so close you could hear them doing dishes, which was why you needed the ocean. She pulled up and held Cyrus's 501 Levis to cover her belly button. Abdomen power was leaking out.

"So?" said Frankie Frank.

"I'll have to move. I'll ruin my credit. I just moved here and I left everything behind in Costa Mesa."

Frankie hooted. When she straightened, the small

refrigerator toppled on its feet and landed upright. Francine hoped the coils weren't broken. Frankie, a tall woman, flexed her muscles, not a threat, but more an autonomic response, like breathing. She ground her teeth and stretched her jaw, then swung her head back and forward in one continuous movement. Her head snapped upright.

"This is me"—Frankie Frank, wrestler, made the snake move on her muscles and came closer—"not caring." She did an imitation of a blond with dimples, fingernail in each cheek to indicate an idiot. Horses know city slickers.

"That makes sense," said Francine.

On either side, seasoned Venetians looked out their windows. This was the Wild West, and Francine was an Orange County matching-outfit bimbo. The wrestler grimaced.

"Okay," said Francine. "We'll talk later."

Hank needed a walk, and she needed the whole Pacific Ocean. Together they went down the red line toward the boardwalk, Hank pulling. For a white fluffball he had powerful upper body muscles. In six weeks, he had become a Venice anarchist, dog school forgotten. The dogs were Communists, and they all recognized each other and repudiated all tricks: roll over, beg, shake hands. Venice dogs and their people were equals. Given her failure as a Venice landlord, there was nothing to do but keep walking. She was no match for rent control. If you were Pentecostal, miracles were an everyday occurrence, but she wasn't. She was thinking how to get more money when she was momentarily distracted by the yodeler.

He was on the beach side of the boardwalk, the side toward China. She had seen him every day since she moved here, because, like her, he was a workaholic.

"Yodel ay ee ooo!" the Venice yodeler yodeled.

He stood on his head all day on a folding chair,

although he did occasionally take breaks. Francine checked her pockets, which were empty. In her bra she found a single dollar bill and dropped it in his Tyrolean hat. His shirt wafted toward his nose, and with one hand he plucked the shirt up to say thank you. His balance was excellent. The shirt wafted back down over his nose and eyes. Francine slowed but as always didn't stand completely still. In some Western movie, some gunman auditions for the job of small-town sheriff but shoots and misses the tin can target. "Can I do it for you moving?" he asks the city fathers, and runs by, making the shot dead center.

"Yodel ay ee ooo!" rang out again, the yodeler obviously a professional from the Swiss Alps, but sooner or later all talent came to Venice. Janis Joplin had sung on this exact beach, and Jim Morrison. In Venice, the air was an inspiration.

Francine turned toward the south, if south was south. The whole coast was crooked. "I have to go," she said.

"Watch out," said the yodeler.

She was just hitting her stride, and the dog was going forward like a happy choo-choo, the forest of legs on the boardwalk having thinned out, when the yodeler stopped mid-arpeggio. When she looked back, he plucked his shirt up. His face had darkened. "Watch out," he said, a little louder.

Two figures were ambling toward her, perhaps five feet away now but who was counting.

"Rumble," said someone from *West Side Story*.

In her peripheral vision, the yodeler stood on his head on the chair, feet in the air. She raised her eyes. Crips or Bloods, the figures were moving toward her and the dog, their flat eyes looking straight through her. She was definitely in their line of egress.

She turned to go home to 31 Paradiso. Blocking her path perhaps the length of two cold bodies away were two more Crips or Bloods, Bloods if the others were Crips, Crips if they were Bloods, but deadly enemies. Now all four Crips and Bloods stopped. Their hands hovered at their pockets.

Francine and her little dog stood inhibiting four men with legs spread who weren't going to move. Hank growled a vicious growl and bared his single fang. He growled again, the growl he normally reserved for children.

"Stop, sweetie," she said softly. "You're going to kill us."

Last week, five people had been killed in a gang shootout in the hood three blocks away. A man on Venice Beach sold a large roll-up map of the neighborhood, extremely useful to tourists. In bright colors, cartoons depicted which streets people were getting shot on, very helpful, which streets were for the enjoyment of tourists. On some streets, for example, little cop cars turned upside down were burning, and bodies lay in blood. Two blocks away, tourists ate cotton candy.

On the boardwalk, it was breathless. Francine and Hank were in the middle. The four men stood in baggy pants, hands in their pockets like Ralph Lauren, palms on the butt end of their hardware, eyes cold.

She must go right or left to get around them, but some madness had gripped her. To the north, the four eyes never looked directly at her, but only through her, yet she sensed they could see every small muscle twitch, the hairs that stood up on her bare arms, something akin to sonar. In the distance where the tourists gathered on the grass at Windward, not a single soul was talking. To the left, the sea and sand remained as beautiful as ever, blue and tan.

"I can move." Francine persisted where she was.

A standoff was in progress.

Where were the police?

She pulled Hank on a short leash.

"Heel," she said in a tone that meant business, like the Businessmen of Rhythm, that tap-dance group.

The shortest distance between two points was a straight line, and she went through two men in the thin space. On her left, her skin brushed against a Blood or Crip, and two dead eyes flamed to life. Danger! She continued. She had always had good judgment about people: a gift of the Spirit, like her father had the gift of wisdom in real estate, like her uncle Sly had the gift of healing missing earlobes, like her mother had the gift of rhythm on the tambourine. Cyrus had the gift of everything. As Francine and the dog moved forward, the Blood or Crip she had brushed touched her elbow with his bare hand and healed her.

"Go!" said the yodeler.

The Crip or Blood continued south. Hood power surged through her.

"Yodel ay ee ooo." The yodeler's voice floated toward her, changed keys, upward, and the beach returned to normal. "Yodel ay ee ooo."

She and the dog moved out, the gang members moved past each other, no death this morning. People flowed around her, shouts in all languages, *Mon Dieu, Vaya con Dios*, and the boardwalk anthem: *Fuck You. No, fuck YOU, motherfucker.*

She shot up Paradiso Avenue, without time to follow the red squiggles. At 31 Francine turned in toward Apartment 2.

The dog was prancing. She moved past the Sierra juniper, where, today, no tennis shoe retracted. Hank sometimes sat inside the window opposite the hiding place and wagged his tail at the complete stranger sleeping outside her window. This was Venice. They cleared the corner of the house, and crossed the ten feet of space that was like the demilitarized zone between Koreas. At Apartment 2, she stepped up one step and knocked three times, a knuckle knock that wasn't kidding.

"Arf," said Hank.

A neighbor in glasses looked out the window.

Cool, she waited, hips slightly forward in the slouch she had been taught by her either Crip or Blood professors. In her head, dead eyes looked at nothing.

She was ready for the blonde, she was ready for the poster, *First Woman to Make a Fist,* et cetera. The music got loud. The door flew open.

"Beat it," said Frankie Frank, wrestler.

"Do you have treats?" Hank inquired.

"The rent check's late and I need it by today." Francine, Venice landlord, longed to use the word *utterly.* "No extensions."

She looked not at but through the snake tattoo, her eyes cold and colder. She felt rather than saw Frankie's biceps rise up like a soufflé.

Hank wagged his tail.

"By midnight," Francine added. She didn't care if she died young. "Otherwise I serve the three-day notice for eviction."

She did care. In one hundred years, Francine Ephesians Didwell hoped to depart Paradiso Avenue with a Hells Angels escort, a successful Venetian landlord.

Drunk on success, Francine floated home and floated up the stairs, where Kitty waited trapped inside. Who would live and who would die? Would Frankie Frank pay rent? She had become a Venetian. She needed to touch someone, and in this she was lucky. She had clients coming tonight, three discount massages. She had put fliers up at Ralph's Grocery Store, the yoga studio, and three laundromats, and in six weeks she had garnered a good base of customers. She had her healing uncle's open channel. To a person, every client surrendered and came back the next week. They needed relief. She had a one-hundred-percent success rate. On the sill of the window through which interesting sounds issued from the secret neighbor, she set out her bottle of half oil and half lotion, proprietary formula, and one eye pillow with buckwheat filler. She plumped the sheepskin. Tonight's first customer was Brad Bryant, a music teacher, third visit. The next was Mr. Wade, who used his right-hand muscles to excess. The third was new, a certain Mrs. Tibbs. The clients all returned because Francine's hands were good. What issued from the palms of some hands and not from others? Who knew?

When Brad Bryant arrived, they started as soon as he was on the table. He wasn't one for small talk. She laid hands on him and rocked him. His breathing deepened, and his fingers played the piano as he went under. Her palms ran up the back and down the back and all around the rhomboids. Her hands took on authority. The tiny Siamese had absorbed the excitement, and she stood poised on the small chair for customers. In one swift move, Brad Bryant unconscious, the cat leaped from a crouch, landed on Hank's back as he ran by, and rode him like a bronco, looking remarkably like Annie Oakley. The Siamese were ancient. Kitty held on while Hank tried everything to throw her off, helpless, insane, both ears flying, out of his mind, but love was agony. Brad Bryant sank deeper. Time flew. Once the massage started, you could assign it to your unconscious and then think about anything you wanted. Like losing your shirt if you couldn't make the mortgage payment. For the Chinese finish, Francine pulled Brad's ears in three places, long life, good luck, health. Then she slapped him lightly on the arm, a friendly slap, to indicate the massage was over.

"I'll be in the kitchen," she told him.

Brad sat up glassy-eyed and looked around to ascertain exactly where he was. Francine listened to his movements from the kitchen. She washed her hands and gave a little jump. Her luck had changed.

"You're a force of nature," Brad Bryant called as the front door closed behind him.

* * *

Four hours after Brad Bryant's arrival, her last customer at last departed, Francine slumped at a table in Van Gogh's Ear, her local coffee shop, exhausted from having executed three rubs at her cheap introductory rate. Upstairs, every table was painted a different cheerful color. It was after midnight, and before her were three cappuccinos, hard to carry up the stairs, but she prided herself on motor skills. Too tired to think, she half lay in a green chair—the table was pink—slurping foam and simultaneously reading newspaper ads for *Men Seeking Women* while she self-massaged her strained right thumb, which was in danger of coming off completely.

"Ouch," she observed.

The building that housed Van Gogh's Ear was the official divide between two neighborhoods, the one with murders to the inland side, and the one with tourists eating cotton candy in the narrow strip along the ocean. Therefore, and especially after dark fell, you had to be careful which door you exited from. Francine made a mental note. Limp, she turned a page, a great physical effort. *Seeking redhead with big breasts and small ankles*, said one ad. *No children*. Francine stuck her swollen right thumb joint into a glass of ice water and slid back on her tailbone without falling off the chair, a calibrated distance. Tonight she had massaged three clients at her still-half-price special offer, three sets of sheets, three sets of *effleurage*, or *saying hello to the skin*, which you did before you went unconscious.

Francine emptied cappuccino number one and licked the cup edge.

For the first time in her career, one hour ago Francine had failed to hypnotize a body on the table, and now she felt a grudging admiration for Mrs. Tibbs, referred from the bulletin board at Ralph's. For sixty minutes Mrs. Tibbs had not shut up or stopped for breath, complaining from Francine's start on her sacrum to the Chinese finish on the ears, not once stopping to surrender any muscle. Which ruined Francine's perfect record of deflating clients down to zero. In the glass of ice water, her right thumb was freezing, and she let it out with a quick kiss of appreciation. But some personalities were dead already. The topics of Mrs. Tibbs's complaints were: the new water-base paints, which had no sticking power; the lack of wind-wings in cars; how women who wore wigs tended to be scurrilous gossips (here her voice got shrill and the tendons in her neck rose up); and on that same note how scrunchies for ponytails came in no color found in nature. Worst of all, the Green Stamp store had closed its doors for good before she could redeem her forty-two collected books for a lovely gray-blue-striped couch and armchair (with ottoman), Green Stamp Book, page 17. To her own amazement, Francine recalled a couch and ottoman from twenty years before. The Green Stamp store had featured it in the window. But were forty-two books enough? In Van Gogh's Ear, alone and happy over two remaining steaming cappuccinos, Francine sat up and arched and curled her back, then closed her eyes and slightly dozed, all Venice around her.

"What's happening?"

When she looked up, a woman was staring, and the look could only be called copasetic, like the Copasetics tap group, which Francine didn't want to think about. White-blond, almost a pixie, half woman, half child, she sat of course not in a chair but on top of a blue table. This was Venice. Her hair, more like chicken fluff, was very short, and tendrils sprouted in all directions. Two legs straddled a large piece of butcher paper upon which she sat drawing stick figures. Francine felt a dark foreboding, like in Shakespeare. Francine's family, the godly Didwells, saw deceit in every person walking down the street. *What is he up to?* one Didwell might say about a perfect stranger. Could you trust anyone? Had Judas betrayed Jesus?

Francine nodded back and shrugged, then picked up her *L.A. Times* and continued using her good pen to mark the list of *Thursday Personals, Men Seeking Women*. Before her visit next week to the Didwells, her family, she needed protection. She was going because her sister Bunny had called a family meeting, something anyone could do, but Bunny was proactive. She ought to be a politician. *Attractive man with good physique seeks woman with same,* said one ad. Francine marked it. She needed a man with substance to buoy her up by putting one hand on her solar plexus after her trip to Monrovia. She went down the list of names and ages, checking height first, five feet ten inches, six feet, six feet adjacent. How tall was adjacent? She needed someone to return to, to confirm she wasn't crazy. Dinner would be sinners versus Christians, Venice Beach meets the Holy City of Monrovia. It would be a mighty battle for the truth. On whose side was voodoo? Would she try to commit suicide? Because BC, Before Cyrus, she had fought to keep her steering wheel from turning into freeway overpasses after every trip home, saved by something at the last minute. The Didwells had an odd effect on her. They were her family.

She crossed out *Jeb, 6'2", please no animals.*

In Van Gogh's Ear, the ads, like last week, were depressing, some men seeking women 25–30, other men seeking women 21–42, others 27–39, but all women *must have sense of humor*. Clearly the men needed a picker-upper. *Please no baggage*, the ads said. *Must like moonlight walks on beach and have good figure.*

After Cyrus died, she had stood in the small room at Cooke Funeral Home looking at his body. To see the body was a great relief, and actually cheerful, because Cyrus wasn't there, that much was clear, so he must be somewhere. She checked the clock on the wall. It was early, and she stood there alone looking at his hair, which had been parted on the wrong side. With her small red comb, she re-parted and combed it the other way, her fingers steady. The world was boring, but on every single day with Cyrus, she felt interested. She patted his chest in the casket, under the auspices of straightening his tie (no one was there), but under the skin of her palm there was no Cyrus. He couldn't smoke. He couldn't tease her. There was Cyrus's body but not Cyrus, his great fine hands folded on what used to be his midriff. Alive, they had looked like the hands of God on the Sistine Chapel ceiling, but dead they looked like gloves. Her brow wrinkled. He looked unreal, as if stuffed socks had been forced into a shirt, the pants yanked closed by brute force. On his body were the clothes he had worn in real life, brought in by her on hangers, but here they looked funny: navy sport jacket and striped shirt, good tan trousers. Above all that was Cyrus's head, the thick hair and enormous eyebrows, the ski-jump nose, and below it his lips, which during life had wiggled just before he laughed, but were now sewn together with a blue thread beginning to slip. Under the lowered half of the coffin were what had been his pelvis, legs, feet in shoes.

"Sit down," said her good friend John Paul Peter Hicks, who had been named as many names as possible out of Scripture.

The comb fell. She threw her arms around him and took in his smell, because he was also a lapsed PK, or preacher's kid. A jazz piano player, he had wild powers of improvisation, common if you have been around the Holy Ghost, and, like her, he was backslidden. Two escapees from the Assembly of God Church, the damned and the damned, they sat together in the small room with the coffin, as they had always helped each other in times of need, although they didn't see each other often because he lived in San Diego. John Paul Peter Hicks sat with his hand near hers, not in a hurry. There was no more she could do for Cyrus. She had re-combed his hair with water, and touched his fingers, which did not seem like fingers. She had dusted off what used to be his chest.

"He moved!" cried John Paul Peter.

Francine giggled, an explosion out her nose, inappropriate and unsophisticated. No one was there yet except them and what had been but wasn't now Cyrus.

"Don't *do* that."

Like most people who had once been saved, John Paul Peter had a drinking problem, but in his case he had solved it. Francine picked up the red comb. They sat with the body in the casket.

"He moved again."

Her head whipped toward the coffin, and she snorted. He moved! He didn't! Cyrus could make her laugh until she begged for mercy. They watched the body carefully, but it did nothing, the face immobile. They looked out the door toward the lobby to see if there were any early party crashers.

"Again!" cried John Paul Peter.

He hooted first, then the two of them hilarious and unable to stop laughing. The viewing room was replete with happiness. Tears rolled from their eyes, and Francine stood up at last and merely touched the body's tie, his favorite, yellow diagonal stripes across a field of blue, tasteful, conservative.

"You're going to land on your feet now, aren't you, Tub Tub?" Cyrus said just one hour before he left forever.

"Of course!" Francine had answered.

In Van Gogh's Ear, Cyrus still dead, Francine returned to the scholarly search for men tall enough to save her from the Didwells. Her right thumb still throbbed from Mrs. Tibbs's neck, which was surely made of rebar. *Man with sensitive nature seeks woman with same, prefer under 5'5" for good times and possible relationship. Must have sense of humor. No dogs please.*

She put down her pen and paper and looked up, a widow.

"So what brings you here?" said the child-woman pixie, who had stopped drawing. Her eyebrows and eyelashes were white-blond, and then the paleness ended in a black cashmere turtleneck, a throwback to the beatniks. It wasn't that she was beautiful, but she was beautiful. She had the kind of glow that Francine's mother, Mrs. Didwell, sometimes emanated, and Francine smiled, an automatic response to light. The force of the woman's personality was quiet but it was powerful, and she seemed to have turned on a switch to make the many colors of the chairs and tables on the second floor of Van Gogh's Ear jump out. But of course Francine was very tired.

"Just working the Personals." Francine held up the newspaper to prove it.

Inside the fluff head something calm looked out, an old soul with a sense of fun, and Francine felt her tendons relax. The child-woman's face was pouty, like a saint's, and while her chest and ears were small, her hips were big, the whole shape like a Bartlett pear. The black cashmere had hanger marks, and with black tights, the look so suited her that you might think she had invented a new *Vogue Hippy*. Francine half turned her chair just as the pear-shaped blithe spirit hopped lightly off the table. There was a wee shake in the earth's energy.

"Julia," said Julia.

She held out a child's hand, and they shook. A familiar smell was in the room, astringent, comforting, like early childhood. The handshake was good. Like her uncle Sly, Francine had the gift of divination through the palm skin.

"Pleased to meet you," Francine said.

Julia picked up the *L.A. Times* Personals section and read Francine's notes out loud: *Maybe, No, No, Give peace a chance, God help us.* Because adopting a cat was easier.

Julia stretched, a complete stretch, her tiny hands in

fists, her black leggings extended, and sat back down, renewed. She was an artist, or a therapist, or possibly a yoga instructor.

"Are you a yoga instructor?" Francine felt her right thumb for swelling.

"Dominatrix."

Preachers' daughters didn't know numerous things about the world of Satan, unlike missionaries' children, who were more sophisticated, living in other countries, the eyes on them less watchful, their experience broader and more sinful. Nothing shocked them. Francine, raised with one goal—do not miss the Rapture—mispronounced many words not found in the King James Bible, while at the same time she could correctly pronounce Habakkuk, Irad, Mehujael. She tried to look world-weary.

"Of course," she said.

They both burst out laughing. They both knew Francine was in septic shock.

"I'm a PK," Francine admitted. "Short for preacher's kid, in the business."

"Queen Julia," the dominatrix announced.

Visible on the blue table she had just vacated was a sketch of something—Julia was no Michelangelo—and if Francine stretched her spine and neck she could see it clearly. A stick drawing of a stick figure sat on a stick throne (her breasts circles) wearing a stick crown with four stick points. But the stick queen was angry, with inverted stick eyebrows. Both feet on the floor, Queen Julia resumed drawing. Francine stared at her. Her nose twitched. But Francine had never met a person in the dominatrix business. Out from beneath the stick crown came stick curls in squiggles, with instructions: *Yellow*, Julia wrote, adding an arrow.

"I almost forgot!" She clapped her teeny tiny hands and drew a royal scepter ending in the cross that Jesus bore to Calvary. She crossed that out and drew a star. She crossed that out and drew either a toaster or a box of Wheaties.

"I'm making a website, which is a thing. People are getting personal computers, and I intend to take advantage of humanity's forward leap."

Francine, PK, stood up and waved her arms, for circulation. She liked moving. "What do you do? *Exactly?*"

"Whatever they need." Julia drew two stick high-heeled thigh boots and a stick whip. "I torture people. For their own good."

"Like God," Francine joked. "Not really! I'm not religious."

"What does an atheist say when he has an orgasm?" The blond pear scooted her chair closer.

"I don't know." Francine crumpled the paper.

"No God! No God!"

They exploded, friends forever, Francine's elbows nearly falling off her pink table, two fallen women, and Van Gogh's Ear rang with their laughter. Men and their members! It was an exotic foreign country you could visit, like being a cowboy on the pampas in Argentina or exploring Antarctica.

"Anyway," said Julia. "It's a calling. Some clients need a slap. Some need to be insulted. It's the dominatrix's job to ascertain this. They all need something. It takes energy to prepare if you want them to relax and follow orders. I only get control freaks."

Francine nodded. Uncle Sly had talked in much the same way about the laying on of hands to heal broken limbs, disease, thumb sucking, sick elm trees. Francine felt herself relaxing. Uncle Sly had had the same ability to be still, to listen with his pores, and to hear whatever was important even if you didn't say it. Her father's brother, he was a faith healer with an eighth-grade education who could do things his two educated preacher brothers couldn't.

One time Sly had come out from Missouri and visited the California Didwells and met Baby Francine, who had no right earlobe.

"God wants her to have an earlobe," the big man said.

Francine waved her arms, because at six months, she wasn't vain. Her left earlobe was perfect, and if her right ear had no lobe she could still kick her legs. Life was grand. The three adults, Sly and her father Clarence and her mother Louella, laid hands on the ear with no flap of skin, and Sly prayed in a loud voice, and nothing happened.

Still Christians, the three Didwells went about their visit. Two weeks later, Louella, bathing her watchful baby daughter, kneeling at the bathtub, straightened her strong back as she held Francine Ephesians.

"Clarence!" she yelled. "Come here quick!"

In Van Gogh's Ear, Francine raised her hands and there both earlobes were. Julia drew a stick foorstool and labeled it *Dyed Pink* as she explained in her voice that was so kind, like something you remembered out of childhood, how she first had to locate the client's soul, almost always barricaded behind bars and wanting rescue. To heal took borrowed energy. A client, Julia explained, couldn't take shit from a weaker personality, and before each appointment she, Julia, personally, must meditate while upside down and eat broth and sing something, maybe from Motown, if only for twenty minutes. For her clients' type of personality, it wasn't easy to let go. If she told them to crawl, they must drop to all fours immediately. Barking was common. (Meowing, obviously, never.) Her clients, men with big responsibilities real or imagined, needed to feel helpless. They were so grateful and so desperate not to be in charge that they sometimes made unintelligible sounds. They craved to be tiny babies. In Julia's upstairs garage apartment in the hood, noise wasn't a problem.

At two-thirty a.m. Francine stood up, exhausted, and wrote her phone number on a napkin. Time flies when you're having fun. When she put the napkin down in front of Julia, she recognized the smell of tea tree oil at the same moment Julia confessed.

"I have your goddamned tap shoes," the dominatrix said.

"From the master class with Gregory Hines." Dizzy, Francine held on to a yellow chair. "But you had long black hair. And black lipstick. Now you're a pixie."

Julia drew what looked like a graham cracker and labeled it Ermine Stole. As an artist, she was terrible. Her hips slid off the table and she landed on her feet, a perfect pear shape, and her small fists rested on two round hips.

"So you're a friend of Eddie Brown?"

Francine dropped her coffee.

"My *man* Eddie Brown?" the dominatrix taunted.

Francine had first wandered into tap one day when she heard sounds coming from a studio. *Bop da de boop, whoosh!* came a language that she recognized. It was her lost tribe of people. She took class that very day in her street shoes, and Jimmie DeFore, hoofer, gave her his old pair of men's white tap shoes as they had the same size foot, broad at the toe. *Shaped like a brick,* said Jimmie. He had just come back from Europe dancing with the great Count Basie. What were the chances? The shoes had big taps that could resonate, the tiniest bird sound or a smash like thunder. For one year she did everything Jimmie DeFore told her and then ran home to show the steps to Cyrus, who watched her face and not her feet no matter how she scolded. He was incorrigible.

"There are three great hoofers living," Jimmie said when he had checked out her ability to keep a beat. "Honi Coles. Eddie Brown. Me."

She hardly breathed.

"Eddie Brown is teaching at the Embassy Hotel up in Los Angeles. You need to go see him."

She took the number he had written down, but only met the great man once. When she came home she stuffed both tap shoes deep in a box marked *Goodwill*, and avoided Jimmie DeFore at all costs. She took detours to avoid his studio. One day, after she moved to Venice, the phone rang in the new old house: there was a surprise Greg Hines class next door in Santa Monica. How Francine got on the tap hotline she had no idea. Jimmie DeFore was in heaven. Francine looked for Jimmie's tap shoes and found them in the box under a pile of old pajamas. She needed something. She drove to Santa Monica and entered, and sat down on the wood and tied the laces.

In the large room of the Westside Ballet Academy there were fifty-four-odd people, but who was counting? She counted again while dancers showed off their best steps, pure anarchy, the little trills or the thrown foot, the nonchalant flash step as if the brain had no idea and was surprised. *Oops! Where did THAT come from?* Amidst fifty-four-odd strangers, Jimmie DeFore's shoes made one small noise, then two. She was warming up her feet and showing off at once, getting her rhythm tuned up, when across the room she saw her doppelgänger, who looked nothing like her.

She peered through someone's elbow.

The doppelgänger, although she was Goth, made Francine stop and stare in admiration. Mad energy came out her feet and pulled her body slightly toward Mother Earth, not heaven. Around the room people could get the steps, but that was not tap dancing. Tap dancing settled. The Goth woman listened to her feet while her body floated over them. Besides that, she had long black hair and black holes for eyes, and was dressed in layers of black lace that hid her shape but yet you saw it; anyone, of any shape, might be a graceful dancer. When the Goth woman waved, Francine did her own step she called a ratatouille with a leap and kick. She added the ornamental flam, a sideways smash at a correct intensity known only to a seasoned dancer. She did it again, now flip the pelvis over and chug two feet forward, make a note to keep the weight ahead to let the body fly. The Goth woman stood still. Next the feet go crazy, clap slide stop.

"Goin' to the Store," said the Goth woman with her black tap shoes, that simplest and best of steps though it must be done just right with a low-down feeling that could melt you into cinders.

All around the room was the clatter of hoofers throwing out their heels and stealing. It was exhilarating, lawless. *Your step today; mine tomorrow*: the tap dancers' creed of honor. The noise was terrible.

The noise stopped.

Greg Hines stood in the doorway.

Class had started. He was one with the floor from the first moment, as if he had been born with wood beneath his feet. The routine was simple yet difficult, with stomps of different changes, and he was exacting.

"*This*," said Gregory, and they did *that*.

"No. Listen."

The music—alternating words and scat sounds, sung by Gregory—was "I've Got You Under My Skin." Without the benefit of actual music, his feet seemed to sing melody. Every dancer concentrated. Sweat dripped on the floor, and once someone shouted. They did the dance again and became soaked, crotch first, next the breastbone and under the arms. Sweat ran down foreheads. Across the room, the Goth woman made each step land, fast or slow, complete, no anxiety. The class did the dance again, again, and Gregory clapped, and sometimes sang, and sometimes said *da da* and then picked up again. *So deep in my heart you're really a part ba dee.* The words were sounds only. Everyone wanted nothing in this life except to keep dancing. Dripping wet, thirsty as shit, all the dancers and their legs and arms and hearts were one country. They had no plans to ever stop.

The master clapped his hands again for silence.

"Form a circle," said the master.

For seconds, no one moved.

Two bodies slithered out sideways with their heads down. Then, a panic took over. Improvisation was a sink-or-swim proposition. Each person had to step out and perform a solo made up on the spot, no place to hide. 1) You had a soul, or, 2) you were garbage. People looked in panic at their neighbors, trying to steal steps while they kept their time, trying to tap and hitting empty air instead due to muscle contractions due to being nervous. Two more bodies busted out the door by walking on the sides of their shoes, as if this made them invisible. One or two hotdoggers looked happy, young men with feet so fast they sounded like machine-gun fire. Francine felt herself being pushed into the large circle.

"One at a time," called Gregory. "Twelve-bar blues. Improvisation."

"Dead man walking," someone whispered.

A slightly acrid smell of nervousness was rising from the bodies. If she died, Francine hoped the hell of Scripture was a figment of her imagination. *If you took all the sand from all the beaches of all the world,* said the old preachers, *and put it in a bucket, that bucket would not complete a grain in the bucket of eternity.* Across the room a woman passed the test. If you could improvise, you were a hoofer's hoofer. In the large room there were no pianos or stringed instruments, just the sound of Gregory's slightly cupped hands, which caused an echo, and even without music the blues was still the blues, twelve bars, plaintive. One man simply grunted for the last eight of his twelve-bar solo.

"Uh uh *uh*," said Gregory.

Thirty-nine souls ahead of Francine walked the plank, their faces puckered in concentration. *The horror! The horror!* one great author had written of improvisation.

"Go," said Gregory. A young man kept the time for six bars and then sat down on the floor.

"Six, seven, eight," said Gregory. He moved on. "Go."

The master came closer with his academic look of glasses and a shabby sweater. Each time he slapped his foot, dancers' bodies reacted. A man with sideburns giggled. The claps moved toward her.

Never keep weight in the center, Francine quickly wrote in her Imaginary Tap Dance Handbook. *Go,* said Gregory. He kept his eyes on the feet, which in tap were the faces. *Go. Go. Go.* Now one woman was the only thing between Francine and her hero.

"Go." In the flesh, Gregory stepped toward her.

For two counts nothing happened.

"Follow my claps," said the master.

On the seventh clap, Francine stepped out in faith. People leaned forward, and across the room, the Goth woman's tiny hand kept time against what must be her hip. The notes were gangsters leaning on the fence, the cat riding the dog's back. They were the crazy breeze you get in Venice. Then it happened. Gregory was dancing with her. He handed her a bass line, and she gave him back a syncopation. When Francine felt more floor around her and looked up, the circle had moved back to give them space.

You dance like Eddie Brown," Gregory whispered.

"Get thee behind me Satan!" Francine shouted.

Both her feet froze instantly. She couldn't move, a solid freeze like the great tyrannicus broctil, no hope of melting. Her arm was out and bent at a right angle, all five fingers spread, the knee open and the foot flexed, a ludicrous position. She looked like a hat rack.

"Miss Popsicle," said someone.

How embarrassing! Her heart had speeded up to a pace that would kill a strong man. She waited to die. In the room at Westside Academy, Gregory kept clapping. He was jazz. Her face, she knew, was purple.

"Show me whatchoo got." He clapped on *two* and *four*.

"Hawlp," she said. Each time she tried to say *help,* her tongue twisted. *Hawlp, hawlp, hawlp!*

Someone said to call an ambulance. *Haaawlp*, her little voice continued. The master's face stayed opposite her own as he clapped his hands slow and easy, in swing time, *ba BAM, ba BAM.* When the siren manifested, her body broke and ran to the door but where was her bag? She might go crazy. Her keys?

"Friend," said the Goth woman. Was she a Quaker?

The smallest hand Francine had ever seen on an adult held out Francine's black dance bag. The Goth had long raven-black hair and bangs and black lipstick and black eyelashes at least an inch long, like spiders, and she reeked of tea tree oil, that astringent. Francine grabbed the bag and keys from the freak hand with its ten tiny chewed black fingernails and dove down the slippery hallway toward oblivion. Halfway, she stopped to rid herself of the white tap shoes and live life barefoot. When two paramedics ran toward her, she disguised herself as a sane person and pointed down the hallway, to be helpful.

"Straight ahead, last door. Please hurry."

A burst of gunfire brought Francine back to Van Gogh's Ear upstairs, where Julia continued sketching. She was drawing fireworks, or perhaps a straw broom. As an artist she was terrible.

"You're not my doppelgänger," Francine said. She

picked up *Men Seeking Women*. "I'm a Venice landlord. I have bread-and-butter units."

Julia shrugged. At this moment, she looked angelic. "At the bottom of the stairs, turn right. If you turn left, you'll be in the hood at night. "

Each stair was a different color, and Francine took them like a lady, one hand on the railing. At the bottom she turned left and burst out into Ghost Town, the place on the cartoon map with cop cars burning. On every corner, figures beckoned. *Crack?* they said. *Goose?* But Francine had her mother's walk, the old walk her mother had in the old days when she used to play the tambourine and hit it on her hip with such gay abandon, before Mr. Didwell made her stop it. When a young corner gangster backed up slightly, Francine nodded. Somewhere glass shattered. She turned many corners, and at each one, dark figures recognized her right to be there. By the time she happened again upon Van Goth's Ear (the safe side) and got her bearings, dawn was breaking in the east.

Where the fuck was Cyrus?

Because other ghosts visited their loved ones. There was Casper the Friendly Ghost, and Heathcliff from *Wuthering Heights*, top shelf, first book. There was the Ghost of Christmas Past. And Topper. And murdered people.

At Paradiso, she walked down the red line left by a painter and turned in at the gate, where something caught her attention. A white envelope stuck out from the green thicket of bamboo trees that lined the front yard on the side by the Pacific Ocean.

Could it be?

The rent check from Frankie Frank, the full amount, signed and dated. Francine unlocked the door, and the animals came out, and they all sat on the three front stairs in front of their square brick house, their heads protected by the gigantic Italian stone pine. She held the check. The tree spread its giant twisted branches over them, and their very own moon shone on the flagstones.

Francine traced the signature of Frankie Frank. When the bank opened at nine a.m., she was going to pay the mortgage.

3
SNOWBALL

Without Cyrus, the Didwells were going to eat her. Francine sped toward Monrovia in her blue Miata to be reunited with her family of origin, two kinds of pickles and the olives from Trader Joe's on the car seat. This would be the first time in nine years that she had seen a single family member (except her father), the first time since she ran away with Cyrus, who was forbidden thereafter to enter the family castle. Ought Mr. Didwell to share jokes with a sinner? The question was rhetorical.

She drove with the top down toward the Holy City of Monrovia, where miracles were common, and where she had completed her childhood after leaving Iowa. Of the four Didwell children, now grown, all except Francine lived near the family compound. In the nine years since she walked out with Cyrus, she hadn't set foot in the old Victorian mansion. Whizzing down the freeway, giant trucks beside her, she prepared herself for what awaited her: the iron dog that sat by the door on the porch to bite you, the music room with the stand that held *Who's Who in Monrovia*, open to you-know-who, and on the wall the framed certificate that proclaimed May 31 Clarence and Louella Didwell Day, signed by the mayor, who joked that they owned half the city of Monrovia. On the 210 freeway all the old familiar exits sped toward Francine in the blue Miata, her hair blowing, big trucks creating a suction field that she resisted. Farther on, in the dining room, you met the large oil portrait of the senior Didwells in their prime (after they got rich), which hung above the small ceramic Didwells on the highboy china closet, Mr. Didwell's ceramic arm around the Mrs., both of them cheek by jowl on the ceramic couch. The flesh-and-blood Didwells would be getting dressed for dinner. Francine drove faster in her sinful Miata. All the Didwell cars were sensible sedans with six-foot ladders for apartment maintenance sticking out the windows. At Santa Anita Avenue she drove off the freeway, past the new Spires Restaurant and the modernization of Monrovia, past Starbucks, and left on Begonia Terrace, up the long hill.

For a month after she met Cyrus, he seemed too tall, his feet too big. She had never met a crew chief from the Arctic Circle. He surveyed wilderness for new roads and sometimes worked in the Yukon Territory. He was quiet, and unperturbed, and wore a beige or yellow cardigan, but there was something untamed in him. He belonged to the wolf family, and she couldn't wrap him around her little finger. She liked to date people who were much like her, which was like being alone except with company. Although she was the veteran of multiple affairs, Cyrus scared her.

When he tried to kiss her, she turned her head, prim, an old Pentecostal trick but unusual for a girl who worked like a maniac to be a sinner. His white-blue eyes looked like the devil's.

They talked all night about philosophy, whether God existed, the nature of happiness, and sometimes spelling. At two a.m., she caved. She was familiar with the mystery of orgasm, she was a sinner, so it was not that much of a mystery, but not a whole experience that rearranged your DNA and curled your hair. She sat up a different person. Was she the first human to experience this? At five a.m., they went out for breakfast. Francine had bacon and eggs with hash browns, extra toast, and three glasses of milk. "You have a big appetite," said Cyrus, watching her chow down and laughing. "Can we have another glass of milk?" he asked the waitress. Sitting there made her happy. When he asked her to go back with him the next week to Alaska, she quit her waitress job and stored her giant bookcase.

"I want to meet your family," Cyrus said before they took off, her car in storage, the truck and camper packed with food, clothes, survey tripod, leather tool belt, tap shoes.

"No you don't."

His eyes of the devil looked at her. "I want to see where you come from."

"No you don't."

But she had arranged a quick and dirty introduction, a meet-and-greet, a fast handshake, all anyone could take, and everyone was waiting. That night, driving the fifty miles north to Monrovia, her stomach churned. In two days, the two of them would drive north up the west coast of America and then up the one thousand three hundred ninety miles of Alcan Highway through the Yukon all the way to Fairbanks, where Cyrus would resume slope-staking roads, his favorite survey job. He loved the angle of a curve. "Francine? Mother and I want you to share your life with us," her father had said just before she brought Cyrus to introduce him. "We feel we don't know you." But a grizzly bear was nothing next to 255 Begonia Terrace. In the beige Ford half-ton truck and camper, as they got closer, Francine's fingers started drumming.

"Cyrus?" She touched his knee. "Don't leave your cigarettes rolled up in your sleeve."

"Check."

"'Never trust a Christian' isn't funny."

"Your breath is sour," Cyrus observed. He was a scientist of sorts. "You really are nervous. I didn't realize."

Cyrus signaled, then turned left onto Begonia Terrace.

For a wild person, he had no idea what he was in for.

"And don't slouch back and stretch your legs out. Christians sit up straight."

Cyrus thought religion was for nut cases, and it followed that he didn't believe in demons. He knew nothing. Mrs. Didwell for her part claimed that all men who weren't born again through Jesus would cut off a girl's arms and legs if given the opportunity, an opportunity exactly like the trip upon which the two were about to embark, the Alcan Highway through Canada to Alaska, one thousand three hundred ninety miles of deserted wilderness. Mrs. Didwell had once described the severed limbs in graphic detail.

"Let's go home," said Francine.

"How bad can it be?" Cyrus kept driving the truck up the hill toward the old Victorian house, his arms relaxed, the San Gabriel Foothills in the windshield.

He pulled over and parked, still an innocent, and there they were, ascending the thirteen stairs past the iron dog, who seemed to lunge although he had been purchased at a yard sale. It was spooky.

Once they were seated in the Didwell living room, with God's associate Mr. Didwell not yet present, things went as well as could be expected: three adults careful, three adults civilized, the meeting of an alien from outer space and two immortals, one backslidden. They waited for the father. Cyrus clearly was a sinner, bound for hell, not going to heaven, but Mrs. Didwell cracked a little after he told her about the Alaska helicopter pilot who had been caught in a whiteout, the worst kind of blizzard, flying with no sense of what was up or down or sideways. He had become disoriented. He was doomed until he saw a fifty-gallon drum on the ground. He peered through driving snow. When he aimed toward it, he bumped down immediately.

It was a Coke can.

"Oh my," said Louella Didwell.

The girl came out in her, her hand fluttered, and she took on more energy: a lightbulb getting brighter. It was an electrical experience shared by her daughters. When Cyrus told how polar bears outsmarted their human hunters and doubled back, Mrs. Didwell and her daughter exchanged glances. They both recognized a keeper.

"Where's Dad?" Francine said.

The gold curtains moved and there Mr. Didwell was. His face looked muscular. *Raise up a child in the way he should go, and when he is old, he will not depart from you*: Scripture. Francine sat still with her knees together. Where was the man who liked a joke? And cut cartoons out of the paper with a scissors? As a child she was allowed to stay up all night and argue with him if she used logic correctly, with strategies flying back and forth across the green-speckled kitchen table. *Is the moon made of blue cheese? Or rocks?* And later on, *You win. You have convinced me*, he might say, or, *You have not convinced me yet*. They argued until Mother called out from the bedroom: *Francine, you think like a man! Go to bed! Both of you.*

The great Mr. Didwell waited.

Cyrus stood up with his hand extended, the wild air all around him. The Didwells didn't have strangers in the house. The atmosphere crackled.

"Sir?" Cyrus stepped forward. "Cyrus Gustafsson."

"Like Greta Garbo?" Mrs. Didwell asked. She had a sinful interest in the cinema. "That movie actress?"

"Fourth cousins. On my mother's side."

Mr. Didwell had drained of color. He looked capable of anything. "A few times, God has let me see what Daddy would be like if Jesus hadn't found him," Mrs. Didwell had said once, both hands up to praise Jesus.

Cyrus stood with his right hand extended. Eventually he dropped it.

Mr. Didwell was a preacher, and as such had a good handshake; his success as shepherd of his flock depended on it. He could shake hands with the best of them. But now both men's hands were at their sides. Nothing relieved the tension, even though Cyrus came from Swedish Western stock—his family had been ranchers—and he was a survey crew boss who had the gift of making situations slow and easy, and he was prepared to like most people.

"I understand the two of you are leaving for Alaska," said Mr. Didwell. His farmer's hands were weapons.

"Yes, sir. The day after tomorrow."

Mrs. Didwell on the couch had become quiet, not her former self but the wife of Mr. Clarence Didwell: first God, then the angels, then the husband, then wife, then the children, then the hired help. The furniture was under everything.

"Will you and my daughter be sharing sleeping quarters?" Mr. Didwell asked in a pleasant enough voice.

Cyrus had one personality for everything. Francine could smell him. "Yes, sir," he drawled, with that cowboy edge. "We will."

In Mr. Didwell's face something had happened. Cyrus remained quiet as he lifted Francine off the couch by one elbow. His Levi's hung low, but his ears had risen up like a rabbit's. He turned with Francine as one body toward the door, and Mr. Didwell watched them, dangerous. The names for penis in the English language are varied: Johnson, Roger the Lodger, tool, boner, pecker, dinger, prick, member, schlong, John Thomas. Both men had one.

"We need to leave," Cyrus said in Francine's ear. "Now."

Francine's parents were her first great love, her father wise as Solomon, her mother a comic genius if Mr. Didwell wasn't in the room. Once Francine had made her mother watch an episode of *I Love Lucy* on TV—they had a television only for the preaching—but Louella Didwell simply sat and stared at Lucy on the screen: one genius checking out another. *Slowly I turned!* cried the bum, *step by step, inch by inch—*

"I don't see what's funny," said Louella, sincerely puzzled.

The lovers moved in slow motion past the piano, his long arm around her as she passed the second fireplace. They continued out the door and past the iron dog and past the flowers in their little pots.

"If I were not a Christian, I would shoot you," Mr. Didwell's voice hit them between two palm trees.

They went to Alaska.

Now, nine years later, blue Miata parked with its wheels braced against the curb, Francine, widow, stood with one fist raised to knock at 255 Begonia Terrace. The lace curtains were new. She gave the iron dog several sidelong glances.

"What ho?" said her only brother, Noah, as he flung open the door. He had broad shoulders and was a natural athlete. He raised both arms in a wide V of welcome, as in vaudeville.

And then she was inside, her senior picture on the old upright piano, the same Persian carpet, her parents who were both eternal coming toward her, Mr. Didwell with the beard she had seen recently, at the Miracle of Seven Sevens in Costa Mesa. Mrs. Didwell, also an athlete, limped just a little. The huge Didwells held their arms out to embrace her after praising God. Her mother smelled like talcum.

"Que pasa?" said Bunny, baby of the family, who lived for concerts: rock' n' roll, not Christian. You could love Jesus and be modern.

"Is the little princess home?" called big sister Ilene from the kitchen. When you were that beautiful, you could be snotty. Nothing looked unbecoming.

"Excuse me," said Bunny, who liked to organize. "I need to get through here. Chop-chop. Move. Dinner's almost ready."

The Didwells were disappointed in their children, not that they didn't love them, of course. With the family seated at the Didwell table, set with the good china, you could feel sin pushing like a fiend to get in through the windows of the one-hundred-year-old Victorian, the Didwells' pride and joy, especially the north wall of small glass panes that looked out on the stunning San Gabriel Mountains, proof of the existence of God and his judgment against all men. In the grand three-story house God had provided, no longer poor, now rich, the adult Didwells still worried. Their children, preacher's kids, lacked the Holy Ghost fire that Louella and Clarence had discovered, separately, when they converted, Mr. Didwell being saved out of the Lutheran church, Mrs. Didwell under the preaching of the great Aimee Semple McPherson. They caught fire and kept going.

Mr. Didwell, now retired, still preached occasionally, while Mrs. Didwell had stopped preaching entirely since the Sunday in the pulpit when she lost her timing and left Hezekiah dangling from a tree, forty minutes over twelve noon, the congregation leaving one by one because their food was burning in the ovens. Her dramatic sense had always been impeccable, but on that Sunday she stepped down forever, an act that seemed to change her personality, make her timid. But oh! What a life of adventure they had had. Their children felt pale in comparison. So in their secret heart the Didwells were dissatisfied. All around them, in the Southern California district, other preachers and their wives had children who grew up to do great things for God, go as missionaries to the Dark Continent, or pastor large churches, or become president of the Bible college. While the Didwell children dangled here on earth, doing nothing outstanding for the kingdom. Not one was a powerhouse. Not one! Alone, in bed, Clarence and Louella shook their heads. In their Christmas letters, they were vague. Francine still lives in Costa Mesa, Ilene continues to use the voice God gave her as a funeral singer (and blesses many!), Bunny loves her work in the field of Christian psychology and often takes additional classes at UCLA, where some of her teachers are Communists! Noah lives just up the street.

To their Christian friends at church they whispered, "Francine isn't living for the Lord," and heads were bowed in intercessory prayer. Hell was real. The Christmas letters were vague because lying about two divorced daughters and one shacking up was an abomination before the Lord, and the Didwells tried, each day, not to sin but to live in purity. The Assembly of God Church didn't condone sin, and divorce and fornication were embarrassing. Ilene had a stepson by her bad marriage, grown and relocated to Pennsylvania, but how on fire was he? In the bed called the Italiano, Clarence and Louella prayed, released from gravity (which seemed to be increasing), and then put on the whole armor of God and went out into the world to fight the devil. The church board agreed with Reverend Didwell that the devil had particularly targeted the City of Monrovia.

"Be ye perfect even as I am perfect," Mr. Didwell said now, while he waited for his sweetheart, who had returned to the bedroom and was still getting ready behind the door even as steam rose off the dishes. When someone's stomach growled, they all looked at Noah. Mr. Didwell's Bible lay beside the food on the built-in buffet in case a point of doctrine arose during dinner, as often happened. The buffet had a long mirror, where Francine looked like she had seen a ghost. Mr. Didwell tapped the Bible. Only sinners called him

Mr. Didwell, mostly tenants in his six apartment buildings; although he was a preacher, he was a financial genius. The saved called him Reverend or Brother. Monrovia was a battleground, and the devil seemed to be winning.

Noah's stomach growled louder.

Hungry faces stared toward the bedroom.

"How go the apartments?" said Mr. Didwell.

"I got all the rent checks," said Francine, and all the Didwells praised God.

Apartment talk was like Esperanto, a language both sinners and Christians could speak. Her siblings jeered at the Venetian method of collecting rent, envelopes in bamboo trees, but Mr. Didwell found it solid. In nine years, despite the wattles on his neck, despite his head collapsing a little forward on his neck, her father's spiritual powers seemed to have expanded. His eyes burned upward with a fierceness, like the eyes of Moses looking at the burning bush. At the table, Francine's muscles screamed for movement. As a child, she had read *Green Mansions*, a novel by William Henry Hudson. Within its covers, Rima, Child of the Jungle, is a wild girl who can talk to birds and wears dresses woven by spiders. She has no human family, but she isn't lonely because she is friends with all the animals, who love her. Smitten with the book, Francine in high school started sitting in the back seat of the car looking for places to jump out. At fifteen, the only options that were open were to marry a preacher and play the piano in church—nothing fancy, chords with the left hand, oom-pa, and melody (with two-note harmony) with the right hand, and you had to keep the time very straight and not swing it, because swing time showed you wanted to sleep with members of the congregation, something called carnal desire—or be a spinster and go to Africa as a lady missionary. There, you couldn't wear high heels because the ground was soggy. There, she would be captured by heathen natives, who would cut her to pieces. At the Didwell table, caged, Francine did isometrics.

"Let's just pray and eat," said Noah, who could no longer abide waiting for Mrs. Didwell. He possessed a high metabolism and consumed enough for three men. He was long and lanky, and named for the only man who obeyed God during the time of the Flood. Scientists were still discovering evidence that proved the Bible true, word for word.

They bowed their heads, and Noah gave thanks to God for almost everything despite his hunger, more pious by the moment while his stomach argued with him. Mysterious shuffling sounds came through the crack beneath the bedroom door while Noah, in his prayer, began a chorus about goodness and light. Of all the children, he was the most fundamentalist, a kind of scholar who had taught himself Latin and Greek. He felt himself enlightened. The oldest sister, Ilene, the movie star, winked, and down the table, the youngest, Bunny, made a list of things to do at work. At nineteen, Ilene had been a siren who drove men insane. She resembled Kim Novak, and the male population fell before her. In Bible college, five hundred miles away, she eloped with a student, a young man who drove an MG, but the Didwells had the marriage annulled, and when Ilene returned home, Francine knew her own boyfriend was toast, gone, history. They all went to Griffith Park, Francine sitting in the front seat with her boyfriend driving, one arm out the window, the newly annulled Ilene in back. Driving home to Monrovia, Ilene sat in the front seat with her hand on Francine's boyfriend's inner thigh, and Francine, sixteen, sat in back, hopeless. Ilene married him, and he had an affair with her best friend, a recent paraplegic from a terrible accident. Paralyzed from the waist down, she still waved her arms and laughed, unyieldingly vivacious. Ilene had sent the best friend's wedding present back to her in a box, the crystal punch bowl smashed to smithereens with a hammer. Ilene was still beautiful.

At the Didwell table, the prayer hurtled on. Mr. Didwell's face contorted with his private supplications to God, mostly to be purified of sin. Prayer was a good time for spying.

"Amen," said Noah, the only man who did what God said.

Hands grabbed food from all around the table—by this time they were ravenous—and the dining room was filling with the satisfying noise of serving spoons on empty plates when the bedroom door opened. All sound stopped.

"Praise God," said Mr. Didwell sonorously, like a trumpet. All eyes followed his. "My girlfriend has arrived."

Indeed, Mrs. Didwell now stood in the bedroom doorway, where she commanded interest merely by virtue of her powerful presence. This was Jesus preaching to the multitudes.

"Mother? Father?" Noah half stood. "You have shown a great example by your long union, still as filled with romance as the day you met. It's a model we children can emulate. And—"

"Has this food been prayed for?" Mrs. Didwell interrupted.

The senior Didwells had recently begun to lose their hearing, a family weakness on both sides, and spoke in voices that made the rooms they lived in quite loud. Mr. Didwell looked sheepish while his girlfriend continued walking slowly, somehow taking command of the room despite her peripheral neuropathy, her charisma undiminished, preaching or no preaching. Her face had grown beautiful in the (to be precise) nine years and one month and fourteen days Francine had been gone, wrinkled but with good bone structure no one would have guessed was there. Nobody chewed. All sat still, hands in their laps, except for Noah, who had risen fully to pull Mrs. Didwell's chair out. Mrs. Didwell could possess a quality that compelled every person present to look at her. Once, Francine had caught her in the bedroom pretending to be Evita Perón, wife of the famous dictator of Argentina. Louella had seen the Broadway *Evita* on a trip to New York with Francine.

"New York is a wicked, wicked city," she pronounced, exiting the theatre into the bright lights and taxis. She was anxious to get back to the hotel, fearing that white slave traders would stick them in the back with needles to make them heroin addicts. Upon her return home, she had checked out every book on Evita Perón in the Monrovia Public Library.

At the dinner table, standing, hand raised, Mrs. Didwell waited for an answer.

"We did say grace." Clarence cupped one hand to his ear.

When she reached down to test a piece of turkey, the dark meat, it had panache, as if from this time forward all the Didwells would eat with their fingers. She brought the morsel to her mouth. She chewed. They waited.

"Tastes about half prayed for," said Mrs. Didwell.

Francine burst out laughing and Noah pulled his mother's chair out. All the Didwells ate and talked about the price of real estate and about God's hand in said real estate. God was interested. All the Didwells loved to eat (they didn't drink, they didn't smoke, they didn't have sex, theoretically). Mrs. Didwell had news of the Laughlons, who brought Bibles into China in two suitcases, highly illegal, and who, as Christians, couldn't lie. What if the Lord came while you lied? You would miss heaven. By faith the Laughlons went through the inspection line, and when the customs officials opened the suitcases and stared at the Bibles (in translation, Wycliffe), *God blinded their eyes*. Two Chinese men in uniforms waved them forward. All the saved Didwells raised their hands to heaven.

"Christ can't come until every man, woman, and child has heard the gospel," Noah affirmed.

"Francine," said Mrs. Didwell, utterly evil, "were you in church on Sunday?"

"Yes."

Everything arrested.

Mrs. Didwell knew Francine was lying, and Francine knew her mother knew, and her mother knew she knew her mother knew. Mrs. Didwell slowly put half a green bean into her mouth. These green beans had been soaked in brown sugar. She enjoyed it and swallowed.

"Where?"

If you pretended hard enough something was real, it wasn't lying. You had to believe it. Francine imagined offering envelopes, hymnbooks, a woman in a blue hat. "On Sawtelle in West Los Angeles. Not Assembly of God."

"I see. What did the preacher preach about?"

Francine pictured it.

"The sin of pride. *Unless the Lord build the house, they labor in vain that build it.*"

Mrs. Didwell leaned forward. "Were there tongues?"

It was a trick question and Francine knew better than to say yes. She was backslidden but had once known the truth: that tongues and the Holy Ghost came after dark—late, if it was summer. Instead of answering, Francine pounced.

"Mother? Sing the 'La La' song."

In slow motion, Mrs. Didwell's features became fluid. "La la la la la!" she sang.

On the high top of the highest china closet—Mrs. Didwell loved all china, good and bad—was a picture in a frame, and Francine entered it. In the picture, Cyrus is alive, albeit fifty miles outside the frame, south, in Costa Mesa, where he still sits eating a baked potato; and in the picture, in Francine's face, her eyes are wild with hope and fear. You can see Cyrus watching.

Bunny had called that afternoon, the phone ringing in Cyrus and Francine's temporary apartment in Costa Mesa, the one they rented to be near Hoag Hospital, a move to ease distance while Cyrus got better despite every prognosis. Doctors know only tidbits. Each day Cyrus sits propped up on pillows, a little better with every passing moment. They can see it, if the doctors can't. The apartment is empty except for the essentials, a bed and table and chairs and one big white chair where Cyrus sits up straight so he can breathe around the fluid that is trying to smother him. Francine rented the place and snuck him in at night, because cancer frightens people.

"Who's on the phone?" says Cyrus from many pillows, propped on his elbows, only his darling head mobile, the limbs at rest. One knee sticks up. Cyrus loves the wilderness, and is stuck in town, in an apartment, no stars, no moose, no grizzlies. He feels like a prisoner. Two nights ago he stopped to rest in front of the medicine chest mirror.

"Jesus H. *Christ*," he said. He stared at his reflection. "I look so bad it scares me."

The doctors had drained his stomach in Hoag Emergency yesterday, but today the stomach sits there again like a raccoon, a foreign presence. It squashes his lungs and makes breathing a hard job. Last week, at Hoag Hospital, they offered him a feeding tube, and he said, "No more invasive procedures"—he was an outdoorsman—after which he walked out of the hospital against doctors' express orders, but he fell in the parking lot and she couldn't lift him. They were alone. He climbed up the side of the car and into it with Francine's help, amid loud grunts from them both, because even with little flesh, bones are heavy. His face was furious. The two renegades went home.

Now Francine turns and cleans him several times a day and a nurse comes every evening. Francine often sits on the bed massaging the metatarsals of his left foot (which is flat, one of her favorite things about him), in case the nerves in the foot hold a secret healing ingredient. When the phone rings, that day, they both light up. Perhaps it is a cure for cancer just now on the news. Insane life burns in her beloved's pale blue eyes.

"Hi," says Bunny Didwell, Francine's little sister.

"How are you?" *Bunny*, Francine mouths toward the bed.

"Just a quick note, FYI," Bunny continues. She is always in a hurry. Francine looks at Cyrus and flaps her fingers in the *blah blah blah* sign. "We're taking the official Didwell family picture in an hour. Just the children. I imagine this will be our official portrait as the offspring. The photographer is kind of famous. Two o'clock sharp and he won't wait, so suit yourself. I have to go. Laszlo, don't tickle!"

Across the room, Cyrus sits in bed beneath his giant eyebrows, long-boned and elegant. He was born for a tuxedo. He has thrown up everything he ate today, and last week feces appeared in his vomit. Indignant, Francine saved it in a jar in the refrigerator to show the doctor. When the doctor said Cyrus was dying, Francine screamed in the doctor's face.

He's not dying!

"You're pretty good in toe-to-toe combat," Cyrus drawled, and pinched her fanny. He must not leave her here alone.

"I'm not dressed," says Francine to Bunny on the telephone.

"One hour and twenty minutes max, whatever. We aren't waiting."

In Costa Mesa, Francine looks around like a trapped animal. "Cyrus! I have to run out for one minute," she calls.

"Why?"

"It's a family photograph. I won't be long and I'll drive fast. Just up and back, zip zip. Three hours maximum."

"What's going on?" says Cyrus. His face is puzzled. He studies her like he always does, still interested to know what makes her tick. She can't walk without him. Who will love you? Panic drives her.

"I'm putting a baked potato in the oven for you, my darling."

They walk to the kitchen with Cyrus holding on to the wall, straight past his big chair, where he sits each afternoon fighting to breathe while he watches the sharks on TV. Their muscles glisten underwater. His eyes are hungry as they circle.

Now he is seated at the counter while she turns the oven on and puts in a potato. She sets out a white plate, a fork, and a napkin. "Here's the salt and pepper. Here's the butter."

Cyrus pulls his robe closer around him.

"This won't take long." She sets the timer. "The bell will go off when the potato's done, and there's lots of butter. I'll get you a blanket, my darling. Wait a minute."

She pulls the raw potato back out and stabs it all over with a small knife. "This will make it cook faster."

"Holes don't cook it faster." Two black holes for eyes look up at her. He still looks debonair, despite the cancer. His voice is amused, despite the hoarseness. "The holes keep the potato from exploding."

Francine stops. She knows her way around a baked potato if nothing else. In almost all respects, Francine isn't a cook: the chicken burns outside while remaining raw within, even the frozen fish sticks refuse to broil or bake correctly, but a baked potato is her *pièce de résistance.* She has variations, the baked potato with cottage cheese, the baked potato filled with salad. She knows the baked potato and the baked potato knows her.

"Makes it cook faster," Francine corrects him gently.

"I'm afraid not. It keeps it from exploding."

That someone so wrong can be so stubborn! Cyrus has the strength of ten men, but she has the strength of eleven.

"Cooks faster," Francine insists.

"Keeps it from exploding."

"Cooks faster!"

Cyrus leans back in his bathrobe, stubble on his chin. His pale blue eyes reflect the DNA he shares with Greta Garbo. "Your grasp of physics is a little thin in terms of your general knowledge."

"Cooks faster!"

"I'm throwing in the towel!"

Cyrus tips his chair too far back.

Happy, Cyrus pulls the butter toward him as Francine runs out the door for the family picture.

That night, when she got home, Cyrus was sitting on the edge of the bed, bones shaking from head to toe.

"La la la la la!" Mrs. Didwell was still singing at the table in Monrovia, because a memory only takes a second. Francine and her mother were just alike, almost the same person. Each one loved fun and was good at it. When Mrs. Didwell finished the song, conversation flowed: Bunny's promotion, thanks to Jesus, a funeral the next day where Ilene planned to sing "The Lord's Prayer." She had been the high school choir sensation, and the year she sang the solo at assembly, her whole skirt had fallen off onstage, at the microphone, which only increased her popularity. Noah mentioned that the universal joint was going on his station wagon, the one he used to do repairs on his apartment building.

"What kind of joint?" said Mrs. Didwell, still eating.

"The universal joint," Noah called out, hands cupped to make a trumpet.

"What's that?" said Mr. Didwell, nearly shouting. They were both losing their hearing at an alarming rate.

"Please pass the fucking mashed potatoes," said the honey voice of Ilene. The deaf Didwells kept eating. All the children paused, in shock, their hearts stopped. Never in twenty-five years had the walls of this house witnessed a cuss word.

Although hands passed dishes and the silver clinked, the table had become electrified, magnetized, dramatized, like a large lit barge floating on the open sea. The Didwell children had never been allowed to swear, not the big words, not the little ones, and no derivation, and no abbreviation. God watched constantly. Their eyes widened while they waited to be struck by lightning, a wild excitement rising in them.

"I'd like some goddamned green beans," said Bunny.

"What was that?" Mrs. Didwell's eyes narrowed, slightly.

"I said I'm gobbling green beans," Bunny yelled, her face red, hysterical.

"I don't see you gobbling." Mrs. Didwell looked around the table.

"Shitty turkey, please," said Francine, participating in the new freedom. Around the table, the swearers felt like they could fly, and although Noah kept his mouth shut, his eyes sparkled with the danger. On natural speed, all their muscles felt spectacular, and they couldn't stop laughing. Mrs. Didwell ate her turkey, her eyes narrow, watching her four children.

"Family meeting in the living room," said Ilene when they recovered. She put her napkin on the table. "Everybody needs to finish eating. Lawyer Donaldson will be here any second."

"Someday you children will be rich," repeated Mr. Didwell.

All sat forward in the living room at the round King Arthur table, posture alert, yellow legal pads (supplied by Bunny) at the ready, pencils (Bunny, ditto) sharpened. A multitasker and workaholic, Bunny had called this almost impromptu meeting to determine whether Mr. Didwell should leave his children real property instead of giving God the real property (insane) and allowing his offspring only a percentage of the profits after the powerhouse Didwells had gone to be with Jesus, assuming there were any profits. *The income will go up and up!* Mr. Didwell often shouted. Bunny, surprise tycoon although she was the family baby, a mover and shaker, wanted each child to have a quarter portion of the principal, the actual real estate, the goose that laid the golden eggs, Mr. Didwell's six apartment buildings. With this house, it was seven, Mr. Didwell's favorite number. Upon the parents' death, each child would receive one-quarter of one-half the net income, for life. Upon the deaths of the children, the property and income would go to the Assembly of God Church. But Bunny, who was practical, had refused to be intimidated. She'd pitched a hissy fit and called the lawyer.

"Father?" said Noah. "Are you comfortable?"

Four yellow legal pads scooched a little.

"I believe so," said Mr. Didwell.

Mr. Didwell was the wealthiest Assembly of God preacher in the world, having been given the gift of wisdom in real estate by God, followed closely by the gift of personal counseling. Mr. Didwell had the Midas touch, and after an initial period of failure, everything he did had turned to gold, so that the bankers down at First Granite Bank on Huntington stood up at attention when he entered, a heady experience for a farm boy from northern Iowa. He was not a powerhouse in the pulpit—it was Louella who could make the fire fall when she preached, strutting back and forth across the platform in her high heels, good legs, a no-makeup Tina Turner—and his congregation in Monrovia was never large, but other ministers had reason to respect him. His gifts were (1) he was trusted, stellar, a man incapable of playing politician, and (2) God told him where to place his dollars.

This afternoon the Didwells sat at the round table, King Arthur and his knights, in expectation of the lawyer. Four yellow legal pads sat waiting, a tiny smiley face with angry eyebrows right now multiplying under Ilene's hand. The maple table at which they sat had been discovered at an estate sale in Pasadena by Mr. Didwell himself. The walls surrounding them were covered with estate-sale paintings that he had eyed and purchased hoping something would be valuable. Mr. Didwell felt that the secret to living to one hundred, his ambition, was to get your blood boiling at least once each day. Twice, he had gone to demonstrations with Bunny, once to hold a sign and protest against a shopping center, once for a march against abortion, where young people had high-fived him. Above his head in the living room hung a large chandelier shaped like a pineapple, purchased after real estate appreciated, the frugal Mrs. Didwell having several times gone crazy before that. The other two chandeliers were shaped like wedding cakes, wide at the bottom. On the floor was an old Persian rug, estate sale also, and under that was the wool purple-and-green paisley wall-to-wall carpet, imported from England, brand-new and laid down through the whole house except the kitchen, and entirely covered by more Persian carpets worth a fortune. Heaven was the Didwells' real home, but as long as they were waiting for the Rapture, they might as well be kind to their feet. For their whole lives, they had scrimped. Rich! On the mantel of the second fireplace sat Francine's card for Mother's Day from last year, mailed from Circle, Alaska, the farthest point you could drive north in the United States if you were a civilian. It was one month before Cyrus collapsed while hiking up a gravel riverbed, precious tripod falling in the stream, unable to keep working, loath to *pull the plug*, as the men said.

"How much longer?" Ilene looked up at the clock.

As if in answer, someone knocked, the four crisp taps of Lawyer Rad Donaldson, and except for Mrs. Didwell all stood up to greet him. Her feet were killing her. Lawyer Donaldson had been a friend of Clarence's for many years, and now his disapproving bulk filled the doorway, looming for a moment, blocking the sun. He had his own successful law firm.

"Greetings in the name of Jesus." His big body displaced space as he moved around three antique chairs. He looked like the football player he had been, barrel chest, close-shaven head, a player for the offense. "Every person," Rad said now, as always, "*every person* who works in my office is a born-again. Without exception."

"Shon da la seeleo," said Mrs. Didwell, speaking in tongues. "Clarence?" she added. "Hold your head up."

"I appreciate you driving all this way from Altadena." Bunny batted her eyes, large ones. Christians could flirt shamelessly, because everybody understood there were no teeth in it. Today, her hair was crazy.

"Now." Rad Donaldson still stood. The seated craned their necks. He shook hands with Sister Didwell. "Isn't God good? Bunny feels the Didwell children should legally possess their own real property after Clarence and Louella decease."

All the children held their yellow tablets still. It was odd to hear the word *decease,* a legal term but nevertheless slightly jarring. The parents would be in heaven, of course. When that happened, the children would be rich, although it wasn't clear by how much, exactly, if any, precisely. Only Bunny had been brave enough to dare it. Of course their parents' death was unimaginable.

"Right now"—Bunny got up to adjust the window shade, then crossed back to the table, then lightly touched the arm of Rad Donaldson; today she sported the hip Christian look, with-it designer jeans and high-heeled spike boots—"right now, all we get after our last parent deceases is some income from the rents from the apartments, but the properties themselves are owned by the Assembly of God Church, which means we own nothing. Which means if we have children, they can't inherit. Which concerns me. I could have children and Francine could and Ilene could and Noah could."

All tried to imagine Bunny pregnant.

"Or what if the income went down?" Francine added. "Like in a recession."

All heads swiveled toward her. The falling-rent doctrine was a lie of Satan. When Rad Donaldson hit the table, Mrs. Didwell jumped. Bunny sparkled upward.

"Your father is a shrewd businessman," said Lawyer Donaldson.

Still standing, he was here, but he had places to go, people to see. Important, he respected Mr. Didwell, and charged him nothing, and would continue to charge nothing while his friend inhabited his mortal body; but of course he would charge the children.

Mr. Didwell wasn't your usual Holy Roller.

"See you if the Lord tarries!" called the other Christians when they met downtown at Myrtle Hardware, shopping side by side with mortals who would be left behind. The horror! But while other saints steadfastly refused to look at billboards showing naked women smoking cigarettes, wanting every moment to be ready for the Sooncoming, Mr. Didwell slyly purchased his first property. It was six bungalows, wood-frame construction, needed paint, nothing down, rents to pay the mortgage. It penciled out. He knew plumbing and electric, which saved money, and he liked to fix things while thinking up his sermons. He had noticed that real estate appreciated, and over time, if you had time, a person could become wealthy. While other Christians watched the sky and planned on imminent departure, Mr. Didwell went long; but his heresy, extreme as it was, went unremarked. He simply shifted paradigms. While others watched and waited, he looked at real estate and made plans to stick around while property appreciated. Money excited him, and no one made a fortune earning wages. *They aren't making any more land,* investors said. Without fanfare, Mr. Didwell found another property, and then another. With money he had strange authority, and the bankers recognized it. He knew where to place his hunches.

"We can do the mortgage," said the loan officer at First Granite Bank, an old Didwell family story, because the church offerings were thin to nothing, "but where do you intend to get the one thousand dollars for the down payment?"

Mr. Didwell crossed his legs. "Why, I intend on borrowing it from you fellows."

First the bank man stared and then he cracked up, and the two men shook hands, the feeling of life unfolding. They gave him mortgage after mortgage, and in twenty years the Didwells owned half the city of Monrovia, as the mayor joked, six properties, all multiple units. Each time Mr. Didwell entered First Granite Bank, all the bankers stood up. Each time a deal closed, all the bankers knelt with Mr. Didwell in their suits, obedient, to thank God. Bankers liked his chutzpah. As for Louella, she stayed ready to meet Jesus in the sky, watching the clouds, refusing to wear earrings, refusing to wear lipstick, refusing to go to movies, all things that might endanger her immediate ascension when the last trumpet sounded. The Christians who went up with Jesus wouldn't need to pass through death, and Louella longed for this. *For Enoch walked with God, and he was not,* Genesis 5:24. Whatever she felt about her helpmeet's bet against the Rapture, she kept her own counsel. She had given up a brilliant career as a fiery preacher to marry him, and she had no regrets. She loved her husband with a slightly mad feeling, like a teenager.

Now Lawyer Donaldson leaned his bulk forward. "Your dad has made some good investments, led by the Lord, and I believe his net worth is about to snowball."

Snowball, wrote Bunny, leader of the campaign to

inherit, her handwriting giant loops.

Snowball, wrote the three others on three yellow legal pads. Several added double underlines. All the children were important.

"Let us, too, remember," said Mr. Didwell, "it is our prerogative to help any of our children when we see fit. Besides your future percentage income, we have helped each and every one of you in some capacity."

"Daddy?" Bunny cleared her throat. "I'm not comfortable not owning anything. We're your children, and I think you ought to leave us real property." Mr. Didwell looked down at the table, his fingers still. He took a moment to consult with God. Lawyer Donaldson continued standing. "Rad has the papers right here and then he can leave. All you have to do is sign them."

"I don't know," said Mr. Didwell. Another personality looked out from behind the preacher, and it had a hint of slyness. "I think I have been very generous with you children. Each and every one."

"Yes!" the voices cried. "You have!"

"Most children receive nothing." The Didwells were both crying, but they were a teary bunch, especially on his side, the northern and central Iowa contingent. Mr. Didwell's eleven brothers and sisters sobbed if a leaf fell, mostly farmers and not a fool among them.

"Noah? Ilene? Bunny? Francine?" Rad's thighs came closer to the table. Francine supported her neck with her right hand to continue looking at him. Somewhere fifty miles east, Venice existed. "Your father is a good man. I've known men who thought they were good men, but your father *is* one. Clarence Maxim"—he used his friend's first and middle names—"you've done a great work for the Kingdom." Rad Donaldson's voice was gentle, like a mother's. "It's all right to leave your children some money."

"What time is it?" said Mrs. Didwell, who was getting bored.

"Five after two. Tell him to leave us the money." Ilene nudged her mother.

But Noah had risen. "Father?" His voice was sonorous, fingers resting on the table, like a preacher. "Souls are lost and dying." He looked at his father. "I vote we give our whole inheritance to God. To spread *euangélion*. The good news."

All the sisters' eyes popped open.

"Noah? You're *rich*," Ilene snarled. "Rich!" cried three sisters.

Bunny stood up. "We should be able to leave our *own* money to God."

"Yes!" cried Francine, a sudden family member. It was fun to be a Didwell, and be rich, and have two sisters and one brother. "Our own money!"

"What time is it now?" said Mrs. Didwell.

"Do something." Ilene nudged her mother again.

"The income will go up and up!" Mr. Didwell shouted. He had come to life, like a young man of twenty, although his head hung forward again. Across the table, he looked mythic. Francine was her father's favorite daughter, although no one admitted it. At the table, the children's fortunes dangled.

"God gave me this money," Mr. Didwell murmured.

"But still," insisted Bunny, "we have so far not owned anything, and this is not right. We're your *children*."

"I've had my say," said Lawyer Donaldson. "Clarence Maxim?" From his great height he pushed a single paper toward his friend, plus something to sign it with. Sleek, black, a gold nib, the pen looked expensive.

"Heavenly Father?" Mr. Didwell ignored the pen and took out his own, a cheap Bic from the drugstore. It wasn't the pen that mattered, but what number you wrote. "I need to decide so Rad can go home to his wife." God and Mr. Didwell pondered.

"Give us half," insisted Bunny. "We're your *children*."

Their futures teetered.

"Half of half." He signed his name.

On the front porch Francine eased past the iron dog, which looked like it would come to life at any minute and bite you. It was extremely loyal to the Didwells. When they were old, the children would be rich, unless Mr. and Mrs. Didwell outlived them. Which was possible.

She counted the thirteen stairs as she went down them.

Cyrus stood in the street, where any passing car could run him over.

"Boom Boom La Tour," he called out, one of a million nicknames he might use each time he came back from the wilderness and held his arms out like Frank Sinatra.

He was dressed in clothes she recognized, jeans and his green Alaska parka, the jeans riding low and bunching at his steel-toed boots. She smiled. As a ghost, he had the same big nose and large ears and unusually long torso. Now he stood with his legs apart, slightly leaning back, his arms loose, his eyes blue. The parka smelled like fir trees. She felt tongue-tied.

Then there it was, his head thrown back, the devil in him laughing although he was Swedish, the decency of his long arms, the precious teeth. When she sniffed again, he had the fresh smell of glacier water over natural gravel. And cigarettes. She stood there watching until a blue Datsun passed between them, during which time Cyrus picked his dinger up and left.

4
SIGNS AND WONDERS

In massage, a client's energy rose off the table like steam from a boiler room, and Mrs. Tibbs was cooking Francine alive. The job of a massage therapist was to take a client down to zero stress, Massage School 101, but in this case Francine might have to kill her. Francine had good hands, but so far, on Mrs. Tibbs, they were doing nothing. The woman wouldn't stop talking. She had complaints about Venice, complaints about the sheets, complaints about the soap Francine used to launder the sheets, also about the cat, who sat high up on the armoire regarding Mrs. Tibbs, whose voice was like chalk on a blackboard, so typical of humans. And what about the lack of parking, the crime, and the humidity, for which the client also blamed Francine? And incidentally—now her voice grew confidential—there were brand-new rings of thieves operating at the Good Luck Grocery apple bin; they bumped against you, then slid one hand in your purse, and bingo! She had twice been flirted with in this way but had jammed her elbow into the offender in time. Francine kept rubbing, but to no avail. The woman was a firewall of resistance. Her second rub today—the first had been a heartbreak victim—Mrs. Tibbs was sucking out Francine's energy at an alarming rate. Soon she would be empty. From time to time, Mrs. Tibbs lifted her face out of the cradle to better express herself. Upon recognizing trouble, Francine had done the usual things to protect her energy: she (1) iced her hands before beginning, (2) built a psychic shield five inches out from her body, and (3) stopped periodically during the massage to shake her hands out and mouth silently, *Get thee behind me, Satan!*

But nothing was working.

"So then," said Mrs. Tibbs, "she told my other cousin, who was the one who told me in the first place, and I took her off the guest list, which if you ask me is good riddance to bad rubbish."

"Breathe," said Francine.

Her hands plodded down Mrs. Tibbs's spine and up her spinus erectus muscles. Francine's lungs and heart were already exhausted, and the massage had just started. A good soldier, she used her pelvis like a headlight, hands directly in front, and dropped her weight instead of pushing it. She made yet another mighty effort to connect to the soul of the body on the table—everybody had one—but Mrs. Tibbs was hyperventilating.

As a child—here the body on the table's breathing quickened when it should be slowing—as a child, she, Mrs. Tibbs, had a pet mouse, Tibbie, whom she had found and befriended. They were very close. Mrs. Tibbs, then a young girl, taught Tibbie to do tricks, to stand on its mousie hind legs and to turn a little wheel. Mouse Tibbie could almost sing the first three notes of "Happy Birthday," in a squeak. They had intended to go all around the world, always together, but Mrs. Tibbs's sister, then a bitch as now, had stolen little Tibbie and deliberately squashed it to death.

Which was the day Mrs. Tibbs stopped speaking to her sister. Forever.

And Mrs. Tibbs began crying.

Francine stopped rubbing. "Jesus Christ. That's terrible."

"Even for a dream it was so real I knew it could happen."

"Wait. You dreamed Mouse—?"

"Yes. And I will not forgive my sister. Ever. You're hurting my shoulder."

Francine removed her hands, to shake them, and say silently *Get thee behind me, Satan*, but now Mrs. Tibbs had risen up, back arched, weight on her elbows, breasts hanging. She stared around wildly.

"What was that?"

And in fact a snore had issued from just outside the Paradiso window, the one where Hank the dog sometimes sat wagging his tail, the green cathedral where a quiet friend slept days. It was her job as a massage therapist to assess energy, and the person in the hiding place was lonely. She could feel it. She sometimes left the curtains open so the person could watch television while Hank's tail wagged madly. Mrs. Tibbs listened for noise. Francine used her palm to smooth out the vastus lateralis, reliably tight.

"There it is again," said Mrs. Tibbs.

"I didn't hear a thing," Francine said loud enough to be heard outside the window. The snoring stopped. Mrs. Tibbs had sunk down on her stomach with her shoulders up around her ears, as if this were a torture situation and she was the victim. Francine's mandate was to make clients relax; she had a license to touch from the city. With that came responsibility. She leaned in harder and swooped farther to connect the calf to the hamstring to the hip bone to the backbone to the shoulder bone, et cetera, one smooth move for healing.

"Ouch!" said Mrs. Tibbs. "Ouch ouch ouch."

"It's time to turn."

This was the point where every single customer complained, and groaned, and cursed. But when Francine braced herself, the wily Mrs. Tibbs turned on her back and passed out completely with her mouth open.

La la la, mouthed Francine, happy again.

Because yesterday, a wild thing had happened.

At ten a.m., out on the boardwalk, Hank still panicked at the legs all around him like a German forest in a fairy tale, with monsters, they stopped to sit down on a bench, their backs facing the ocean, storefronts ahead of them, sun on their faces. She felt hope there for the first time since Cyrus left her, a pilgrim on earth who had at last found a country. With her hand on Hank's neck, the bench warm, they sat looking at life streaming by them.

"Do you live in a house?" said a bum.

He was with another bum, and Francine sat up straight, and also leaned a little forward, to demonstrate that Venice was a democracy. Unfortunately she had no money on her. She had been giving change out freely, until she finally had to start explaining to each street person who asked that she had already contributed so many times that day, and that she still had to buy groceries. Sometimes she mentioned the mortgage.

The bum and the other bum waited, both sets of watery eyes staring.

"Yes, I live in a house," she said. She was prepared to say how many times she had contributed, but the bums didn't seem interested. "We just moved here."

"You have to get up," said the first bum.

"What?"

"Get up." The second bum was stomping his foot like a racehorse, patience at an end, explaining life to an idiot. "We don't have a house." He spoke each word slowly. "This bench is ours. We need it to sit on."

She jumped up, and the bums sat down, and she rejoiced that every day in Venice was a Harvard education. The bums made sense. She spoke their language. In Venice, there was always someone you could talk to. Together with Hank, she walked south along the ocean, one main reason she had moved here, because the ocean looked exactly like Iowa, flat and empty, the place she had lived when she was happy and the world was normal. Every time she looked, she half expected to see a Holstein cow standing on the blue water.

"Tibbie! Mousie!" Mrs. Tibbs snarled, and brought Francine back into reality, the living room, massage client, money. On the table, clients sometimes had strange reactions. Francine reached down into her gut to pass some joy to Mrs. Tibbs, which was her calling as a therapist.

Why I am a hedonist, Francine had written, Bible college freshman. Dr. Scott Fitzgerald, his real name, had made his Christian students write a paper, "My Philosophy of Life." The class was Philosophy 101, so it wasn't surprising. All the students—she was peeking—wrote about the day that Jesus found them: *I asked Christ into my heart on April 20, 1963, and I want a closer walk with Jesus. Why I am a hedonist*, Francine continued, pen moving fast. She quoted Scripture, *Make me an instrument of Thy joy*, and *David danced before the Lord*, and she quoted *The Odyssey, the ancient wine-dark sea*, and also *A jug of wine, a loaf of bread, and thou*, from somewhere. She expected to be reprimanded, or possibly expelled; but Dr. Scott Fitzgerald gave her an A+ on her paper, which forever made her soft on Christianity. Now Francine, a hedonist by constitution, pulled up on Mrs. Tibbs's waist, fingers against the spine, and sleeping Mrs. Tibbs gave two peeps. Francine went around the C curve of the hip of Mrs. Tibbs, who, according to her eyeballs, was still dreaming.

"The tidal wave!" growled Mrs. Tibbs, and briefly reared up, then collapsed. The skin of her eyelids rippled.

"Cucurrucucu." Francine added the eye pillow, two ounces of buckwheat wrapped in satin. "Breathe."

Mrs. Tibbs went under and then rose from the waist. The eye pillow tumbled.

"Alaska, 1964. In Prudhoe Bay there was an elementary school just off the beach. When the water rushed out—it sucks out to sea for just a minute—all the little children ran out of their class down to the beach, the ocean floor exposed, it was so interesting! The teachers didn't understand it. It was too late. The water rushed back with a mighty roar and took the children with it." Mrs. Tibbs waved her gnarled hands, to demonstrate. Her sparse hair shook. "When the wave receded, the beach was empty."

Francine looked down at Mrs. Tibbs with a sudden, virile hatred. Her happy hedonistic views were leaking out the doors and windows. Her fingers kept rubbing. She did Mrs. Tibbs's forearm, moving faster. A wave could even now be moving up Paradiso, no time to flee. And in the wall of water, caught in front, her dog and cat, their claws scrabbling.

Mommy! Mommy! Their eyes bugged out.

"You're done," said Francine to her client. She stepped back, hands out, as though contaminated. "Massage free. Compliments of me."

"Well I never—"

"Done," Francine repeated. "Drink plenty of water."

Exhausted, Mrs. Tibbs toast, gone, eighty-sixed, Francine and Hank went to the beach to let the water heal them. Francine walked north because last week, while going south, she had seen the dominatrix Julia, tied to a large cross on the sand side of Ocean Front Walk, tiara sparkling in the sun, wearing a bra and medium-rise bikini pants and garter belt, singing a song, her hat out on the boardwalk with a sign that said MONEY HONEY. Francine backed up to disappear into the crowd. She was no hoofer. Hoofing was dead. Francine hurried north (if north was north) past the man selling cartoon maps of Venice, past the Silver Mime, who nodded. Huge pit bulls came forward on extender leashes managed by Crips and Bloods, but Hank pranced through on a special dispensation. A homeless man near Rose Avenue had told Francine that Hank was the Dalai Lama, and that if she treated the Dalai Lama well, luck would follow, and also of course the opposite. On the beach the air was fresh, and she inhaled big gobfuls. The regulars were out, the upside-down yodeler, who had changed locations, the gentleman with no distinguishing characteristics who walked up and down, the gorgeous fortune-teller who talked about the anatomical parts of her past boyfriends, the real-deal fortune-teller Mary. Francine waved at a shopkeeper.

"No," said Hank the anarchist to every direction she pulled him in. What had happened to his third-place ribbon from dog school training in Orange County? Last week, she had thrown away his collar for a harness because he would rather choke than obey her. For a small dog, he had shoulders like Attila the Hun. So far he knew fifteen words but not how to spell them, which gave Francine a slight advantage, temporarily, possibly.

"Carry me," he said, and promptly sat down. People streamed around her.

"No." She pulled on his harness.

"Don't yank little Fluffy," said a bystander, and Hank wagged his tail. "What kind of mother are you?" the kook added. Francine and the dog stared at each other. At home, at every chance, he climbed up on the table to eat Rolodex cards and thus discourage her from talking on the telephone. He wanted her to play ball. He sometimes snarled and ran around the bed to keep her off it when she was tired.

On Venice Beach, Hank won. She picked him up, the king of all he surveyed.

At Paradiso three drunks watched Hank where they lay on their elbows. They wished to be rocked. She ascended the slight rise in land, no tidal wave as yet, and at the blob in the red line directly outside 31, she put Hank down to open up the gate.

When she turned around, the dog was missing.

"Hank?" she called.

There was only one sidewalk. She looked up and down it. The sky was a perfect blue. No hawk held Hank in its talons.

"Please find Hank," Francine asked Jesus.

On Paradiso, not even a bougainvillea flower moved.

She sped down the path beside the house toward the alley. Last week, Hank had stuck his head through the fence's iron bars, and her World Gym bodybuilder neighbor had to come and pry the bars apart, a scene out of a Popeye cartoon. "Hank!" she called out. On the beach, on Monday, he had climbed into a car with Crips or Bloods, who decided to let him out, impressed by his sheer derring-do. "Hank!" Behind the four apartments, the alley was empty. She raced up to Pacific Avenue but no white fur lay crushed in the gutter. She ran around and back down the red line to the place where she had started.

"Hank!"

Venice sat before her, empty, still, as if no hell-raiser named Hank had ever been dubbed the Dalai Lama. She turned in a full circle. Next door, at 33, a man high on a ladder reached out into thin air, one foot dangling. She had noticed him yesterday.

"Have you seen a small white dog?"

The man looked down. He had a short white beard and held a paint can and a paintbrush.

"A small white dog is right behind you," he called out, in a thick German accent.

She whirled. "Hank!" She picked him up, cursing him horribly, making his tail wag.

"I saw the pig," said Hank, excited.

"Thank you!" she called up, but the acrobat was coming down, paint can in one hand, one finger on the ladder like a daddy-long-legs spider. With his other hand he reached for cigarettes and lit one while he traveled. He smoked with just his mouth, using his teeth to hold the cigarette. She had seen him there all week, she realized. His foot touched the ground.

"I am Ilya Storch." He put the paint can down and held out his hand.

She had her uncle Sly's gift of discernment of character by what came out the palm of the hand. Why she trusted the man Ilya with her life, she had no idea.

"Thank you for finding my dog."

"Your dog found you."

Her energy had returned as though she had never been totally drained and on the verge of collapse. She stood up straighter. The terrible Mrs. Tibbs had done her best, but the strange man restored her. They sat down on the small curb across the peaceful sidewalk and watched the bougainvillea while Ilya smoked and she inhaled little sniffs, which didn't count if you had quit. Cyrus smoked until the last minute. On the curb, she stretched her legs and feet.

"I've seen you on your ladder. Working. I just moved here. Most men around here can't fix anything."

"Oh! I see they are damned with you."

"They wear ponytails and shoes with no socks, and they talk about the acting parts they might get. They can't stop."

"They are good for decoration only," agreed Ilya. "Which is why I am so busy. You live here, because I see you every day and hear your cat meowing. I have no time for animals. Who needs them?"

"Are you German?"

Ilya smoked his cigarette. "Yes. German."

"Everything is breaking," said Francine. "To spite me."

"Don't say *everything is breaking*." Ilya ground his

cigarette out in disgust. He lit another. "Say what. Exactly."

Francine Didwell laughed, abruptly. They were fighting like an old married couple. She took three steps down the red line and did a little pivot.

"The bathtub is leaking through the floor in Apartment 4 behind the house. I bought *Plumbing for Dummies*, but my brain disconnected." She rubbed her head and dropped Hank's leash and then grabbed it. "It looked like Russian."

"No," said Ilya, studying her. "You are not the type for it. Some females are good at fixing what is broken, but you have no aptitude. You should stay away before you fuck up everything. I cannot help everyone, but I will help you."

They were already going up the narrow stairs of the apartment building, four small one-bedroom units, or maybe singles, a knock on Apartment 4—plumbing emergency!—using her key, going down the narrow hallway, but Ilya was very impatient. She walked faster. Ilya tapped the walls as he went, energy like a fountain. Something to fix made him catch fire.

"Where is the bathtub? Get out of the way, please."

In the small space, he knelt and turned the bathtub faucet, each finger intelligent. Plumbing was man against darkness. Hank remained alert, eager to understand the mysteries of apartment maintenance. Last week, she had hired a plumber from the Yellow Pages, but the plumber was an actor with a ponytail who got an audition and had to cancel. The next plumber knew all the parts of plumbing, but the way water ran didn't transport him. He was a stand-up comic. Ilya leaned forward, practically tender, turning the faucet on and off, color rising in his face from each clue. Once he nodded. Francine sat on the toilet holding Hank and feeling safe. Ilya could be a kind of husband. Now he rose from squatting, and she pulled Hank into the small hallway. Everything was narrow at the beach except the wide Paradiso sidewalk: the squashed apartments, the small paths, the lot itself.

"You are always in the way, I can see that."

"Can you fix it?"

"It is simple, I go in from behind this small space and replace the pipe." He grew more animated. "To remove the tiles is not necessary. Then I patch the ceiling below where the drip is coming through, and you paint it, this does not take genius. I cannot do everything."

On the sidewalk he lit one more cigarette. He wiggled the fence to see if it was stable, and she yelled at him to stop it.

"Don't worry. I am cheap and you have to fix things. Otherwise the government will come down on you."

"There is one loopy thing," said Francine. "The height of silliness."

"Do not beat around the bush!"

"In the unlikely event a tidal wave came up the street." She tried to look blasé. In the sunlight she could see the wall of water rushing toward her, Hank and Kitty inside, their eyes bulging, little feet clawing helplessly. She pointed at the roof, where if you got up there the twenty-five feet could save you from the water. She felt her life ebbing. "I have a roof, but I can't get on it. My bedroom has a crawl space, but I can't get the top off. The screws are welded shut."

Ilya looked at her sideways, a German who could handle crazy. "Yes, I see with you everything is an emergency." He picked up the six-foot ladder she had leaning inside the fence. "Ladders walk, so do not leave outside. I have to tell you everything." He pushed inside the front door and Francine followed. "I will save you from the tidal wave, but for the rest I come back day after tomorrow." He moved briskly through the kitchen and up the stairwell, no time for bullshit. "I give you the number. Do not call me before afternoon. I stay up all night and sleep in mornings. I read Edgar Cayce."

In the bedroom ceiling, he unscrewed the screws, and when he lifted the trap door, all their problems were beneath them. On the roof, everything was peaceful. Birds flew across their home the sky. The two humans climbed the six-foot ladder to stand there, all the roofs of Venice spread out before the calm Pacific Ocean. Seagulls drifted on the air currents. At the edge, Ilya went closer, his toes over the roof into thin air, Francine slightly behind him. Down the wall just below them, a right foot in a tennis shoe emerged from the cave of the Sierra juniper, then retracted.

"Is Venice cat burglar," Ilya said.

"What?"

"All Venetians know this. Nobody sees him. The police cannot catch him. Three times he is cornered and three times he vanishes in front of them."

And indeed Francine had felt outlaw energy outside the window. No wonder he slept days. He worked nights! The cat burglar, Ilya continued, had grown up here as a child, and knew the streets and alleys. He had left for three years to ride the rodeo in Colorado. Then, out of nowhere, he had come home to suddenly appear on rooftops all over the walk streets. The police—here Ilya's voice grew confidential—were going crazy.

"In twenty-seven days the cat burglar has robbed thirty-two houses. He is a hard worker, to rob and—how do you say, to *fence the goods*. Two times the police have caught him, and both times he vanishes in front of them, poof poof. For this, the police have become berserk. They want only to catch him."

"Should I tell someone? A priest?"

"So he gets killed or worse? This is impossible. He comes with house. Now you are Venice citizen."

Descending the ladder, they continued past the window looking on the yard and down the staircase, one sharp turn, elegant if you were that type, together passing by the badlands just outside the window, the cat burglar's hideout. As Ilya walked, he wrote in pencil in a little book, which he slid into his shirt pocket, then gave it a pat. "This is my brain, so I cannot lose it."

"I'd like to put a tile floor in the kitchen," Francine said, to keep him there. She had three friends in Venice: Ilya, the cat burglar, and Julia, whom she avoided.

But Ilya was done with her. He went out the door and followed the red line inland toward Pacific Avenue to the next gate, went in, climbed up the ladder, and hung off it, one foot dangling.

If someone owned you, were you a slave? Because Francine worried. Francine sat in Venice at the table that served as a desk, unable to pay bills until tomorrow when she became a Didwell Revocable Living Trust Fund Baby. She checked her watch. Her birthday was in two hours. She put down Southern California Gas and straightened the whole stack of fourteen, flaps still open. From now on, while in the Holy City of Monrovia she must always be a good Didwell, and pretend to go to church, and never mention the name of Cyrus, and honor Mr. Didwell's status: perfect as God is perfect. She stood up, the fourteen white envelopes open and hungry. She had made her bed and she would lie in it.

It had all started in the old old house where she lived in Costa Mesa, when she opened the door and there stood Ned Horsely. Except for his Newport Beach Casual attire (Bermuda shorts, a pink linen shirt, expensive sandals), he looked like a boxer.

He hadn't yet knocked.

"Hello. This is your lucky day. Ned Horsely, realtor."

"I'm not interested."

He had a pit bull by his side, and they say pit bulls are sweet, but not this one. Around this pit bull's huge neck was a huge spiked collar. When Hank wagged his tail, the pit bull refused to roll over, and this ought to have been a warning.

"I want to buy your property to build six condominiums. I'm willing to pay top dollar."

"It's not for sale. I just purchased it." Francine backed up and closed the door.

He knocked.

She opened it.

He named a price.

"Shit," said Francine.

After he left, she collected her keys and purse and sunglasses. "Back in a jiffy pop," she told the animals. She got on the freeway and headed north.

She had never realized a place like Venice existed until she stumbled on it that day, before she knew Cyrus would save her. Venice stood there like a person. In those days she had been trying to find Hollywood; there was a concert with a trumpet player from Southern California Bible College, her alma mater, and she was driving her old slate-blue 1950 Plymouth with the sunroof and DeLuxe dashboard—Mr. Didwell loved to buy his daughters antique cars, because cars that old could appreciate—unaware that shortly she would meet her true love. Ilene had a 1942 Nash, Bunny had a Cadillac with giant fins, and all three cars were unreliable. On that day, on various streets in Los Angeles—it was hard to turn corners—Hollywood evaded her. Even when she was a child in Iowa two blocks from home her sense of direction had been terrible. On that day she was off by twenty miles, so when she saw the first flash of brilliant Pacific Ocean, it disoriented her. Where was she? Down each fat sidewalk was a flash of deep blue water. She almost crashed the Plymouth and recovered only because she had good reflexes. From her car she estimated you could hold your breath, and run, and hit the ocean in thirty seconds.

"*Zut alors!*" she said, as she was at that time trying out new personalities.

There was no place to park so she kept driving, her head going *left! left! left! left! left! left!* In between each flash of deep blue sea, she fought the Plymouth. In this place, a person could be alone. Down each sidewalk, no cars allowed, she saw huge bursts of bougainvillea, and then at the bottom of *each street*, there the water was, flat, empty, looking like Iowa. Each street had shabby houses. Seven cats, not together, rested in silhouette against blue water.

The next year when she tried to drive back, she couldn't find it.

"Earth to Francine," said Ned Horsely when he appeared the next day at eight-thirty in the morning and knocked again, pit bull standing by his side. He named a higher price.

She named a higher one.

"Done," said Ned Horsely.

She blinked. It had been easy! She was a real estate mogul.

"Sign here," said Ned Horsely in Costa Mesa, and handed her a gold pen. "And here. Initial this."

She did it.

"Oh my. Venice. The nude beach," cried her mother, and dropped the telephone.

"Mom? Are you there?" Francine heard the toaster pop in Monrovia. "The nude beach closed in 1973."

"How do," came her father's voice on the extension.

"Francine wants to move to the nude beaches out in Venice."

"They're closed!"

"*Come now and let us reason together*, we read in Scripture." Mr. Didwell scooted himself the butter. "God gave us brains to use. How big is the lot you have now?"

"Three hundred by seventy. Feet."

"And how big are these lots out by the ocean?"

"Little."

"I would gauge twenty-five by ninety. If that. You're trading half an acre for something the size of a postage stamp."

"I don't care," said Francine.

"Los Angeles has rent control!" Mr. Didwell shouted, and his fist pounded the table.

"I've thought of that," she said, which she hadn't. Rent control was of the devil. Nobody owned anything.

"With rent control you can't evict," said her mother. "It's Communistic. Prostitutes. Drug ringleaders live there. You own the building and you can't raise rents."

But under rent control people breathed. People lived there. You could see the ocean. Under rent control in Venice she had seen people laughing. People ate pizza. Bougainvillea shot out in the blue air.

"God? Unblind her eyes," said Mr. Didwell.

Francine closed her eyes. *God, please let me move to Venice.*

The Didwells didn't own her. In between their violent spates of logic, she drove to Venice every day after massages, older and wiser, with a map on the passenger seat in her blue Miata that had power steering. There, she went on foot up one walk street and down the next, each small world more wonderful than the street before it. She walked until the house found her. It was a small brick house with an upstairs to look out of, and a small yard for the animals protected by a tree with giant limbs, the kind of tree that watched over its people, and a juniper that shot straight up. Behind all that was another building with four numbered doors and a stairwell up the middle. Those must be apartments. In the small yard was a red sign that said FOR SALE BY OWNER, with a telephone number.

"Hello, Tree," said Francine. She had a good feeling.

The owner turned out to be two realtors, she learned when she called them from the pay phone next to the tattoo shop on the corner by the ocean.

"Eliana," yelled a person named Babe Light. "Do we want to sell Paradiso?"

"Never sell a property on a walk street," yelled Eliana.

Francine laughed out loud. Were they realtors or weren't they? They were lawless, like gangsters. Francine watched the people on the boardwalk.

"She has the money. She's in escrow," Babe noted.

"That place is a cash cow," yelled Eliana.

Babe Light prevailed, and Francine signed the papers that same Saturday. And then they waited. Both escrows were scheduled to close in forty-five days, a simultaneous closing, and everything was going smoothly until three days before closing when Ned Horsely telephoned Francine in Costa Mesa, where she was pacing the floor with all her boxes packed. The one exception was the table and sheets for her last massages. Several clients had wept. She was planning where in Venice to put the little Persian carpet when the phone rang.

"I'm lowering my offer," Ned Horsely said, loud and clear. He named a disaster figure.

"Are you crazy?"

Minutes later she strode into Ned Horsely's office, dog not walked, dishes not washed, on the warpath. Through a door she could see the pit bull at the desk next to Ned Horsely, who didn't bother to get up. "I'm lowering my offer," he repeated.

"You can't do that. Escrow's started."

"I can and I did."

Francine backed up a step, and the pit bull started toward her. "I won't sell." She stuck out her foot, then drew it in. In tap, your toes were extremely precious. "The deal's off."

"If you don't sell me the property—" Ned Horsely leaned back in his chair and lit a cigarette. The pit bull menaced. They worked together. The cigarette went out. He relit it. Francine waited. "If you don't sell to me, I'm going to slap a *lis pendens* on your property. It casts a shadow over title so you can't sell it to a third party. Any buyer will go away, and your equity will tank. You'll be tied up in court forever." He held the smoke in while he talked, which made his voice sound like a robot's. "Take it or leave it."

On the beige wall by the exit door was an oil spoof of *The Last Supper*. Twelve realtors in assorted sports jackets sit at a long table, some half standing with their fists lifted, some toasting. All lean toward the head, where one man sits: the broker. The picture, which was raucous (twelve drunks), was called *The Closing*. Was Ned Horsely Jesus?

Back home, in the old white house of seven sevens, hours into the night, Francine worked the numbers. Cyrus wasn't available to talk to no matter how many times she looked up. The dog had fifteen words, but not *escrow, mortgage*. Finally, at midnight, she called the Didwells of Monrovia. While the phone rang, Francine braced herself against their *Praise God!*s at her failure to move to Venice. She hung up and redialed. Without Cyrus, who on earth loved her? When Mr. Didwell answered, Francine began to sob.

"The house fell out of escrow. Ned Horsely lowered his offer. I can't afford it."

"Mother, pick up the phone," said Mr. Didwell.

"Just a minute!" Mrs. Didwell called. "Things are falling off the table."

"Is that right?" said Mr. Didwell periodically when

she spilled it all out after both parents were at their stations. There were small crunching sounds, because Mr. Didwell was a midnight snacker, sometimes milk-toast with brown sugar, but more often mashed potatoes fried dark brown outside with melted Velveeta cheese inside, his own creation: Chee-Tater Patties. He thought he could patent it. Between hiccups that had seized Francine's throat from out of nowhere—she never had them—she sobbed and told them everything, the vicious pit bull, the terrible painting that made fun of Jesus. (Who was Judas?) The hiccups were coming stronger, and Mrs. Didwell said a woman on a ship had needed to be flown off for just this reason. Hiccups were dangerous. "It's a very serious condition. It's nothing to joke with."

"That painting was sacrilegious!" Francine finished.

"People will be people," said Mr. Didwell.

"Hic," said Francine. "He can't do that. Lower his offer."

"Well," said Mr. Didwell. "He can and he did."

In Costa Mesa, Francine sat holding the small Persian rug with all her boxes stacked around her. The dog and cat looked worried. In Costa Mesa, every street was a street where Cyrus had once walked but now he didn't.

"My thinking is this," said Mr. Didwell. "Why not go ahead and buy it?"

"I beg your pardon?"

"We may have a little news," said Mr. Didwell.

"A surprise," added her mother.

Her father announced in his reasonable voice that the fact was she could now afford to buy the house in Venice because of a happy coincidence. Starting on Francine's approaching birthday, announced her father, she would come into a surprise, a percentage portion of the Didwell income. Now! Immediately, instead of at the death of Mr. and Mrs. Didwell. The yearly amount would exactly match the cost of Ned Horsely's drop in price; but in Pentecost, miracles happen. "This is not for you alone," he continued. "We do things for all our children as we see fit. Ilene has money."

"But Daddy?" Francine felt frightened. "You hate Venice."

"But yet again, as pointed out by you"—Mr. Didwell's reasoned voice had once talked down an armed masked robber in his church office—"Venice is Los Angeles's only beach. People like to be near the water."

"Not everyone," said Mrs. Didwell.

"Venice has rent control."

"The point is, the value will go up and up." Mr. Didwell cleared his throat again. Money excited him. "Twenty years from now your neighbors will be jealous."

Since she was eighteen, Francine had never been dependent on the Didwells for her daily bread. On the one hand, all Holy Rollers lived by miracles—Francine's earlobe in the bathtub, not to mention Mr. Didwell's murderous driving, not to mention Moses in the Bible parting the Red Sea or the burning bush which was God. Yet, what exactly were the chances she would get the Didwell money at the precise moment in time that Ned Horsely dropped his buying price? For the exact right amount? Had someone called the realtor and suggested it? So that she would always toe the family line?

"But Daddy. The exact amount I need?" Who was Judas in the painting called *The Closing* if Ned Horsely was Jesus? "At the exact moment I need it?"

"Signs and wonders," Mrs. Didwell murmured. "Hallelujah! God is able."

In Monrovia, the toaster suddenly popped, and Francine jumped.

"There go your hiccups," said Mrs. Didwell.

"Daddy?" Francine swallowed. "Did you call Ned Horsely? And tell him to drop the offer? So I would always need the money?"

"I did not," said Mr. Didwell. "That is the truth, the whole truth, and nothing but the truth."

To tell the truth was the whole center of Mr. Didwell's salvation, and he preached against lying with a passion that neared madness. "What a baby!" he'd say if he dedicated an ugly infant.

"Are you still there?" said Mrs. Didwell on the telephone in Monrovia.

"Daughter? What say you?"

"For life?" Francine scrunched her face harder. Her childhood was full of signs and wonders, but also powers and principalities, which were of Satan. She threw salt over her shoulder.

"This would be for life," Mr. Didwell answered. "So I think you would rest easy."

"Hankie." His tail wagged. "Bark if you want Venice," Francine enunciated as if talking to a person hard of hearing, accent on the first syllable. She needed the money.

"*Ve*-nice," Hank barked clearly.

"*Yes!*" cried the daughter to her parents. The toaster popped. Again? "Oh my God. I mean goodness. Thank you for your generosity."

Clarence and Louella were weeping, they were all a family, and Francine had income on her birthday every year *for life*. For life! In her mind, in the new house, she moved the small Persian carpet to different places, and in each place it looked fantastic, the deepest red imaginable. It was a Christmas present from the Didwells, one to every child, straight from Jerusalem, from the time in their prime when they had walked where Jesus walked and bargained with the Arabs and Mrs. Didwell had been kicked out for being pushy, her proudest moment.

Francine stopped doing little jumps on one foot and then the other. This old scarred wood was just slightly bouncy, like a trampoline.

"I'm extremely grateful to you," she said to the telephone. *"Extremely."*

"I hope so." Louella Didwell blew her nose, and the toaster popped yet again. The Didwells were night owls. The old ceramic butter dish slid across Formica. "I surely *hope* so."

In Venice Beach, birthday tomorrow, Francine savored her last day of freedom. Tomorrow she would start to be a good Didwell.

On the night Cyrus died and the two coroner's helpers who spoke no English, only Bronx, wheeled him from the bedroom, knocking him on the door frame, they tilted the gurney upright. He was tall, and the front door was a sharp angle.

He was completely covered by the brown blanket courtesy of Pierce Brothers Mortuary, a brown blanket that began slipping as they battled the threshold. They were uncoordinated. It began slipping down his face like he was doing a striptease; Cyrus knew exactly how to make her laugh until she couldn't breathe. First his thick hair was revealed, then the smart forehead and wild eyebrows. The nose made a hook to hold the blanket there a little longer; the suspense was hilarious. From where she sat on the credenza down the hall, she laughed on. Now the brown blanket slid to show the one deep vertical crack in each cheek, a result of extreme weather, and then his lips and the chin he had freshly shaved earlier this evening.

When the last wheel thumped, he turned the corner.

5
LE CLUB HOT

On her birthday, soon-to-be trust-fund-baby Francine Ephesians Didwell forgot her purse, then her sunglasses. She had to go back in the house four times, twice for getting to the car only to realize the cat still rode her shoulder. The Siamese can hypnotize at will. Today she was nervous. Would her father keep his money promise? Truth was the root of his salvation. Each time she started out for the Holy City of Monrovia, a new wave of forgetfulness made her even later. The last straw was that in the nick of time she remembered the pickles and olives, and had to walk back a fifth time from her good parking place at the top of Westminster. Family secrets are a hard burden to carry, but many people carry them, and the main thing is never to think about it *in the presence of the family*. And if in the presence something should drift in, do not make eye contact. It was obscene and it was naughty. It was evil. For the sixth time, Francine told the animals, "See you in a jiffy pop"—they ignored her—and turned her back on the art deco security screens, checked them twice, and started down the red line to her blue Miata—hooker blue—to officially celebrate her thirty-seventh birthday and become a rich woman and pay the mortgage. For life! She would return to Venice a real estate mogul. The day was beautiful. No good could come from thinking the Didwells planned to tie her to the furnace.

"Move it," said Frankie Frank, Apartment 2, the snake tattoo on her arms bulging, en route to Gold's Gym. Her muscles had grown larger.

"Thank you for the rent," said Francine, and Frankie Frank gave her the finger.

Francine walked fast, her head down, no cat, hell-bent for Monrovia, and stopped.

The smell of tea tree oil made her look up.

The dominatrix stood just ahead in her tiara, holding two white men's oxfords, taps glistening. Had the dominatrix come to torture her? The tiara sauntered forward. Since encountering Julia at Van Gogh's Ear, Francine had turned the other way each time she spotted the performance artist/dominatrix/hoofer on the Venice boardwalk.

"Catch!" Julia shouted.

One tap shoe came flying toward her, and Francine caught it, pure reflex.

"Ouch," she complained.

Now, the dominatrix was so close Francine could see her little white eyelashes.

"Your energy is coming out your back!" Julia pointed.

Francine looked over her shoulder. "It is not."

"Go tap dance at *Le Club Hot* in Paris! It's a jazz club. Hoofers can make up steps." Julia threw the other shoe, and Francine pulled it in. "Your hero Eddie Brown danced there."

It was as if a knife struck Francine. As she backed up, the shoes fell to the sidewalk.

"I'm a Didwell!" she was shouting. Francine pushed past Julia's shoulder. She spotted her blue Miata. "Of the real estate Didwells!"

She was rich! She kept running. On Pacific Avenue she crossed without looking, pickles and olives jiggling, and cars swerved around her. She got in her blue Miata and drove toward Monrovia trying not to think about what happened.

In truth, Mr. Didwell had tried. He was a man of God, and the Didwells had just left Iowa, and California was full of perverts. Every billboard along every street displayed giant naked women. Some were smoking. All wore lipstick. A farm boy who had made it all the way to the ministry, Mr. Didwell strove every day to be perfect, as God is perfect. Because it was possible.

"Louella!" he had pleaded when Francine was ten years old—he called his wife by her first name, or Bride, or My Valentine—pleaded not once but on multiple occasions, his voice slightly hoarse. Francine was ten, Ilene thirteen, and Noah toddled on fat legs until he fell down. "Do not let the girls run around unclothed!"

"They're wearing underpants." Folding towels, Louella smoothed out a wayward corner. All the Didwells wanted to be perfect, as God is perfect.

"There are men in this house!" Mr. Didwell thundered, but his voice made all the women smile, in secret.

To Mrs. Didwell and the girls, his order was ridiculous. If bare flesh drove men insane, it meant men who came to the door, not those who lived here. The amused females paid him no attention.

"Come here a minute," said her father one night as Francine went through the kitchen to the bathroom. It was the middle of the night when all children were allowed to sleep, uninterrupted. Francine loved dreaming. Blurry, Mr. Didwell rose from the chair, a tall figure.

Safe, asleep, dreaming of her pillow, she followed, obedient. Soon she could go back to her pillow. In her underpants her right hip bumped the kitchen table. When she tried to see the clock, the numbers blurred into each other. Whereas Francine loved to sleep, Mr. Didwell was a night owl and rather a bad insomniac. Sometimes he dressed up in his Sunday suit, a tie and pressed shirt, and even cufflinks and shoes and socks at two a.m., and lay sideways on the bed trying to trick his mind into going to sleep, it was a nap, as

Louella slept curled up, Mr. Didwell perpendicular, her head above him. You could hear her slightly snoring, which she claimed she didn't. It was comforting.

In the kitchen, the Didwells' kitchen bedroom door was closed as Mr. Didwell directed his daughter forward to the bathroom. Tonight he was dressed not for insomnia but in his work clothes, a paint-stained short-sleeved shirt and slacks, the clothes he wore to fix things around the house while he thought up new sermons, usually three a week. He went through the bathroom door and his daughter followed.

They might be going for mercurochrome, because Francine was always falling. She had one million scrapes from jumping over boxes and chairs: anything that gave you that sailing-through-the-air feeling. It was a wild animal sensation.

"Here," said Mr. Didwell.

She blundered forward.

"Stand on the toilet."

A father was like God, or directly under God, and Mother was under him, and after that the children. In heaven there would be no animals.

She took two steps up, sleepy.

A hand was going up between her legs directly to the place her mother said must be privately aired out. *We mustn't touch*, her mother said. A father was like God, who continued his investigation. Dust sat on the medicine cabinet top, a new world she could clearly see, and one wrapper from Wrigley's gum, Doublemint. The Didwells sometimes chewed it, and also Spearmint. Her father, who was God's assistant, or a kind of right-hand man, continued working. In Iowa, her best friend Linda Andrews was undoubtedly asleep in bed. There were no animals in heaven. God was adamant. On the toilet, very still, Francine studied the green wrapper.

"I've seen the way you look at me," her father said. His fingers on her pants and then inside, where it was scientifically impossible. Fingers wiggled inside her stomach. "Pretending you're asleep and parading through the kitchen in your underpants." On the small shelf, the wrapper waited. Ilene liked Juicy Fruit. "I'm your father, and as your father I intend to scare the living daylights out of you." The top of his head had beads of sweat where his hair was thinning. He sometimes wrapped a towel around it and used steam over the sink to make new hair grow. "I need to scare you silly. Right here right now." His hand drew out of her body and he pulled her pants up. "I hope I succeeded." He looked agitated, and his hair was messy. "I hope you learned your lesson."

Francine had to believe him.

"I learned my lesson."

She stepped down, naked through the kitchen in her underpants, her father behind her. A father had to discipline his children. A father had to warn them about evil. How lucky Francine was to have two godly parents who loved her. The next afternoon, she took her daily nap in Mother's bedroom, required by the doctor to cure wetting the bed. She must sleep from three to four, no ifs, ands, or buts, and she could listen to her mother's music box play "The Hawaiian Wedding Song" and stretch out on the glorious nubs of the chenille peacock bedspread. The Didwells owned what was the most beautiful bed in Iowa or California, with curves, her mother said, to match the size of humans.

Francine lay with one foot on the side rail, one hand on the headboard curve, and her head next to Mr. Peacock's. She smoothed Mr. Peacock's tail and was about to drift off when the doorknob turned on the door to the dining room.

Her father entered.

"Would you like a backrub?" said Mr. Didwell.

"No," said Francine, frightened for no reason she could name. Her father was a Christian.

"The Hawaiian Wedding Song" was slowing down. She

scooted away and he walked forward.

"Turn over on your stomach."

"No thank you."

He had on his church clothes, pink tie and his suit for visiting the sick and other dignitary events. Mother was at Women's Missionary Council, of which she was the president. After Francine promised to go to sleep, she had heard her mother drive out, spitting gravel. When Mr. Didwell leaned over the bed, the fat half of the pink tie fell toward her.

"Turn over," said Mr. Didwell.

"No."

For a man, the tie was an unusual color; but Mother said he wore it, and not it him. *He it and not it him*, Francine repeated. Mr. Didwell sat down on the peacock's feathers.

"I know you like backrubs," Mr. Didwell said.

"I don't want one."

But a good girl never said no to her father. Francine tried not to be naughty every minute of the day and night in case Jesus came. What would Jesus do? When the big hands, farmer's hands and hands that turned the Bible pages, rolled her over she didn't disobey again. Mr. Didwell was God's agent on earth. When the big hand went under her blouse and along her back, she tried not to panic. With force, he moved her arms from her ribs out to the side. She moved them back. He moved them out. One hand reached up under her chest and pinched her nipple. A sound like wind was coming out his mouth. His other hand pushed up under her Bluebird skirt. Only sinners were allowed to wear Capris, and all the Didwell women eschewed them.

"Oh, you like to wiggle," said Mr. Didwell.

When he turned her on her side, a bad man looked out of his eyeballs. Although it was her father's face, the devil had him in his clutches. The vile sinner watched her and she lay not breathing.

"Can't you take a joke?" laughed her father.

And he knew her, said Scripture.

He lay down and pushed his front to her front. His breath sounded like a fiery furnace. His tongue forced open her teeth and pushed inside her mouth (all manner of filth, she would get sick!), putting a thousand germs in, tuberculosis, the flu. Coughing. His body smashed her body closer. Francine Ephesians went rigid. Her soul dove down her esophagus, too deep to reach. When the old devil lifted her arm, it fell like a toy soldier's. Now her father jumped up with his hair on fire. Sweat ran off the end of his nose. His pink tie tickled once and then went to the door, where Mr. Didwell stopped. With one hand on the doorknob, he turned back.

"A man could go to jail for what I did."

Mr. Didwell's eyes watched Francine to see if she would run and tell her mother. She couldn't tell the police, who were going to hell, and ditto the firemen and ditto her new teacher, who wasn't Mrs. Roisen. Mrs. Roisen was in Iowa. Her one friend Linda Andrews also lived there. But Mr. Didwell was watching to see if she would ruin the family. She needed to be a hero. It was like Atlas holding up the earth.

He smoothed down his hair as he stood waiting.

"To jail. For years," said Mr. Didwell.

On the freeway, she passed Baldwin Avenue. She got off at Santa Anita, and turned left on Begonia.

All money came directly from God to Mr. Didwell to disperse as he saw fit, and to get some, Francine sat quietly at the table while Mr. Didwell asked God to bless the food, a longish ordeal. She tapped her fingers. The picture taken while Cyrus sat eating a baked potato fifty miles south stared back from the second china closet. Eyes closed, the Didwells pretended he never existed.

At the table's other end, her mother's finger waggled at her second daughter, unredeemed, who was again peeking during prayer. But so was Mrs. Didwell! Eyes closed, Francine pulled on her XXX large sweatshirt to make it bigger and more sexless. Mr. Didwell had a second cousin, female, who was living in sin with her beloved. "Those two have been shacked up *thirty-one years*," he liked to say, shaking his head. In Francine's right cheek, a pre-prayer olive waited to be eaten. The trust fund check would come after dinner, once a year *for life*, made out to *Francine Didwell*. On the table, pickles and olives glistened in their little dishes, and the ham sent out its aroma, all the Didwells waiting for Mr. Didwell to stop praying. Now he thanked God for Francine's birth, and salvation full and free, and all the real estate God had given him. In closing, he reminded God about the drunken bar in Duarte that was applying for legal status to become a church in order to avoid paying taxes, and all the Christians said *Amen*, and all the Didwells reached for serving spoons.

They dug in.

The only time Francine ate home-cooked food was in Monrovia, and like the old days before Cyrus she would receive a bill for twenty-five percent of the raw groceries, cooked at no charge by her sisters. Fair was fair. After dinner all three girls would do the dishes. Delicious warm ham went around the table, and turkey stuffing, although there was no turkey, but Mrs. Didwell insisted. All the Didwells had big teeth, except Ilene, of course, whose teeth looked like small pearls, expensive ones. Completely dazed, Francine sat still and chewed and listened. If they hurried, she could put her check in the bank before closing. What could go wrong? Had time stopped? She watched the clock while landlord tips flew around the table, this one from Noah: When buying paint for the apartment walls, interior, always get five gallons of the same batch number. Because each batch varied slightly in its color. With the same batch, when someone moved, you could then retouch a wall without repainting the whole thing. Bunny pulled a yellow legal pad out of thin air and wrote *Same Batch #*. The Didwells always used Dunn-Edwards Navajo on their apartments, although Francine had discovered Swiss Coffee, which Ilya said was warmer. Venice existed. This table was an encyclopedia of rental knowledge. Besides his biblical exegesis, Noah performed his own repairs. All three girls could paint a house interior with no drips, as instructed by Mr. Didwell, who loved to tinker. Today the Didwell house was cleared for company, no small plane propeller to block the path through furniture, no half-refinished butter churner on the table, the rooms almost slick, like something in a magazine.

"Well well well." At the table head, Mr. Didwell put down his fork with a click, and all heads came up. His chair was the only one with arms. The husband was the head of the family, and above him the angels, and above them God. The wife was beneath the husband, and the children were on the bottom. "On this day, thirty-eight years ago, God gave us Francine."

"Thirty-seven," said Francine. She raised one hand, as if to introduce herself, and her teeth crunched a red radish.

"Thirty-seven," said Mr. Didwell. "I stand corrected."

"Daddy thinks Francine is looking older," Mrs. Didwell mentioned.

"She wants to live at the beach," added Noah. "And not Monrovia."

"She may end up the richest Didwell yet." Mr. Didwell talked down to the birthday girl directly. "I believe you may have been correct in your assumptions. Venice is Los Angeles's only real access to the ocean."

Mrs. Didwell spilled her water, and Noah jumped up.

In the next chair, Bunny put one arm of forgiveness around Francine, who had gone AWOL, run off with a man, and done exactly what she wanted. But family was the only thing that could be trusted. "I love my family!" Bunny was fond of saying. She had refinished all six chairs on which they sat, another gift, first the wood and then new leather upholstery. All the Didwells were handy.

"My baby girl!" Louella Didwell sat up straight, happy. "I remember holding you. You had just been born!"

In Mrs. Didwell's face, a switch had flipped, and a woman who moments before had blended with the wallpaper was now impossible to look away from. Her face emitted wattage. In high school, Louella Eggers had been older-looking and shy, so shy she had thrown up not once, not twice, but three times when forced to stand before the class in Public Speaking. One memorable day, she spattered the teacher Mrs. Lindstrom's new shoes, and afterward, those bodies close to her moved back whenever Louella Eggers took the floor. Each time she stood up to speak, Mrs. Lindstrom insisted the girl take the metal trash can with her. People giggled. Louella, high school student, lived in desperate fear, and then her whole life changed in an instant. Louella Eggers Got Happy.

She had been saved for several years, converted along with her mother by Aimee Semple McPherson's preaching. Aimee Semple was dramatic, roaring right out to the edge of the platform on a motorcycle, in a leather jacket, screeching on the brakes and holding out one arm the moment before she went over the edge. "Stop! You're on your way to hell!" she cried out. Years later, the Supremes took their famous movement from her. Salvation was to go to heaven, but the Holy Ghost was for dangerous living. The evidence of getting it was falling on your back to speak in tongues, which was a language only understood in heaven. Once you had it, you had power:

the power to preach, the power to not be afraid. Louella, faithful, prayed every night to get it but the Holy Ghost eluded her.

"Let go, Louella!" the people sitting with her at the altar would cry, one hand on her back. Sunday morning was for sermons, but nighttime was for the Holy Spirit, who tended to be noisy, the third person of the Trinity, a wind who blew where it would. All around her, at the altar, people spoke in tongues, some lying prostrate. "Let go! Let go and let God! Let go! Let go!"

One night the power struck. It was no different from any other night, but she went down hard and landed on her back with her arms up. People's legs stood around her like trees, and she recognized the purple buckled shoes of Sister Aimee Semple stepping over bodies. The shoes paused next to her, the thrill of a lifetime. Someone, she remembered, pulled her blouse down, but this Louella Eggers was eternal, past earthly concerns. *And ye shall have power, when that the Holy Ghost is come upon you*, Scripture promised. A strange force took her jaw and she was babbling, praising God in heavenly language. The Christians all around her faded into nothing. Her arms, straight up, never became weary. It lasted into the wee hours. When she got up, just a few Christians were left, sitting around her, the women sidesaddle in their skirts, the men with their legs crossed. For a minute she lay still to listen to the Christians' sweet exhausted sounds. When she went to school the next day, it was her turn to make a speech. She got up and walked with her paper to the front of the room.

"The Amazon River," she said.

Several students sniggered, and those in the front row moved their legs sideways. With her foot, Mrs. Lindstrom pushed the trash can closer to the vomiter. Louella looked out at the class, looked at Mrs. Lindstrom.

"I don't want to talk about the Amazon River," she announced.

Then she gave a sermon to remember. She talked about Jesus and the evil Herod, King of the Jews, and as she talked, she loosened up, acting out the parts, smoking cigarettes to illustrate sinners, once even doing the Charleston, which she didn't know she knew. She tipped an invisible hat. She did imitations of her father. In the classroom, mouths fell open, and the teacher stared at her. They hoped Louella Eggers would talk forever. That day two students converted, one after math and one during gym period, both girls, and from that day forth, people came toward Louella. She went to Bible college, preaching on students' day, which drew recognition from the big guns. Upon graduation, on the recommendation of three famous preachers, she booked several meetings, and the news spread. She booked more meetings to preach across the country, traveling by train. Once, invited forward to see how the train ran, she converted the conductor. She was booked for a solid year in advance when she met Clarence Maxim Didwell, a one-night engagement at his pioneer church, pioneer meaning tiny. She preached to fifteen people. *Where two or three are gathered together*, said Jesus. The two young ordained ministers shook hands, as Christian singles do. They were shy. That night, alone in bed, she heard actual wedding bells. Within one month she had canceled all her future bookings and her hope for future preaching glory. They were a couple. Their love letters referred only to Jesus and fields that were white to harvest.

"Oh!" cried Louella in Monrovia. The Didwells all leaned forward helplessly, drawn by her animal magnetism. Francine braced herself with all ten fingers. "I remember holding you—we named you Francine after my college roommate Francine Waters, who brought the gospel to Israel—and we offered you to God. Daddy held you high up to the ceiling, and we called Grandmother Eggers on the phone in California. Oh! Long distance was expensive, and we woke her up, but she knew Jesus. She was converted under Aimee Semple McPherson's preaching." Mrs. Didwell stopped briefly and addressed the ceiling. "Lord! We claim Francine!" She turned to her daughter at the table in Monrovia and resumed normal speech. "I don't believe you were on earth a half hour yet. Directly across the street was the Tall Corn Hotel." Mrs. Didwell looked beyond them. She could see it. "*Tall Corn*. You were screaming, but Daddy held you even higher and we consecrated you to God right then and there. Hallelujah! He has promised us the desires of our heart."

At the table, the original Didwells had vaporized, temporarily in eternity, hands raised, no longer mortal. *Enoch walked with God, and he was not*, Mrs. Didwell was fond of quoting, and she hoped to go up in the Rapture and thus avoid death. Louella was more fun than anyone Francine knew, she laughed until she gasped for air, and took dangerous chances. She was a hedonist exactly like her daughter. Once, in Monrovia, a bank robber had jumped into her car at a red light. "Go straight, lady," he said. "Sorry, I'm turning right," Louella told him.

The bank robber got out.

At the Didwell table, back on earth, Louella continued. "In that room, looking out that window, that Tall Corn Hotel across the street, we knew instantly that you would do great things for God." Her hands rose to her Savior, and she closed her eyes. "Mighty things!"

There was an awkward silence at the table, as Francine hadn't done great things for God yet. Bunny snickered. They were finishing their ice cream singing "Happy Birthday" in four-part harmony—Ilene's voice carried, pure and beautiful—when they heard the awful screech of tires. Something laid rubber up Begonia Terrace.

"I'll check on that—" Noah got up and took a bowl of ice cream with him. He was a hungry man. The Didwells sat back, and Mrs. Didwell passed out the newspaper articles she clipped and saved for her individual children: Francine's tips for tricking burglars (leave a light on); "Hiking Trails of the San Gabriel Valley," Noah; "Put Your Best Foot Forward," Bunny. Ilene's was turned upside down so she could read the comics. The girls were putting away their clippings and stealing tiny bites of white cake with butter frosting when Louella jerked up. Noah's tall frame filled the archway.

"They took the dog," he said.

At first his words didn't make sense. The dog had been there for fifteen years, a Rottweiler who looked so real no one came near him.

The Didwell children jumped up at once and sprinted to the door. The older Didwells followed slowly, as Mrs. Didwell had to transfer to her walker, helped by her husband. At the sight of all four grown kids running, Louella and Clarence giggled. What fun they had experienced in their life working for Jesus. What adventure! They had fun even when Mrs. Didwell had her headaches, or when Mr. Didwell smelled up the kitchen cleaning fish after the day boat brought him back and he drove two full boxes home. Because it was for better or for worse. Ahead of them, fast and fleet, the children reached the door and piled out.

The porch was empty.

Dark paint stared back in an oval shape the size of a Rottweiler in a seated position. The dog was wrought iron. Who could move him? Even with his mouth closed you knew he had sharp teeth that could rip you asunder. Every time you passed you noticed him and walked more carefully, even Mrs. Didwell, and the paper boy refused to come farther than the two giant palm trees. He threw the paper. The dog was impossible to lift alone, or even push, but persons had come up on the porch and taken him while the Didwells were eating dinner, and God had not struck them dead. The three sisters' eyes met.

"The dog is gone." Mr. Didwell stood holding his napkin. "Gone as a two-dollar bill. I venture we won't see him again."

"I don't know what's going to happen to us." Mrs. Didwell's voice had taken on a treble-clef sound, and she leaned against her boyfriend's elbow. Up Begonia Terrace you could see hostile armies descending. "They came while we were sitting at the table."

"That dog certainly looked real," said Mr. Didwell.

Every other Didwell nodded.

"Oh, the nerve," said Mrs. Didwell, coming back to life. "The gall. Those people came right up these stairs and didn't make a single solitary sound. How many did it take to lift him?"

"Do re mi fa so la ti do." On the front porch, Ilene kissed her parents. "I have a wedding, and I'm singing 'O Promise Me.' I have to get dressed." Her sisters kept their mouths closed—for *wedding* read *date*. Men fell in Ilene's path like trees. When she dusted off her hands, it was a pretty gesture with no hint of her peasant roots. "The Presbyterians," she lied. She rolled her eyes and looked absolutely darling. "Ta-ta, people."

But no one moved. Though the dog was made of iron, it had the size and look of blood and muscle, and it had an eerie stillness of the moment before attack. All the Didwells stood like giant Dumbos. Next to them, sinners looked small, Francine thought, except for Cyrus, who looked bigger. But the dog, discovered by Mr. Didwell at a yard sale—yard sales helped him to relax, and he liked talking to people—the dog had guarded them for years. Was it more than fifteen? Even people passing on the sidewalk stopped and did a double take while the Didwells watched them out the front windows. Then the people hurried on, but they always looked back. Still, thieves had come *this close* to the Didwells' inner sanctum. Even people who had touched the dog and felt the metal were afraid of it.

"Thruppt!" came Mrs. Didwell's special sound made with her tongue, the sound that paralyzed you like a snake. All the Didwells helplessly turned toward her index finger. She was now fighting unseen forces. "We need to go back in the living room and get down on our knees this minute. God knows where that dog is and who took it."

The sisters groaned.

"Prayer changes things," said Mrs. Didwell.

The Didwells trailed inside and knelt, food still on plates. Noah had simply sat back down to dinner and continued eating. All the Didwell children were headstrong, and it did no good to argue with them. One member short, Mrs. Didwell addressed the throne of grace and pled a miracle would bring the dog back. God had promised! While the daughters fidgeted, Mrs. Didwell raised her head to connect with a power that would see where the dog was. Mrs. Didwell wanted it back.

"Smite Thine enemies!" cried Mrs. Didwell, who now looked like a teenager. Francine stared at her. The two preachers raised their hands to heaven while the girls reached for their purses and found their keys. "You are the God who parted the Red Sea. You are the God who knocked Absalom off his horse and won the victory. Hallelujah!"

All rose at twenty past three o'clock. Some power had either listened or not; the dog was still gone. One by one they brushed off their knees and straightened out their clothes, but Mrs. Didwell simply addressed God.

"The dog needs to be in your service, God. Not in the service of thugs. We claim Jack for you."

"Jack?" said Mr. Didwell.

"I call him Jack. In private."

"God knows who you're referring to," said Bunny.

"We're done here. Let's go."

"Toot toot," said Francine's father, his arm out the window of the big black Lincoln Continental. Growing up, they had a pink Pontiac. "Get in. Time and the bank wait for no man."

Since the amount was large and the occasion was of the utmost importance, momentous, they were driving to the bank together to get the windfall. Noah wanted to go along to share his latest theory with his father, but when Mrs. Didwell chimed in, "Let them go. Francine loves to get her daddy's counsel," he took three more bites and walked off without a word to drive home and trade commodities. Mr. Didwell was out of checks, and the bank closed in thirty minutes. He liked flying by the seat of his pants, as did his daughter when she could, two daredevils, and this served them better than circumspection, although Mr. Didwell thought of himself as rational. As they drove down Begonia Terrace toward the flatlands, Francine counted on her fingers. The actual check could take up to five days to clear after she deposited it. This was the moment of decision, like in salvation. She was officially a Didwell, but she assured herself that she would still be Francine. If the roof leaked, she would fix it! *For life*, her father said about the trust fund, although if Cyrus were still alive, it would not have happened. In five days there would be money for the mortgage, water and electric, the little things that came up, like if the sink got plugged up. She no longer had to worry; plus, she only had to be a Christian in the hours she visited Monrovia. Whizzing by out the window was her life when she was suicidal from before she met Cyrus, her high school stomping ground, her mother's phrase, which the Reverend Mrs. Didwell sometimes used in preaching, *the devil's stomping ground*. Geographically, the land sloped south, the way they were descending, and continued sloping south as they passed Foothill Boulevard, where the houses became more modest. *North of Foothill,* said the Didwell apartment ads. They stopped at a red light.

"The cow's still there," said Francine.

Father and daughter chuckled.

A life-sized plastic Holstein, black and white, stood across from the red light at the far curb. The cow stood there as a landmark for all Monrovians, and at night the owner dragged it in. Chuck's Drive-Thru Dairy had been selling milk since the day that homesick Francine plopped down here from Iowa at ten years old, a plastic cow better than no cow at all. From day one, Francine felt lust each time she passed it: she missed the tall cornstalks, the smell of clods of black dirt. She missed her best friend Linda Andrews.

The light turned green. They looked left out the window.

When Francine reached high school, the cow was involved in a scandal. It turned out the dairy owners had been dealing drugs for fifteen years. They had a sophisticated system. If the cow faced east, they had cocaine, and if the cow faced west, the drug addicts kept going. As a farmer and a businessman, Mr. Didwell couldn't help admiring them, but as a man of God, he shook his head and disapproved entirely. Satan was clever. As they passed, both Didwells gave a snort, not loud, but a snort nevertheless. Except for preaching, farming was the occupation of the Didwell branch of the family. Mr. Didwell and his daughter wiped their eyes.

"The bank will come up any minute now." Without signaling, Mr. Didwell changed lanes, and a bus almost hit them. He had a homicidal driving style, and yet had never gotten a ticket, one more proof of God's existence and special affection for the Didwells of Monrovia. Jesus watched them every minute. Mr. Didwell threw on the brakes, and Francine's palms hit the dash. "It's good to have a chance to chat," he added. "You and I don't have much time together." In the crosswalk, a pedestrian jumped back and shook his fist; Mr. Didwell raised one hand and waved back. "How go the apartments?"

"Apartment 2 wants me to install a ceiling fan." Francine held the dashboard. "I told her fine. Also all the screens are rusting, but it's near the beach, so the salt air makes them go kablooey. Immediately. Another water heater may be going on the fritz."

"What is it doing?"

"Leaking."

"These things are normal," said Mr. Didwell. "Now, capital expenses can be overwhelming, but the rents will rise to cover them. You're buying appreciation. *Nobody ever got rich punching a time clock*," they finished together.

At First Granite Bank, they parked, not dead or maimed yet by Mr. Didwell's driving. Cyrus claimed the way a person drove revealed the degree of their mental health. Mr. Didwell killed the ignition but stopped her when she reached out for the door. "I think we should pray before we enter."

They bowed their heads.

In his prayer Mr. Didwell asked that she would use the funds she was about to receive wisely, and honor God. He reminded God to smite the bar in Duarte. Perhaps, someday, she could build a deck, redwood was best, and have a rocking chair there when she got old. As soon as she had the check in hand, she planned to repair the loose step in the staircase of the apartment building—Frankie Frank was complaining (again)—and also buy one good brown purse that looked better the more it aged. Many didn't appreciate the subtleties of brown, which was like tree trunks. She felt almost giddy. There was a town called Good Cheer, Iowa. Moments from being a trust fund baby *for life*, she made her toes stop counting the five days to wait, and listened to Mr. Didwell pray that all would hear the gospel.

"Amen," said Mr. Didwell.

"Jack the dog," she said.

"And find Jack if it is Your will to find him."

"It's ten to five." Francine spoke up, because it was ten to five. How long did it take to get the money?

Reverend Didwell turned toward her. "God has been good to me," he said, sliding his seat back, and she stiffened slightly. One of his characteristics was that he liked to torture people. "I own half the city of Monrovia. Figuratively speaking. A man going from rags to riches because he honored God and lived a long life that was righteous."

A car is like a little universe, especially with the windows closed. For one incessant moment, they sat there while time moved closer to the bank closing. She needed money. A single ant crossed the console of the Lincoln Continental, going from passenger to driver side. He seemed intent on his journey.

"I wonder what he hopes to accomplish," said Mr. Didwell.

"I wonder," said his daughter.

"You need to get right with God," said her father.

The depression that was always waiting since her father walked in the bedroom in a suit just like the suit he now wore had filled the car in the snap of two fingers, poison gas. She held her breath.

"If you do not repent," he continued—each word was a horror—"your life will be a misery. It will be wasted. *We've only one life, 'twill soon be past, and only what's done for Christ will last*. No one knows when life could be cut short. Mother and I pray for you with hearts that are broken."

The ant toiled on across the dashboard. Francine wanted power, like the power her mother had when she received the Holy Ghost, the power to handle deadly serpents and drink any deadly thing *and it shall not hurt you*. She was an improviser who couldn't improvise. Then she heard her voice speaking.

"You should not have done what you did in the bedroom." Francine enunciated each word carefully. "When I was little. On Mother's bed. The Italiano."

On the dashboard, the ant scurried. In the rearview mirror, in another world, their neighbor Mrs. Braithwhite parked and got out.

"We were in love!" A nutty Mr. Didwell hit the steering wheel.

The ant continued.

"We were in love." He hit the steering wheel again, again, again, each hit violent. Mrs. Braithwhite locked her car, a cipher. She always wore white gloves in public. Mr. Didwell hit the steering wheel without ceasing. "Scripture clearly tells us that this is wrong!"

"We weren't in love." Her voice continued.

"The old devil looks for any opening." When he hit the steering wheel again, his hand misfired, and the horn sounded. "We ought not to have done what we did."

The horn had attracted the attention of Mrs. Braithwhite, cosmetologist, retired, who did Mrs. Didwell's hair, and she waved. They both waved back. She was a sinner despite many invitations to know Jesus. Her bungalow, next door, uphill, was one of six that Mrs. Didwell craved to own; real estate was like a sickness. Mrs. Braithwhite's white gloves lifted up her purse in salutation. She disappeared into the bank.

"God has forgiven me!" her father shouted. His color had returned. His cheeks were feverish. His eyes glittered. He opened the car door.

You murdered me." Her voice was soft. "I have these rhythms in my head. I could have danced at *Le Club Hot* in

Paris. I got ears."

"I don't like the way you clap," said Mr. Didwell.

"I want therapy." There was an awful silence. One would live and one would die. "I want you to pay for it."

Mr. Didwell pulled his foot into the car from the asphalt parking lot. He closed the door. "Well, I declare. With the money we're giving you, I think you can most certainly afford it." His face grew urban. Mr. Didwell put his hat on at a jaunty angle. "Let's face facts. The fact of the matter is, in your thirty-eight years on the planet, many other things have happened to you."

"Thirty-seven," Francine corrected him.

"Thirty-seven. Life's everyday frustrations and disappointments, which take their toll. Yet reason tells us you would then be asking me to pay for those events as well. And would this be fair to me? It would not."

The ant reached the center of the windshield and then resumed the first direction. With her thumb, Francine reached out and squashed it.

"I don't care," said Francine.

When they reached the bank to make Francine a rich woman, they heard the big door lock. Yet God was able. When Mr. Didwell waved his farmer's hand, a money man in a business suit unlocked the door. Mr. Didwell introduced his daughter. The bankers shook her hand, the daughter of the man who owned half the city. After a short wait, a bank clerk handed her a business check that had the right amount of zeros to make up for the perfidy of Ned Horsely, with *Francine Didwell* spelled correctly, with the year and date right, today, her exact birthday.

Mr. Didwell signed it.

They all shook hands, and one man joked that all the landlords waited to raise their rents until Mr. Didwell gave the signal.

In the car, the ant lay murdered.

"How much does it cost?" said Mr. Didwell.

"I don't know. Sixty dollars. Ninety dollars."

"Twelve sessions." Mr. Didwell stared out at the concrete block wall adjacent to First Granite Bank. A teller came out the door carrying her purse. "I have to preach a funeral at ten o'clock tomorrow. I'll bring the money to you in Venice sometime in the p.m. Surely before six o'clock." His finger twitched. "So you can go ahead and get the ball rolling."

"Thank you."

Father and daughter looked out the windshield up Begonia Avenue toward the mountains.

They drove up the hill past all the houses of her youth, past the Monrovia High School Marching Band, and Francine put her hair out the window. The check was in her purse and could be deposited tomorrow. The murdered ant cried out for justice. *The grace of our Lord Jesus Christ be with your spirit*, she said, privately, because the Assemblies of God didn't believe in animals in heaven. But they were wrong! She didn't push her luck.

"Whose funeral?"

"Old Sister Aronson."

"Melissa? Because there were two sisters who were maiden ladies."

"Betty."

They drove past the dairy.

"Betty was pretty. She taught me how to make a French braid at that water baptism up on the East Fork River. Before we built the baptismal. That was fun."

"It was," said Mr. Didwell.

6
POMONA

"What the *fuck*?" yelled Bunny Didwell. "What the fucking fuck fuck *fuck*?"

On the walk street Paradiso, the homeless charismatic singer Pinkwell dropped his beer bottle, and glass shattered all over the pavement. As always, he wore a long, black, once-expensive wool coat and red boots. His voice had old magic that paralyzed the tourists and the locals, but Bunny had rattled him. While Francine watched, the head of giant yellow hair came through the gate, though rumor had it that the Didwells were one-teenieth Negro. Francine stood frozen with all four front doors wide open, too late to hide. What was Bunny Didwell doing on Paradiso? Where had she parked? Like any badlands, Venice was full of people not wanting to be found. In Venice, you could run and you could also hide, no problem. Francine wet her lips, exactly like her mother. At least the check had cleared, with all the zeros that said Didwell Revocable Living Trust. It took five days, but this morning, it had cleared at once when she begged her bank to call First Granite Bank, where Mr. Didwell was a personage. The mortgage paid, her house safe, she stood in her living room. She blinked. Besides the bills she mailed, she needed earthquake insurance. Before the earthquake.

"Fuck you, fuck you, fuck you," came Bunny's voice across the yard, out of control even for Venice. In the tree above them, several birds flew elsewhere. Now Hank was growling. "I'm sick of you and your shenanigans. I'm sick of you being the black sheep and waltzing in at the last minute after nine years of doing nothing. *We're* the ones who go to church and honor Mom and Dad and do all their goddamned medications at the doctor. And then count them. Fuck you."

Francine jumped. Bunny was swearing?

"*You* do what you want and get a house, boom, and then you sell it for no reason, and then you come home and Mother laughs and you sit there looking pink-cheeked. What makes *you* so special?"

Francine stood, looking down three steps at Bunny's leather boots, which touched the little white flowers that Francine had planted in between the flagstones. Two worlds were colliding.

"I'm not going anywhere until you answer," Bunny added.

All eight doors were open, four wood and four art deco security—claustrophobic, Francine was also Rima, Child of the Jungle—and at this moment her sister Bunny was standing with her legs spread and one hand on each hip. It looked like steam was coming off her head, but it was probably stray kinky blond hairs. Today she was wearing skin-tight jeans and spike-high-heeled boots and at least a pound of hippie jewelry. Was this the 1960s? She shook her pile of gold, a hair disaster.

"And I'm not done," she added.

The dog had now attached himself to Bunny's boot. He pumped, with vigor, on and on with no thought of tomorrow, possibly inspired by her excitement and gripping her leather ankle with both paws.

"Get off!"

When she kicked him, he fell back, and then was on her like a boomerang. She kicked. He lunged, a zealot, rejection but a welcome obstacle. He jiggled up and down each time she shook her foot.

"Hank," said Francine. "Stop it."

The dog did his own thing. In only six weeks, he had become a Venetian, dog school training discarded lock, stock, and barrel. Last week, on the boardwalk, a long-distance rider had fallen off his bicycle, all thin tires and Spandex and a bright blue water bottle, spread-eagled on the concrete, in temporary shock. *Opportunity knocks but once*, said Hank's face. He broke from the leash—his neck was powerful from being stubborn—and began humping the long-distance rider's defined calf, the rider still out of breath but gasping, "Fuck you fuck you," all the onlookers cheering Hank, King of the Boardwalk, until she pulled him off. Venetians could be cruel to people who wore outfits. Now, in the yard, Francine plucked the dog and took him struggling through the door and locked him in the kitchen, fence up.

"Fuck you," said Bunny Didwell. "You have unmarried sex out in the open for nine years without even trying to hide it. You run off to Alaska and Dad doesn't disown you. Then you waltz in for your birthday and go on about the Tall Corn Hotel. Who cares about Iowa?"

"That was Mother."

"I'm not done! And Dad says, 'How go the apartments?' Then you talk about your stupid rent checks."

On the sidewalk, local shaman Mr. Venice passed, walking his Schwinn bicycle, more rust than paint, today dressed in pink hibiscus, his beak nose pointing toward Pacific Avenue. His face was lost, as always, in contemplation of all the things that bugged Francine on a daily basis. How long was life? Did Cyrus have a girlfriend in the afterlife? Someday, hope against hope, the seer would speak out.

Bunny came up the steps and continued past Francine into the mostly empty living room. On the table through the archway, daisies wilted. From the bookshelf, the characters who had raised Francine watched her sister. Hank growled from the kitchen and exposed the single fang he used to terrify children. It made them scream.

"Who do you think you are?" said Bunny.

She wasn't talking to the dog, but to Francine, who refused to be a Didwell. Because the Didwells were a kind of royalty. Francine stared back at her and at the two (beaded!) earrings that looked out of place even though you could wear anything in Venice. Because Bunny was an outsider, and not a real Didwell at all, just the California version, not the Iowa one that knew how soil smelled. For instance, she had never splashed out in the wading pool behind the Iowa house, the weeping willow branches all around you, or climbed through them sideways after the tornado when the tree blocked the back door and their mother let them leave it and pretend it was a green castle. Palm trees were nothing. People were always trying to climb into the A-list Didwell family, and Francine couldn't help that Bunny was born in California.

"You think you're the golden child but you're just selfish," continued Bunny. "You get away with murder but those days are over! I'm sick of you one thousand percent." She produced a Twinkie from her purse and put it in her mouth, then went on. She was a multitasker. "*We* go with Dad to church so he knows we're saved, and *we* take Dad grocery shopping so he can drive the stupid cart down the aisles like a maniac and wreak havoc. You're not loyal to Monrovia. *We* go to the mall and look for scarves for Mother." She stopped to gasp for air. "I'm sick of you and all your little princess stunts. I'm sick of how you walk in and the whole world gets so *formal*. End of sentence. Period."

"*Jesus.* But I—"

"*You* don't get to talk. I'm talking. *I'm just getting started.* I already paid my trainer, but I left and came here because somebody had to tell you that you ruin everything. You walk in and the whole room gets formal and Mom and Dad look different. May I have a glass of water?"

In the kitchen, Francine got one from the ceramic jug on three oak legs. *Glug glug* went the water.

"You're a flake." Bunny drank and gave the glass back. "More please. You're a flake and you always have been and you always will be. And you're selfish! So I came to inform you. This is an edict." Bunny licked her fingers. "From me. You're going to stay with Mom and Dad this weekend and every weekend from now on. They're getting elderly. And you're taking Dad to church on Sunday since Mother's too nervous to go out. This is nonnegotiable. You can sleep in Ilene's old room in Aunt Velma's antique bed, which is worth a fortune." Francine handed Bunny several paper towels off the roll on the refrigerator. "And be sure to change the sheets. No ifs, ands, or buts about it."

Francine would rather die than sleep one night inside the yellow Victorian house where the crime took place. Outside the window, the cat burglar had just come home, as confirmed by Hank's breaking through the fence and wagging his tail under the front side window. Bunny, clueless, drank her water, plus half another glass. Bunny wiped her fingers on the paper towels. Once, Bunny had a boyfriend who turned out to be married. When Bunny discovered his perfidy, she drove to his house and called him out from the front sidewalk, his wife at the door, her husband, the offender, hiding behind her helpless. "Ask your husband who I am, why don't you?" Bunny shouted. "Ask him! Ask him!" In the large empty Venice living room, as Bunny stepped closer, the daisies in the Mason jar wilted some more, which might or might not have been a coincidence. Francine had never noticed what enormous teeth she had.

"No." Francine refilled her sister's glass.

"I'm not asking." Bunny took it.

Francine shrugged. She looked toward her book family, all the characters reclining on the bookshelf side by side: *Under the Volcano, The Day of the Jackal,* the dancers in *The Collected Poems of W. B. Yeats*. From the bookshelf, the Consul watched, disinterested, and had another drink, and went back to his snotty neighbor watering his flower beds, a Mr. Quincey.

Bunny put her glass down with a dramatic thunk. "Oh, you're charming. *Charming.* Just because you can make Mother sing her wedding song doesn't mean she's happy."

"It doesn't?" said Bad Mousie.

With a crack, Bunny slapped her.

Venice was quiet.

There was no violence in the Didwell family, except for the horse thief who'd been hanged in Ohio and the gold miner great-uncle Theodore who'd killed his partner, but that was alleged. The Didwells weren't criminals. Bunny stared down at her hand while Francine stared out at her sister. In one of the seven mirrors—two from antique stores, four from the alley, one from her life with Cyrus—Francine could see her cheek reddening. The finger marks were muggy, and now the whole handprint was filling in, as though two girls were coloring. But Francine had lost her innocence while Bunny was still in her mother's tummy, and therefore their paths hadn't crossed as children. Bunny stood still, the violent hand lifted.

"Every time you come home, things get weirder!" Bunny sobbed. Her right hand was still lifted, not part of her body. "We always talk and laugh and sing and Noah wears a funny hat until you walk in the door. Then you and Dad go running to the bank and Noah stomps out? And Daddy won't talk to Mother? We all walk on eggshells."

Bunny sneezed, which kept the room from exploding. Some hilarity lurched up from deep within her. She half giggled. "Ha ha ha! What did Daddy *do*? *Molest* you?"

"Yup."

Not a pin dropped. Francine stood exposed as the child bride she was. Until this moment her father had been the only person who knew what happened, except Cyrus, and Cyrus was busy with new activities. *Soon you will take a long vacation*, said the fortune cookie at the Chinese restaurant where they ate their last meal in public. Bunny stood blinking, Mr. Didwell presiding over all of them. His greatness went before him and around him and also after him.

Next door, someone slammed a window.

"Oh my God," said Bunny. She kept blinking. "Oh my God oh my God. *Oh my God.* I believe you."

They stared back and forth, two sets of blue eyes, Bunny's turquoise, Francine's cornflower.

Then they laughed, as if they had been sisters forever, completely inappropriate, but the Didwells were great laughers, every one of them. It was a comedy of errors, like in Shakespeare, second bookshelf from the bottom. The first shelf was empty, which was the better part of wisdom if your dog sometimes didn't get his walk due to emergencies. All the Didwells laughed like crazy, Mr. Didwell holding up *Reader's Digest* and announcing, "Laughter: The Best Medicine," Mrs. Didwell doing sinner imitations, Noah laughing at private jokes that only he got but they all cracked up watching him, Ilene laughing at anything. Didwellian, the sisters laughed and held each other, and fell on the massage table, and got up.

"You need a couch!" screamed Bunny, and off they went again.

They staggered outside to Paradiso and wandered up the line of red paint, east, toward Pacific Avenue. Bunny held her newfound sister Francine in a death grip by the elbow. Tears rolled down her cheeks and sparkled.

"I'm going to be there for you no matter what ever

happens. Rain or shine. Thick or thin."

"The postman's creed."

They cracked up again.

"I'm not kidding."

"Don't tell Daddy I told you." Francine pulled away. "He's on his way right now to help me."

They both jumped in the sudden fear that Mr. Didwell would step out from behind a clump of bougainvillea. No black fedora appeared anywhere. When a gorgeous muscleman en route to Gold's Gym turned around to ogle Bunny, she ignored him.

"He's going to pay for therapy for me."

Bunny screamed. "No kidding."

Both girls hooted. Because the Didwells didn't believe in therapy, even though Bunny was a therapist. They believed in sin and they believed in salvation. They checked the area again to make sure Mr. Didwell wasn't manifesting.

"He's bringing cash. Today. He didn't want to write a check."

"Paper trail!" the sisters screamed together. They ran east across busy Pacific Avenue, cars whizzing so close they could feel the speed, but all the Didwells in the royal family had immunity from being hit. God protected them. On the far curb, safe as usual, Bunny stopped. Her bright eyes pierced the blue sky and clashed with it. She peered up harder.

"Oh. My. God. *That's* why he's leaving all his money to the Assembly of God Church. So God will let him into heaven."

"Yes. Or else to impress the district officials down in Springfield. And protect his reputation on earth. It's a stroke of business genius."

"Eeeeeeeeeeeeek!"

They ducked, but it was merely Marlin, Francine's neighbor, who was coming from the mailbox. They went up and down the many small streets, lost in Venice, Francine amazed to have a witness. She leaned against Bunny. Her sister had parked in the only place you couldn't, PARKING FOR MEXICANS ONLY, with three spaces. It was a handmade sign that even the gang members respected. Just as they almost reached the red Mustang (with black interior), a dark blue car shot past, something old and foreign—a Volvo? a Peugeot?—with a shine so high they saw themselves reflected, two Didwells arm in arm, and then Bunny squealed and pointed at the bumper sticker. It proclaimed, in large black letters: SCHLESWIG-HOLSTEIN: LOVE IT OR LEAVE IT!

Two Monrovian Schleswig-Holsteinians, they bent double. They laughed and hit Bunny's sweet red ride, laughed while she popped her purse in. Not since Francine was a teenager had she laughed so hard at anything, not even at the Didwell table. She had laughed this hard with Cyrus. To laugh this hard, you had to be young, young, young girls coming home from church in the back seat of a car with their legs tangled, whose legs were whose? And you had to touch (so many girls, no seat belts) the knees in their grown-up nylon stockings to identify yourself by when you felt your fingers, love and life ahead, and then went screaming off again. Or if you were in love, of course.

An open mind is like a sieve, they heard the fulsome voice of Mrs. Didwell. *Everything falls out.*

They had grown up in Schleswig-Holstein, and they knew its every hill and valley, and now they knew they weren't crazy. They were ex-patriots. Francine needed to get back and prepare to meet her father. Soon to be normal, she hugged her little sister. She had a father.

"Don't tell Daddy I was here," Bunny reminded her. "He would *kill* me."

"Welcome to Schleswig-Holstein!" they both cried, and cracked up.

* * *

The cat was sometimes called Kitty and sometimes called Caddy, but never Kitty-Caddy, which would be demeaning to so elegant a creature. She was both tiny and magnificent, and she went through the world with perfect confidence, leaping onto strangers' shoulders, greeting doggies. Francine lived in terror something would molest her. Caddy had been named out of Faulkner's *The Sound and the Fury*, where Caddy is the gorgeous sister who loves two things: her brother, and to run away. With Caddy on her shoulder, Francine went outside to look for Mr. Didwell.

So far the red line was empty.

Anytime she was alone with Mr. Didwell, Francine feared his other personality, and to be ready, she smoothed down the giant sweatshirt purchased on the boardwalk just this morning to hide her shape completely. When Caddy wiggled, Francine squeezed tightly. Beneath the tent of a sweatshirt were several old T-shirts from the rag box (one needed washing), and on her legs were three pairs of sweatpants. Her own flesh lay hidden underneath thick layers. She felt gigantic. Her hair was ugly. Because the sinner is at fault, no matter what the problem.

She looked up and down the empty sidewalk.

Except for First Granite Bank, one day ago, Francine hadn't been alone with Mr. Didwell since before she ran off with Cyrus, whose presence had infuriated him. In those days he used to trap her in the car and say weird things, with all the windows rolled up and no witnesses. He had a change of personality. *We should get to know each other better,* he might say, she in her mid-twenties, on the Sundays when she visited from her sad apartments. Each living space was darker than the last for reasons she couldn't understand. *I don't see you much. We should talk about our lives and share experiences.*

Now, you believe in this free love. Am I correct? Copulating with every Tom, Dick, and Harry? In any position whatsoever? I'm interested to know about your philosophical position.

"Fuck you!" called a free Venetian who in no way resembled Mr. Didwell. Francine retreated up the stairs into the house and paced the floor with Caddy on her shoulder.

Mr. Didwell liked black coffee. Francine threw out the sitting pot and made a fresh one, and rearranged the cookies she had bought, his downfall, Fig Newtons. At 3:17, she rearranged the Fig Newtons into a chaos pattern and someone knocked.

"Welcome!"

But it was Ilya Storch, genius handyman. "Now in America at last we find the Loch Ness monster. Your clothes are so big your arms have to stick out."

He loomed in the doorway, and with him, standing like a person, loomed what looked like a box spring for a single bed. She peered past him, a little worried about Mr. Didwell's parking skills, as he was an erratic driver and some Venetians weren't all that copasetic, especially in the deep hood.

"If my father appears, you have to vanish instantly. He wears a black fedora."

"Yes. I will click my fingers. I am genie."

Ilya came inside, both hands dragging the bare single or possibly three-quarter box spring, which looked new. Was Ilya moving in?

"Where did you get that?"

"In the alley. Venice Furniture Exchange."

Upstairs, still in boxes marked MISCELLANEOUS, she had two extra pillows and some blankets. He could set up shop in the small basement. In fact, most houses in the walk streets had small mystery basements, perhaps seven feet by eleven feet, but who was counting, cool in summer. For wine? For potatoes? You entered from the kitchen. Because this house was one of the originals, from the day Venice started. He dragged the box spring to the kitchen and opened the basement door. She already had one roommate, the cat burglar. She pulled out the neck of her sweatshirt, which was choking her. Why not another? Not to mention the Spirit of the House, which had traveled from Costa Mesa.

"We use this to weed out your boyfriends who are disasters." Ilya disappeared with the box spring down the steep stairs, the low ceiling notwithstanding, and around the sharp corner, which was logistically impossible. Yet like a swan he floated through, and if anything, the box spring sighed with pleasure. Everything had a soul. "So," he called up the stairs in his German accent after all these years. "When your date comes from the newspaper, before you leave to waste time eating useless dinner, you can ask him to please bring this box spring up the stairs. He will flex his muscles. He will brag that it is no problem. If he cannot bring the box spring around this sharp corner, you must kick him to the curb, because he has no spatial understanding. Then you can try again." Ilya emerged, and used her fresh tea towel to dust his hands, and looked down the steep narrow staircase with the low ceiling and sharp turn at the bottom from whence he had come.

The clock said 3:27, exactly. Francine did need a boyfriend, to protect her from the Didwells, the taller the better. So far, each date out of the *L.A. Times* Personals had been a disaster, like the man who only looked at himself in store windows, like the man who talked for three hours without taking a breath, like the man who had some promise but said she didn't cry and therefore he could no longer see her. He was a lawyer. Where was Cyrus? She touched her cheek where she could still feel Bunny's slap. Then, without warning, she started crying and confessed to Ilya.

"My father's bringing money. To get therapy. He's a preacher and he—"

"I am not Dr. Ruth to think about your crazy family."

"But my father—"

"I must be at the Rose Café in fifteen minutes. I do not care about your people problems. I have no time for Chatty Cathy. Today I must sand the Rose Café floors and make them like new with good varnish, this is polyurethane, but I am able to find oil-base. In a minute I will go because to paint varnish is better in natural light. But without blither-blather, first we must go up on the roof to check your rain gutter for trash. Otherwise your roof will leak and I do not have time for everything. Hurry please, and do not get in front of me. I have varnish and the Rose Café is waiting. I do not have time to waste my life with piddle-paddle."

Ilya vanished up the stairs, and she raced behind him.

She followed him through the bedroom up the ladder through the crawl space onto the roof, her escape hatch for the tidal wave. When she got her footing, Ilya was flinging things off in all directions. A pigeon body followed a Coke can.

They had no bag! They had no latex gloves for hygiene.

He threw the trash, she waved her arms to stop him, more work for her, he didn't listen. When he stood up, he deemed her incapable of helping.

"You will only fuck it up." He tossed a Nike tennis shoe in good condition.

When he had cleared the gutters, they sat down on the front roof edge, but there was still no sign of Mr. Didwell. You could see the whole ocean, and their feet dangled. Someone moaned from a window. Around them, birds took off and landed.

"He'll be here any minute," said Francine. "He must be parking."

Ilya lit a Camel. To calm her nerves, Francine pretended to smoke with him while they waited for Mr. Didwell. Ilya blew out smoke, and she blew out imaginary nothing.

"I have to go now," Ilya said. He didn't move.

In the huge Italian stone pine, a teenage possum watched them from a large limb just out of reach. Every night, the adolescent joined Francine and Caddy and Hank in the bedroom from just outside the large square window. The possum's eyes were piercing.

"I do not like animals," said Ilya.

When the telephone rang, Ilya was first down the ladder and the stairs and then they ran neck and neck into the living room. Ilya was faster because he was a gossip. Where was the phone? Without a cord it was hard to find. Ilya grabbed it first, then handed it across the table, like a butler.

"I'm at a phone booth in Pomona," a voice, sinister, whispered.

What was happening? Pomona was farther east than Monrovia! In the phone booth, she could almost see him huddled, collar up to hide his face. She squeezed the receiver. She calculated how long it would take to get from Pomona to Venice. Because her therapist had a twenty-four-hour cancellation policy.

"I feel like I'm cheating on your mother," said the telephone receiver.

The voice was hoarse, like someone awakened from deep sleep, but the sound was amplified. He must have both hands around the mouthpiece. Were the two of them a couple? Was she his girlfriend? Her father had promised.

"You said you'd bring the money," said his daughter. "I have Fig Newtons." She held one up.

But the phone was dead, which meant Mr. Didwell was now speeding toward her. He had said he would be here, and he would be here. Mr. Didwell always told the truth, which was the root of his salvation. To her horror Francine saw the art deco security screen door stood slightly open from Ilya's mattress. She witnessed Caddy fly out the opening and streak across the yard and jump the fence: not a good omen.

"Caddy!" cried Ilya.

They ran out the door and down the red line toward the crowded boardwalk looking for a small white feline with brown markings. The cat was sitting on the actual boardwalk looking up at the Silver Mime, judging if she could make the leap onto his arm and thence his shoulder.

"Caddy!" Ilya cried.

Francine wrote *Help* in her Imaginary Tap Dance Notebook. She grabbed Caddy and scolded her and kissed her head.

She blinked.

A man wearing his Sunday suit stepped away where he had just hung up the phone outside the tattoo parlor, and that man was Mr. Didwell. The face was chagrined, his features caught between a rock and a hard place. He wore his usual fedora, tilted at a rakish angle, but his Sunday tie was skewered. Liar! He dropped his change and bent to pick it up and Francine stared.

"What's wrong?" said Ilya.

On Venice Beach, Reverend Didwell straightened, and in that moment, his eyes met those of Francine Ephesians Didwell. Anything might happen. He was a man with nowhere left to turn. His face contorted, badly, like an epileptic. Then he turned and strode inland, his arms swinging. A fire truck blocked her view, and when it passed, Venice was empty.

"That was my father."

Ilya nodded. The actual cat purred on her shoulder.

"He isn't in Pomona."

She needed her mother. She started up the sidewalk Paradiso, then ran. At 31, Caddy jumped off her shoulder. Ilya came in and locked the door while the cat watched him. Francine picked up the cordless phone where it had fallen.

She punched in the number of her childhood home. Her father was a mild-mannered person, unless the devil whispered to him. *From time to time God has allowed me to see what Daddy would be like if Jesus hadn't found him*, Mrs. Didwell had said only from time to time. The phone was ringing and Ilya bent to listen.

"*Praise God*," said the answering machine. "*This is the day that the Lord hath made.*"

The voice was that of Noah, who was proxy for the Didwells on the answering machine recording. Mrs. Didwell, in a crafty move, felt a younger voice would repel thieves, now that the dog was missing. Ilya was very still.

In Noah's recorded voice, emotion rose on wings of glory. "*I will rejoice and be glad in it!* This is the Didwell residence. Please leave a message."

Beep.

"Daddy?" Anyone who heard the phone could hear her. "My appointment is tomorrow. You forgot to bring the money," said Bad Mousie.

She hung up.

"Now I am leaving," Ilya said.

But he stood rooted.

Before Cyrus saved her (life was Before Cyrus and After Cyrus, or BC and AC), during her lost period, speeding back home from a family visit in Monrovia to whatever sad apartment in her white Ford Falcon, she always had the impulse to drift her car into an eighteen-wheeler and see what happened. But Cyrus made her want to live. Ilya used a putty knife to scrape bare wood around the kitchen doorway.

"You're late for the Rose Café."

"I have to take care of you," said Ilya. "You are helpless."

When the phone rang, she lunged to grab it. It radiated danger. No one spoke.

"Dad?" she said.

"Well, you've surely done it now," said a third Mr. Didwell, one she had never met before. This one was a stranger. The telephone receiver radiated danger. Ilya quietly came closer to hear clearly. Fury emanated from Mr. Didwell's breathing. "I arrived home." No toaster popped. "I should inform you. Your mother is the one who listened to the message."

"Dad. I only said you forgot to bring the money."

"I'm afraid I told your mother everything. A Christian can't lie!" He had strong vocal cords from denouncing Satan in the pulpit. Now his voice cracked and came out in little pieces. Mr. Didwell made a sound like a whale. "I hope you're happy. I've tried to protect you and make excuses for you, but I fear all that is now impossible. I would have to say your mother hates you. She is violent in her mind."

Francine cringed.

Mr. Didwell had told his wife a whopper.

"I do not imagine she will again speak to you."

"Daddy?" Francine whispered.

What kept people's bodies upright? How would she live? Ilya scraped more wood. Her old massage school teacher Marcel had said that no one knows what life force is, but it exists. Why was she standing? By logic, her body should fall down immediately.

"Who's going to take care of me?" screamed a fourth, or fifth, or sixth Mr. Didwell. Waves of sound came out of the telephone and landed on her sweatshirt.

"Not me," said Francine. "I'm your daughter."

When Francine looked up, the light was fading. Her ugly outer clothes lay dropped where she had left them, no need for protection from her father's secret personality. Her same sister Bunny stood in the same doorway wearing the same clothes as earlier today as if the world had not ended. At last, out of politeness, Francine dragged herself to get the key off of its long nail behind the door and open the art deco security screen, a huge effort. Ilya with his can of oil-based varnish had departed for the Rose Café, and the cat burglar was out robbing houses while there was still light. He had become fearless. Tail inert, Hank looked up at Bunny and didn't hump her calf, perhaps sensing the seriousness of the situation.

"Dad didn't bring the money," said Francine. She was frightened.

Bunny jumped sideways. "Is he gone? But. Listen listen listen." As she spoke, her earrings jangled.

Since when did Christians tart up? Whereas Francine, sinner, wore no makeup. Except lipstick. She had none on now, and in two of the seven mirrors, she looked like something the cat dragged in. She hoped Cyrus couldn't see her.

"Please pay attention." Bunny's eyebrows stuck out every which way, as they did when she was excited. "I think I had a vision," she continued, and immediately began crying, "I love love love my family."

The old argument of young men having dreams and old men seeing visions was a hot topic of debate in Pentecostalism, not Evangelicalism. Evangelicals were clueless, as they didn't have the electric presence of the Holy Ghost. It was like walking around blind and feeling objects. In any case, Noah loved to argue the dream/vision problem, or was it the other way around? Young men had visions? What was the difference? In other news, the Assemblies of God Church had been ordaining women to preach since 1935, which was very forward-thinking. Bunny was gearing up for something.

"Help," said Francine.

"*The Didwell Healing Cruise*," Bunny enunciated. She swung her arm out, palm up, like Vanna White on TV, while she allowed each word to penetrate. "I think I may have found my calling." She smoothed her eyebrows.

"I was sitting in my office," she went on, her voice in awe, her hair in shock, "and it just came to me." Hank listened and did the downward dog stretch named after him. So far, there were no words he recognized. Bunny's turquoise eyes looked like a prophet's. She looked toward heaven.

"I had just come back from taking my break, this week is my favorite schedule, Emergency Room Rotation, and I was just sitting there when I had this bright idea. I have a lot of them. I think I'm like the painter Picasso in that respect. Anyhow." Bunny picked up a Fig Newton, looked at her stomach sideways in a mirror, and replaced it.

"So. My patient is in crisis, but the idea bursts into my head and it just gets brighter."

Francine had a bad feeling. Because who would believe her? No one else had seen him.

"My patient went on all through her suicide attempts, failed, obviously, and started in on her desire to burn down forests, but I told her *next time*. I said *good work*. I immediately got up and drove here at ninety miles per hour."

Francine gazed down at the clothes dropped on the floor, but it took too much energy to pick them up. She wished Hank would attack her sister's leg. Instead, his head cocked, he tried to increase his vocabulary.

"Picture this. A ship. Us. The Caribbean." Bunny's voice was rising in crescendo. Francine checked to see if the wilted flowers had come back to life—not yet. "The Didwell Healing Cruise to get a tan and help the family heal and confront Daddy." In the air, as if by magic, Bunny had created a Las Vegas marquee with one hand. You could see it in your imagination, in living color. "Daddy may not be willing to counsel with any people outside the family. Sinners look to him for guidance. But." She fluffed her hair. "Duh! *I'm a therapist.*

What are the chances? I lead groups. I'm a professional. We can have sessions on the deck in the a.m., including Noah, and keep it in the family, and individual counseling when it gets shady. We can do role-playing. You can be Daddy. Daddy can be you. We can do it all inside the family. Sinners would love to see the Didwells fallen! Plus we can get a tan. The duration of a week to ten days is my thinking."

Francine started laughing.

"Hear me out."

Francine backed up against the wall and tightened her solar plexus, an old trick from her dancer days. *Always swivel from the hip* was one note in her Imaginary Tap Dance Handbook. Hank stood up, his ears alert. Bunny had energy enough for a whole village. Once, she had stenciled all the walls in her three-bedroom home with scripture from the King James Version, the only language the Didwells knew, *Thy Word is a lamp unto my feet, and a light unto my path.* The week after, she took a one-day course in furniture upholstery, then reupholstered all the chairs in her house and continued unabated to the Didwell house and the eight chairs at its formal dining room table. She loved her parents, and she loved upholstery. Directly after, without resting, with the help of people from Dobson Paints (who offered her a job), she re-stuccoed the front of her one-story residence though it wasn't even crumbling. Now she produced a yellow legal pad out of nowhere, with a list. Demon forces had supplied it, with a pen. No power on earth could make you board a ship.

"*Rage pillows.*" Bunny tapped the first item on the list. "You hit them and say bad words, although frankly, Daddy probably wouldn't. I'm thinking September."

"You aren't allowed to blaspheme Daddy," Francine said.

"Don't be silly, silly. Obviously, we can't say the word

molested."

"*Obviously.*"

"Because it's tricky. We can say *ill-advised.*" Bunny filled the yellow pad at lightning speed. "We can say *inappropriate.* We can say *Perhaps a better choice would be.* God, my brain is going crazy." For a minute with her turquoise eyeballs, she looked like someone from outer space. She bit on the pencil. "We can say *confusing.*"

"No." Francine crossed her arms.

"Put a fleece before the Lord," said Bunny.

A fleece was something Christians put before the Lord, from the Old Testament. You put it out at night. In the morning, if it was wet, you ceased and desisted with your earthly plan. But if it was dry! You went to battle. You could use a chamois or a towel, and of course, in California, the Christians didn't use fleeces but had watered them down to metaphors, the exact kind of thing that allowed them to wear lipstick. On the table, the Fig Newtons sat uneaten by Mr. Didwell. Francine kicked a T-shirt sideways.

"No fleece."

"I love my family! Daddy will tell the truth, and Mom will cry, and we can all forgive each other and be happy. Like after the Civil War. Like a country. We almost are. We have fifty-three first cousins in Minnesota."

Francine flared up, momentarily animated. "Our cousin James isn't in Minnesota. He lives up in Sacramento. Uncle Eliot's boy by his second marriage."

Out of breath, Bunny bent forward and put both hands on her knees to get air. She looked fantastic. At that moment, someone whistled from Paradiso, audible through all the open doors. "Workin' out is workin' out!" the someone added from the sidewalk. Bunny waved back.

It had been sweet to have a sister, if only for one afternoon. Francine already missed her.

"No."

Bunny shimmied. "We can come home black! Every afternoon Mom and Dad take naps, and we can sneak on the top deck in our bikinis." Bunny held out her arms, and Francine reciprocated without thinking. The Didwells had fish-white skin on both parents' sides. "We can come home with killer tan lines if we have the right bikinis. We can look fantastic."

"No," said Francine.

"You're my only sister." Bunny's big hair shook with sobs. "I don't want to lose you."

"I'm not your only sister."

"Whatever."

Francine walked Bunny to her car in PARKING FOR MEXICANS ONLY. The three spaces tended to be empty. Walking, their joints moved alike. On her yellow legal pad, Bunny continued making notes, *Take sunglasses. Coppertone!* Two men of Latin origin were sauntering toward them, and Francine's hackles rose, because you had to be very careful. The women were inside the hood itself, which was hardly their territory. As the men came even, on the sidewalk, one of them, covered in tattoos and wearing a crucifix, stopped opposite the red Mustang.

"You a Mexican?"

"Who wants to know?" Bunny leaned one hip against the car.

Francine stood still, alive for who knew how many more seconds. But Bunny's inner light had come on, in the way of Didwell women. She stepped onto the sidewalk and tossed her earrings. One ringed finger traced the ultra-defined pectoral muscle of the man in the tight T-shirt.

"Listen." She looked up. "You boys be good now." Her light filled Venice. "Don't shoot."

7
THE SECOND COMING IN SPIRES RESTAURANT

Francine ran up the white stairs, two at a time, no hands on the railing, in order to keep her appointment with Sarah Sitwell, PhD, LMFT, CGP. Her energy was coming out her back! For some reason Francine believed Julia, despite or because of her black bag of torture items. Besides being mean, the dominatrix possessed some weird kindness. On the wall by the top stair, there was a small sign with an address from the yellow pages, 3202½ North Pickles Street, Santa Monica, California. The word *Pickles* was encouraging. According to her watch, Francine was seven minutes early.

In the small foyer, two pictures of coffee cups on the walls, Francine didn't sit down, but worked to calm her nerves by taking short steps in a circle backwards. The great hoofer Bill "Bo Jangles" Robinson, in order to hone his skills, had practiced every move in four directions, and his tap sounds were consistent, no weak brothers. What was she doing? She was no hoofer. When a door beside the water cooler opened, Francine walked sedately through it into a large room that contained a couch, a chair, a woman standing.

"I'm Sarah."

Her head was slightly cocked, and she wore brown from head to toe, with brown hair and brown eyes, all different browns, and all the windows looked out into trees, as if this were a giant oak. Rima, Child of the Jungle, Francine sat herself exactly in the middle of a small couch, and the woman sat opposite, a low table with Kleenex in between them, but Kleenex would not be needed. Francine wasn't a crier.

"What brings you here?" said Sarah.

"My father molested me." Francine ripped a box of tissues out of Sarah's hand where she was just extending it. "I'm a slut. He had to stop me. *Oh! You like to wiggle,* he said just before it started."

Sarah waited.

"Just your garden variety molestation, the usual, blah blah blah. After he did it he shoved his tongue inside my mouth and started shaking. His tie was pink." Francine looked up at Sarah Sitwell. "My father is so powerful that once an angel brought him chicken. I think he put a curse on me. I just want to tap dance."

"I don't believe in curses," said Sarah.

Francine stood up. A sinner, Sarah's eyes were blinded, plus she had no signs and wonders at her fingertips. Francine touched her earlobe that had once been missing. Purse tight, she glided toward a small sign that said EXIT.

"Our time isn't up," said Sarah.

Francine stopped gliding.

"No one can make you tap dance," said Sarah. "You have to take it."

Stay down, said the imaginary Mr. Didwell.

When Francine's tap teacher, Jimmie DeFore, who gave her the white shoes said *There are three great hoofers living: Honi Coles. Eddie Brown. Me*, she went home and called up Eddie Brown as her teacher instructed. The great hoofer was teaching at the Embassy Hotel in downtown Los Angeles.

"What you want?" a voice snarled when she dialed the phone. She didn't hang up.

"Do you teach tap?" she asked the master. She hoped

it was the master. Who knew? This man was cranky.

"Be there at one o'clock tomorrow," he yelled. "The Embassy Hotel. Ninth and Figueroa." He slammed down the telephone.

The next day there was Eddie Brown, as unmistakable as Jesus, across the street, black skin and a brown derby hat, good bones in his face, a tired king leaning on the wall under the gold dome of the Embassy Hotel. Elegant, he seemed on the point of death, exhausted. A dance bag weighted down one shoulder. When she walked toward him, he pushed off the wall, and his brown derby hat went with him.

"Eddie Brown?" For some reason she held out her two white men's oxfords, taps forward.

His slow eyes blinked, and he looked at her briefly. He concluded that she was a great rhinoceros.

"You're lucky you ain't late," he snarled.

He turned and went into the hotel. Francine followed at a safe distance. Tall and fine-boned, he moved with natural grace, but it was obvious he was too tired to have left the house, too tired to stand up altogether. At any second he might collapse. When they reached the elevator, creaky, everything in this hotel old, he dropped his whole back against the button, chin down. The antique car screeched to a stop.

"Follow me," said Eddie, his chin on his collarbone.

Up they went, Eddie's elbow leaning on the P for Penthouse. Together they rose, the cables screaming, Eddie breathing, his mouth open. Was this the wrong number? As they passed floor seven, his head in its brown derby hat rose off his chest.

"I wish I had a chocolate muffin," he said, bitterness in each word.

Eddie's head dropped with a conk onto his collarbone again. Francine stood prepared to catch him if he fell over. He was somewhere between nothing and eighty, and each breath might be his last. She was grateful when the door opened. Having come this far, still holding her shoes, she followed his long legs and short torso down a long hallway with red plush carpet, a very deep red, thick and old. They turned a corner and came to a red staircase ascending. Behind them was a ghostly red plush auditorium with steeply inclined seats, the stage far at the bottom, empty. At a wide swinging double door, a grunt came from a place so deep inside him that Francine shuddered. He turned and pushed through backward. She blinked.

"Hoo-*ie*," said Eddie as he walked into the huge, bright room.

The glorious hardwood floor covered the length and breadth of the whole Embassy Hotel, with one wall all industrial windows that skewered out to make horizontal perches for the city pigeons, who sat in rows and watched the dancers. Hoofers, Eddie and Francine moved across the gleaming floor toward four gray folding chairs that sat unoccupied. Eddie collapsed into one of them, and his bag dropped with a gunshot crack. Francine jumped. Eddie's upper body fell forward over his long thighs, head dangling between his knees. Was he dead? The tips of his long fingers trailed the floor. His back expanded and contracted with his breathing.

"Are you all right?" Francine said. "Shall I call a doctor?"

His spine rose, his spine fell. To their right was a portable ballet bar and a pair of ballet slippers, pink, abandoned on the floor. She stood slightly bent forward. After some time, very slowly, torso on his knees, Eddie Brown reached one arm out and pulled his dance bag toward him, his fingers creeping inside, his head dropped almost to the floor. Why did his brown derby hat not fall off? He extracted two men's loafers, taps on the soles and heels. They were beautifully made, their leather purple from years of polish. He pulled them toward him inch by inch by inch. With the top of his derby nearly touching his ankles, Eddie took his left foot and then his right out of its street shoe and deposited each one inside its purple loafer.

"I got these shoes in 1958," he said. The master's voice had grown younger.

Francine counted on her fingers. "Twenty-seven years. My God."

"Damn right."

Eddie Brown unfolded, much like an accordion. First his head came up and then his neck, his knees straightening, and when he was standing, he took off his brown derby hat. Looking down at the pink ballet shoes, he spat.

"*Bal*-let." He did a little rhythm with his feet while his head and shoulders looked down to see what his shoes were doing. His right foot slapped the floor, once, twice, a musician testing his wood, which must be oak. Or maple. His foot slapped it like a badger. "*Bal*-let. Don't nobody want to see that shit."

Eddie Brown began to walk, tuning up his loafers, following the purple shoes wherever they took him. With each step, he was defying physics. By the time he reached the center of the room, he was filled with helium. He floated up like a balloon, both feet leaving the earth and coming down with strands of sound that were impossible, as light as rain. He floated up again and landed with a *shigadeeboom*.

"*Uh*. That ain't right." He jumped again and landed with a slight but distinct variation.

"Huh?" said Francine.

"Don't talk," he yelled while jumping up and landing with sixteen sounds—if she had not miscounted. Excitement filled her belly. "Just dance. Now echo me." He made four sounds and waited for the echo.

The first four notes were Beethoven's Fifth Symphony,

mysterious, with power to raise the dead, and then her brain disintegrated. More steps flew out of his feet, and her brain gave up and rolled over. Her feet acted crazy. He did another drum roll, and she did a pathetic imitation, one good note only. His head came up.

"That ain't bad. Echo me."

She echoed him.

"Echo me now."

She was drowning in a sea of intricately constructed taps, too much to remember, but she grabbed each one while looking at his back and tried to be him: hops, slides, slaps, stamps, stomps, the sound occasionally true, exactly. He sang "Peg o' My Heart" to count the measures. "When you finish, that's how you know you got a chorus," he said. Sometimes he grunted. He never got tired, and sometimes he floated up as if he were a feather. Something was running him. He jumped and landed. She tried to follow his clean toe sounds, heels sounds, slides that turned the opposite direction. He jumped, a man in his prime, and when he landed, a pigeon flew by his head.

He shook his fist and missed it. "Get out of here!" He flapped his arms to chase it to the window. He turned toward her. He pointed.

"Now do the dance on your own." Eddie did a boogaloo and slammed his body to a stop, a human exclamation point.

"Me?" said Francine.

"One." He clapped. "Two." He clapped. "*You* know what to do. Eight-and-a-*ho*."

If she practiced she might someday play the floor like a xylophone. She could hear something in her feet. She made mistakes and misremembered steps and made steps up that came out of nowhere. Sometimes she had a syncopation that made you see prairie, but Eddie was from Kansas City.

Two Midwesterners, she danced and he listened. Sometimes he stepped in to help her. "That ain't it," he called sometimes, and then he led. "You got to put the accents in!" he yelled, suddenly furious, and then she did it. In the upstairs ballroom of the Embassy Hotel, nothing else mattered. On they went, and pigeons watched them. When they finished, both of them were dripping wet. He put both hands on his high hips.

"You got ears, you can hear," said Eddie Brown. He was a master. "You got steps inside you. You can make up what you don't remember. Now you come back here this time every Tuesday. I'm going to work with you for free and you can take me grocery shopping. I like Stater Bros."

In Santa Monica, standing opposite the woman, Sarah, Francine looked down at her two feet.

"I didn't answer him. I ran out and I never went back." Francine let out a raucous laugh, like a demon. "Now Eddie Brown is up in heaven."

Sarah slid open the garden door, a different door from the one Francine had come through.

"I saw a dancer the moment you walked in." Sarah percolated. "I'm going to say something I've never said about another human being. I want you to hear it."

"What?" said Francine.

"Your father is a slut."

Francine burst into giggles. Mr. Didwell? Whom they called Solomon? Who was righteous? Who was like God?

Sarah remained in place. "Watch your step between the flagstones."

In the garden were the old flowers: hibiscus, geraniums, begonias, gladiolas. Not surprisingly, there were no gardenias, the best smell on earth. Difficult, yet they bloomed for Mrs. Didwell and burst out all over her yard. Her wedding flowers had been a whole bouquet of nothing else. And like that, Francine missed her mother.

* * *

Francine sat in a soup of indecision outside Spires Restaurant, city of Monrovia, Huntington Boulevard. Mrs. Didwell wanted to apologize. Bunny had appeared in a third visit on the night their father didn't bring the money. It seemed Mrs. Didwell wanted to apologize in person.

"Oh my God," Bunny had gasped, dramatic as usual. When Francine let her in, the cat ran up her shoulder.

"Eeeek!"

Francine retrieved Caddy, front paws first.

"I just came from Mom and Dad's." Bunny was panting. "I left here, and on the way home I whooshed up to Monrovia. Mom was hysterical. Oh my *God*," she repeated, swearing again, but then she was a modern Christian, not the lion-fighting kid. Mrs. Didwell had contempt for Christians who wanted to be relevant.

Bunny straightened. "When I pulled up, all the neighbors were outside, and Mother was throwing the good lace tablecloth off the porch, the one they use when they have preachers over. It landed on the grass, and she screamed, 'Nobody touch it!' One corner hung off a gardenia. When I went in, she couldn't talk, which is unheard of. She can always talk. She kept crying and strutting around the house and hitting things with her palm like she thought the whole house was a tambourine, like back before Dad made her stop playing because it looked sinful. She hit the cupboard and the kitchen island. And the dining room table. Her whole life nobody could walk faster than her, not even Noah. In the car Dad went screeching out the driveway and then screeched back in. I hope he didn't hit someone. She's determined."

"No," Francine answered.

Mr. Venice wheeled his bike by, going toward the park, night-blooming jasmine trailing from his head and looped into the frame and handlebars.

"She wants to apologize to you. The Monrovia Spires Restaurant. Two o'clock tomorrow."

"No way José."

"Suit yourself." Bunny stepped into her therapist personality. "No problemo." She was a Christian, but her clients were mostly sinners. "You have your path and Mother has hers. I'll give her the message. She was crying so hard she was choking. She wants to see your face to ask forgiveness. Whatever."

"I'm not going."

Outside Monrovia's Spires Restaurant, the Miata top down, sun on her head, Francine gunned the engine. She was going. She wasn't going. She backed the car up, she pulled forward. Bunny had surely dropped their mother off at two o'clock sharp, no one could beat Bunny at efficiency, and it was now according to the clock two-thirty. And creeping. On the one hand, Francine longed to tell her mother how frightened she had been that day, leaving the bedroom, pink hands going chair to chair to hold her up, passing the kitchen where her erstwhile father sat with one foot crossed over his knee, newspaper wholly opened out.

The soup of indecision simmered.

On the other hand, why should she forgive her mother anything? Who had abandoned her at only ten years old and made her live like a hunted animal? Because the week after it happened, Mrs. Didwell screamed at her at Family Worship, "Francine! Put your knees together!" But it was *Francine* who struggled each day to be perfect as God is perfect. She had closed her knees while Mr. Didwell looked down at his Bible.

Francine turned the ignition off.

But, against all reason! Of all the Didwells, Louella was the most fun to be with, a secret hedonist. She and Francine laughed themselves sick, and that time they visited New York they had beaten off three thugs.

Walking down a dark street on the Lower East Side—they were naïve, a cab had let them out—they realized that it was midnight. Their address was on Third Avenue. This was East Third Street, they now saw by streetlight. One hundred feet ahead stood three large men, one leaning back against the streetlight, all three bodies in the universal posture of malevolence. The three men waited for the ladies, their eyes glinting. It would be death to run away. But suddenly a lightness took her mother.

"Follow me," said Louella.

Fear thrilled through her daughter.

Mrs. Didwell, who never danced or wiggled, broke out in the Charleston, a sudden natural show-stopping dancer, her knees and hands flapping (she had good legs), her high voice singing gibberish, her eyes crazy as she charged toward the men. The would-be attackers straightened up and pulled their bellies in to let the women pass, and Francine and her mother laughed all night. Mrs. Didwell was possessed, the Holy Ghost and power, and they were safe on any street in New York City.

In Monrovia, Francine pushed up out of the Miata.

When she entered Spires Restaurant, she saw her mother's back at once, the Queen of England waiting for her audience. Careful, Francine walked toward her. Mrs. Didwell slightly tweaked one shoulder to remind her daughter she had eyes in the back of her head. Francine continued down the aisle toward the booth where Mrs. Didwell sat the way she always sat, feet crossed at the ankles, hands crossed on the table. Her legs and hands were her best features. Her face was plain, but she became a beauty when she was excited.

"Hello," said both women at the exact same moment.

At nearly three o'clock, the restaurant was still crowded, with no chance of privacy; it was Chicken Friday, chicken dishes twenty-five percent off. Francine scooted into the booth amidst the clink of silverware, the din of loud voices. Across the table Mrs. Didwell eyed a passing uniform, her master-seamstress eyes automatically broadening the shoulders, adding lapels, adjusting the hem. Although she had renounced the world, she had a killer sense of fashion. To this day she insisted that curls around Francine's face would light her up, and also a touch of white, a white collar or a white scarf.

Today, dressed all in black, no baggy clothes, her long hair straight, Francine tossed her mane back. She had many snap-on white lace collars, gifts from Mrs. Didwell, but she refused to wear them. The more she refused, the more her mother gave her. Two sets of identical blue eyes moved up and down the menu as if lunch were the Ten Commandments set in stone, each item life or death. Mrs. Didwell was considering the chicken fried steak, the thing she always ordered after she considered the whole menu, but then again they had been too poor for years to eat in restaurants and consider anything. She closed her menu. Just because God had suddenly made them wealthy, she didn't throw money away on expensive outfits like the Black Angus Steakhouse down the street. She asked Francine about the traffic.

"Are you ready?" said their waitress, Betsy.

They looked up, both Didwells smiling, as a preacher's family always had to be on fire for God. Sinner Betsy wrote their orders down and popped her gum, and Mrs. Didwell took Betsy's uniform in at the waist two inches. Her fashion sense never slept. Long and lanky, Betsy would look better with short hair and bangs.

"Might we have more napkins?" Mrs. Didwell inquired. She had always had an ear for language, and she paid attention in school, and after marriage she gently taught her husband subtle linguistic differences, the use of *who* and *whom.* He claimed it was the other way around.

"Napkins." Betsy popped her gum and nodded.

Next the women discussed humidity. Both could agree that they intensely disliked extreme heat but moisture in the air was what defeated you. In the sky outside Spires Restaurant, Mrs. Didwell checked for Jesus, but the Second Coming wasn't yet happening. Many modern Christians didn't think about it, but Louella held up the standards. Now she set her lips that lipstick had never cheapened. Should Francine start? Should Mrs. Didwell? Her mother could be cruel, yet those fine hands had also rubbed Francine's back each night in childhood and listened to her minute-by-minute reports of nothing to report at grade school. Francine felt in mortal danger. Mrs. Didwell eyed the Sweet'N Low, a handy sugar substitute she kept at home next to the toaster. She loved a bargain. Albeit rich, she loved free things, and God didn't care how many Sweet'N Lows you took if you bought something. She slipped five in her pocket.

"Here you go," said Betsy.

The food saved them, as if the restaurant had been awaiting their arrival; but in Pentecost, miracles are normal. The women were grateful not to talk, just chew, Francine on a fish something. Should she say *I forgive you* and be gracious? Because to have your husband cheat on you, in your own bed, with your own daughter, was too grotesque. Who could imagine it? It was beyond the thinkable. She hoped her mother hadn't called the district superintendent to have her father kicked out of the Assembly of God Church, ordination papers revoked. Francine's heart beat fast. Could she forgive her mother? Today? This century?

Mrs. Didwell cut and put aside small bites, then cut them once more in half, her method of maintaining her girlish figure. When she finished, she motioned. "*Waitress?*"

Betsy appeared, dirty plates in hand, more on her forearm, four glasses in four fingers.

"*Napkins*. Will you take our dishes?"

Betsy balanced the four glasses on the plates on her left arm, then stacked their own plates and lifted, an *artiste*. So far Mrs. Didwell hadn't grabbed her by the collar: *Do you know Jesus?* Monrovians walked past their table, sinners from other churches and some from no church at all. Without food to chew, a nervousness had settled on the women. Who would break the silence? For twenty-seven years, a wound had festered, but this day was Waterloo. Mrs. Didwell rubbed her lips together to wet them. Dishes clattered. The women looked across the table, not a hair moving. Neither blinked; and then Mrs. Didwell ran the table.

"It is my understanding you wish to apologize to me," said Mrs. Didwell.

"I beg your pardon?" said her daughter.

In Francine's mind she saw the comic possibilities, some Shakespearean tragicomedy, something hilarious, as in all the books she loved. It was important to hold on to the hysterical aspect. At the next booth, a strange man winked at Francine. What were they doing in a public coffee shop? The Didwell family's code of privacy was epic.

"*You're* here to apologize to *me*." Francine's index finger was pointing at her mother. *You* to *me*, the finger indicated.

A new waitress leaned over, her bosom large, her uniform obscuring everything. "I need to switch your sugar for a full one," she said, and they waited until she'd finished. "Ladies? Dessert?"

They ignored her, and still the Rapture didn't burst out of the clouds to end the conversation, Mrs. Didwell going up with her feet together and Francine left here at the fifth booth from the entrance. A former waitress, she always counted. Mrs. Didwell kept her hands clasped, loosely, feet crossed at the ankle. The minutes ticked toward death and no one spoke. The young Mrs. Didwell, Bible school graduate with ordination papers, had put all her eggs in one basket. She was then Louella Eggers. Only twenty-three, she had a brilliant career as a traveling evangelist, a rising star, so in demand her calendar was full for one year out. Her preaching could make tired people jump. But then one night she preached at Clarence Didwell's church, and God pointed at the young pastor. Louella looked where God directed. That night, they took a long ride, and Clarence ran out of gas.

Soon they were engaged. *Souls*, said their love letters. *Helpmeet*, they wrote by hand.

They were married.

They had no money, and sometimes ate milk and bread, but that first year they bought an actual bed so beautiful that Mrs. Didwell cried each time she saw it. The Italiano was expensive, purchased on time with money borrowed from the relatives, but it was the center of their marriage and worth every penny. Louella polished it, and even after forty years it had not one scratch. It included two dressers and night tables, but the bed itself was elegant and simple, a harmony of subtle curves, an act of faith *which is the evidence of things not seen*, like the marriage God gave them. The bed was either holy, or Mrs. Didwell's life was wasted.

The bell rang. "Number seven! Get your order," a cook yelled. It was never good to piss the cook off. They had the power to hold your orders. Francine and Mrs. Didwell floated.

"Your father has bad asthma," Mrs. Didwell said finally, and in a flash Francine saw that her father, Mr. Didwell, who couldn't lie, had told the whopper. At the table, Mrs. Didwell's grand romance propelled her. She now enunciated each word, as if she were revealing a great secret. "His breathing can, from time to time, get very noisy."

Mrs. Didwell slid two Sweet'N Lows into her purse. "He's had it since that brick fell on him several years before we met, outside Good Cheer, Iowa, where he was building the new parsonage. From cinderblock. So now his breathing gets quite disturbed and dramatic. Daddy said he loves you but that you misunderstood completely."

"It wasn't his breathing!" Francine shouted. *Taps are poems,* she wrote carefully in her Imaginary Tap Handbook.

"We both admire your strong imagination." *Napkins,* Mrs. Didwell signaled.

"Daddy is a liar," said Francine Didwell.

Mrs. Didwell thought about her posture. She had always had good legs, and Mr. Didwell was attracted to them. She crossed and recrossed these now. If Mr. Didwell was a liar, God was dead. There was no middle ground. Mrs. Didwell picked her fork up. Betsy had left it. The bed Mrs. Didwell polished each week to its original perfection was the temple of their marriage, the fountain of youth to which they returned each night as strangers again. Mrs. Didwell stood on the edge of a great precipice. *I am the way, the truth, and the life,* said Jesus. Tough, Louella Eggers Didwell leaned forward. She needed the truth. She slid two more Sweet'N Lows into her purse. Of course, *this* daughter refused to go to church and she spread her legs with men. Not to mention she had lost the antique stove that Mrs. Didwell loved by leaving it in an old apartment (a red enamel pinstripe on the perimeter). But the collars! Mrs. Didwell's heart hardened toward her daughter. Over the years Mrs. Didwell had given Francine fourteen, white lace, snap-ons, one from Aunt Amelia, one with little blue flowers, and where were they? Left in some apartment? At the thought of all the collars, Mrs. Didwell's heart exploded.

"You will tell me now *exactly* what happened." A little speck of froth came out of Mrs. Didwell's mouth. Mrs. Didwell smiled. She leaned across the table, its surface as vast as Africa, where souls were perishing. When Francine tried to talk, no voice came out. You could not tarnish Mr. Didwell. She would be struck by lightning. She would be put into a mental institution. The words were filth. "You will tell me and tell me now"—Mrs. Didwell's eyes were like a falcon's, her life in the balance—"and then *I* will decide what happened."

"You weren't there," Francine whispered.

In Spires Restaurant, nothing moved. Their booth was a Broadway musical. The waitresses no longer delivered food, the cooks no longer cooked. The Didwells were God's star family; yet here in Spires they were as helpless as people in a hurricane. Francine stared into outer darkness.

Daddy molested me, wrote Francine on a napkin.

She slid it across the table and Mrs. Didwell put it on a dirty plate and the waitress came and swooped it up. Someone asked if they would like dessert.

"No thank you," said both Didwells.

Mrs. Didwell lifted up her reading glasses and plucked a piece of paper from her lap, where she had kept it hidden.

"I have here something." The ancient newsprint was folded twice, and torn a little along the creases. While all eyes watched, her hands smoothed the sections open. How long had she had it? The top-secret weapon had been waiting—years or decades—and Francine stared along with the other people in the restaurant. With the flats of her hands Mrs. Didwell smoothed the irregular paper, a scissors-cut with one short and one long column. She adjusted her glasses.

"'Several years ago I received a letter which I feel the need to reprint,'" she read in her preaching voice, and people listened, mysteriously mesmerized. Her preaching voice made her Evita. "This is Ann Landers talking." Mrs. Didwell's eyes behind her glasses now looked mischievous. She and Ann Landers were girlfriends. The warmth that now emanated from her personality was narcotic, and Francine leaned along with others. She had grown up in the Didwell house, where armies of the Lord marched forth against the devil, smoke and guns on every front, every moment in the trenches. Who would live? Who would fall into the lake of fire? When Mrs. Didwell dropped her eyes, Francine felt rising fury.

"Now, this is the letter. 'Many years ago I told a lie about my father,'" Mrs. Didwell read. She took her time. Her voice had resonance. "'I said that he had sexually molested me, and I destroyed my family. To this day I do not know what possessed me. My father was a good man who had done nothing wrong, but I was young and angry at something I don't remember even now. My parents' life was ruined. His friends shunned him, and although he kept his job he was detested.' This next is in parentheses," said Mrs. Didwell. "'(I would do anything to fix it. Anything!)'" She looked up. "'My father died a broken man, while my mother has never forgiven me. I would give up all I have to change what I did. All of it! I feel I am responsible. I live in hell for the monstrous lie I told, and I do not think I will be forgiven. Signed. A miserable creature. Bonnie.'"

When she had finished, Mrs. Didwell folded up the paper. A little white paste sat in the corners of her mouth, and she dabbed them with her tongue. She brushed crumbs off the table just in front of her, each movement dainty.

In the car they drove up Begonia Terrace toward the mountains with Mrs. Didwell's hairdo blowing, past the dairy.

"Say you love me!" Francine could feel her mind was going to shatter like Humpty Dumpty. She was dying. "Say you love me!" she screeched at her mother.

"Daddy and all those other men you molested!" Mrs. Didwell shouted. Because she was a preacher, her voice carried. Her eyes looked straight ahead up Begonia.

"Say you love me!" Mrs. Didwell couldn't hear her.

Francine grabbed her mother's arm and held on. On the night Mr. Didwell left the bedroom, ten-year-old Francine had crept back to her own bed and pulled the covers up, no mother, no father, no Ilene, no Noah, no baby in Mother's stomach. She was alone in outer space. "Say you love me!" Her voice sounded crazy. "Say you love me!" They crossed the light at Foothill. "Say you love me!"

Past the cleaners, the angle of Begonia steepened.

"I have always admired that chimney on the right," said her mother. "Slow way down. It wouldn't fit our house. But still."

In the driveway, Francine got out and helped her mother exit. The Miata was a low car, and difficult, and there was a condition called Miata Shoulder from pulling yourself out.

"Oof," said Mrs. Didwell.

Together they walked past the ancient bougainvillea, the old purple color, up the north steps to the porch, where Francine stopped. The door was open.

"Goodbye," said Francine.

Mrs. Didwell turned with her mouth open. "Aren't you coming in to say hello to Daddy?"

In the blue Miata, top down, Francine laid rubber down the street and hit the freeway at a sharp angle out into the fast lane, where she had an open road. She hit ninety and the car drifted.

8
PILLS

The blue-and-yellow capsules were such an instant and complete relief that Francine wondered how she had ever lived without them. At Chauzer Impermanente Sunset on the way home from the Didwells, the closest ER, she explained to the doctor in an award-winning performance that a veritable hatchet was breaking her skull in two. She made herself believe it. By faith you could create an instant migraine. Her neighbor, one Peter across the alley, had given her two blue-and-yellow capsules one day when she had a headache, and within fifteen minutes the whole sky had changed to something glorious. Every little scrap of trash held promise. The headache had introduced her to a world of happiness: a cocktail prescription drug made of narcotics and barbiturates. Francine had dabbled in pills in the pre-Cyrus years when she was famous Waitress Seven, fastest hash house slinger in Santa Ana, California. People came in just to watch the blur of speed that was her six tables. The mini-Benzedrine that her colleague Nellie handed out in tinfoil packs of five before the breakfast shift gave you an optimistic outlook on the day: *happy pills*, Nellie named the foil cylinders she only sold at one per shift per waitress, and only after you clocked in; nothing for recreation. The pleasure in combining ketchups! In talking people's heads off as their eyes went glassy. The dry mouth, so delicious. But one day Francine stopped. She simply stopped, which proved she was no drug addict.

"What's going on?" said each new nice doctor.

"Headache," Francine breathed out.

She never overacted. The trick was never to lie. Belief brought a strange power with it, which was how faith worked, which was why Christians didn't allow themselves to be influenced by unbelievers. In Chauzer Impermanente, she used her faith skills. Her shoulders slumped. Her bones quivered, a little.

"What do you usually take?"

"I don't know." She talked like a ventriloquist. "Blue and yellow."

The doctor named it.

"Maybe," said Francine. She slumped down one more vertebra.

"Take one, and if needed, two," said each nice doctor. Each one patted her shoulder. "You'll feel better shortly."

In fifteen minutes she was happy.

The blue-and-yellow pills were oblong, and more beautiful than anything designed by Michelangelo. With each dose, two (the label said one, but labels were conservative), she had six hours to be happy, and then she took another dose, and sometimes a third. Sometimes she lost count, and had to estimate. When the last dose of the day faded, she ate one heavy meal, takeout pulled pork from Versailles Restaurant and beer, two Coronas, and as her eyelids closed, she begged her lungs to keep breathing and closed her eyes into a great darkness.

In the morning, still alive, she swallowed two more blue-and-yellow new friends.

It turned out not to be difficult to get them, all-hours visits to the Chauzer Emergency Room, and being honest—pain was pain—was her success formula, her pure soul looking straight into the doctor's flashlight, not pretending. Pain was pain, period. Prescription pain pills had been designed by real doctors for maximum relief when you needed a small vacation. Francine's use of the cocktail was only temporary—they called it that, a cocktail pill—or at least her daily use. How often was healthy? Because stress would kill you. While deciding, she took the pills every day. The supply rooms, called ERs, were open twenty-four hours, and all freeways led to Chauzer. Within two weeks, she knew each pill exit: Woodman, Sunset, Harbor, Jefferson, Signal Hill, Cherry, Agoura Hills. *Pills! Pills! Pills!* the big green exit signs cried out in large white letters. At Chauzer, there was always the risk of being refused, but faith was the substance of things hoped for. Pain was pain was pain. Like a miracle, each time, the doctor put a kind hand on her shoulder.

"Thank you," Francine barely mumbled.

Each nice gentleman handed her a piece of paper, small but of inestimable value. The scribbled writing was the ticket to staying upright. Each time, Francine was careful to keep her posture casual, to relax her fingers from their death grip on the small flimsy scrip. Each time, she gave it to the pharmacist and yawned, her heart pounding so loud she had to back up. Like God, the pharmacist always looked suspicious. The pharmacist in his white coat behind the window handed you the Chauzer paper bag, no need to check, the thirty pills inside in their plastic amber bottle, and in that moment when his hand let go, the actual, legal vesting changed and you were the owner of record. The check was cashed, the money was in the bank, no one could take your bliss. Once the handoff had been made, Francine felt happy just to hold the paper bag. *Pills! Pills! Pills!* sang choirs of angels. To be safe, Francine continued to look tortured for several seconds. Then, owner of record, she turned down whatever Chauzer hallway, the Woodman or Sunset or La Cienega, the same linoleum tile hallway. With the precious bag in hand, the precious pills inside the precious bag, she might, for twisted pleasure, skip the first drinking fountain. She might even skip the ladies' bathroom. In such cases, at the exit door she found herself running toward her blue Miata, where she never traveled without water for swallowing. If she got the pills at Chauzer Sunset, by the time she hit Crenshaw driving west on the 10, she was singing songs from *Camelot*, belting at the top of her lungs, unmindful of who stared. *I know it sounds a bit bizarre!* Her hand thumped the steering wheel. *But in Camelot!* Thump, thump, thump. *Camelot!* Three thumps. *That's how conditions are.*

The pills produced clean feelings, and the clean feelings were simple, unadulterated by things that were the opposite of happiness. The pills made you want to clean the kitchen tiles so carefully that no microscopic speck remained, of anything. The pills were blue and yellow, and she took up to three doses per day, which became four doses unless she took more. So far she hadn't accidentally paralyzed her diaphragm, always a possibility, but with the optimism the pills gave her, it seemed unlikely. On pills, the animals blended in with the furniture until from time to time she noticed four eyes looking at her. To keep them safe, she put out three gigantic pans of water and a cooking pot with cat food, and in the largest skillet she poured dog kibble. She touched their heads when they got in her way, and sometimes she said "Mommy loves you."

The pills filled Francine with clairvoyant wisdom, so that insights flew all around her head, and every several minutes no matter which tile she was cleaning she put down her sponge—a delicious lemon yellow—to write down the mysterious knowledge on scraps of paper that would inform her when she quit, soon, at some point in the future. Epiphanies came out her ears. *There are no borders*, she wrote, feverish. *Butterflies are people. Bordello red is not a color, but a feeling! Yellow.* Her letters came out in gigantic loops. She filed the scraps of paper in a hanging folder with a tab marked *!!!*, easy to spot while rushing by the filing cabinet, third drawer up, no time to bend over.

Two hours after the second dose kicked in, Francine was a Didwell. What had she been thinking? She called her sister.

"The Didwell Family Healing Cruise? I'm going."

"Oh my God," said Bunny.

That very afternoon the sisters went berserk and went shopping. The Didwells were one of the great families, like the Kennedys of Kennebunkport, or Bunnekinkport, or the Rockefellers, or the rich Kreske family that lived up the street in high school and everybody tried to see inside their house on Halloween. Most often, Bunny came to Venice, as Francine couldn't remember which day was which. On the Venice boardwalk, they bought the items necessary for any cruise: fourteen pairs of chartreuse sunglasses, extras for breakage, flip-flops in medium and large, suntan lotion. Between them they had fourteen sets of bikinis, polka dots, stripes, et cetera, each one cut to flaunt your figure. They strutted on the beach in their bikinis. At Your Name on a Piece of Rice, they bought one for *Clarence, Louella, Ilene, Francine, Noah, Bunny,* and a tiny dark blue velvet bag in order not to lose them. Bunny tucked it in the pocket of her handbag, outside lower.

"I have ideas," Bunny mentioned every time she came, and each idea was different. Today, Mr. Venice walked his bike, machine and guru dressed in pink hibiscus. Bunny continued. "Like a little book of Didwell sayings. *Didwell Speak.*"

Let's adopt a wait-and-see attitude.

No ifs ands or buts about it.

No one ever got rich punching a time clock.

"Rise and shine!" both girls screamed, making a drunk wake up horrified.

"Good one," Bunny scribbled. "And a list of everyone's heroic acts. Like that time Dad got robbed in the church office and he made the burglar bow his head and pray before he left. And then the man sent back the wallet but without the money."

"And how you saved the neighbor's baby."

"And the time Mom almost lifted the refrigerator."

"And the time I ran away with Cyrus."

"Don't say *Cyrus.*" They kept walking. "Dad will freak."

They decided to announce on Noah's birthday, although Mr. Didwell's was next Thursday, because they wanted hats. They had found the personally inscribed baseball caps this afternoon at Mad Hats, and come up with the name while they stood talking to each other.

"Didwell Something. Didwell Happiness. Didwell Forever. Didwells Are Wonderful."

"Didwell Country," said a passing man who looked homeless—apparently to hush them up, he couldn't take it—and they stood there with their mouths open.

"Didwell Country," Bunny finally repeated.

They decided on mauve with blue stitching—the homeless person wasn't there to help them—and paid on the spot. They would announce in three weeks, and put a hat on every head, and throw confetti.

"Suntan oil," said Bunny.

It was The Didwell Healing Cruise *and Bible Study* because, with those words, Mr. Didwell would be willing to foot the bill and pay for everything. They must not insult him *personally*, Bunny repeated, but be respectful. Parishioners looked up to him as far away as Iowa. To their right, the Pacific Ocean looked like Iowa, as if a Guernsey would appear and start to moo. Last week, in Starbucks, when Francine got a drink of water from the glass urn, she forgot to turn off the spigot and stood staring at it while people stared at her as if she were a crazy person. But these things happened.

At PARKING FOR MEXICANS ONLY, Bunny stuffed in packages, including many lipsticks. Which looked better in the bright sun? Bunny waved and put a finger to her lips. "Mum's the word! Noah's birthday."

It didn't have to be love, but Francine needed a boyfriend to come home to from the Didwell Healing Cruise, now officially *and Bible Study*, 6'2" or taller. Every Thursday since she moved to Venice she had deconstructed the *L.A. Times* Personals, *sense of humor a plus, children ok*, et cetera. All the ads said *No Baggage, No Baggage Please, Please No Baggage*. Although the names were different, the actual humans seemed like the same human, the same eyes, nose, ears, mouth, the same boring conversations; but on certain nights a warm body felt good when the pills wore off and left her falling through space. Once, she put in her own ad, *Seeking Big Spirit*, but no Cyrus materialized. After sex that was the same sex, she might get out of bed to write down some new insight on whatever paper was nearby. *FUN HEALS BACTERIA. Strawberries! Don't kill bugs. Butterflies are listening.* She drank glasses of water. *Bees are friends to mankind! MASSAGES FOR GANG MEMBERS. Learn to speak all languages.*

"Couch," she said out loud one afternoon when she was cleaning.

Because a couch would be a place to entertain prospective boyfriends over 6'2" and show them she had no baggage, and had a sense of humor, et cetera, et cetera. "Say no more," she said to herself. She got her keys and purse and told Hank and Kitty that she would see them in a jiffy pop and jumped on the 405 freeway to Orange County, where there was parking. She drove fast to get there before the pills wore off, and she could no longer remember why she came.

She looked up.

In Costa Mesa, which she had almost bypassed—you could end up in San Diego, and she was singing *Camelot*—she drove to Homes R Us and chose one of many empty parking spaces and ran across the lot to the front door, which slid open without her touching it. She scurried up and down the aisles, her head darting left and right, but every couch was the wrong couch, too bland, too rigid. Some had buttons. Did no couch have some *pizzazz*? In the ladies' room she took a fourth or seventh dose.

When she came out, there the couch was. Enormous purple flowers stood up out of a black background.

"How," said Francine, as if each purple flower were a wild Indian.

She sat down and stretched her arm along the puffy back. A brown couch was where she fell in love with Cyrus, where they looked up words in the dictionary, an activity that seemed both perverse and sexual. On the same brown couch they sat and saw the mouse who found the marijuana wander out from underneath it to cruise the living room in big loops while they watched it like concerned parents. For a moment she lay back against the pillows.

"I want this couch," she told the taller of the two men in identical green shirts.

He looked at his watch. "Of course."

"I want it delivered tonight."

The second green shirt smiled. "Perhaps early as next week. Thursday."

"I can pay."

They traveled north by freeway, the red truck with the couch sticking out, Francine in her blue Miata. From the top of Paradiso Avenue, the men from Homes R Us ran the couch down the red line to the gate, and when Francine peeked over, it occurred to her that she should have measured.

"Hank and Kitty? Surprise!"

The men set it down, a monstrosity, as it turned out, too big to fit across the living room and face the garden, so they tilted it on the diagonal. The cat and dog stood staring, leaning on each other.

It was only midnight, and Francine riffled through her Rolodex to M for Men. The couch flowers were terrible. Each card held another boring date, each mouth the same with the same things to say, all the arms identical, all the fingers, identical biceps and abdominals. In and out went all the penises. Hank tried to get on the bed with all the men who slept over; however, no one wanted to be a father. Francine picked out a card and dialed the number.

"Dubois," she said when he arrived. The only light was the moon and one streetlight. On the couch, the giant flowers waited to devour them utterly. "Come in."

His skin was black, the color of slavery, and his past was clothed in secrecy, as if she had no business asking. *Climb ev'ry mountain/Ford ev'ry stream/Follow ev'ry rainbow*, her white choir sang in high school, but not Dubois. They sat down on the new couch, a shopping mistake even in the dark, but pills made you go crazy. Hank jumped up next to him, because the cat burglar was working.

"Yo," said Dubois.

"Put your hand here on my midriff." Francine lifted her blouse.

"Okay." Dubois complied.

Since Cyrus died, his casket in the ground—she had rapped twice on it as it was lowered, very British, which she wasn't—she had sustained a large hole in her midriff, larger than a grapefruit but smaller than a bowling ball, which hurt at all times, day and night, nor did the pills stop it. The exposed red insides felt the bite of fresh cold air. But each time she looked, to her amazement there was no jagged edge, only smooth skin.

"Don't move your hand," said Francine.

"No problem," Dubois answered.

In Monrovia for Mr. Didwell's birthday, the dinner at Spires Restaurant had sunk beneath the ocean water like the city of Atlantis. The blue-and-yellow pills were fabulous. Mr. Didwell was again God's righteous man on earth and Francine had more pills in her purse. In the bosom of her family, she was seated under the oil painting of the Didwells in their prime. Cyrus was disappearing, the long craggy face, even his hands, the way the wrist articulated. The real Didwell faces beamed in a circle.

Bunny kicked her. *Conference*, she mouthed across the table. Her turquoise eyes jerked toward the kitchen.

"What's going on?" said Mrs. Didwell.

By the sink, the sisters put their heads close together.

"Just FYI," Bunny whispered. "At two-thirty we have an interview. Rattle dishes."

Francine did so.

"Mother fell down, which is a perfect reason to hire a helper, and I'm taking full advantage. We can employ her as a Cruise Companion, to keep Mom and Dad from falling overboard. Of course, the interviewee knows nothing. It's just between the two of us and Daddy. Watch her and try to see if she's the type who would get seasick."

The cruise was coming! The Didwell Country hats would arrive soon, and Bunny had made cabin reservations, and Mr. Didwell had sent the deposit. They must remember to buy confetti! To make the announcement. On her yellow legal pad, Bunny wrote down *Blow whistles*.

"Bring more iced tea!" cried Mr. Didwell.

When she sat down again, Francine sucked more mashed potatoes with extra butter through her teeth, then took another forkful. Down the table, Francine's black olives shone in their green dish. Today she had also brought pimientos, and a large assortment of pickles: sweet, half dill, full dill whole and full dill halves, dill slices, relish. Next week, Ilene and Bunny each would send a separate bill for groceries split four ways among the children. Her own anti-cooking stance was militant. Marriage had ruined her mother's chances to be the tambourine hit of her generation. Louella's rhythm had once sent shivers up the spines of all who heard it. Louella hit it on her wrist. Louella hit it on her hip, which jutted out to meet the instrument despite her best intentions. Anyone who watched began to move their hips and shoulders, unable to hold them steady. She had kept on playing to praise the Lord until one day in Iowa, Ilene and Francine remembered, Mr. Didwell put his foot down.

"Put it away and leave it."

"Oh," said Mrs. Didwell.

"It's not seemly for a pastor's wife to play it. It looks suggestive."

"But Clarence!"

"No ifs, ands or buts about it," finished Mr. Didwell, and that was that. He was directly under God. Orders were orders.

At the dinner table Francine used her mental powers to drift. Time was difficult on pills (as when she had to run down to the corner newsstand to know what day it was), and also numbers. *Persimmons have no nuts*, she wrote quickly on a napkin that she folded over. Turkey made its way around the table, and Mrs. Didwell slid one small piece onto her plate. She slid a quick second. Because of tiny rips in the flesh of her esophagus, Doctor Love had forbidden her to eat food except when blended into a liquid, which wasn't delicious; then again, he was Jewish.

"When I'm gone, you children will be rich," Mr. Didwell was saying. The subject today, as all days, besides which churches were doing what, was how to make a fortune.

"Dad!" Ilene cried. "Stop it. It's your birthday." She pretended to smoke a cigarette. When the Didwells looked, she threw it on the floor.

"Ilene's right, Daddy. You aren't going anywhere," Bunny chimed in.

"'Enoch walked with God, *and he was not,* for God took him,'" Noah quoted, "Genesis five: twenty-four."

Mrs. Didwell praised the Lord. To pass through death, but without dying!

Francine had pills for all occasions secreted in her bra, her purse, the glove compartment of her car, the trunk, and three pills stuffed into the pocket of her pants, the secret pocket in front that made her buy them. She felt there now and found them. You needed to be prepared for any eventuality: a flat tire, a revolution, pirates boarding an ocean liner. The Didwells made plans for eternity.

"Excuse me," said Francine.

When she came back from the bathroom, two more friends inside her, warmth radiated from the napkins. It radiated from the oil painting of the Didwells in their prime, and beneath it from the ceramic couple, and on the wall from the framed proof that May 31 was Clarence and Louella Didwell Day in the City of Monrovia; and in a chair at either end of this table were the Didwells in the flesh, each one a powerhouse for Jesus. Some children had boring parents. Francine made silly secret hand signals (stolen from the Crips or Bloods) to Bunny across the table, and to each one, Bunny nodded. When the girls caught Mrs. Didwell staring at them, each one burst out laughing. It was thrilling.

"Francine? How go the Venice units?"

Francine sat up. She was a sinner, but real estate was the language she had in common with her family. She cleared her throat.

"People seem to want to live there." AIRPLANES ARE DANCERS TOO, she wrote in big letters. She blinked, to focus. "The apartments aren't fancy but they're near the ocean. When I rented Apartment 3, the guy left me and ran down to the beach to see how high the surf was."

"All those surfers need to get to heaven," Mrs. Didwell interrupted. She stopped chewing her forbidden turkey and half stood up. "Francine! You're right there. You can start a beachfront meeting and tell the surfers about Jesus every Sunday morning. Oh! How I wish I could jump up and give a sermon. And walk faster than everyone."

"'Bring them in! From the fields of sin!'" came Noah's rich tenor.

All the children except Noah rolled their eyes, because the girls were modern and they fit into regular society. The oil-painting Didwells were still led by the Holy Ghost, *a wind that blows where it will.* If the Holy Ghost said *Buy this house*, they did it. Anything might happen! Real Christians were like wolves.

"Bread-and-butter units are indeed the thing to buy," said Mr. Didwell, in conclusion. All the Didwells had their rental property. "You can take your fancy units. Of course they might make you feel luxurious. They might make you feel mighty important. But consider this. Along comes a recession. Everyone moves down a level, and there you are with those same fancy apartments empty."

"Stuck with them." Noah leaned back and crossed his arms, satisfied the foolish landlords had found justice.

"People?" Bunny's voice cut glass, and they sat up as one body. She tapped her water glass with a clean butter knife. "It's Dad's birthday, and the family is gathered. Can everybody please stop being rude?"

From the kitchen, the cake floated through the air with all the candles lit. It was carried by the beautiful Kim Novak, aka Ilene. Francine touched two pills in her pocket.

"Daddy?" Bunny stood up. "Would you like to say how old you are?"

"No," said Mr. Didwell.

They sang "Happy Birthday" as a family, the sound much improved without their father although no one would dare say it: Ilene soprano, Francine alto, Noah baritone, Bunny and Mrs. Didwell mouthing. Their voices hung in the air a moment. They might have been the Singing Didwells.

"I can tell you this. I plan to live to be one hundred." Mr. Didwell reached under the table, and his farmer's hand lifted up a red book, rather small, a yard-sale treasure—all the Didwells shopped there. "*How to Live to Be 100.* This book sits down and shows me how to do it. Step by step."

All the children dropped their eyes and calculated how old they would be when Mr. Didwell turned one hundred—old! old! Against doctor's express orders, Mrs. Didwell snuck another smidge of turkey she had saved beneath her napkin. She had the Holy Ghost, and she was careful when she swallowed. Mr. Didwell blew the candles out in one big heft of air—the big bad wolf—while all the children clapped and Mrs. Didwell watched them.

"*How to Live to Be 100.*" Noah paused, the resident genius. "How old was the man who wrote it?"

When they exploded, Noah blushed, his bon mot a success. He often said that he would like to marry and have children, but as yet he hadn't found a person who completely met his standards. They were too shy, or wore puff sleeves, or were Christian but not progressive, or were the wrong height, or eyed the Didwell money, or only pretended to love the hiking trails up in the canyons behind Monrovia.

"Newsflash," Bunny interrupted. "Hurry and eat your cake. Someone's coming at two-thirty."

"What's going on?" said Mrs. Didwell. Her eyes narrowed.

"Mother?" Bunny stood up. "We need a helper."

"I don't want strangers in the house." Mrs. Didwell made a sound, her signature, half maya bird, half hyena, a trill with her tongue. It was electric. It got everyone's attention. She was the ruler of a mighty nation.

"Mom and Dad took a small spill," said Noah.

"Mom?" Bunny moved around the table and put both hands on Mrs. Didwell's shoulders. "The two of you were helpless."

"Oh! It was fun." Mrs. Didwell appeared to soften, but the children knew her better. They watched for what was coming. She didn't pull away from Bunny's fingers. "I was using my walker. Oh, my feet hurt terribly! Daddy came behind to help me and he got impatient."

"Not *impatient*," said Mr. Didwell.

"So he pushed me and I went over, and he went over right on top of me. His glasses fell out of his pocket. There we were, unable to move or do anything."

"I didn't push." Mr. Didwell didn't scowl, but he put on his wise face, the one he used to counsel parishioners, and in this aspect he was very popular. He was no fiery preacher—that was Louella's gift, the hard truth—but more than one member of the congregation had referred to him as Solomon. God had given him the gift of wisdom in matters spiritual as well as matters of making dollars multiply.

"Then it struck our funny bones. It was like a picnic!" Mrs. Didwell's face had brightened, like when she was preaching, and her hands flew thither and yon, and your eyeballs followed them. Her soul was in flight. In a quick epiphany, Francine recognized the strong resemblance that had nagged her since she was in her teens. Yes! Louella's face was like Aretha Franklin's, plain and open with a certain come-hither.

"We laughed until our stomachs hurt. Tears were rolling out of our eyes. We couldn't find Daddy's glasses. We laughed until your brother came to practice the piano, and then we kept on laughing. Clarence? Do you remember our first date when you ran out of gas? We didn't get back to the church until two a.m. It was a scandal."

"It was an accident," clarified Clarence.

"I believed your father but the pastor didn't." Once more Louella giggled, so much like a girl that the Didwells leaned forward. Although her face was plain, she had an overpowering sense of fun that both attracted and crazed Mr. Didwell. "He doesn't believe him to this day."

Bunny kicked Francine under the table.

"People!" said Bunny, and all sat up. She was a natural leader. "The applicant will be here in twenty minutes. Mom and Dad are getting older are the facts. But I think we should ask God's guidance."

Head bowed, Francine had just peeked to see what the other girls were doing when the doorbell rang.

"Who could that be?" said Bunny.

The doorbell rang again, as if the ringer was impatient.

"Oh, for heaven's sake. She's early." Bunny threw her napkin down and stood. She was a Christian, but even our Lord Jesus had a temper when he threw the moneychangers out. "I told the woman two-thirty precisely for this interview. Not two-ten. Not two-fifteen." Mrs. Didwell watched in silence. "Not a promising beginning."

The doorbell rang a third time.

"Hold your horses," Mr. Didwell counseled.

Hold your horses, Bunny mouthed, and walked to open the door while she wrote *Hold your horses* for *Didwell Speak*, the dictionary.

"What's going on?" said Mrs. Didwell.

The woman who stood waiting on the porch outside

was black. She wasn't brown. In the sun her ebony skin glistened, and in her ears were tiny gold hoop earrings and one small diamond. Modern Christians did sometimes wear jewelry on their ears instead of neck and wrists only. It depended on the pastor. While the family stood risen, their ice cream melting, the cake as yet untouched, Noah straightened. He was a soldier who had heard a bugle call from a distant point. *Thy people shall be my people*, said Ruth in the Bible. Outside, the woman's face was beautiful. The shape of her shaved head was perfect. The charge inside the house extended from the woman to the place where Noah stood, a strange look on his face, transforming it from something pinched into a handsome canvas—intelligent forehead, a neck that could bend to a five-star restaurant menu.

"I'm Yaram," said the wondrous creature.

"What sort of name is that?" said Mr. Didwell, who was interested.

"My parents came from Senegal, where it means *my body* in the local language, Wolof. They speak it but I don't."

"We had missionaries there," said Louella, but no one heard her.

The woman's head moved left, a structural wonder.

"Come in," said Noah. His true love moved like a cheetah, or was it a lynx? Cyrus had moved like a coyote.

In the living room, Yaram bent over to examine handmade scenic tiles in the fireplace, turn of the century, the colors muted, deep. Noah bent over with her. Yaram's long finger touched a fireplace tile that held a shepherd, staff made out of tile that was impossibly thin, impossibly green.

"I said two-thirty on the nose." Bunny stepped forward. "In any case, we need someone as soon as possible. To keep tabs on Mom and Dad while everyone is doing other things."

"We don't need tabs," said Mr. Didwell.

But in an unexpected wrinkle, Noah was becoming a

man about town, in slow-motion photography. His posture was realigning before their eyes, his shoulders dropping. You could almost see him with a top hat in one hand, in a tuxedo with pants that were long enough. Yaram, named from Senegal, explained that she had her degree in architecture from the University of Southern California. She might or might not continue to a master's.

"Yes," said Noah.

Her head moved back and forth on her long neck when she spoke, and on certain points Noah nodded, as if the two of them were in cahoots already. His clothing had a new and well-cut look about the shoulders.

"Would you like to see the kitchen?" Noah moved past Bunny.

He showed Yaram the pantry designed by Mrs. Didwell, her pride and joy, hidden behind the kitchen door. Yaram admired it. One soup can deep, it was a brilliant use of wasted space and showed exactly what you had to eat. With one arm, he pointed to the beautiful San Gabriel Mountains out the window over the sink. Her fine head nodded. Noah's only purpose was to save Yaram from invading Huns, or earthquakes and the mudslides they brought with them, or a scourge of locusts. Bunny continued. Yes, Yaram could be free to start on Tuesday. Mrs. Didwell watched them. Mystery filled the kitchen.

"We separate the trash," Mrs. Didwell said to her daughter-in-law, potential, and took one more forbidden piece of turkey from the counter, strictly against doctor's orders. She chewed it and licked her finger. "To save the planet."

In a daring feat—you could see the two of them were on another plane—Noah led the lynx or panther out the kitchen door and stopped two feet short of Ilene's bedroom door, preserved of course. The children might want to stay over. This room was the biggest since she was the oldest. Noah's voice took flight, explaining how all the woodwork was original, where they got each antique. In the Didwell house, the air had shifted. The Didwells strained to listen as the goddess teased him and his new happy voice protested. The girls had more than once tried to take Noah shopping, but despite new clothes, he managed to put the wrong thing with the wrong thing. Where he stood with Yaram, so far still visible, he waved both arms, including the one spattered with paint. His pants were still too short, his short-sleeved plaid shirt still with its bleach stain, but as they turned to go through, he seemed to have pants so elegant they sloped down to his shoe tips. Yaram's fingers almost touched his elbow. They disappeared through the doorway. Yaram shouted with laughter.

All the Didwells tried to listen, Mrs. Didwell from the red antique stool that had been her mother's. Mr. Didwell dropped a fork, and the others shushed him.

From the depths of the back room came Yaram's silly giggle.

On the day Francine met Cyrus, she thought he might kill her. He had sat down in her station where she was a hash house waitress, the best in the West, bar none. He leaned back and watched her. He drank more coffee and she kept an eye on him.

After an hour, he leaned forward. "Would you like to have dinner?"

"I'd love to!" Francine responded.

They went to Alaska. Nothing could rattle Cyrus, one tough motherfucker, although it did rattle him when he was dying. Just before he went unconscious, she was sitting on their bed, where he lay propped up on pillows, and he held her hand and pressed it hard. A surveyor of the wilderness, he relished being lost or meeting a moose or a bear. He liked trouble.

He looked up.

"I'm scared," he said.

She searched the bedroom for a cure for cancer.

"I'm scared too," she said.

Then they put their foreheads together and rolled them back and forth, like kissing.

From the back room, Yaram giggled. Would the two come out engaged? Francine took the two last pills from her hidden pocket and closed the bathroom door behind her. Would she overdose? After swallowing, she jumped up and down, she did deep knee bends to increase her circulation, and did twists. She touched her toes, and when she came out, Bunny met her.

"We can be the Didwell Sisters!" Bunny shook her.

"What?" said Francine.

"Like Daddy! And Uncle Sly."

As a young man, Clarence Didwell had left the farm to ride the rails as a hobo. With his knapsack on his back, he was on his way to Alaska to pan for gold when the train passed through Kansas City, Kansas. At the stockyard, he jumped off. Eighteen years old, he rolled and landed, then dusted himself off. He wanted to see his older brother, Sly, who, according to the rumors, had religion; but despite that, he was crazy for Sly. He admired him. They had a bond as the two oldest boys of ten children.

"I'm off for Alaska," said young Clarence to his older brother.

"You ought to come to church with me tonight before you leave," said Sly, and because Clarence respected Sly, he thought it was the least he could do. They went to church, a storefront outfit, with sawdust on the floor and uncomfortable wooden benches, but the boys were young and full of energy and had their whole lives before them and welcomed hardship. Their mother was a Lutheran who enjoyed her life of little sins and hoped her oldest boy would come to his senses. The brothers listened to the sermon, which was boring, and then the preacher gave the altar call. People flooded toward the front.

"You ought to come down to the altar," said Sly. A large man, he never walked but lumbered. Sly had kindness.

Clarence wanted to be polite, and he was going to Alaska, but what was twenty minutes? He was much thinner than his brother, like a stick figure. In Minnesota, they had fished together in Crooked Creek a thousand times, trout mostly.

"Only for a minute," he said.

"I got canned food in that room I stay in. We can sit and catch up on the things that happened."

They walked forward together toward the altar. *Jack Spratt could eat no fat, His wife could eat no lean.* One big and one skinny, they both knelt down, and at some point God struck thin Clarence Didwell and struck him hard. Lightning leaped through his limbs. He was new from head to foot. He experienced salvation full and free, and when he got up, he didn't know where he was except that *something happened.* Big brother Sly's arm was next to him. Shaking, he followed it out to the car—the building was now empty—and they sat in the large Studebaker. Ripped lining hung down from the ceiling.

"You got saved," said Sly. "And now you ain't a sinner."

Clarence shook even harder.

"We are going to set the world on fire for God." The key clicked. The engine started, and died. Sly tried again. This time, the engine turned over. "The Didwell Brothers will preach the gospel back and forth across the whole country."

"When?" said Clarence, newly saved. By minutes.

"Starting tonight. We are going to build a reputation. Sinners will convert. The Didwell Brothers are going to set the world on fire together."

"We don't have any money," said skinny Clarence.

"God will provide the money!"

"We don't have any gas," said Clarence.

"God will provide the gas!"

In Monrovia, Francine stared out at the kitchen. Tap dance was not a field of possibility. Cyrus was dead.

"Be The Didwell Sisters and do what?" said Francine.

"Heal families, silly." Bunny shimmied. "I'll be the psychologist and you can be the prodigal come home. And poster child."

Something had flipped, but who cared when you were happy? She was a mighty Didwell. She had a sister. She might take swimming lessons.

"Oh my God," said Bunny. "I think I have some of Mother's gift, that electromagnetic personality."

The Didwell Sisters raced through the kitchen and through the dining room and stopped by the piano, where they let go. They did the Watusi, the boogaloo, the twist, the mashed potato. Francine grabbed a cello neck from high school and let go immediately. Cellos were delicate. Francine felt happy, and there were more pills where those came from.

"Dance therapy!"

They moved around the corner where no one could see them and twisted down to the ground and back up. They struck obscene poses. They kicked their legs and flung their heads. Their second wind made them dance even harder. They were whirling dervishes! Pouring sweat, breathing hard, the Didwell Sisters strutted around the Louis Quatorze chair. They moved their hips.

A scream from the kitchen stopped them.

They ran like wolverines, like cheetahs, like women who were crazy. Mrs. Didwell was still alive but she was choking. Her eyes were bulging. Between worlds, she leaned forward, helpless, sweat on her face, clutching Ilene, whose rubber gloves wouldn't come off. Someone yelled to call 911, and Bunny pounded on her back, and they all prayed, including

Francine. You couldn't live without a mother! Mrs. Didwell's arms flailed. As her face began to sag, Yaram's long smooth shadow flew across the kitchen. Long smooth arms crossed underneath the choker's breasts.

Bang! Like a wrestler, Yaram jerked her.

Nothing happened.

Bang! Yaram jerked harder.

Mr. Turkey flew and landed on the kitchen counter, grim against the white tile from the remodel. All the children had grown up in the old kitchen. Mrs. Didwell made loud noises, nothing ladylike, and took in air in gulps, and the family raised their hands to Jesus, and kissed Mrs. Didwell's cheeks, Yaram stepping backwards and folding her beautiful arms.

Noah stood in his new personality.

Mrs. Didwell raised her head slowly, one foot on the second rung of the red stool, built to last. A napkin remained on her lap, and she unfolded it. For a moment her bright eyes were grateful. When she straightened, her face was determined. Her smile was neutral.

"And where do *you* attend church?" she asked Yaram.

"Church?" Yaram lifted one long delicious finger off the list of medications she was holding, what time to take each, then put the blue folder in the drawer. An orange had fallen from its hanging basket on the island counter—a feature of the remodel, Mr. Didwell's idea—and Yaram replaced it, a neat person. "My whole family are atheists, but we respect all religions. My parents are sociology professors. What time shall I come on Tuesday? Also, I like to go to see my family for a few days over New Year's. In Massachusetts."

"Have you met Jesus?" said Mrs. Didwell.

Noah stepped up behind Yaram. Francine could see their children's features would be marvelous, do not doubt it. The joke was cruel. An atheist inside the Didwell home was just as possible as pigs flying. The devil tried each day to undermine your faith, to make you doubt the truth of heaven. Your name was written in the Lamb's Book of Life: Louella Aida Eggers Didwell, Clarence Maxim Didwell, Noah Steadman Didwell; Rebecca Louella Eastman-Didwell, probably; Ilene Duchess Singhorn (she had not kept her own last name in marriage), a possibility. Even a moment's doubt could send you straight to hell if the Lord came.

"Get out," Francine whispered to her brother.

Yaram touched her bald head, a woman who could make an ordinary purse catch fire. Her diamond sparkled. The gentleman behind her smiled as the young couple moved toward their surprising future.

"I'm afraid we won't be needing anyone," said Bunny.

On the porch, confused, Yaram still smiled, her face brilliant, the air blue, her head bald, small gold hoop earrings.

"What?" she said.

For a moment, Noah pushed through the doorframe. Yaram was slowly going down the stairs, one foot and then the other. Noah's clothes looked silly. Francine waved, but Yaram couldn't see her.

"Close the door," said somebody.

In the bowls, the ice cream was melted, but the cake remained to be eaten. Mrs. Didwell touched her throat. When the devil entered, you had to plead the blood, which was powerful. In the hymnbooks on the sideboard, under T*opical Index*, was the heading *Blood Songs*.

"Turn to two forty-three," said Mrs. Didwell.

The family sang them all, in order, all four verses. In a circle at the table they sat up straight, heaven triumphant. Ilene let fly the melody, Francine two notes below her, while Noah tried to fill the baritone. His voice got stronger. Oh, the harmony! They let it linger. Bunny kept quiet, but she had other talents. The Didwells clapped on every number.

"Mother, you're off," said Mr. Didwell.

Mrs. Didwell's two palms hit the belly of the beat, once more, twice more, and were quiet.

Mr. Didwell took the lead, his clapping terrible, hilarious, like splats of mud against the melody. Mrs. Didwell strove to follow him as best she could. Love was funny. They sang the Blood Songs through, and when they were edified, they stood up to go to their own houses.

"Note to myself: form an L.L.C." Bunny added.

Francine quit the pills every single night, and every morning come rain or shine she decided to quit tomorrow. Still not awake, she would walk downstairs to the pill cupboard and swallow two; and all day, every day, she continued swallowing. Between the first thought and the hand going to her mouth there was no stopping. She was the puppet, and the demon who pulled her strings was bigger. It was unequal. Sometimes, after dark, she flushed the blue-and-yellow capsules down the toilet; once, she threw them from the top floor of the Hunt Hotel in Santa Monica. Some days she buried them in the yard while reciting Edna St. Vincent Millay, or Kierkegaard (the leap of faith), or once T. S. Eliot about children. It was discouraging, or would be, if not for the pills. Each morning following her pledge the night before, she dug them up, or drove the freeways to her regular pill exits: Woodman, Sunset, Cadillac. She quit on days that were her lucky numbers—11, 22, 17—and on small holidays. When the pills wore off, life was terrible. It was true that she had been falling down in public, often choking, and there was the time she turned in front of an eighteen-wheeler and her license plate got slightly dented by the cab. She swallowed more pills. Every night when she collapsed after carnitas and two beers, her diaphragm moved so slowly she simply forgot to breathe, then she caught herself and woke up gasping one more time. Every night she prayed to wake up the next morning. The next morning the blue-and-yellow capsules made her happy. Time was long, as when she waited for the next fix—*dose*, these were from a doctor—and time was short, as when the Starbucks cashier got pregnant and had her baby in three days, start to finish. Francine continued dating from the *L.A. Times* Personals section, hoping to find someone to put his hand against her when the pills wore off and she felt death. Dating was hard work, dressing up in one of her five outfits, which she rotated. Job? Whatever. Travel? Blah blah Nepal blah blah Kathmandu. Favorite movie? Who cared? Her dates, if they stayed over, got up at three a.m. while Hank jumped around the bed on his hind legs, a human pogo stick, and barked without stopping and without inflection. It drove each of them crazy. "How long do these dogs live?" they sometimes asked before they put on their socks and left, good riddance to bad rubbish.

On pills your pupils grew large, which was how they were the afternoon she saw dear Ilya, too late to put on sunglasses. She had come face to face while exiting the door of Small World Books, her arms loaded down with fiction from the W section: Wambaugh, Waugh, Wharton, et cetera. *Research W!* she'd written on a scrap of paper somewhere. When she looked up, there Ilya stood staring.

"What is wrong with you?" He peered out of his brilliant eyes, a six-foot ladder balanced on his shoulder.

"I feel fantastico." With the sun in her eyes, it was difficult to read his expression, plus she might be levitating. Plus sparks flew all around her. A Crip or Blood stepped sideways to avoid her. When she reached out toward Ilya, two books fell to the boardwalk, but no one helped her. "Let's redecorate the living room." She wiped her forehead with her forearm and then couldn't remember whether she had. Pills made her so thirsty she would kill for water. "And after that, knock out some walls, and also build a roof deck so you can see the ocean. Also I plan to get a bunny. And build a cage. And also create two parking spaces."

The pink Hare Krishna passed between them.

"You are of no interest to me." Ilya watched her from three feet away, but it was a great psychic distance. What of their plans to put pot racks in the apartments? He was the thing that made being a landlord possible.

In the white beard, the pink mouth opened. "I have no time for people who are silly. I did this in Algeria." Ilya walked off, taking his brain of a handyman with him, no handyman advice on health or love life or drips, or even admonitions from the great Edgar Cayce. On Ilya's shoulder, his six-foot ladder floated like a feather due to his feeling for physics.

"I'm going on a cruise ship," she informed him. "With my family!"

His beard turned. "Do not call me. I am busy."

Tonight, the terrible Mrs. Tibbs was on the table, Francine's single remaining client—the rest had mysteriously disappeared. Francine effleuraged the whole back, saying hello to the skin very carefully, still in her date dress #3, the evening a disaster. She had fallen down while trying to lean in for a kiss. On pills, Mrs. Tibbs's flesh felt totally inanimate, like a bag of stuffing. Francine felt no connection. She had sashayed down the Paradiso red line in her Chinese Laundry high heels only to find her client on the porch, another victory at being wronged that made her look ecstatic. Francine didn't ask how long she had been waiting. The *W* books sat scattered on the ugly couch next to two newspaper clippings from Mrs. Didwell, "Dress for Success" and "Girl Beaten After Leaving Library Park." Mrs. Tibbs was able to squeeze by the horrid couch sideways.

"*Les fleurs du mal*," said Mrs. Tibbs, who could surprise you.

"I'll let you get undressed. Start on your stomach, please."

When Francine entered, Mrs. Tibbs's head popped up like a turtle's. Francine gentled it down. The client was complaining, through the faceplate, about the ugly shoes she had been forced to wear in childhood, with long brown laces that had to be double-tied. Because the whole experience had scarred her.

"Breathe," said Francine.

In her black dress, sleeveless voile—pills made you go shopping—Francine did thumb kneads on the sacrum, but she was getting tired already. In fact she felt utterly exhausted. The terrible Mrs. Tibbs was draining off her energy. Her voice that shattered nerve sheathing went on about her upstairs neighbors who clomped around in order to annoy her. Next was the long line at the DMV, and next was how the newspaper was getting thinner. The neighbors upstairs were named Smith, which clearly was an alias. Mrs. Tibbs had called the police, and what had the police done? Nothing. Francine's energy leaked out until her fingers stopped.

"The hand should never leave the client," said Mrs. Tibbs. The head popped up.

With a small crash, Hank broke through the doggie fence in the kitchen entryway, his ears flying, and scudded across the wood floor to the front window, where the cat burglar had just come home. Apparently.

"I wouldn't have come if I knew your dog was that undisciplined," said the client. "Can I get a refund? I'm allergic."

And with that, she went to sleep and started snoring. Francine sat down and looked at her for twenty minutes. Then she got up.

"Time to turn."

To her astonishment, Mrs. Tibbs turned without complaint. Francine gently placed the buckwheat eye pillow over her eyes, slight scent of lavender.

"Don't crush my eyeballs. I hold you responsible."

"Rivet," said a voice outside the window, the cat burglar's way to say hello; but he was shy; even, possibly autistic.

"What was that?" said Mrs. Tibbs with her eyes closed.

"Old pipes. They have to burp." To her surprise, Francine found herself in tears, strangely moved to have a friend who walked on roofs. The cat burglar couldn't talk and she couldn't tap dance. They understood each other. The Sierra juniper outside the window had one hidden entry, and yesterday Francine had slipped in two *Time* magazines and *Under the Volcano*.

"You need to move into a safe neighborhood," said Mrs. Tibbs.

"Rivet," said the cat burglar.

No one had ever seen his face directly. Some said he had a moustache, some said an eye patch. Some said he was mute. The police had almost caught him twice, in grabbing distance of the back of his shirt before he vanished into thin air. Hands on Mrs. Tibbs's quadriceps, Francine kneaded with professional intent to keep off a sense of foreboding. She herself did absolutely nothing illegal, ever, no street drugs, no daring left turns, for fear she would be locked in a small cell and go crazy. She took giant steps around the massage table to remind herself of freedom.

"Are you aware that what you call your Persian carpet is not from that country?"

"Breathe."

Francine blinked and tried hard to concentrate: effleurage the new skin, think of the client because they can feel it, don't push but drop your weight, the result of which feels completely different.

"I'm going to stretch your leg out from the hip. Relax and take a big breath in. Giant breath out. *Haaaaaaa.*"

But which leg had she finished? Right? Left? Both? On pills, it was a conundrum. She picked up Mrs. Tibbs's right ankle and leaned back into space. An opening in either sacroiliac joint might make Mrs. Tibbs forget which leg was which.

"Ah," said Mrs. Tibbs. "Oh. Indeed. My aching feet."

Francine leaned farther back on faith.

"Mmmm," hummed her client. "Oh. Ah."

Francine leaned slightly farther.

The floor came up to meet her, as in a cartoon. She got her wind. Above her, staring down, Mrs. Tibbs's face appeared immense. Her forehead glowered. Francine sat where she was, no need to scramble to her feet. But now Mrs. Tibbs was jumping off the table, a spry Mrs. Tibbs, nimble, running on her tiptoes with the sheet trailing behind like a goddess. She came back and got her clothes, then disappeared around the corner.

"I won't charge you," Francine called out, professional.

On the floor, it was very peaceful. Mrs. Tibbs stalked out the door with her nose raised, a fresh umbrage, and Francine waved, one hand high enough for Mrs. Tibbs to see her. Hopefully. Night sounds came in: a gunshot somewhere in the distance, the sound of someone doing dishes. She wished she could hear crickets.

"Ima fuck him up," said some passing Venetian.

She could no longer stand it.

She swallowed two pills as a farewell—the pills had spirits—and also to feel good when she started a clean way of life. *Today is the first day of the rest of your life*, some Hallmark card said. In a cute hoodie over her black dress, she zipped all remaining pills into the left pocket only. There would be no turning back. The pills were coming on when she left without the dog, down the red line and north up the boardwalk. With each step she felt more joyful. When she reached Rose Avenue, she continued lightly to the little spit that extended toward the ocean. With her hand in her pocket, she got ready. It was here that her mother's tambourine teacher, the great preacher Aimee Semple McPherson, had come walking out of the ocean after her thrilling disappearance with her lover. Although Mrs. Didwell denied it. A rosy love for all the Christians and sinners came over Francine. A gospel group was singing "Jesus on the Mainline." How precious life was. On the bike path just ahead (*the heart and soul of Venice!* she wrote in the margin of her Imaginary Tap Dance Handbook), a blond female was roller-skating toward her, both arms out, her long hair floating behind her. She was flying, wind on her abdomen, and she looked exactly like Francine Ephesians Didwell.

"She's going down," said a voice from somewhere.

She was never going to quit, and the pills she had intended to throw in the surf went back into her pocket with a small zip. Water lapped around her. In the amber bottle, twenty-two blue-and-yellow dancing girls were rescued. With the moon shining on the water, death seemed real, almost as if it could really happen, not a silly worry, not neurotic, but as if you really would lie in the ground unable to move, *Climb ev'ry mountain!* over. You! It was the feeling that you might die, not your grandparents or famous people in history, you. YOU! As if they weren't kidding.

9
SCHLESWIG AND HOLSTEIN

On what turned out to be a Thursday, nothing special, Francine woke up, still alive, at something o'clock in the afternoon, whatever day it was, and blundered off the bed and down the stairs to the source of life that was the pill cupboard. As she reached the cupboard door, she waited for her hand to rise but it did not rise. Her legs kept walking forward. She peered at her right foot, perplexed. She had quit the blue-and-yellow pills forever the night before, as usual, the earnest vows, the prayer to keep her breathing until morning, the resolution to drink wheatgrass juice and only think positive thoughts (the Inspirations!!!) and be absolutely fabulous. At this point she no longer had the hope needed to throw the pills off piers, either Venice or Santa Monica, or ride the outside elevator up to the top of the Hunt Hotel and hurl them into space. She would die soon, if not last night, tonight, or the night after. It was coming. In the familiar kitchen, she continued walking forward.

Was the puppet master on vacation?

A vaudevillian, she backed up to the cupboard in question. Nothing happened. There was a tiny rip in the window of reality, and she stepped through it. She took one giant step from *Monty Python*.

She kept walking.

In the dining room, she passed the table with Bunny's note, pink stationery in a pink envelope that upset her every time the pills wore thin. She picked it up and opened it. There was a pink handwritten bill for Mr. Didwell's birthday dinner—each child paid one quarter—but what cost each of them $90? A sinner dare not ask a Christian. Times four children? The bill was in Bunny's lavender pen, the cute curlicues. Bunny circled every *i* instead of dotting it, and without pills the curlicues seemed criminal. $360 for all four children? For one dinner? Out loud, she read items one through seven: Parmesan, brown sugar, turkey, green beans, butter. She picked up the note and waved it.

Number six said *Item, $90.*

By dusk, she needed to buy protection, like in *The Friends of Eddie Coyle*, one of the books that raised her. Surreal, she got her keys, her blood starting to ask *What? What? What?* Still no pills inside her, she drove five miles to Brotman Hospital. She had seen the underworld denizens hanging out at this hour on party night, a Saturday, Fuck Me with a Spoon Anonymous, or some Anonymous, there were a million. It was something. Inside, the brainwashing had started. The large room was packed to the gills with people who looked dangerous. A visitor, she spotted what appeared to be an empty seat on the extreme front right, which meant she had to walk in front of all the sinners. A preacher's daughter!

"I'm new here," she whispered to her neighbor, which was what you did in church to be welcomed warmly.

The goons on either side ignored her totally, both unfriendly specimens besides being unfashionable. Who did they think they were? Francine stuck out her new boot, a celebration boot from receiving her trust money. The woman on her right was wearing red, white, and blue, a human flag topped off with henna hair. On Francine's left a balding man with glasses wouldn't even qualify to meet her on a date for Starbucks coffee. Francine crossed her legs and tossed her long blond hair, two of her three most attractive gestures. To pass the time, she mentally went over Bunny's pink note. The nerve! The awful color! There at the bottom had been the word *item*—$90? Times four children? What was *item*?

Francine looked up.

At the podium on a high stage a man was saying that he crashed his Mercedes, flat-lined at the hospital, then lost his job as a Hollywood producer and his wife divorced him, and all the brain-dead souls on both sides were laughing. Did no one take being the dregs of society seriously?

What the fuck cost ninety dollars?

Because the Didwells didn't eat thirty-thousand-year-old excavated mastodon. The envelope had a red rose on the return part and on the sheet of paper was a red rose. *Times four children?* Ahead on a high stool, a demented woman in a hot pink turtleneck waved her hot pink arms, making her bracelets clang, and no one shut her up.

"And then I paddled down the Amazon," the idiot speaker droned on.

And why call it *item*? The Didwells didn't eat Albanian roast pig. They didn't eat imported Spanish lemon drops. Onstage, the speaker had received four DUIs, then married two women the same week, both unsuspecting. The Didwells didn't drink expensive bourbon. The woman in hot pink on the high stool was beginning to look epileptic. At the podium the speaker now had gone to France and commandeered a train, then run and pissed on the eternal flame, then the gendarmes came and something happened. Each time she multiplied it, four times ninety was three hundred sixty dollars. For one *item*? For one *dinner*? The Didwells didn't eat exotic antelope from the Himalayan glaciers. She was talking to herself and gesturing when all the bald fat snooty types stood up and clasped hands, on one side dry, on one side clammy.

"I'm Francine," said Francine, sotto voce. "And you are?"

The woman snubbed her!

Francine started through the crowd of low-lifers toward Venice, where in the cupboard thirty-four blue-and-yellow capsules waited to save her. In the crowd of bodies was an opening and she barged through it.

"Here."

Someone in huaraches pushed a flat black disc into her hand. She looked. It said 10 MINUTES. It was plastic! Did they call this jewelry?

"Get a sponsor," said a man in loafers who squeezed her elbow.

She had almost reached the exit, then her car, then the cupboard, when she smelled tea tree. She tried to punt but two small feet with stems in leggings blocked her. The body was pear-shaped. Francine tried to feint around her, but a tiny hand reached out and grabbed her.

"Friend," said Julia.

Francine burst into tears. It was embarrassing but she couldn't stop. Around her, people laughed and chatted, as if crack-ups in this space were normal. She cried harder.

"Everyone snubbed me," she blubbered. "I tried to be friendly."

Julia's small hand pointed at the hot pink woman. "You were sitting in the deaf- mute section. That's the sign language interpreter."

Francine laughed but then, she couldn't stop. She started crying.

The dominatrix, old soul, floated. Was she never in a hurry? Her black tights bulged at the hip, her white hair stuck straight out, her face was innocent, as if she were the Virgin Mary or Joan of Arc or Madame Curie who discovered radium. Her black turtleneck was cashmere.

"I'm not addicted. Francine clutched the round black (plastic!) disc and looked for the nearest trash can. She explained the obvious to Julia. "I only take pills if I have a job to do, or have to clean, or I'm tired, or fireworks are going off, or I go to Monrovia. I'm a preacher's daughter. Stress will kill you."

"Get a sponsor." Another body touched her forearm. "Somebody who has what you want."

"Go home and flush your pills and call me," Julia said. "Tonight."

"All thirty-four of them?"

At home, she watched her hand flush them but just as they went down the hatch, she realized the cat was missing. She stuck her hand in but the toilet bowl was empty. When had she heard or seen the Siamese? Because on pills, time bled together. In the kitchen, Hank stared back at her, his eyes like a stuffed animal.

"Kitty?" she called sweetly.

The cat wasn't on the refrigerator, and the cat wasn't in the window. She wasn't upstairs on the dresser. Had the cat been gone hours or days? Francine ran through the living room. She called out the door and ran down to the beach and ran back. Three mason jars with dead flowers sat unattended, two with putrid water, one dry completely.

She called Julia.

"Help," she managed.

"I think she got mad at me and ran away from home and now a killer has her!" Julia stood in the living room and didn't talk but only listened. "Siamese have to be worshiped. It's their birthright." Francine burst into tears. "I was loaded."

While Francine talked, the women made signs with a laundry pen. *Lost Cat! Red Collar! Reward! $$$!* With Francine's heavy-duty stapler, her one tool besides duct tape, they walked the streets of Venice and put up fliers. The moon was full. In Venice, the Satanists had rituals. And gang members tied cats into burlap bags to train pit bulls to be killers. *Kitty!*

the women yelled. The cat's mother listened for the right meow. When she called *Kitty!* other cats came out to meet her.

At three a.m., when they heard singing up ahead, Francine broke into a run and grabbed Pinkwell. He kept singing. *If you ever change your mind/About leavin' me behind!*

"My cat is missing."

He stopped singing. On the grass, Pinkwell tipped his hat, as elegant as always.

"La Petite Madame Butterfly."

His entourage watched and waited. Everybody knew Pinkwell, and he knew everybody. The homeless population knew exactly what went on, because nobody saw them. Now Pinkwell stepped out from the grassy knoll with his guitar strapped to his chest. It was never off him. Several of his acolytes struggled to their feet from where they lay drunk, and waited for guidance. Those who were passed out would remain sleeping until the sprinklers woke them up at four a.m.

"The Queen of Venice. I saw the signs. I already sent people out to look and listen."

They were quiet, but no cat voice pierced the boardwalk.

Sometimes Pinkwell sat outside 31 Paradiso and listened to the cat for professional reasons. He was a singer, but not just any singer. Pinkwell had the curse of being able to stop you in your tracks and make you forget what you were thinking. Tonight, as always, he wore a black wool full-length topcoat, once very expensive, and dark red cowboy boots. His hair was impressive, long and black and dirty. Even the cops liked Pinkwell. Instead of citing him for being drunk in public, they all bullshitted while he drank his beer and leaned against a car that wasn't his. Besides having ears to the ground, he had that je ne sais quoi that was perhaps the magnetism from the actual earth, and he made everyone wake up around him. He probably would someday kill himself, but he made others happy.

"A fellow is burning cats," said Pinkwell after some deliberation.

"Kitty?" Francine looked up and down the beach.

"They found two in dumpsters, burned to a crisp. One had a black tail."

When Francine heard, Julia put out a small hand as if to catch her.

"It wasn't Madame Butterfly. The other didn't have a collar with a buckle."

An acolyte handed her a dirty hankie and she thanked him, then turned away and kept hyperventilating. Pinkwell was saying that no one knew where the pervert lived. In his black coat he walked with the two women up the boardwalk, and his followers who were awake walked after him. At every building and at every window she could reach, Francine meowed. She called, "Kitty!" There was a pervert somewhere. When the two women walked home, the sun rising, posters with Caddy's name and *Red collar!* were stapled to every pole and fence. Was Caddy calling for her mother? There was the parking space where Francine had found Caddy beneath a Cadillac. There was the tree she climbed and Francine climbed after her. When they got home, the *L.A. Times* boy was tossing papers willy nilly at houses. The search party walked up to the red line at 31 and stopped.

"We'll look later today," Julia said. "*Vaya con dios*."

"Deploy," said the homeless singer Eddie to his army.

Then, all hell broke loose and Francine's euphoric period was done, over, toast. She couldn't live without the pills. Her neck screamed, her eyeballs had knives in them, and her legs jerked when she lay down. She couldn't sleep. She got up and watched infomercials advertising mattresses, the only thing on TV but the pictures on the screen were moving. Her nerve endings were jangled. Chauzer Impermanente was only a freeway ride away, and yet she didn't drive there.

In this state she drove to Noah's birthday party in Monrovia, eyes straight ahead and both hands on the wheel. The cat hadn't come home and was either burned or being used to incite pit bulls. In Venice, her front door was ajar, anchored by a can of tuna. Getting closer to her fate, she tried not to think about the future. She had *said* she would go on the cruise and she *would* go on the cruise. The tickets were bought and it was too late to back out. What was water? H_2O. How could it hurt you? At the house she had once visited with Cyrus, Francine went up the thirteen stairs with her olives and pickles, stone cold sober. Her left eye twitched. She walked across the faded place where Jack the iron dog had been. When she raised her hand to knock, the door swung open. Was this a haunted mansion?

"What ho?" said Noah.

The woman who stood behind him smiling broadly (despite red lipstick, could she be a California Christian?) was quite beautiful, dark hair pulled severely back. One tooth was missing. Had Noah found a wife? Yaram was bound for hell along with her parents.

"I work here," the woman said, nodding. "I love Jesus."

It took one pillhead to know another. The woman was loaded. In her hand she held a yellow plastic pitcher, ostensibly to water plants—the Didwells had many: wandering Jew, spider ferns, the pretty ones with little white marks, also creeping Charlie, some perched on high stands, others hanging—but the pitcher was empty. At the creeping Charlie, she tilted the yellow submarine, but only air came out. Slowly she tilted the pitcher farther. Did no one see there was no water?

"Oh!" cried Mrs. Didwell from the archway. Because of

company, she was using a cane, not her walker, her hair done, and of course face clean of lipstick to praise Jesus. Noah had been born exactly thirty-two years ago today in Iowa. "Muriel? This is our second daughter, Francine Ephesians. Francine, this is Muriel, our helper."

"How goes life?" Noah continued.

He had waited two weeks in agony and then persuaded Yaram to meet with him, engagement ring in hand, and fallen on one knee to make her his bride and defy his family. Slowly she raised her left hand. Yaram was a bride already. She had been married. The two lovers stared at one another. Finally, he rose to his feet. The star-crossed couple pledged never to speak again, and Noah as a consequence had now devoted himself to minerals and rocks found in the vicinity where Jesus walked. But Noah's face had changed. It was leaner, full of knowledge, like a soldier who has witnessed what cannot possibly be possible. He took a rock out of his pocket.

"Quartz," he said.

Bunny waved and ran across the dining room and clutched her only sister. "I inscribed leather notebooks for each family member for our workshops!"

Francine felt sick. She lurched past the piano and around the dining room table into the kitchen and threw up in the sink.

"Are you pregnant with someone's illegitimate child?" called Mrs. Didwell.

When Francine straightened, Bunny whispered that she would announce the cruise after dessert, every detail taken care of, hats and confetti hidden in a bag beneath the table. Bunny wrote a bright idea on her yellow legal pad. Francine unloaded her pickles and olives into pretty dishes, and went into the bathroom to rinse her mouth out. The cruise lasted one week, but the Didwell Sisters™ was forever. What had she been thinking? The difference between pills and no pills was a completely different person. Who was she when she took them? Who was she when she didn't? When she returned to the dining room, for a moment all the Didwells looked slightly demented.

"Let us pray," said Mr. Didwell.

"Don't pinch me!" Ilene kicked Noah.

"Dear heavenly Father," said Mr. Didwell. "Thank you for sending Noah Steadman."

All heads bowed.

Without the blue-and-yellow helpers, Francine felt like she was on an LSD trip—she had never taken acid—and she poked down inside her bra to feel the 10 MINUTE chip where she had stashed it. Her palms were sweating. Bunny had devised a new game called Miracle! to name the times in family history when the impossible had happened, like Francine's baby earlobe, or the time the thief sent Mr. Didwell's wallet back. Mr. Didwell thanked God for the new STOP sign at Colorado.

Francine did isometrics.

On the Didwell table, placed amidst the food at intervals, were three small bowls in which Mrs. Didwell's gardenias floated, emitting their incomparable aroma. Louella's wedding bouquet had been gardenias, period, and nothing else. It was a fashion departure that scandalized Grandmother Didwell, nor had that side of the family recovered. On the wall, the clock ticked toward the cruise departure. In his prayer, still going, Mr. Didwell thanked God again that Noah had been born, and that he had been given a fine mind. Noah's face was starting to relax, the pain of Yaram easing so you could see his essential sweetness. Mr. Didwell explained to God the rigors Noah encountered in Satan's world: the scoffers he must face, the atheists, the daily threats to his purity. When Mr. Didwell mentioned Yaram's name, a wave of pain washed over Noah. Behind Mr. Didwell, helper Muriel was staring at a lampshade, happy and lobotomized. In his prayer, Mr. Didwell reminded God that any Christian could slide out of the Lamb's Book of Life and land in hell before the cock crowed. He finished with a plea that God bless Noah and keep him and make His face to shine upon him.

"Clarence? *Dog*," said Mrs. Didwell.

Mr. Didwell asked God to find the dog whose name God knew, because God was omniscient.

"Jack," said Noah.

The pot roast fell apart and was head-shakingly delicious, Noah's favorite, with the little onions, potatoes, and carrots placed around it in the juices. The piece of quartz sat beside his water glass. Francine got up to get more napkins, although no napkins were needed. She couldn't sit still. She walked into the kitchen and doubled back and went into the kitchen and came back again. She had to keep moving.

"What's wrong with you?" said Mrs. Didwell.

"Nothing."

But in the mirror on the sideboard, when she sat down to eat mashed potatoes, she looked wild-eyed.

"You look terrible," said Mrs. Didwell.

Her eyeballs held knives. *Give me pills*, the blood demanded. *Bitch*, the blood said. *I will kill you.* When Francine reached into her cleavage to locate the black plastic chip that said 10 MINUTES, Mrs. Didwell caught her.

"Hands," said her mother.

While Bunny crackled with excitement, they talked of Noah's childhood, the cute things he had said, and his success in the community of Christian scientists. Because of his incisive paper *What Does Language Mean?*, Noah had been asked to give a speech in Atlanta, Georgia, on Creation Theory: Is a day a day? Is a day an aeon? Bunny's eyebrows had grown fuller with anticipation. Noah took more pot roast. On his plate, Noah had built a dam of mashed yams with brown sugar, and pimiento olives for a border (Francine's contribution), and pot-roast gravy for a lake. He ate with his right hand while his left hand reached for butter. As a scientist, he had little time for nonsense. Still, gravy had begun to leak out the backside of the project and the yam wall was softening. From time to time, he turned the piece of quartz over. Disaster got closer. Mother's headache pills sat quietly in the kitchen, twenty-three if she had not miscounted last time she was here, and Francine got up and walked there and shook four pills into her hand and made a fist around them. She went back to the table and used her free hand to resume eating.

"Everybody eat faster!" Bunny's eyes were neon. "I can't stand it."

"What's going on?" said Mrs. Didwell.

Just last week, Bunny had placed ads in two Christian magazines concerning the Didwell Sisters L.L.C. cruises starting in December; one couple had signed up already. The initial Didwell cruise was only the acorn that would become the oak tree. Bunny hoped they could go international, and to this end she was trying to learn Italian. Bunny wanted to hire a videographer who would tape Francine's witness account about the peace of being reunited with her family. *Meow*, said Kitty from the dumpster. Muriel had moved on to dusting the lampshade at which she had been staring. They were moving toward dessert, and Francine opened her fist. The little pill eyes sparkled. Who besides your family knew the time the four siblings pretended there was a call from a man in Algeria seeking salvation? And ran in the kitchen and told Daddy? And he got excited? And who else knew car trips every summer to Minnesota to visit your sinner grandmother, Grandma Didwell? She had a fishing mania, and once she got her pole cast and her feet in Crooked Creek, no power could get her back to be a wife and mother and cook dinner. She could catch fish all day long if sunstroke didn't get her. When Mrs. Didwell looked up, her eyes had sharpened, crazy like a fox.

"We have an announcement!" Bunny burst out. Muriel almost dropped the cake, which God made land safely on the table.

"Hold your horses," said Mr. Didwell.

Mrs. Didwell watched her daughters.

Noah blew his candles out, and they applauded.

"Make a wish," said someone.

"*The Didwell Healing Cruise!*" Bunny shouted. She held out both arms, engorged with excitement.

"Healing from what?" said Mrs. Didwell, but no one heard her.

"Everyone be quiet!" Bunny climbed up on her chair and balanced. She held up a banner, gold on black.

With her free hand, Francine stuffed more olives in her mouth. She added a pickle.

"Pay attention. *And Bible Study!*" Still balanced on her chair, Bunny passed out hats, the pièces de résistance, magenta with blue stitching. The minute she took the pills, copasetic, Francine could join the Didwell Healing Cruise and hit rage pillows. She and Bunny had bikinis. Without the Didwells, who would love her? DIDWELL COUNTRY, they read out loud. Hands put their brims on toward the front, but Noah insisted on putting his on with the writing in back. A freethinker! *Didwell Country*. Their heads moved as they looked at each other. The color made the Didwell eyes pop. Bunny's chest got bigger. Francine got ready to be loaded. Still standing on the chair she had upholstered, Bunny waved her arms and almost lost her balance.

"I hope your shoes are off," said Mrs. Didwell.

"The Didwell Healing Cruise and Bible Study. Surprise! And Daddy's paying. We leave *as a family* in three weeks, from New York City." The hats were taken off and looked at, and then the Didwells put them back on, Noah's backwards. "We all have berth numbers and everything. The family will fly together."

"What translation of the Bible?" Noah interrupted.

"I wanted Revised Standard Version, but Daddy said King James."

"Original Greek!" Noah shouted.

"What ocean?" Ilene smelled men.

"The Caribbean," Bunny said. Hats bobbed around the table while the Didwells hooted and cheered. Noah wore the banner cape-fashion. The table was hilarious. "And little grains of rice with our names on them."

"Didwell ice cream!" Noah shouted.

"Three weeks, people!" Bunny shook her can-do personality. She had the famous fish-white Didwell skin, her arms spread in glory. "Twenty-one days until we praise God on the open sea, so get ready. We have Didwell beach towels. And Mom and Dad's budget book from when they were first married. I found it in the attic. *Ice cream, 13 cents*."

When Muriel began to clear the cake, Ilene grabbed it with both hands.

"What's *wrong* with you? We have to eat it! Bring a knife. Bring water."

"We have events planned for every day, exercises to get to know each other, plus a forum every afternoon to bring up grievances." In her compact, Ilene checked her face to see what those who fell in love with her would see at their first glance. The compact clicked shut. "From two to four. The emphasis is on togetherness. And forgiveness. And greatness."

"Forgive your enemies seventy times seven," Noah added.

"Healing from *what*?" repeated Mrs. Didwell.

Bunny clapped her hands for silence.

"Get ready, get set," she said, except her voice was serious. Ilene put down the cutting knife. Bunny jumped off the chair and skipped around the table. Bunny moved like Oral Roberts and Mick Jagger rolled into one, a Christian superstar.

Bunny yanked Francine's pill arm toward the ceiling.

"Francine and I are going to heal families at sea, and ask Jesus to help us, and use psychology." She pulled their arms higher, engorged with excitement. "Francine will be the poster child and I will be the charismatic leader." Bunny was crying. "And spokesperson."

In his cape, Noah made a drum roll on the lace tablecloth.

"Meet the Didwell Sisters!" Bunny blew her nose. "Like the Didwell Brothers. The famous evangelistic team!"

Mr. Didwell cleared his throat.

"I never told the end, and I feel that I would like to." Mr. Didwell looked out at his family.

"You were a hobo," Bunny interrupted. "You met Sly and you got saved. And that night you sat out in the car and took off preaching. And you became the Didwell Brothers."

"Not exactly," said Mr. Didwell. "Not precisely."

"Hurry!" Bunny said. "I have confetti."

"We sat in that old Studebaker and it was cold. Well, I was new to this thing, and I was shaking. He was older. The stuffing was coming out the roof. Sly said, *The Didwell Boys are going to preach the gospel. We're leaving tonight. The Didwell Brothers are going to be famous.*"

"I said, *But Sly. We don't have any money.*"

"God will provide the money!" the children shouted.

"*But Sly. We don't have any gas.*"

"God will provide the gas!"

"Then," said Mr. Didwell, "Sly started driving. We

went up a little hill and over a stone bridge, and Sly took his hands off the steering wheel. He has that booming voice. He held both hands up."

"God is driving this car!" Sly shouted.

"Right then we went over the edge of the stone bridge and plunged down an embankment and came to a stop right side up and smack in the middle of a tennis court. The prosperous people of Kansas City were running around with tennis racquets and screaming, and someone started toward us.

"Sly got out.

"He's a big man, a huge man, and so is everything about him. He lifted both arms. '*God will strike dead anyone who touches this car!*'

"He stepped forward.

"The little men in white coats came and took him, and Dad had to come down in the truck and drive me back to Minnesota."

There was silence in the house. At the table, no one touched their silverware. "It's a wonder I remained a Christian. When I think about it," Mr. Didwell added.

If given the opportunity, always shake hands with a preacher. That is the quality that makes them one. They have the warmth of ten men or women. When Bunny let go, Francine opened her hand and let the pills fall on the expensive Persian carpet. Francine reached out and shook her father's hand; he was still sitting, but this was what church people did, you could feel the spirit through the palm skin, forget hugging.

"They sang a hymn and went out," said her father every Sunday morning service just before the Christians went home to dinner, which was pot roast. Mr. Didwell had risen to his feet to shake hands better. Much of handshaking is posture. Father and daughter finished shaking hands, very satisfying, but she had learned from the best.

"I'm not going on the cruise," announced Francine to the assembled hats. She looked at Bunny who had confetti ready to let loose, too late to stop it. It snowed down over their heads that said DIDWELL COUNTRY. Francine continued. "I'm not going on the one-week healing. I'm not going on the Didwell Sisters™."

Bunny's eyes were glitter.

"Oh, you're going," said Bunny sweetly.

The Didwells partook of birthday cake and ice cream. They were used to drama, both the Old and New Testaments, the plagues of locusts, the fire by night, Lazarus. Strong emotions were relaxing. Mrs. Didwell ate some pot roast she had hidden. They leaned back in their chairs, Jesus was real, and crossed their legs and continued what they were doing.

Bunny turned her back to them—she faced the Didwell portrait—and when she turned around again, she was feral.

"Francine? You have your own path, so whatever." Under the baseball cap, her mouth was stretched in a wide smile. The room had darkened. "Have fun in your life in Venice." She swallowed. "I have a ton of things to do."

So the unconscious is a wild country, and who knows what lives there? For several minutes, nothing happened. Francine saw by Bunny's changing posture that she had become psychotic, like all the Didwells, like all humans. Mrs. Didwell's bedroom door was almost always closed (the sacred space that held the bed, her private holy of holies for worship and regeneration, her hotline to the Throne of Grace), but Muriel had left the door open. The shining headboard caught the summer light, because Mrs. Didwell polished the bed on Tuesdays. The younger heads in baseball caps with some confetti followed Bunny's gaze. Mr. Didwell, who was hard of hearing, took more pot roast gravy.

"Daddy," said Francine.

"Mother's bed is going into storage," Bunny said. Her

tone was efficient.

Noah speared his cake but didn't eat it.

The others blinked.

"The Italiano," Noah said. He made an Italian gesture.

"Now we have workers. And they need to get around it," said Bunny.

"We only have one worker," Noah pointed out.

Bunny never started anything she couldn't finish. When she stretched, her arms had gotten longer. "It makes more sense to have single beds that raise up and lower down. With bars on either side so Mom and Dad don't fall out." Mrs. Didwell's face was changing into little separate areas. "It's a well-known fact of sociology that people as they age need extra room around them. I can get my friend Jake to come by and do the packing. He has special blankets, and he's a Christian. Wait." She pulled out her yellow legal pad. "Tomorrow I have stuff to do. Wednesday."

"The bed has not a single scratch on it." Mrs. Didwell clawed the air, as if she couldn't breathe, then sank back. Her grammar was perfect. Mr. Didwell claimed he had instructed her in speech, but it was the opposite. The bed had been their rendezvous for fifty years, before the children came, and much later when their bones began to hurt, they could be young by simply lying on their backs on it. Mrs. Didwell could touch her husband merely by moving one finger. She got her strength. All four tiny babies had come home there, plus one who had not come home but died inside her. The headboard curves were the children's first view of the world. The bed had been named Morning, although only Mrs. Didwell knew it.

"I'm going to call him." Bunny picked up the telephone receiver.

"Mother will grow old without the bed." Francine pointed toward the chenille bedspread.

"You don't have the right to interrupt." Bunny smiled a

gracious smile. "Not now. Not ever."

"I'm not growing old," said Mrs. Didwell.

"Well well well," said Mr. Didwell, who could hear nothing. He made two ear trumpets with his big hands. "Some people say that old discoloration on a hardwood floor from dogs is a reason to replace it, but I say it adds value. I call it *history*."

For one second, Mrs. Didwell looked eviscerated, cheeks hollow. Her life had been exciting, and she could have been a criminal, but she chose Jesus. Or Jesus chose her. Now, leaving aside her cane, she stood up and took three steps toward the north door, whose visage looked out on the San Gabriel Mountains. During their time in Iowa, she had sorely missed their contours. Sorely. At the little antique table with intact red painted piping, she opened the little drawer and took the key ring: lock, unlock, trunk.

"Mother?" Bunny approached. "What are you doing?"

Mrs. Didwell stood with her arms out for balance.

In the Didwell dining room, there was only the sound of breathing. No one moved.

"I would like to go for a drive," said Mrs. Didwell. "Why don't we take the Lincoln Continental. Muriel?"

Muriel turned to deal with this new problem. It nearly always worked if you said *I love Jesus*. Her face struggled to understand what they were doing. As the north door stood open, you could feel the little breeze that made the screen door go bump. Just beyond the stairs the beautiful one-hundred-year-old bougainvillea rose, and Mrs. Didwell started toward it. She was using both arms like rudders.

"Mother," said Mr. Didwell, who had risen. "Muriel ought not to drive you."

Which should have stopped her. The husband was under God, and under him the angels, and under them the wife, ad nauseam. She continued.

"Are you coming back?" said Mr. Didwell.

"We shall see," Louella answered.

Muriel stepped out and stumbled—who knew how she drove?—and Bunny blocked the door, and someone said to grab the keys, but all were stopped by Mrs. Didwell. Who could preach. Mrs. Didwell was a preaching snob, and no one was as good as she, except perhaps C. M. Ward (Francine had met him), perhaps the great Cotton Mather. When it came to preaching, Mrs. Didwell knew the Holy Ghost when someone had it. She knew the windbags and she knew the empty vessels.

"Mother? Sit down," said Bunny.

"Get out of my way," said Mrs. Didwell.

"We have a gig," said Julia, standing in Venice in the living room on Paradiso. Today she was wearing her tiara. "The Puffin Hotel."

"Where's the cat?" Francine unclutched her black 10 MINUTE chip and sat up. She still slept downstairs on the terrible couch with the door cracked open. She blinked. The cat was dead.

Two white tap shoes slid across the floor and crashed into the sofa.

"What day is it?"

Julia threw her pear-shaped body weight on the enormous furniture item with enormous purple people-eating flowers, then shot up as if stung by a bee. *Bees are philosophers,* Francine had written in her delirium. Her skin still itched. She wanted pills. Relief was just a car ride away, but she didn't take it. In a strange state of mind where she could feel things, she was loath to give it up. Today the dominatrix glared down at the large purple flowers and again tried to sit, but to all appearances, one large flower propelled her up and forward.

"Get on your feet. We're a duo."

Unwieldly hope filled Francine.

"My God, that couch is ugly." Julia dispelled the bad energy by shaking her arms from the shoulder. Next she shimmied. "One gig for one tap duo. Paying. We have three days to get ready."

"What?" said Francine.

"We have a name. Schleswig and Holstein. Like the bumper sticker on that blue Peugeot that parks on Horizon. Schleswig because I'm Jewish, and Holstein for you because you're from Iowa."

Francine rubbed her eyes. "Who said I'm from Iowa?"

"Please." Julia rolled her old-soul eyeballs.

She had flipped into a headstand so fast it was like osmosis. One minute Francine was looking at her face, the next minute at the pink soles of her feet. Her top and bottom had simply switched places, as if the floor were now the ceiling.

"We have rehearsal and we need the space," said Julia, upside-down short blond hair sticking straight out. Her cheeks were ruddy. "You have to throw yourself out into traffic. Paying gig. Puffin Hotel. Move it."

Francine blinked. For a moment, she scrolled through the great tap duos in history: Coles and Atkins, Astaire and Rogers, the Nicholas Brothers, Click and Clack the Tappet Brothers. The partners had to have a certain kind of duo energy. Was three days impossible? The numbers she knew were "Organ Grinder's Swing" by Bob Scheerer, Sam Weber's or Dianne Walker's "Shim Sham" (my step today, yours tomorrow), and the Eddie Brown BS Chorus, which was the standard of all beauty when done in duo synchronization. Francine stood up and stood on one foot. For a hoofer there were no obstacles! Look at Astaire's tap dance drum solo. Look at Harold Nicholas running up the wall. Francine clicked her fingers. She knew the Louis DaPron, part of the one with the giant kicks, the syncopation only Bob Carroll could master because he was a genius and loved his dog—if you mastered that syncopation you could die happy, but not yet—and Leon Collins Routine #2.

Don't nauseate my step! called the great Leon Collins from eternity.

"We have three days to learn the choreography. Start to finish."

Julia flipped into a right-side-up position, tiara intact, and plopped down on the couch again, but now she bounced back up. A flower had apparently bitten her. The couch faced the doors and garden on its diagonal tilt so you could squeeze by it. Mrs. Tibbs had not come back since the massage fiasco. Pear-shaped but still petite, Julia rolled up her sleeves. She pointed her child's finger. The flowers glared back, each flower face malevolent.

"Out. Number one, we get rid of this monstrosity. This couch is toxic at its very heart, and it's in our rehearsal space. How did you even locate something so demonic?"

"Don't say *demons*." Francine reprimanded her. "And besides, it was expensive. I put it on my credit card. I'm still paying on it."

"Lift."

"You aren't my AA sponsor." Francine stood with both arms hanging. "You aren't anything. Hail Nun," she added. She had seen that on a T-shirt on the boardwalk yesterday.

Julia shrugged one small bossy shoulder. "Lift. Use both your hands. And tighten your abdominals."

It was fun to do what someone said, as if you were a small child and the world was normal. First their knees bent, and they lifted from their abdominals, and the couch unstuck itself and went with them. Julia's high white forehead had a strange authority, and Francine followed what she could see, two pale blond eyebrows. Down the three stairs they struggled, still no pills, a duo already, each feeling the other's heat, turn, dip, lift, out the gate, which Mr. Venice stepped forward to open, one hand on his bike, his mind thinking great thoughts, his mouth closed. Today his theme was night-blooming jasmine. Maurice, the screenwriter who lived next door, was stretched out on the sidewalk with his eyes closed. This was where his ideas came to him. The duo negotiated by him, then cut south through the vacant lot two numbers up. The Manson Family had once lived on this street, as had numerous poets. The street took only those it wanted. Now the couch was getting heavy. As they neared the Venice Furniture Exchange alley, cars cruised by, Beverly Hills decorators. It was the most democratic spot in Venice, but fraught with competition: homeless people, middle-income people on a budget, antique scouts. Here you could sometimes see vans and pickups waiting for good pieces. Last week a man who was moving out had lost a bookcase only moments before he left the neighborhood. He'd raced back in to take a whiz, his bladder full up, and when he sped back to the alley, it was empty: no ten-foot bookcase (golden oak, recessed lighting) had ever been there. It had been less than sixty seconds. Francine, personally, had found two good floor lamps, one solid brass, plus her table.

Francine and Julia were about to drop the couch forever. They had almost set the legs down when two young hoodlums burst from the tattoo parlor in front of the ocean.

"Hold it!" they yelled, running toward the tap duo.

The back door to their tattoo shop stood wide open. Francine stopped. Through the open doorway you could see the whole Pacific Ocean and simply step into it. It was another country where you could be anything. The water sparkled. Out beyond the waves was the large flat world looking so much like Iowa that at any moment a Holstein might appear. Each time you came out the gate and your head swiveled right, the ocean was a different color, like grasses when they moved on the prairie. Up the actual alley, the two tattoo hoodlums ran harder, knees pumping. They arrived with tattoos up and down their arms and chests and necks, and very sweaty. The couch feet didn't so much as touch the asphalt.

"Nice ink," said one of them to the flowers, and then the couch was running inland toward Pacific Avenue.

"I need an answer about our gig." Julia's tiara sparkled. "The Puffin Hotel. Tap duo. Yes or no? I have cancer."

"You have cancer?"

"Lymphoma. I've had it for years. It comes and goes, so I have to hurry. I may be gone by the next chance." She shook her head like a racehorse. "No pressure."

Through the open door of the tattoo parlor the Pacific Ocean sparkled. Francine hadn't worn tap shoes since her fiasco with Gregory Hines. This gig waited to be taken. Out the front of the tattoo parlor, a new world beckoned.

"No making up my own steps? You beside me?"

Julia laughed, an old soul in the alley. "Trust me."

"No," said Francine.

"*Que será, será.*" Julia waved a magic wand she had produced from somewhere. Her tiara sparkled.

Cyrus stood just beyond the trash can, arms crossed over his chest, one foot over the other, leaning back on thin air, the same large nose, the old amusement on his face, and Francine felt happy. She didn't touch him. Between them, one man and one woman, the old tension sizzled.

"Holes make the potato cook faster," she insisted.

"Keep it from exploding."

Francine leaped in the air and down the bountiful sidewalk and through the gate and up inside the house. Her muscles felt immortal.

At 31 Paradiso Avenue, behind the impenetrable art deco security screen doors, Francine's old friend Ilya Storch squatted, working at a burned electrical outlet. Ilya had managed to forgive her for throwing her life away. She had tried to kiss his cheek when he returned, but Ilya didn't like feelings.

"Next I must fix the toilet handle which sticks upstairs."

"Ilya? Thank you."

"Quiet, woman. Still I see I have no coffee."

She heated water while he checked a pencil point against his face—it was sharp—and wrote *8 x 14*.

"This notebook is my brain. I cannot lose it."

Last week he wrote pencil measurements on the freshly painted (Swiss Coffee) wall by the kitchen. He drove her crazy. He was twisting new wires in a socket hole (red on red, blue on blue, Hank made mental notes) when his hands stopped working.

"Your silly cat is back," he said.

The cat stood in the flesh outside the art deco security screen door. She stood watching them with her feet together, stripped of her red collar, her neck naked, filthy, as beautiful a cat as ever said, *Meow. I want tuna.* She lifted up one paw and put it down beside the other.

"Open the door," croaked Ilya.

When she stepped in, the smell of kerosene wafted off her, and they knew she had escaped the cat pyromaniac by twisting out of her red collar, *CADDY*, 310-276-5555. Francine got the tuna, Ilya got the cream. In celebration, they watched her chow down. The dried kerosene and filth made her fur spiky, but before they cleaned her with a wet rag, they rested. Life was sweet. They made a bed of warm towels fresh out of the dryer, and put her in between them, and slid down on the floor on either side to keep her safe. In the middle of their welcome home party the cat arose and streaked out the open door, greased lightning. The humans made it to their feet in time to see her tail vanish over the front gate.

"No no no no no," said Francine.

In the four hours that Caddy (also known as Remedios the Beauty, also Nefertiti Queen of the Nile, also Kitty) was gone, Francine turned into an old woman. Her life force was drained. She left up the posters she had not yet taken down, pictures of Kitty and her red collar like a diamond necklace. REWARD! *Lost her collar*, she wrote on the posters with black magic marker. *Any amount*, Francine slashed under REWARD! When the cat burglar came home to his hideout between the front window and the Sierra juniper, for the first time Hank's tail failed to wag. The dog stared out at nothing, his chin lowered to the floor.

"We should go back down to the boardwalk," Francine said. "That cat is crazy."

Ilya picked up an electric faceplate. "Is not my problem." He hit a nail where there wasn't one. "Animals. Who needs them."

When it was dark, Ilya still there, the three sat on the floor. They hadn't found her. In his hideout outside the front window, the cat burglar sneezed. They would commence searching in a few minutes. Francine turned her flashlight on and off to test the batteries.

Hank's ears lifted.

The tiny cat stood outside the screen, her pretty feet together. She held her lost red collar firmly between her teeth—she had gone back!—the buckle still buckled. It was filthy.

Francine ran to open the door, but Caddy stepped around her in a cloud of kerosene. Her fur was wet. If someone lit a match she would go up in flames. Unperturbed, a fashion model—had she stepped out of *Vogue*?—she moved past the happy dog, his wagging tail, the red collar hanging squarely from her teeth, an occasional clink when the buckle hit wood, until she reached the first window. At the cat burglar's lair she leapt onto the sill, her fine teeth holding her lost collar. She was counting coup. The cat burglar would normally be away at work in the dark, but he was home nursing his cold. Sneezing was dangerous. Caddy waited on the windowsill and held the prize above his head, only the thin screen between them. She preened, one daredevil to another.

Meow, said Kitty.

Outside the screen, something was rising, a salute by baseball cap with a crown that said L.A. CLIPPERS, first the top of it and soon the brim, and now the actual cat burglar fingers, a first sighting of part of the man who evaded the police day after day. The infamous hand rose higher. Between his first finger and thumb, when he stretched his hand open, a tattooed horse leaped through the air with all four legs spread. The common people laughed to see it. The screen between them, the cat and the cat burglar communed at eye level: the great Butch Cassidy meets the great Sundance Kid.

The cat was Francine's AA sponsor.

Late that night, Francine and Caddy ran out the door, one riding the other's shoulder. Ilya had left for a midnight job replacing tiles at Dhaba Cuisine of India. "*We are Siamese if you please*," two voices belted, one human voice (inferior) and one meower, running up the red line and across Pacific Avenue on through the crooked streets of Venice, better than any pills. Life took courage. Occasionally Francine did a running spin, and the cat hung on for dear life, and adjusted her weight like the extreme athlete she was. She was a thrill-seeker. Francine didn't exactly know where Julia lived—Howland? Grand?—it was in the canals in a garage apartment where her clients could make all the visceral sounds they wanted. Francine used the Venice doorbell system of calling Julia's name.

"Up here," a voice called out from beside a huge pine tree.

At the top of the stairs the door was open.

Julia was balanced in a headstand near but not on the wall. Her white-blond hair fell sideways. She didn't blink. An old soul, she took in the cat. Her small feet remained flexed. In the little adjacent kitchen, some herbal smell drifted from something simmering on the stove. It was soup. There was space beside the dominatrix. Francine threw herself upside down and after several tries managed to keep her feet up, although she rested on her elbows and not her head. The cat purred somewhere.

"Yes," said Francine, upside down. Their heads had to stay straight ahead in order not to break their necks. "The Puffin Hotel. A tap duo. Schleswig and Holstein."

"Here we go," said Julia.

10
HOOFIN' AT THE PUFFIN

A period of industry ensued. For three days, the hoofers practiced for their flagship engagement: the Puffin Hotel, Schleswig and Holstein. There were whole hours where Francine never thought of pills and then a pleasant voice might enter her head: *Shall we get high?* The voice sounded wholesome, like Betty Crocker. At other times her head screamed: WHAT COST $90??? Despite all alarums, she practiced day and night, in the shower, at two a.m. when she got up to go to the bathroom. The steps tied her to life. She counted: toe punch *here*, flap on *two*. As long as you had choreography, no forces could drag you to the blue Miata to the freeway to the Chauzer at Woodman. They had seventy-two hours to perfect five dances, no wrong directions, no sloppy notes. With the carpet rolled up and the couch gone, Schleswig and Holstein worked every day all day, canceling their clients. (Francine currently had none.) Holstein wrote tips in her Imaginary Tap Dance Handbook, tricks she had heard from the great dancers over the years: *Tina Turner is explosive because she holds her energy IN* (Jim Taylor); or *Legs crossed, legs crossed* (Richard Kuller); or *Drop from the ball of the foot to make the heel ring* (Denise Scheerer); or Sam Weber, *To go faster you just have to relax. See?* There are such times in people's lives, and for three days Francine worked as if she were a farmer (only people in the Midwest could be trusted) and the livestock needed feeding, the crops harvesting. One time her grandfather Didwell, a wiry man, had pulled a bull home twelve miles by the horns after purchasing it. Once, for old times' sake, Francine looked in the hanging file of Inspirations (marked *!!!*), which, as it turned out when she went through napkin after napkin, told her nothing, because happiness was apparently irrational. Each morning she put on her white Capezios and began again, you had to know the steps so well you didn't think but only acted, the heel drop *here*, the five-point riff exactly one-half beat after the *two*, embedded in your brain like DNA.

On the third day, no pills, they ran the show in the living room in sequence without stopping. If they made mistakes, they smiled wider. In case of an encore, they had Alfred Desio's "Sunny Side of the Street," as tasty a dance as ever lived. *The pelvis leads, the limbs follow*, Francine wrote in her Imaginary Tap Dance Handbook, tip courtesy of Hama, dancer.

They had five numbers that Francine knew both backwards and forwards. One was "Basie's Boogie" (Jim Taylor), but at the end the hand grip leaning back on one flexed foot was tremulous. She must be mindful not to miss the exact point of balance on the heel, or she might fall over. (Should they keep it? YES. They were mad hatters. They were adventurers.) Next was the Eddie Brown BS Chorus, not the 1927 BS Chorus—*That old thing!* they could hear Eddie shouting on the eternity-to-living telephone. *This has CLASS.* Besides that they had Bob Scheerer's "Organ Grinder's Swing," tricky, but swing threw you into the next step if you would let it. Next to last came Leon Collins Routine #2, and you sat into it, breathing, breathing. They got their second wind. In the seven mirrors in her living room they strove to see their body parts, impossible to see the whole, an arm here, a neck and chin there.

They couldn't jump into the splits, of course, or run up walls, or wiggle their knees like Arthur Duncan. Not wunderkinder, not child prodigies, not even spring chickens, yet they had all their teeth, and their knees were good, and they had sophistication and the knowledge of the school of hard knocks and its underlying sadness that hoofing required. The skeletons were suspended, not muscled up. They weren't a duo yet, not Coles and Atkins, but occasionally they heard a beast with two heads, and the corners of their mouths rose. Dead choreographers surrounded them and were never satisfied with the execution of each of their particular creations. Each dead face cried, *Why me, God?* Blessedly, the living choreographers couldn't see them. Leonard Reed looked down and to their surprise encouraged them by waving.

The grand finale was "Begin the Beguine."

"Don't blow the turns," said Julia.

Their muscles weak from lactic acid, their brains fried from overwork, they flapped into the famous steps Fred Astaire and Eleanor Powell had done, seven fantastic turns to finish. Tonight, Schleswig and Holstein would soak their whole bodies in Epsom salts and then massage their tired arches. Who cared who was Fred? Who cared who was Eleanor? This was 1993, soon to be 1994, the farthest humans had been in what we call time. They were alive. They flung up their legs in the three syncopated flings, Ba da *BA*! Ba da *BA*, Ba da *BA!* They jumped into the squiggle and did the feet on fire. They entered the dread final turns where each time Francine might or might not lose her balance.

She crashed into the cat burglar's window.

"*Damn* it."

"You'll be fine," said Julia. She threw herself on the floor, where arms and legs and head made one five-pointed star. "You'll do it at the Puffin."

"I need to practice." Francine did a turn and crashed into the archway wall.

"Don't push the river." Julia lay with her arms and legs splayed out.

Francine collapsed. By faith she rested.

Julia's chest rose and fell, as if their show were not tomorrow.

All at once she moved. Her arms went down, her feet flew up, and she was in a headstand on the one stretch of bare wall without a mirror. She looked normal except reversed, her zaftig hips where once her chest had been. Her fine short hair was slowly tilting. Her toes wiggled. "Hank. Newspaper!"

The happy dog ran out the open door and down the steps, a job to do—he understood part of the language they spoke, *beach, walk, food, kitty catty, furnace, newspaper, bed, salami. Bad dog* made him happy. He leapt the three front stairs to fetch the *L.A. Times*, which was a job demanding creativity and cunning, and most of all determination, because the bulk was too large, his legs too short, and with every step it fell out of his mouth. Francine bit her fingers.

"Help him," someone said.

Hank's head appeared over the next-to-top step and flung the paper toward her (get four legs up, get a bite, fling the paper). When he reached the top, he got the paper in his teeth and dropped it in triumph at Julia's feet, or in this case her head, and they all clapped. His tail wagged.

"Is more than one way to skin a cat." Ilya nodded.

Today, the German was working on the wall furnace, the cover off, Hank as his assistant. He had been illegal here for many years, because the paperwork required to become a citizen annoyed him and interfered with his ability to think of ways to solve the problems that plagued houses. Hank again took up his post, watching Ilya's every move with concentration against the day when he, the dog, took over. Now his eyes grew fierce: *firewall, pilot.*

Julia commenced the Sunday crossword puzzle standing on her head, using a pen, arms forward, the newspaper folded. Each time she clicked her pen and wrote a letter, her body adjusted slightly, the muscles in her abdomen appearing and disappearing, and they all watched her as if to hold her up. Her blond-white hair had settled at a hard right angle.

"What's a twelve-letter word for *bubbly*?" she said from her upside-down position. Her voice had a languid quality. How did people do the crossword with the Puffin less than twenty hours (but who was counting)? "Fizzy? Sparkling? Twelve. Twelve. Twelve." On her head, Julia snapped her fingers. "Effervescent!"

Francine stayed where she had plopped down on her fanny up against the child's wardrobe. "I wish I could do eighteen turns," she said. "Nineteen."

No one looked up. They all sat there, Ilya who could be deported at any moment, Julia, who could die, the cat burglar, who had just come home and was making little noises.

"I wish I could speak," Hank barked, but all shushed him. He suddenly looked very lonely. "I open my mouth and out comes *woof*."

Only the cat already did exactly what she wanted.

As if to be on your head was natural, Julia lifted up the paper and resumed her work, everything upside down, her balance as perfect as it was when she was standing on her feet, which was a form of being ambidextrous.

"River in Louisiana," Julia called out to the others. "Eleven letters."

"I also missed it today where I do it when I take the paper my neighbor has discarded. There is no need to buy extra." Ilya lifted the furnace cover and put it back, his dog assistant watching. This went here, and that hooked that way. "This is number twenty-three across with one *f* in the middle."

Upside down, Julia held the paper farther out, squinted. No one knew the answer. On the little chair for customers, the cat had jumped up with the dog and lay purring loudly enough to wake the neighbors. Mr. Venice wheeled his bike up Paradiso Avenue, enfolded by the pale yellow hibiscus. Francine tried to see what he was thinking. Was it physics? Mathematics? Was it *Finnegans Wake* by James Joyce? Upside down, Julia brought the paper closer.

"Yikes. I have everything but this river." She tapped her pen. Her hair stuck out sideways. "I have *ch* in the middle."

The cat burglar sneezed outside the thin screen. "Atch!"

His friends who lived inside the thin screen all looked at one another. A sneeze in his line of work was a matter of life and death. A sneeze could tank you. What if the wife woke up? The husband? The kids? And because you sneezed, you went to jail, with only six feet of space to stretch your legs in? Francine took huge steps around the living room.

"Atch. Atch."

Hank wagged his tail at each one-half iteration.

"Sneeze the sneeze!" Ilya suddenly picked up his chisel. Hank studied the tool, and his eyes made a mental note: small, flat, smelled oily. "Hit the nail on the head!" Ilya erupted. He was a little like a madman. "Fire the cannon!"

"Atch. Atch. Atch."

"He's saying something." Francine tiptoed to the window, where Kitty joined her and sat, purring.

"Atchafalaya," said a voice. It was a whisper, but a whisper with ferocity, as though he had laryngitis. You could feel the power behind it. He cleared his throat. The whisper was punctuated with a squeak. "Atchafalaya."

Ilya sprang up from his crouch—everyone an acrobat—and clapped his hands once just as Julia circus freak fell out of her headstand and landed without effort. She slapped the newspaper.

"Atchafalaya." Ilya jabbed the crossword with his finger. "I know this river. It is in your state of Louisiana or Florida."

"Twenty-three across. Nine, ten, eleven letters," Julia counted.

There they sat, the crossword finished, old Indian spirits all around them, police looking for the cat burglar, Hank's hump victims hoping he would expire, Francine's family crazy, worries within and worries without.

Mr. Venice passed in the other direction. The hibiscus pale yellow seemed the most beautiful color in all creation. Francine quivered.

"This sceptered isle," she said. Which was Shakespeare. From the shelf, she removed the book and found it, page 1023.

"*This royal throne of kings, this sceptered isle, This earth of majesty, this seat of Mars, This other Eden, demi-paradise, This fortress built by Nature for herself Against infection and the hand of war, This happy breed of men, this little world, This precious stone set in the silver sea.* This Venice."

Los Angeles had become a renters' market due to a slight recession, and every day Francine looked at the neighbors' faces to see whether she should panic. No one was renting, and Apartment 3 had stood empty for two weeks, negative cash flow, her bank funds dwindling. So far three (count them) interested parties had come to look: a man who didn't believe in banks; a man who wrote the date and full rent on a check, and signed it, and tantalized her when he held it out, and then asked, "Does it have a swimming pool?" Didn't he see the ocean? Was this Malibu?; and a musician who tried to rent it on the spot, no credit check. He was willing to leave his slightly broken keyboard as a deposit. If you fixed it, it was worth a fortune. Francine tapped her pencil. According to *Landlord* magazine, one way to survive during any downturn was to bake fresh bread and hide it in the oven and then rent your apartment subliminally.

Francine unstacked the gas and water and other bills,

total of nine, then counted them again. Tomorrow, she planned to pay them all thanks to the Didwell Living Trust, Revocable. She covered all bills with a pretty dishtowel.

As it turned out, on her pill vacation she had drastically lowered two existing rents, Apartment 2 and Apartment 4, during a particularly high pill dose when she felt besotted with love for anything in front of her and happened to meet two tenants. Frankie Frank was one of them. *Mankind sings!* she wrote at that time on a napkin she put in the Inspiration file. But under rent control, the rents, once lowered, could not be re-raised. When she asked Frankie Frank to revert to the original rent on a voluntary basis, explaining all the worries landlords have (rising expenses, plumbing disasters, the cost of trash), the blond wrestler started laughing and did not stop as Francine retreated down the narrow path that marked the property, and now each time Frankie Frank saw her, she started in again, bent double. *When sorrows come, they come not single spies, but in battalions* was another Shakespeare saying she had flagged, but when she tried to find it, the yellow sticky was in *A Midsummer Night's Dream*. Did the gods think Frankie Frank was hilarious?

To calm her nerves, Francine moved into the living room in Dansko clogs to run the show from start to finish out into the dark beyond the two doors that were always open. She was Rima, Child of the Jungle. *Jesus! Help me turn!* she prayed or swore, whichever. She prayed she didn't go veering off into someone's soup. It was thirteen hours and twenty minutes until the Puffin.

On Leon Collins Routine #2 the imaginary audience applauded.

At Beguine, the seven turns, finale, she flipped on the porch light to help spot the lavender geranium. You needed color. Shoulders down, lower ribs in, sternum lifted, don't forget the stomach, legs together energetically, tuck the butt, get your weight on top of the turning leg or even slightly forward, knee turned out, tighten your cha-*choo*, twist opposite, and unwind like a whirling dervish, spot geranium.

"Stop!" came Julia's voice from the sidewalk.

A blond head appeared. "Get your purse. We're leaving. Now."

Tonight the dominatrix looked like a bird in a vision, in a white coat made entirely out of feathers. Her face was without makeup, only fresh skin, and her hair was pale blond fluff like a chick's. As she came through the door, the cat flew through the air across the room to land on her shoulder, not a *trompe l'oeil* but proof that Siamese cats can fly. Julia had on alligator boots that must have cost a fortune.

"Sale at Barney's," she said in the monotone of rich people. "Forget your purse. We're late." One small finger indicated the open door.

"But I'm—"

"Keys. Chop-chop."

Francine got her keys from the long nail behind the door. Outside, halfway up the red line toward Pacific Avenue, they realized the cat was still on Julia's shoulder.

"Shit."

They ran home and threw the cat across the living room (Caddy purred) and ran back and leaped into Julia's small black Mercedes. Sometime Julia drove a Jaguar, other times a jalopy. Sometimes she drove a motorcycle. Was she an heiress? Or a derelict? They peeled rubber and arrived at the Friends Church in Santa Monica in what seemed like seconds. They were still breathing. Julia was either a great or a terrible driver. Through a mighty wooden door appeared a large, dark space with nearly invisible folding chairs gathered in rows of six by finger count. If you peered, a small box stage emerged out of almost total darkness.

"What is this?"

"My performance piece." Julia unbuttoned the three top buttons on her blouse. "I have to take the podium."

"Your what? When do you sleep?"

Julia undid a fourth button. "I have cancer. I have to hurry."

All molested children recognize their fellow travelers, and even in the dark Francine could see the trembly ladies waiting. KICK ME, said their icky vibrations. They sat with their thoracic vertebrae slumped and their chins forward. Julia had tricked her into coming. Francine felt furious. On her fingers, she counted all the things she hated: the dominatrix, Christmas tree tinsel, directions that came with anything, affirmations that you taped up to the mirror—*I am beautiful!*—but most of all she hated victims. She was not one. Her father hadn't so much as nicked her. She was a soldier in the French Foreign Legion. She stood with her arms crossed and her legs spread.

"Boobs," she muttered.

The stage lights came up abruptly.

She wasn't staying.

The first thing you saw with light on the small box stage (with stairs) was Julia, front and center, a white bird dramatic in her feathers. When she raised one arm, she showed a flash of nipple. No one gasped. This was the Friends Church, Santa Monica. No one believed in anything.

"Tonight we have six guests," said Julia.

To her right, in three folding chairs squashed close together—the stage was tiny—sat the three depressives, white, female, two crying already, expensive purses at their feet in Neiman Marcus shoes. This was West Los Angeles. Their legs were all crossed at the foot to prove they had done nothing criminal. *Poor me!* cried their ankles. To Julia's left, in three more folding chairs, were three bad motherfuckers. Black, the men sat slouched in long athletic postures, knees apart, feet far forward. One pair of white tennis shoes was blinding.

Two stratospheres collided.

Queen Julia shifted in her white feathers, her blouse unbuttoned. No one hooted. This was art. She leaned toward the microphone. One nipple protruded. "Our first guest is Alice Chase."

"Blah blah blah," said Francine. She plugged her ears with her fingers and sat down in the only chair available.

A bad motherfucker, Francine leaned back. Mr. Didwell hadn't so much as touched her quintessential being, no harm no foul. The last laugh was on him. From time to time, when she unplugged her ears, she heard one of the three complainers droning on about penises, fingers, little tears, bruised tender skin. On and on the women's mouths moved, but Francine was a gangster. She saluted. Her father's perfidy or hands had rolled off her like water.

"And then he said, *Let's tickle*," said Princess Number Two.

If the women didn't shut up, she would kill them. The giant babies were draining her life force. Her spine sagged. Somewhere she had read a story about soldiers who were tricked by the enemy into giving blood to save their comrades. In a tent, the enemy hooked the unsuspecting men up and talked to them while their blood drained out onto the ground behind them. They emptied them. When each man was dead, they took the next one.

"On Tuesday they shot my little brother Devereaux," came a deep male voice out of the dark.

One of the three motherfuckers was standing at the podium. The sound of his voice lingered in the auditorium.

Francine lifted one hand in greeting.

He was so black you could hardly see him. He was the man in the white tennis shoes who had been sitting on the far right end. His voice traveled out as if he were on the radio and you were in a car traveling at night, everything dark around you.

"Shot him dead from out of a car window," the voice continued. The man at the podium was just a shine and flash of his feet when he moved. "Devereaux was standing up on Crenshaw outside the door of Club Bip listening to jazz. It's that club that has the big blue bird painted high up on the wall. Devereaux liked it."

In the man, nothing moved, but you could see things pushing out from inside him. The whole room waited.

"That bird is so high nobody can reach it. Sometimes my brother brings his trumpet, but on Tuesday he did not. Sometimes he gets a fake ID if they have a slow night. He just turned fifteen. Once, they let him sit in on 'Take the A Train.' He never got over it. But Tuesday he had to stand outside." At the Friends Church, they saw the man look out and see nothing. "I guess they were busy. Where Devereaux stood out on the street, he could hear Mr. Wynton Marsalis. He liked it under that blue bird. It has a red beak, and once you see it, you don't ever forget." Devereaux's brother looked up briefly. "Devereaux does that thing when he gets excited, some horn riff, all the fingers come straight out like he can't stop it. Spastic." Devereaux's brother wet his lips, succinctly. "At the funeral, Lester Monroe played his trumpet."

Devereaux's brother's grip tightened on the podium. For a moment, he seemed to forget the audience was there. It was quiet. No one moved.

"They fuck you, and then they just keep on fucking you."

The speaker turned his head to acknowledge the three women, and Francine joined them. She was black. She wasn't crazy. She had been black ever since the day her father walked into the bedroom.

The smell of tea tree oil alerted Francine, and when the

light came up, there was Julia. Her blouse was buttoned up. She was respectable. She was a businesswoman.

"When I'm onstage, I get this overpowering urge to bare my chest." Julia looked puzzled. "Why is that?"

"You're an exhibitionist?"

They laughed, friends to the end, and then Schleswig and Holstein each went home to get what sleep they could. The Puffin was tomorrow.

With false eyelashes, Francine looked instantly like Zsa Zsa Gabor. At the Puffin Hotel, she batted them in reflecting surfaces, the piano, a chrome vase. Everything in the lobby was bright and shiny, glittering in a way that was the polar opposite of Venice, like Monaco. To either side of the reception main door, on pedestals, were two brass horses facing inward, each a foot tall, rearing up on their hind legs, all their muscles tensed to guard a Chinese gong that sat between them. Although small, they were so magnificent you didn't notice it. The gong had been upstaged. Francine was longing to put her finger on a flank when a voice made her jump.

No touching, said the loudspeaker.

There were white flowers everywhere, different kinds, white roses, white gladiolas, obviously no daisies. (This wasn't daisy country.) At a grand piano, lid up, a man in a tuxedo sat playing, but the music was inconsequential. One whole wall, the back wall, was glass, enormous, and you could see a large courtyard complete with its own lake, and the lake was complete with its own small island. Around the lake sat little tables with people enjoying cocktails.

"Well, hello there," said a handsome Beverly Hillsian.

"Hel*lo*," said Zsa Zsa. She batted her new eyelashes, extra long, feathered.

To be this beautiful was interesting, but on the other

hand, her muscles were cooling off rapidly. Julia had gone to find the manager. For inspiration, Francine stood looking at her reflection in the Chinese gong, blurry, a horse on either side, and tried to rear up on her toes to feel her flanks. In the gong, she winked one lash. She gave up. To stretch her hamstrings she leaned forward to touch her toes. Every time she put on tap shoes, she felt clean, even bent double. With her head upside down, fancy feet walked all around her.

Two tap shoes appeared, stopped walking.

"They're sending down the manager," said Julia. This was their moment. Her arms swiveled to either side to stretch her intercostals. "It's getting late."

As if in answer to a prayer, someone was headed toward them across the giant lobby, and both dancers pulled up on their hips to look professional. Each on one hip, they waited. They were Schleswig and Holstein, professional duo. They each placed one hand on the hip bone. They each raised a chin, slightly. The light coming in from outside was blinding where the sun flashed on the water that surrounded the small island.

Francine squinted.

Larry Clarke, Welcome! said the name tag of the gentleman who at this moment was shaking both their hands with too much vigor. There was something wrong in it. The handshaking grew wilder.

"What?" said Julia.

He deigned to explain that he was the Puffin Hotel manager. His eyebrows knitted. He was just another poor Joe with a job to do.

"Spit it out." The dominatrix waited.

Mr. *Larry Clarke, Welcome!* was explaining how the venue had been changed, last minute really, it was unforeseen, the dolt who double-booked their spot had been let go, Los Angeles was dead to him, the banquet room had been taken over by rug salesmen. Rug salesmen! Their presentation on

Berber carpet had begun already.

While Julia stared him down, Francine took the opportunity to stretch in every direction, first bending one knee and then the other. She did rib cage isolations. What cost $90? Because the Didwells didn't eat diamond-encrusted oysters. Mr. Larry Clarke went on explaining. In the blurry Chinese gong reflection, a white limousine pulled up and spewed out people. It was an emergency, the manager went on, he was very sorry, they might even in *fact* be lucky, he emphasized the word, as it was a lovely day.

You're not thinking what I'm thinking, Schleswig and Holstein said by mental telepathy. They were a duo already.

Mr. Larry Clarke held out his arm to indicate the great outdoors.

"No," said Francine.

"A floating stage?" Julia was saying. "An island? On an artificial lake? Are you kidding? We're tap dancers. We have to balance."

Mr. Larry Clarke's eyes turned steely.

"You'll be fine." He touched his nose. "I understood you were professionals." And, he said, the time had been moved forward by about forty minutes.

"We need a run-through," said Francine.

"We need a sound check." This from Julia.

"Insurance waiver." He held out the paper and they signed it. His eyebrows lifted, and with that, their introduction music started. "To get there you go out that door"—he pointed—"over the little bridge that leads across the water to the island. It has a gate that sticks, so simply kick it."

His fingers snapped toward the desk.

Mr. Larry Clarke! Emergency!

"A hotel never sleeps." He looked back over his shoulder. "You two pack a wallop. Tremendous talent."

"No improvisation," Francine whispered. "Swear it."

"Quiet," said Julia.

They checked the laces on their shoes, straightened up. The music pushed them. They twisted their torsos while running. They shook their arms and fingers. Their tops were sleeveless vests with sequins, one blue and one plum *(colors of the Didwell Country hats!* Francine thought at the last minute. Only the crazy Didwells believed in omens). The bridge was built like those in the Venice canals near Paradiso Avenue, the ones where you walked your dog, a rise and descent, but with metal on their shoes it was slippery. They grabbed onto the rails and pulled, and their fresh red fingernail polish flashed in the sun. Julia kicked the gate. They were almost to center stage when a small rogue wave caught them and they slid, holding on to each other, outside arms lifted.

The Associated Real Estate Appraisers on retreat applauded.

"Here we go," said Julia.

They hit the *one* of "Basie's Boogie."

Standing still, they looked like opposites; however, when they moved, they looked like sisters. At the nearest table, by the lake's edge, a woman sat sipping her tall drink, which sported a red umbrella. When they both saw it, there was no need to exchange glances. This they could spot on every turn and not fall in the water.

Red umbrella! Red umbrella! Red umbrella!

The routines raced by in a world where time was speeded up. Her nerves had made Francine lighter, as if she were a grasshopper, and she danced with Julia as if they were two parts of the same beast. They were connected. Every time the stage—it floated—made a small adjustment, their muscles adjusted with it. This must be how Kitty felt when she rode Francine's shoulder. If they made mistakes, they overrode them, and their feet hit every note with a flash abandon, but they knew exactly what foot came next. They threw their arms up when planned; they shimmied on the *four*. They trusted one another's instincts; they were a duo. When they clapped their hands beneath their thighs on Leon Collins Routine #2, the crowd half stood up and then sat down. They jumped and beat their feet like hummingbirds, landed with sixteen distinct sounds, exactly. They smiled. "Organ Grinder's Swing" demanded panache, but by that time they had panache, moving their heads like steamy flamenco dancers. When the two turns plus one came, they nailed each sweet rotation, *umbrella umbrella umbrella*. They were halfway through Leon Collins Routine #2, "Begin the Beguine" looming, seven turns, each one meant to be spectacular. Francine's left false eyelash had come loose. She ripped it off and tossed it in the water. She prepared her abdominals, both transverse and horizontal. She tucked her sacrum for the grand finale.

"Ladies and gentlemen! Messieurs and Mesdames! A change of plans." The cherubic face of Julia gleamed with sinister intent. "An original number made up on the spot. No net!" She clapped. "Francine Ephesians Didwell." Julia pulled her neckline lower. "Hoofer."

Francine stepped out. Julia, dominatrix, had tricked her. A second chance! For a moment, Francine thought she saw her father, but on second glance, it was someone else entirely. But when she tried to move she saw more Mr. Didwells, each one dressed like a real estate appraiser. She rubbed her eyes.

"Christ on a cracker," came Julia's voice from somewhere. She sounded bored. "*Do* something. I have fucking cancer."

Francine Ephesians Didwell, hopeless sinner, shimmied.

If her father came to kill her then he would kill her, if not today, tomorrow, or maybe never. It didn't matter.

One, two, said Eddie Brown from heaven. *You know what to do.*

She did one shuffle, and then her feet said *HELL no! This way*. They did a toe stand and jumped her into a slide that almost put her in the water. She windmilled backwards, and the audience applauded. Her hips wiggled and she threw both arms up like a stripper.

In heaven, Eddie snapped his fingers.

"Rivet," said a potted palm tree.

"Hi!" said Francine.

She had never seen the gentleman in his entirety. Under the L.A. Clippers baseball hat, the cat burglar appeared to have freckles. He edged sideways. The spoons he held up glistened in the sun. With one hand he vibrated them, and with the other hand he hit them for emphasis. It was an arcane art he must have learned in Colorado. Under his freckles now he sported the seersucker suit that she had spotted this morning, neatly folded, on a trash can in the alley at the Venice Furniture Exchange, where many Venetians did their shopping. One sleeve was ripped off at the elbow. When her feet did a Maxi Ford, he hit the spoons in timing that was perfect, one push-beat later.

"Rivet!" the cat burglar shouted.

A rush passed through her whole skeleton, all the bones connected to one another, as in hip bone connected to the thigh bone. *Boogaloo*, said the pelvis. Her shoulders shimmied. She snapped her fingers. Her feet cavorted! They were bossy. They told a few jokes. As steps kept emerging from her feet, the cat burglar weaved expertly among the tables. People handed him more silverware. He rattled two spoons in one hand and slapped them for emphasis with the other. His *Rivet!*s grew syncopated. Francine watched for police, but none manifested. A band, they talked in taps and *Rivet!*s about life, itself, how he liked to brush his teeth in houses he broke into, how he always carried his own toothbrush, for the vigorous bristles. *There are more things in heaven and earth,*

Horatio, than are dreamt of in your philosophy, Shakespeare, second shelf from bottom, page 1014. She told him rhubarb is delicious when pulled out of the black dirt of Iowa. The cat burglar's voice was so deep and resonant he might yet have a third career as a radio announcer.

"Rivet!" yelled a waiter.

"That's what I'm talkin' about," a man in glasses added.

To wrap it up, she did Goin' to the Store, it looked like you were going to the store for bread and milk and peanut butter, and then Falling Off the Log, bent forward (so far her nose almost touched the ground) to his *Rivet!*s *(Rivet! Rivet!).* Two sinners' arms were flung above their heads, the water between them.

"Atchafalaya!" the cat burglar shouted.

"River in Louisiana!" a real estate appraiser yelled.

They did a final *Rivet!,* three tap grace notes, one small chug to finish. Tap is sad. When she held out her hand to present her fellow band member for his applause, the cat burglar had vanished. She looked around, then took a bow so low she almost fell over. She could die happy.

Julia grabbed Francine's hand, and they bowed once more.

"Let's go home," said Julia.

At the desk, they received their envelope marked "Schleswig and Holstein." They made their way across the lobby, paid entertainers. Someone had given Julia a card and asked them to dance at a bar mitzvah. More money! Francine, hoofer, smiled at a plant she believed was called mother-in-law's tongue. Just before they reached the hotel entrance, they ran into a gaggle of policemen (three) plus *Larry Clarke, Welcome!,* all pointing and talking at once.

Francine's right false eyelash widened.

The policemen stood with their arms hanging near their guns, like cowboys.

On either side of the gong, the twin pedestals were empty.

"Two brass horses thus high each," Mr. Larry Clarke was saying, and with his hands he indicated an exact measurement, about a foot.

The largest gentleman in uniform scribbled something.

"They're on loan from a dealer," Mr. Larry Clarke continued. "Quite valuable. The two of them are rearing up on their hind legs. What the fuck, excuse my language. Whatever motherfucker did this must be brought to justice."

"You have camera feed?" said a second cop.

Schleswig and Holstein tiptoed forward.

"We checked it. No one could take those horses unless someone passed in front and then the felon hid behind them. Pretty impossible."

"Nearly impossible," said the third.

The hoofers walked down to the garage to Julia's car, which tonight, for some reason, was a banged-up Toyota. They got in, and closed the doors, and locked them, and checked the windows.

"In plain daylight!" Julia high-fived, and the two pulled their arms in, on the chance the cops were watching. "That young man needs to be careful."

11
HEAVEN

Exhausted from her triumph at the Puffin, Francine fell into bed without brushing her teeth, and at some ungodly hour she sat up sweating from a nightmare in which a demon was trying to peel her from the bed and her fingers couldn't grip the fitted sheet. In the real world she held still, panting, a slightly worried dog and cat watching her. As with any nightmare, it was a relief to wake up and find everything was ordinary. She scratched two alert heads and moved her legs against the three-hundred-count Egyptian cotton.

"Demons aren't real," she said and threw back the covers.

Her Puffin clothes, glittery blue top and black jazz pants, lay drying out on a white spindle chair next to her white shoes, all still wet from sweat. Tonight, she had been born a hoofer at the Puffin. She sat up. In the newest mirror from the Venice Furniture Exchange, her right false eyelash made her face look half Zsa Zsa Gabor and half Puritan. Schleswig and Holstein had a gig next week, a Yom Kippur or bris or Hava Nagila. She couldn't remember.

Had someone knocked? The clock said three a.m.

She jumped and reached for her pig pajamas to go downstairs and prove no one was there, and then get a drink of the good water in the cooler. Her tongue felt parched, which was how your tongue would feel in hell if you believed in hell. The PJ ensemble was new, from the store Homework on Main Street, a fresh look for a free life in Venice. She stepped into the bottoms and rolled the waist over. The pig top was so huge there was no necessity of unbuttoning it. A sound made her whirl, but it was the little possum staring from the branch outside the square four-foot open window.

"How are you?" said Francine Ephesians.

Only the crazy Didwells believed in curses. The PJs were XXX large, the way she liked them, drowning inside, soft flannel, the pink pigs busy against a background of pale yellow, using real pots and pans with their tails sticking out behind their aprons. These pigs were cooking dinner. This being her first occasion to wear them, the pajamas still had their creases, the famous Nick & Noras. They were intended to be elegant for any occasion.

She applied lipstick blind and started down into the living room.

There were several ways to cast out demons: put your hands on both sides of the head and say in a demon-terrifying voice, *I REBUKE YOU*, then pause, then hold the temples tightly and call, *COME OUT!!* (Uncle Sly's method), or have the person blow the demon into a brown paper bag until it popped, as practiced by the Church of the Brown Paper Bag in Christ, but this method had been discredited by many people she loved, including Sister Everett, her father's secretary of (lo these) many years. The third method was to cry out, *I plead the blood of Jesus!* The blood was powerful. In the back of the hymnbook—page two forty-three—under the *Topical Index*, her whole family loved the list called *Blood Songs*.

"I plead the blood of Jesus!" she called out into the stairwell.

The PJ arms hung well below her fingers. In her Dansko clogs, which looked dorky with these pajamas—she was a snob—her two feet made a soft thud on the wood, as in the old art of sand dancing. She descended at her leisure, one in a long line of hussies and nymphomaniacs who ruined the careers of great men: Delilah, Jezebel, and also Salome, who danced before the king and demanded the head of John the Baptist on a platter, and they brought it. *Soft*, she wrote in her Imaginary Tap Dance Handbook. She tried to resist, but everything was rhythm. She held on to the railing Ilya had installed last week: *If you fall, you will break your neck. I have to watch you.* Francine had told the animals to stay, but Hank ran ahead while Kitty vanished altogether. In Venice, this behavior was typical.

Daughter, Mr. Didwell's letters said during the life she lived with Cyrus, who had saved her. Who called her Pilgrim. The letters came once a week, or twice a month, no matter where she and Cyrus traveled for his work, at which he was the best because of how he loved earth formations: dirt, rock. He surveyed land in all terrains, and countries meant nothing. Land was land. Yet the letters always found her, General Delivery, Middle of Nowhere. Someone always told them where she was, God or else private detectives. *Daughter,* the letters said. *You are living for the devil. What filth your life contains Mother and I tremble to think, but we still love you. God loves you.*

She always opened them.

Daughter. You have become a slattern, and your mother and I are heartbroken. The devil has you in his clutches, daughter. But there is still time to turn back to the Lord, said his cursive handwriting, which she recognized.

Daughter, they began again. *You work for Satan. Your mother and I cannot bear to think about the unspeakable things that you are doing. We had high hopes for you. Now who would want you? No decent person. If you do not turn back to God, I fear your time is limited. I am sorry to say we think of you with the utmost disgust.*

Daughter?

Time is running out.

A stranger waited on the porch with his eyes closed. Through the inner doors, open as usual, and the double art deco security screen doors, the person looked to be of normal height, with no deformities. The clock said three-o-seven.

"Grrr," said Hank.

The prior owner of 31, a Mr. Dick, what an odd name, had put in all four art deco security screen doors, each with steel bars spaced at five-inch increments, the proper width to prevent a child from squeezing through, as Babe Light had explained during escrow, but all this did nothing against powers and principalities.

When the man looked up, his gaze went through her eyes into her brain. She stopped briefly to roll over her waistband a second time—the legs were gigantic—and walked her Sunday School teacher walk toward the phone on the massage table, to call the police, but through the art deco security screen door his eyes told her to drop it, and she watched herself obey. He looked like someone from Iowa, not from a farm but from a small town, a drifter or an encyclopedia salesman. Hank was misbehaving, running in circles going bug-fuck crazy. He bared his fang.

"I'm Jones," said the demon. "Do you have a hammer I can borrow?"

"Hammer," she repeated.

"I'm your neighbor." Jones pointed to the house across the fat sidewalk, where she knew the Neigarts lived. She nodded. The short sleeves of his white dress shirt were yellowed at the armpits from too many washings, perfectly ironed but shiny. On the skin of his arms, blue veins showed.

"When I'm done I'll put the hammer here," said Jones. He bent his knees and touched the top plank of the porch, these were redwood, and termites wouldn't eat them. His tender fingers touched the place where he would leave the object. "That way, I won't have to wake you up tomorrow morning."

Hank was jumping so high on his short legs his face met hers at eye level.

Jones winked. The dog growled. "I'm building a bench."

A nice girl, she turned toward the kitchen. It would be rude to point out to his face that he was lying. She walked past the bookcase where the characters that raised her stared out, some with their hands lifted. She would be a dead body when the sun rose. She passed the nine bills covered by a pretty dish towel. She floated through the kitchen door toward the hammer. Hank was attached to the leg of her pajamas and she dragged him.

"I don't have all night," called Jones from the porch.

When she was gone, the Didwells would be perfect. *Be not deceived; God is not mocked; for whatsoever a man soweth, that shall he also reap*, said God, a supporter of Mr. Didwell. *Sinners never prosper*, said the Didwell code of honor; but tonight she had kicked it at the Puffin. She had wiggled! She had flaunted! She had let her hip bones go in circles. She was Delilah! A slut, she stepped past the refrigerator closer to the death drawer. She moved on with her small bones lifted, space equals energy. At the cool ceramic good water jug on three oak legs, she stopped briefly, *last chance for gas in the desert*. She drank three glasses of water one after another. Water ran down her chin and dripped onto the linoleum.

"Do you plan to be buried with Cyrus in Alaska?" Mrs. Didwell had called to ask three days after Francine got home from his funeral. Francine softened. It was a miracle that her mother had acknowledged Cyrus's existence. Francine thought about the lowering casket. She had rapped on it three times, a crisp goodbye, as if she were British.

"Yes."

"I will need an exact map to the cemetery and the spot inside it," said her mother.

"Why?" said Francine.

"So I may visit you from time to time," Mrs. Didwell answered.

"But Mom! You'll die first!"

"I wouldn't be too sure," said Mrs. Didwell.

Francine upended the glass and placed it on the shelf with special care.

At the far end of the kitchen was the junk drawer Ilya had fixed so that it opened smoothly. She slid it twice more, a salute to his expertise. The hammer was in back; she moved items she seldom used, including an egg slicer. She wasn't a cook, but who knew when you might try to make a chef's salad? She took out rubber bands. She moved a red feather. Hank was dangling off her sleeve by his teeth like a dog in a cartoon.

Julia! Take the animals, she printed with magic marker on the sink tiles. The police would find it.

"I will tear you limb from limb if you don't stop," said Hankie.

The dog had let go, and he bit her. She tried to disengage him from her PJ leg, which was ripping. They were new! "Take care of your kitty," she told Hank. "She's a runaway." She pointed. "Both of you go hide. This instant."

"Mommy?" said Hankie.

The hammer might have been made for her, it fit her hand so perfectly, the neat shape and heft, almost an antique and with little nails embedded in the handle. She swung it unexpectedly against the wall and cracked the drywall. *Sorry*, said Francine. *Sorry sorry sorry.* Of course she would miss Ilya. The hammer was a gift from the great Mr. Didwell. The two of them—she and the hammer, not her father—had done good work together: hanging pictures and pounding in nails that stuck out (about one million). On her way back to eternity she waved at the Consul in his place in the bookcase.

"Hubba hubba," called Jones. "Get a move on."

At the double art deco security screen doors, she reached behind the inner doors to get the key on its long nail, out of reach where no intruder's hand could grab it. Ilya planned to install a brass hook on Tuesday. Hank was hanging from the good sleeve of her new PJs. *Always throw from the hip*, she wrote in her Imaginary Tap Dance Handbook. This lock was a Schlage, with German precision. When she directed the Schlage key, Jones's Midwestern face ignited with wild anticipation. Francine put the key in the lock but didn't turn it.

"Ima kill you now you stupid bitch," said Jones, who was impatient. He did a decent jitterbug. "Fucking slut."

At the word *slut,* she awoke.

"My father is a slut," she said.

She opened the door and hit him with the hammer. His arms windmilled for balance. She hit him again and blood came out his forehead. He grabbed her forearm.

"Get out!" she yelled.

He tumbled down the stairs and took her with him. He landed half-upright against the birdcage. When she kicked him, he grabbed her ankle. She threw the hammer. They heard it land. A certain smell was wafting up into her nostrils.

"Oh my God," said Francine. She sniffed. "You're the cat pyromaniac." The odor of kerosene was making her dizzy. "You're not a demon."

"Well now." Jones flushed with pleasure. "I is and I isn't."

"Police!" she yelled.

While he held her ankle, the cat ran down the steps and streaked across the yard. Caddy was a hopeless escapee in the way that some people are hopeless gamblers. The cat shot up over the fence, and was history.

"Run!" Francine ordered Hankie.

Jones jumped up and she ran up the stairs. Jones caught her.

"Let's go back inside and have some fun," Jones snarled with what appeared to be parsley hanging from his left canine. When he talked, the parsley moved. "First you and then that cat and then dear Fluffy."

Hank sank his teeth into the leg. Blood spurted out his jeans onto the flagstones and the little white flowers Francine had planted.

Jones kicked and the dog went flying.

"Run!" Francine ordered Hankie.

Planted on all four legs, Hank shrieked a shriek whose sound would surely break their eardrums. Both fighters crumpled up. At last the sound stopped. They stood up straight.

Pinned against the art deco security screen door she wedged one Dansko clog against the second bar to hold it closed. She was a human bolt. Her only hope was to be rescued.

"Crips and Bloods!" she yelled.

Ima burn your house down when I'm finished," said the cat pyromaniac. Who on earth ate parsley in the middle of the night?

It was the best of times, it was the worst of times, said one of the books that raised her. The killer tried to pull her off the second bar from center, but so far her muscles held her. Her quadriceps had begun shaking, overloaded with lactic acid. She was alive so far, but if her foot inside her Dansko shoe came loose from the steel bar, the door would open. Her foot slipped a millimeter.

"Fun fun fun," said Jones. The parsley wiggled.

The Didwells were mud wrestlers, each and every one. All the Didwells loved adventure, Mrs. Didwell had her earthquakes, Mr. Didwell had been held up four times and come out each time looking fresher. The smell of kerosene was overwhelming. If someone lit a cigarette, they would incinerate. Jones pushed her head into the wood next to the porch light while his other hand wrenched her arm behind her. She didn't yell. They were both sweating, their hands slipping on each other's skin. Francine's legs were shaking like the legs of someone having a seizure. Her single remaining eyelash dangled by one thread so that she looked at him through a curtain.

"On the street they call me Fellowship," he crooned in between gasps. Should someone pass, it would look like they were kissing in the warmth of the porch light, his hand over her mouth, the heat of passion, which it was, his face so close bile came up her throat. One small burp of garlic hit her. When he smashed her face, she tasted blood. He smashed again, but dancers have high pain thresholds.

"When are you going to hit me?" Francine managed.

On top the fence toward the ocean, if west was west, the cat burglar was moving one foot at a time, and in the air he swung a lasso. Francine kept a poker face. He had changed into his black clothes, and Jones's back was to him. The artist proceeded like he was strolling down the Champs-Élysées. He swung the circle wider, no doubt a roping skill left over from his youthful Colorado rodeo days. Francine glued her eyes to the parsley while out the corner of her eye the rope came ever closer. It was silent. The killer twisted her nose.

"I like me a wildcat." The parsley kissed her.

When the lasso jerked, the perp fell sideways with his arms pinned at the shoulder, and when he tried to rise, his ankle bent and he cursed. On his knees he pulled the rope off and crawled toward the gate past the hammer. From the fence, Marcel Marceau stepped off into the air and landed precisely on a flagstone. Jones reached up for the gate latch, and who should be balanced on top but Caddy, her nails for ballast, *I am Siamese if you please, I am Siamese if you don't please.* His face exploded into rage. From the yard they watched him jump on one foot holding on to fences down Paradiso Avenue.

Hank's tail was wagging up a storm.

"I heard you scream," said the cat burglar.

He told Hank that he, the dog, had done a good job, how he himself had been up on a roof on Breeze Avenue, three blocks away, and yet the bloodcurdling sound reached him. Hank listened carefully. The basso profundo voice sometimes boomed, and sometimes became a whisper, but he was a work in progress. The cat burglar explained how he had recognized the message, how Hank had seized the moment. Hank stared and added more words to his repertoire: *bloodcurdling, seized the moment.*

Contentment settled on the yard over which the Italian stone pine presided. It, too, was human. An almost full moon shone through the giant convoluted limbs. Francine's eyelash had finally fallen off, and it was a relief to have her Pentecostal face back. Upon looking down, both dancers admired their toes, hers bare, his showing through his thin shoes, all the little bones (twenty-four) and joints (thirty-three, twenty articulated) and muscles—who knew?—each foot holding up a body for a lifetime, not to mention jumping. They were grateful. The cat burglar pointed to her cheek, and she nodded to indicate she knew about the blood. He prepared to make like a tree and leave, which was his special gift.

"You saved my life," said Francine. "Thank you."

The cat burglar searched through the things he had to say in social conversation. As he worked alone, he very often talked to no one.

"I wish I had spaghetti," he proffered.

"How about them Dodgers," Francine replied.

In other news: In Monrovia, Ilene had been caught in the

Aztec Bar on Foothill Boulevard singing to lushes. They sat at the bar and at tables, and watched her while they drank their whiskey. As Francine hadn't been murdered, she had come to Bunny's birthday dinner—for the children, these dinners were de rigueur—and sat salivating while she watched the butter on the mashed potatoes melting and waited for someone to say grace, without which no Didwell could ever begin eating. To encourage conversation, Bunny was placing little pictures of herself, each from a different epoch, up against each water glass. The song Ilene had sung was "Fever," a jazz tune that had lustful lyrics, and Noah at the dinner table was recounting what had gone on in surprisingly good detail. When he'd first seen Ilene's car parked up the hill behind a tree, his suspicions were aroused. Once inside, he saw her there, secret green earrings, hands held out in invitation.

"I'm disappointed that you wear earrings," said Mrs. Didwell.

"People. It's my birthday." Bunny tapped her glass with a spoon. "This is rude. I think everyone should learn some manners."

"Does anyone know what Phoenicia would be called now?" Noah continued.

"Israel," said Mr. Didwell.

In this house, around this table, no Puffin Hotel existed. Today, Mr. Didwell wore his casual clothes, a plaid shirt with suspenders. Francine looked at her feet. To celebrate her Puffin triumph, she had gone out and spent mad money on new shoes, beige rope cloth wedgies with straps all over. She flexed. She pointed. Since Yaram got married, Noah had expanded his study of the rocks in Jesus's time to botany; and his article "What Grows Here?" was being published. Ilene excused herself and went back through the kitchen. When she returned and sat down, her lips were painted cherry red. Eyes widened.

"Don't everybody stare." Ilene looked around the table.

Science says that matter, by its nature, is disintegrating, the little particles moving farther apart, and only energy can hold the mass together. Without sufficient energy, the parts disintegrate into a black hole that sucks in everything. What happened happened fast on Bunny's birthday.

Beneath the oil-painting Didwells on the wall behind her, Francine stretched her latissimus dorsi and reached into her bra to touch the black plastic chip that said 10 MINUTES. She was done with pills. She hoped. Forever.

While Bunny balanced photographs, the family salivated. The food tortured them. Mrs. Didwell sneezed once and with the napkin stole some ham, which was forbidden. She was at home with a mild case of bronchitis, waiting for it to be over so she could go to the hospital to get a pin in her hip so she could walk again. The accident when she ran out the door with Muriel had been unfortunate, but no one spoke about her singular rebellion. Now, at the table, the hungry were getting restless. Ilene and Bunny were both formidable cooks. Of course they couldn't eat until they prayed, and they couldn't pray until the last picture was in place. Francine's own specialties, pickles and olives, sat in pretty dishes and looked delicious. Against the final glass Bunny placed the last snapshot of some decade of her life, not all but mostly young: toddler, infant, college graduation. Francine had Bunny as a teenager, laughing with her four Eggers cousins. Noah turned his picture of Bunny to stand on her head.

"So, each person can pick their picture up and tell a story about that time in my life," said Bunny. "Like a talking scrapbook. It's an idea I woke up with in my bed this morning."

"I'm starving," said Noah.

Mr. Didwell thanked the Lord that Bunny was born with all her toes and fingers, and that she loved the Lord and served Him. As far as Francine could tell, all had their eyes closed except

Ilene and Muriel, the helper, who stood doing nothing holding a feather duster. Mrs. Didwell's bedroom door was closed. Back at the table (opposite her husband, the head and foot), Mrs. Didwell sat, a pleasant vacant look on her face, wrapped in an afghan that she fingered while her husband thanked God for that of which they were about to partake, finally.

"Amen," said Mr. Didwell.

Noah dug in.

In lipstick, Ilene looked more than normally like Kim Novak. She held up her picture, Bunny in her rabbit costume, perhaps three years old, the famous hopping incident for which she had been nicknamed. Ilene said something with her red mouth moving.

"That time you made Eggs Benedict," Francine plunged in, and waved her picture. "The hollandaise—"

"Do *you* hear someone talking?" Bunny asked flatly.

"My precious birthday girl," said Mrs. Didwell, who could be deaf when it suited her. She liked having all her children under one roof, fighting or not. Since Francine walked in the door, Bunny had been pretending not to see or hear her. Now the whole family pretended not to notice.

"Next picture," said Bunny.

While food disappeared, people held their pictures up and talked, Bunny as a newborn, the little sounds she made, her tiny toes and fingers. On this, her day, the female Didwell light came out of her face. How strong her baby kicks! Her darling personality! Mrs. Didwell said the usual things, her first precious moments, how Mr. Didwell held her up to God, Mrs. Didwell terrified she might fall! Ilene's red lips said she had found her sister's baby bracelet and a jeweler had extended it, to make it larger.

Bunny, birthday girl, held her wrist up for all to see: R-E-B-E-C-C-A. But no one in their right mind would call her anything but Bunny.

"*Tis ara houtos estin?*" said Noah, who was always learning Greek or Latin. Today he had flash cards. "The language of the original text is essential to make viable scientific biblical discoveries."

Bunny ignored him. "How much did I weigh?"

Although it was forbidden, Mrs. Didwell took another tiny bite of ham as the plate passed her. Since the day she choked, and even earlier, in fact for all her life since Jesus brought salvation, He had been watching over her so no harm could befall her. She could eat what she wanted. Successfully, she swallowed.

Bunny waited.

"Seven pounds, two ounces. Or was that Ilene? Noah weighed nine pounds, one ounce. Which meant he would be tall."

"Mom? Dad?" Bunny took off the Rebecca baby bracelet and put it back on. "What about when I came home the first day?"

"*Hoti kai hoi anemoi kai he thalatta houpakouai auto,*" Noah finished.

They talked about the day that Mrs. Didwell brought the (only) California Didwell back to Begonia Terrace (Mrs. Didwell came from mountains), Mr. Didwell driving the pink Pontiac (here Bunny clapped her hands once, and the bracelet jiggled), the three older children jumping under the two majestic palm trees. How happy the big sisters were! Bunny's incandescence grew brighter. She leaned back in her chair, a force of nature but relaxed now, at least at this moment.

"I love Jesus!" shouted Muriel.

"So, what else about my childhood?" Bunny looked around the table, tucked into the bosom of her family. Sun came through the windows. "Everyone can tell more stories. Like when I first started walking and I walked up and kicked the mayor. Was that funny?"

"Funny like Bozo the Clown," said Noah.

Bunny kicked him underneath the table.

"Oh my!" cried Louella. "When you walked, your curls bounced and even strangers tried to touch them. I invited them to church, of course. We got the attendance up to one hundred and seven one Easter."

"Our parents have had a great romance," Noah announced, and tapped the card next to his plate. "*Euaggelion.*"

Still aglow, her hair turning slightly frizzy, Bunny asked that they hold hands to celebrate being a normal family. Others were not so fortunate. While Noah stole a piece of ham, and then another, Bunny thanked God that He had seen her through two divorces, the men worthless, yet as a Didwell family member, she endured every blow of Satan. "Like Moses," she added. When Mr. Didwell wiped his eyes, for some reason you could see the farmer in him. Only Bunny was a native, as Mrs. Didwell had been carrying her when the family arrived in California.

"It was so embarrassing," remembered Mrs. Didwell.

All heads turned.

"To be pregnant at my age, forty-*seven*, and arrive and present myself in a new pastorate, my stomach sticking out to here."

"What?" said Bunny.

"We drove in from Iowa late Saturday night—"

"It was freezing!" Ilene threw her head back and clapped her hands.

"And Sunday morning, Daddy couldn't find his shoes. He had to preach! He drove from Iowa to California in his bedroom slippers because it was comfortable."

At her end of the table, Ilene let go a laugh that infected them all, loud, clear, capable of stardom. All the Didwells liked to have fun. They were hedonists. "We left them in

Iowa! We got in late the night before, and we dumped all the boxes out all over the floor. All the stores were closed, of course. Muriel?"

"Paprika!" Muriel shouted.

"Never mind." Now the incandescence had moved from Bunny the birthday girl to Mrs. Didwell, and all heads swiveled toward the young Louella. "Your father"—she was tickled—"preached the first time in his bedroom slippers."

All the Iowans exploded.

Bunny waited, counting seconds. The family laughed so hard they choked and had to wipe their eyes.

Bunny snapped her baby bracelet.

"When we tried out for the church, I wasn't showing." Mrs. Didwell's gestures changed, a lively version of herself, the Evita of Pentecost, not Argentina. Whenever she preached, her wrinkles vanished. Her cheeks plumped. "We flew here for the tryout and we prayed hard on the plane, and Daddy witnessed to a lawyer who knelt down right there and got saved. We will meet him up in heaven. His name is Dithers. Hallelujah!" Mrs. Didwell refreshed her lips, which lipstick had never smirched.

"We children stayed in Minnesota," Noah added.

The real Didwells remembered how they stayed in Caledonia with their uncle Walt, that was his name, another preacher, Louella's brother. Preaching was the only worthwhile occupation. Clarence had two brothers who were preachers, saved out of the Lutheran Church, where their Lutheran mother died without repenting. Francine had adored her.

"Oh my." In Louella's face, the skin had become even fresher. "They hired your father on the spot when he tried out and I looked normal. Then I showed up for the first Sunday with my stomach out to here with Bunny. At my age. I was humiliated. Muriel? Dishes."

"Jesus is the sweetest name I know," said Muriel, mouth

open.

From Bunny, a tiny growling sound issued.

"The whole church could see that Daddy and I were still having relations."

Ilene rolled her eyes, and Bunny's nostrils flared a little. Louella ignored her.

"Oh, it was embarrassing. Our private lives out for everyone to see. What did they think of me? I had to show up every Sunday with my stomach shouting, *Look! Look!* Announcing."

As the dinner plates were cleared, someone carried in clean forks for dessert.

"Who has the cake?" said Bunny.

Noah pulled his food back to him. "That time at Uncle Walt's in Minnesota, and they had that scary basement, and it had a tunnel. With a bear hiding in it."

"Run. *Eeeek!*" squealed Ilene and Francine, nine and twelve years old, upon which Bunny stood up and slammed one hand on the table.

The butter jumped.

"This whole family is incredibly rude to talk about the other stuff from Iowa." When Bunny sat down, she started crying. It was her actual birthday. "Mom, what else? Did I have a baby blanket?"

"We bought it new," said Mrs. Didwell.

But Mr. Didwell had bad hearing, a fairly recent development. It wasn't his fault he missed the pathos of the situation. He put one hand to his ear, to make a trumpet.

"Francine? How go things in Venice Beach?" All the family pivoted, transfixed by their dilemma. It was Bunny's birthday, but Mr. Didwell was directly under God, the head, and couldn't be questioned. Under Mr. Didwell came the wife, and then the children. But what did Scripture say about a hearing aid that didn't work? Noah considered Greek while the others sat helpless. "No broken water heaters? All the tenants paying rent? All five furnaces working?" There was a silence. "Most can be repaired unless the firewall has a hole in it."

Francine did hesitate. But. How could a Didwell refuse the Gothic? Her very Irish/Scottish/Norwegian/German/Negro genes cried out to tell the story. Bunny seemed to levitate, but it was just that her hair had risen like a soufflé.

"Monday someone tried to kill me," said Francine.

And with that the lost sheep was home, a Didwell family member, her name written in the Lamb's Book of Life. She would get in by association. She told of Jones, the moon through the Italian stone pine tree, how a razor (a spontaneous addition) stuck out of his hand and caught the moonlight. The Old Testament had instilled an appetite for a juicy story. Esther sleeping with the king, sent there by her uncle Mordecai, Absalom's hair caught in a tree while his steed galloped off, 2 Samuel 18:9. You could learn from Scripture.

"Go from the start," called Noah.

She told the true story, with several embellishments, which weren't the same as lies, safe in bed asleep at whatever o'clock, the almost full moon showing through the twisted branches of the pine (she had once seen a raccoon walking across her window), the rude awakening that pulled her from her deep sleep, impossible to wake up as she was in childhood.

"Oh my my my," said Mrs. Didwell.

From the kitchen Muriel entered, the cake in one hand, paprika in the other. The candles needed to be lit, plus where were the knife and glass of water? But in the story the killer was leering. Bunny had lost her color. They had time.

"Oh! My skin has shivers," Mrs. Didwell murmured. "Where is Jack? I wish God would find him."

Francine told how the killer looked like he could be from Iowa, one eye on her audience to be a listener with them. "I held them right here in the palm of my hand!" Mrs. Didwell would say when she remembered her own preaching. Because preachers were hypnotic. Francine told about the killer's soft arms, which had hidden tendons. Between his teeth was what looked like parsley. When Hank screamed the scream, the Didwells jumped back and Mrs. Didwell's arms flew up, a compliment. Francine told how the killer pinned her arm behind her.

"God find Jack," prayed Mrs. Didwell.

But now Francine's feet were scudding, one Dansko clog slipping by the next steel bar, when what should happen but the unbelievable, the cat burglar balancing on the fence with his arms out. When he swung the lasso, several Didwells raised their arms to heaven. Because the Didwells lived, daily, with the supernatural. Francine added blood dripping.

"What is this cat burglar's name?" Mr. Didwell cupped two hands to make two trumpets.

Francine stopped, flummoxed. "I don't know. Cat burglar."

"Cat burglar?"

"He doesn't talk. I only know he likes spaghetti."

"I see," said Mr. Didwell.

But in his face some fervid curiosity had come alive. He studied his daughter closely.

"I believe you have the Holy Ghost," said Mr. Didwell. He stared while Muriel put water on the table. She added a knife. "Something is different."

Around the table, forks slammed down and eyes slammed open. You could be cast out of the church for doctrinal violations. Rules were rules. *No man cometh to the Father but by me*, said Jesus.

Mr. Didwell had always been a heretic when it was warranted. Even though a model citizen, he lived his truth, like the time he wore a beard (which was forbidden) to General

Council and the preacher from Sierra Madre threatened to knock him down and the other preachers held the arms of the preacher from Sierra Madre. Or the bums he picked up on the street and took out for steak, any one of whom might murder him. At table, all the Didwells sat on pins and needles. Because salvation was only when Jesus stood outside and knocked on your heart's door and you said, *Enter*. It looked like a door in a garden. *Because strait is the gate, and narrow is the way, which leadeth unto life, and few there be that find it*. In Monrovia, Mr. Didwell watched his daughter. At the table, ice cream arrived, but no one noticed. Mr. Didwell, the head, had always been a heretic, but not a lunatic, and if you made an exception you might as well let in Catholics. Bunny was the one who picked up her spoon first. No one dared to contradict him. They all waited.

"I declare we will see you in heaven." He took a bite of ice cream.

The crash they heard was Bunny's chair. It fell against the china closet and didn't break the glass, but then the exquisite ceramic Mr. and Mrs. Didwell toppled on its side. By the grace of God, Francine caught it. The chair lay sideways, upholstered by Bunny. On the bottom, brass tacks sat in a neat row. They glowed. The next sound was the front door slamming, followed by four car tires laying rubber up the hill. At the table, they waited to cut the cake.

"She'll be back," said Mrs. Didwell.

A good preacher, perhaps a great one, she knew how her stories ended. She held out her plate, and Noah dipped the knife in water.

"Just a tiny slice for me," she cautioned.

* * *

The cake dishes were cleaned, and there were no crumbs, *no not one*, as the songster said, left on the table. Francine wiped it one more time, leaning hard to stretch and restretch her latissimus dorsi muscles. She needed to practice. Left alone for too long, the muscles would start to atrophy, and Schleswig and Holstein had a job next Saturday. The man with the winning bumper sticker SCHLESWIG-HOLSTEIN: LOVE IT OR LEAVE IT! had stopped to chat, and so she had invited him. She did a perfect pirouette, landed. Through her mother's slightly open bedroom door, the Italiano that had been the center of the house had been dismantled and tipped up against the walls. The rails were leaning one way, the mattress another. One end of a new hospital bed showed through the door, the white sculpture of her mother's toes under the sheet, while beyond it in the center of the room on one more of one bazillion Persian carpets, thick dust sat in shape of the dear bed itself, which Mrs. Didwell secretly called Morning. In the Italiano a girl took a fright. She touched the sheeted foot of Mrs. Didwell, who was lightly snoring. All the other children had gone home, and Mr. Didwell had retired to his study.

"Boo!" said Bunny.

The hairs stood up on Francine's neck.

Bunny Didwell stood by the piano, her arms crossed, taller than usual, the Ice Queen from a fairy tale, the kind that made you know trouble was just around the corner. The temperature of the air had fallen. Had Francine just noticed? And this despite the bright blue sky that showed out the windows over the San Gabriel Mountains. With every step that Francine took toward the door, Bunny's features got more prominent.

"I've decided to distance myself from you and Daddy." Her voice was formal, like a news reporter. "I'm too close to the situation."

"Got it." Francine double-checked her purse for car keys. Her constant fear that the Didwells would lock her in was crazy. "Happy Birthday. There's cake in the kitchen."

"I'm starting my own cruise boutique. *How to be an Entrepreneur.* Two clients have signed up already."

"Happy Birthday."

But when Francine stepped out, Bunny put one Christian fuck-me boot forward to block her. Did they have sex, the modern Christians? Was it just teasing? Did Bunny's clients at Chauzer Permanente die and go to hell? And did she warn them? Above all, what cost ninety dollars? As Bunny continued not to move her foot, Venice grew dimmer. A sheen of leadership had fallen over Ms. Bunny Didwell, like a 1960s form-fitting sheath, and Francine could see why she succeeded at work, and was promoted. Like Francine, she had missed inheriting Mrs. Didwell's sylphlike fingers, and had Mr. Didwell's farmer's hands, good hands for baling hay; but she wore a plethora of rings in defiance of her own digits. In the dining room it was so cold, Francine had goose bumps. Bunny snapped her Rebecca baby bracelet with her farm thumb and first finger.

"Apropos of nothing," she said, mispronouncing it.

To keep from disappearing, Francine did a shuffle in her wedgies.

"FYI." Bunny liked to shorten words, which gave her extra time to go on dates and attend those continuing education classes she needed for promotion. She was a master genius of efficiency. "Ahem. We have all Daddy's money." She giggled. "All three checkbooks."

The sisters were so close their eyelashes almost touched. Bunny's were black, sticky. In Iowa, mascara had been forbidden because when the Holy Ghost descended, tears would smear it all over your cheeks. But Bunny was a California Christian. She used an eyelash-extending product. Her lashes looked like metal spiders.

"The children had a family meeting, and we agreed you aren't a very nice person. We voted you out. So there won't be any money from the Didwell Living Trust next year. Revocable. After that we'll see. We have expenses." Bunny watched her. "I'm telling you this out of the goodness of my heart in case you need to know for your own financial planning."

Francine stood homeless.

"Oh! I love you and I hate you!" Bunny charged and threw both arms around her only sister. All the Didwells cried like crazy. "You make me so *mad*." She hugged Francine so hard she almost smothered her. She blew her own nose. "I suppose"—her voice grew soft—"I suppose you could go to each child individually and apologize."

Francine broke free. "*Apologize?*"

"They don't let perverts into heaven," Bunny whispered. "Dad is godly." Her eyes were rigid, and for a moment she looked extreme, like Jones, the cat pyromaniac. She looked around. "We're not dying. End of sentence. Period. The Didwell family is going up, and nothing you can do can ruin it. You can't make us doubt the truth of our salvation."

"*Apologize?*" repeated Francine.

Bunny came so close their noses tickled.

"You want science? And no God watching over you? And you're on your own? And when you die you're dead?" Bunny shook her. "Don't you want to see Grandmother?"

"Of course I do," said Francine.

"We're on the Faith Line! It's a railroad. By faith you can make heaven but you have to get on board. First you believe and then you see it. In a million years we five will still be walking around up there. You have to believe until your muscles shake."

"You think I did it?" Francine's arm hit the piano.

"Do the math. You're the sinner."

Francine thought of the two subjects that most troubled her. One was Mr. Venice, and his deep thoughts on life; and the other was *What cost $90?*

"What cost ninety dollars?" Francine shouted.

"I beg your pardon?" said Bunny.

"At Noah's birthday dinner." When Francine pushed toward her, Bunny stepped back. She looked confused. "Because your bill on that pink stationery said *Item, $90.* The Didwells don't eat caviar. They don't smoke cigars from Australia." Francine stopped for breath. "Four children times ninety is three hundred and sixty dollars. The Didwells don't drink champagne. What is *item*?"

Bunny threw here head back and let rip, a Christian's laugh, the laugh of someone who was going to live forever. She smoothed her clothing. "All your little visits to Daddy," Bunny sniggered.

Francine slapped that bitch. It was a sound that traveled through Mr. Didwell's study door, which had four panels.

"What's going on?" he called.

Bunny was toast. Mr. Didwell honored all his children equally. Francine rapped on the study door just as Bunny reached into her pocket, withdrew a cough drop, and began sucking it with the panache of a sinner smoking a cigarette. Both sisters breathed audibly. Power was the family's business, spiritual and otherwise.

"Ye may enter," called Mr. Didwell.

He was sitting on a rolling chair around the corner. It was here that he dispensed wisdom. He discussed what God wanted, and finances, and car engines, and salt versus pepper. He was bent over his desk, his neck collapsed over his papers. The desk was a plain contraption, but it got the job done, and he liked it—it isn't the fancy pen, it's the number you write down—and Mr. Didwell put aside the contract he was reading. He swiveled. He knew the value of hard work, and he enjoyed it, and enjoyed being exhausted. He was a farm boy and a city boy. He looked up insofar as possible. His collapsed neck and spine were making him into a human S. His head struggled to stay up, but it was no use. The bald dome tilted farther forward.

"If I may give you some advice. Don't ever allow your study to get out of hand." He gestured at the multitude of papers on his desk, a right mess. Old parishioners still worshiped him, even as far away as Iowa. "You can never hope to dig your way out."

"Dad?" Francine sat down on the red stool that had been Grandmother Eggers's, moved from the kitchen for Mr. Didwell to fix. It was one of two things she hoped to acquire when her folks went to heaven. The other was her sinner (Lutheran) Grandmother Didwell's painting of the sandhills of North Dakota with a farmhouse and pond in the foreground. Beneath her, Francine slid the clever recessed footstool out and placed her hoofer instruments on the rubber scuds so the arches were symmetrical. It was quiet in the study.

"Dad?" Her father's favorite daughter pushed her hair back. "Bunny said next year I won't get any money." She invoked reason. "But you said the money was for life, which is why I went ahead and got the new high Venice mortgage. You said buy it." Mr. Didwell moved some papers. "Dad?"

"I find the best solution for cockroaches is a little boric acid." Mr. Didwell turned over a magnifying glass that he took good care of. He was still curious about the world even though his spine and neck prevented him from looking up. "Cockroaches are smart, but you have to be smarter."

Francine started. Mr. Didwell was letting his children do his dirty work. Had *Noah* called Ned Horsely?

"For some reason the children seem to hate you. I'm getting old. I'm afraid I can't settle disputes among you."

When his chair on wheels rolled back, he was beneath her. His bald pate bent over his knees and twisted sideways with the strands of hair that he combed over. His eyes twinkled.

"Adam and Eve walked in the garden nekkid," he said

in his farm-boy pronunciation, and held the Bible up and pointed at the passage. "You see here in Genesis?" His skull grinned up at her, his eyeballs snapping. They were two damned souls on vacation. He rolled his chair and the arm stopped at her knee. His eyes were hot coals.

"Nekkid!" He cackled once. He cackled twice. He pointed with his farmer's finger. "Nekkid! Nekkid! Nekkid!"

When she got up to go, her legs were Jell-O. She put one foot in front of the other. She had almost reached the doorknob when his voice reached her.

"Are you leaving?" He was entirely normal. "I see. May the Lord bless you and keep you."

By the front door, there Bunny was.

"Are you all right?" Bunny touched her. "Did something happen?

Bunny was her only sister, which was entirely real while it lasted. The pill hunger touched Francine occasionally, but oh well. Life is dangerous. She didn't take them. She felt the Didwell family magnetism.

"I'm fine," said Francine. She needed air. "I have to go. Excuse me."

12
SEAN THOMPSON COME HOME

Back in Venice, Francine found parking near to (but not in) PARKING FOR MEXICANS ONLY. She walked down the red line toward the ocean. She smelled ozone. The ghosts of Digger Indians, or Hoopa-Kali-Maka, lingered in Venice and went out on the sand at sunset, which was peaceful. No Crips or Bloods leaned on the fence to compliment the cat, her sponsor. She reached up for the latch and heaved a sigh of relief at greeting Hank and Kitty and the cat burglar (if he was in) when she saw a body sitting on her porch. It was the unbearable Mrs. Tibbs, her greatest massage failure.

"I'm giving you one more chance!" Mrs. Tibbs stretched out her palm to show the splinter she had picked up on Francine's three redwood steps. "I don't have a tetanus shot. If I get lockjaw, it will be your fault."

Lockjaw would be a blessing. But massage is a calling, and it brings certain obligations. While she washed her hands, Mrs. Tibbs got on the table, voice loud like a propaganda bullhorn. Francine used another squirt of liquid soap to stall for time. Hank King of the Boardwalk watched her carefully. They needed money. They had to live here. They were Venetians. Hank had friends down on the boardwalk, including a Vietnamese pig who squealed when she saw him. Unlucky Apartment 3 was empty. A man had called to rent it for one night, he needed to make a movie, he would be quiet.

"A movie about what?" said Francine.

"A nun," said the director. "It has a bed, right?"

"No," said Francine.

"I'm freezing here," called Mrs. Tibbs, who lay naked covered only by a sheet. Although it was summer.

Francine ran holy hands up and down Mrs. Tibbs's back, the muscles moving as Mrs. Tibbs said things in English. *Blah blah blah her best friend Louise couldn't keep her mouth shut/had again embarrassed her, giving away state secrets/couldn't keep it in his pants/the post office all were idiots/poet so-called.* Francine performed by rote all the motions learned in massage school, effleurage, *saying hello to the skin*, thumb kneading, always push the blood toward the heart, lean on your hands, let your hips act as your headlights, place your pelvis straight behind the headlights.

"Your hands feel funny," said Mrs. Tibbs, whose intelligence was maddening. "Am I supposed to pay for this fiasco?"

"Breathe," Francine told her.

She was an orphan. In Cyrus's last hours, they had spoken about the change that was coming. It was coming. With dark outside the window, Francine sat on the bed next to his long bones. An hour ago, Cyrus had stopped smoking.

Francine and Cyrus sat there alert to something.

"I don't want to lose you," Cyrus said.

The two held hands. The sound of the neighbors fighting floated in the window.

"You make me want to live," she finally managed, which, until she met him, had not been true. But she wasn't sure he heard her because he had thrown himself down flat where heretofore he couldn't breathe in that position.

Girls are nice but oh what icing comes with Oreos, Mrs. Tibbs said in between snores.

In her mind, Francine hit her with a shovel.

When Cyrus died, Francine had gotten up to take a walk into the living room and just come in the bedroom door, and Cyrus waited. He simply threw up and didn't swallow. She reached out and touched his leg, but any electric charge had ceased to flow. It was like the leg of a table.

"I don't know where I am," said Cyrus from the great beyond a few feet left of the bed, her left, not his.

"You're okay, darling," she said.

She called the doctor, who called the coroner, who had to come when someone died at home without medical personnel. The paramedics came in and left, and two policemen arrived to wait with her for the coroner. The apartment was a beehive of activity. The police were seated down the hall while she stood in the doorway of the bedroom guarding his body. He was obviously not in it.

How would she live?

I like Oreos, said Mrs. Tibbs, distinctly. Mrs. Tibbs was on her back, relaxed for the first time in history, one arm hanging off the table.

In massage school, her teacher Paolo had taught them this truth: You didn't need to feel good about the person on the table, you just needed to feel something. The night he got the hundred-dollar tip, the love of his life had broken up with him. So it shouldn't have been surprising when the good Mrs. Tibbs reared up like a vampire from a coffin.

"He *swings* me right!" she cried.

Francine jumped back.

The client sat up. The difficult Mrs. Tibbs had been reborn as a party girl. She laughed a high laugh. The best self often comes out in massage, one of its health benefits. The new self swung her arms up in a ballroom dance position, arthritic hands cupped on some partner's arms and shoulder. Her face was fresh. When the glad Mrs. Tibbs swung right, Francine ran to stabilize the table, which was the lightweight version, aluminum, three hundred dollars more, but easier to carry.

"He *swings* me left!"

Francine raced around the table to steady it.

"You may call me Imelda," continued Mrs. Tibbs, ballroom dancer, a devil-may-care personality. "I cut the rug on the weekends, Friday and Saturday." She batted her eyes, one hand against her chest to hold up her ballroom dress, or in this case, sheet. With gusto, she changed arm and head positions for a tango.

"I have outfits."

Francine could indeed see the yellow crinoline in her description, also the red sheath with slit leg. "I am always on the lookout," Mrs. Tibbs explained about her shopping. *No one knows what life force is,* her teacher added. *The blood is there. The bones are there. Without life force all the muscles in the world can't keep the body upright. The skeleton falls down in a heap.* Francine continued her little job, to massage the anterior tibialis, left leg. Mrs. Tibbs's favorite was the green skirt that twirled out. She had eye shadow to match, also cloth high heels dyed the same exact color. Francine ducked and grabbed the table as Mrs. Tibbs swung out for the finale.

"He *swings* me in a circle!" she cried.

Francine had finished Mrs. Tibbs's foot, careful around the bunion, and was about to change legs. But first she must connect the body parts in one long swoop, ankle to collarbone. She was putting her weight on both feet and following her pelvis when a shot rang out, or else a firecracker.

"Oh no no no no no," said Francine.

Men in police clothes lined Paradiso Avenue when Francine looked left from behind the back door. They stood side by side and faced her while the red line whistled beneath their spread-out boots. The men lined up were actual policemen. When Francine crept forward down the path to Paradiso past the great Sierra juniper, the cat burglar's hideout, she saw that the line of uniforms stretched all the way to Speedway at the beach. This was not a police Broadway musical.

Down the narrow corridors between houses, the other way, more men with guns filled the alley.

Paradiso Avenue was surrounded.

There must be one hundred bodies. The policemen's uniformed legs were spread, and their black boots were almost touching the man next to them. Their guns were holstered, their hands ready to grab them, some hands with their fingers twitching in anticipation. Out on Paradiso the red line squiggled beneath them.

"They got someone," said Pinkwell. His guitar was strapped across his chest, but he wasn't singing today. In his long black coat and long hair and red boots, he stood with his entourage behind him. All were quiet.

Their quarry had become a mythic figure, and this time they had brought in dogs. Everyone was out, the surfers, Mr. Venice, the man with no distinguishing characteristics, either a Crip or Blood, who knew the colors? Also those residents who worked at home: psychics, screenwriters. The dogs had cornered or not cornered the cat burglar when he ran into a basement across the alley, then made a run for 31 Paradiso. Some said he was on the roof, others said he was barricaded and shooting at the police. All men in uniforms were turned in the direction of Apartment 1, diagonal bedroom window.

Francine began to edge around the building.

Someone had spotted a figure on her neighbor's roof an hour ago and phoned the police. Who thought it was a prank. The nut-job informer phoned again. The police said they were busy. They said if they had time. But when they finally showed up, the man was climbing out the window of the second story.

"They didn't listen to the guy who called at first. They get a million crank calls. It was some fellow goes by the name of Friend. Or Fellowship. Some fucking thing."

"Fucking tourist," said a neighbor.

She speeded up.

The neighborhood was quiet. There were no more gunshots. Francine took stealth steps in order not to draw the attention of two policemen stationed on the alley to block the crime scene. They were twins, each one without a neck. They turned only with difficulty, and even then they had to turn their whole body. They moved like toy soldiers. Each time they tilted her way, Francine tried to look bored. When it was safe, she took long strides in her new rope platform wedgies.

"Call an ambulance," yelled some Venetian.

"Scum don't get 911," one twin yelled back, unable to turn his head on no neck.

"Sean Thompson," said Ilya. "His name is Sean Thompson."

Between the buildings it was peaceful now that the cops were blocked from sight. Francine continued moving toward Apartment 1, diagonal window. The cat burglar could make himself invisible. In the hope nothing could catch him, she proceeded past the metal cage that held the water heater (one small hole, as from a bullet) and walked in her new shoes around the corner, being careful. They were brand-new, by Chinese Laundry.

Around the corner, Sean Thompson lay where he had fallen. It was surprising to see him on his stomach, arms out. His head faced left toward the Apartment 1 pale green stucco wall. He was the perfect size for robbing houses, medium, and his gun lay in the dirt six feet away where the force of being hit had flung it. The gun, small and gray, looked too insignificant to be dangerous. It wasn't malignant. It wasn't fancy. His arms lay spread as wide as possible, because, like her, he was claustrophobic. Eternity beat jail, no question there, unambiguous. Francine squatted down on her new platform wedgies.

"I brought you spaghetti," she told him.

Today Sean Thompson was wearing a plaid Western shirt, the kind with snaps at either wrist, and a pool of blood lay underneath him. Francine could smell it. Except for that, he looked fit.

"And Parmesan cheese to go with it," she continued. Sean Thompson's eyes flickered. She closed her own eyes to imagine a restaurant with red-checkered tablecloths. "These drippy candles are a mess, but they are worth it." His back went up and down in even smaller eighths of inches. She continued. "Do you like the red wine?"

His shoulders released.

But when she used her shirt to wipe the perspiration from his forehead, he shuddered. She readjusted her feet. The pool of blood was getting near her shoes. Where was the goddamned ambulance? She described the pasta twirling on their spoons, the sound of Caruso's voice singing opera. Through the thin skin of Sean Thompson's eyelids, she could see the tiny muscles moving, which she knew from massage lore meant his cat burglar's mind was busy.

"My, this Parmesan delivers," Francine said. His eyelids smoothed out.

"Who ratted me out?" His dry lips formed the words with difficulty.

"I don't know." She tried lying, but he knew her. He lived outside her window.

"The misfit?" His lip cracked from smiling.

"He calls himself Fellowship."

He stretched his thumb and finger and they watched the tattooed horse leap forward. They loved freedom. A high, keening noise was traveling down the corridor from the window beneath the cat burglar's hideout, where Hank knew what was happening.

"We killed at the Puffin," said Sean Thompson's lips which barely moved. His ear seemed to be bleeding. "We can die now."

Their fingers intertwined and his breathing got easier.

"What the hell is going on back here?" said a nasty voice from above her.

It wasn't God. It was one half of the twin police set. Because he was all muscle, his arms and legs stuck out. Above his head with no neck, the corridor of bright blue sky remained bright blue.

"Stand up and move away slowly."

The intrusion was a mighty one for them both. She came out of her squat slowly, but one hand unsnapped the snap on Sean Thompson's sleeve, because it was too tight and cut off the blood flow.

Upstairs, from her bathroom window, she watched over the cat burglar Sean Thompson. They yanked his wrists behind his back (horse and all) and then locked on handcuffs.

"Ouch!" she yelled.

Death wasn't as exact as you might expect, just an indeterminate time. Hank was quiet. After it had been a while, she got her white tap shoes, and her keys, and started out the door. She wanted to go where she could hit the floor.

"I'll be back in a jiffy pop," she told the animals.

On Crenshaw Boulevard she located the blue bird painted on the building, exactly as described by Devereaux's brother. Even on tiptoe she couldn't reach it. She went in and found a vacant table on the dance floor, and no one immediately took her order. All around her in the Club Bip *'twas brillig*, as the English whoozit said in some book that had raised her. Friends called out to each other, all dressed in splendid clothing. On the stage a big band blew, and people sat around the dance floor, their black bodies hardly moving, but sending waves of energy. Earlier, after dark, when the police had carried off Sean Thompson's body, Frankie Frank had come out of Apartment 2 and Francine joined her. The two Venetians hosed down the blood left by the city. Francine sat with her knees together, feet together in their rope wedgies. She had thrown her Dansko shoes in the dumpster. One tap shoe was stuffed underneath each arm with only the heels protruding.

"Excuse me, miss?" said Francine to the waitress.

The waitress ignored her. The band played two more crazy numbers, "Satin Doll" and something she didn't know. She heard tap master Alfred Desio say, *When you get nervous, listen to the music.* The stand-up acoustic bassist was a tall thin man. Each time his long black fingers plucked the strings, his dreadlocks moved. He moved like her mother! The music pushed and pulled him as if he were Louella playing the tambourine for Jesus.

When the waitress passed, Francine sat upright. She cleared her throat. She raised her hand.

"Excuse me. Miss?"

The waitress kept walking.

The band took its break, and the chatter increased in volume. She ought to leave, but this small place on Crenshaw set the bar for jazz. Outside the door, Devereaux had listened to Wynton Marsalis. In the entryway there was a gallery of pictures of musicians, all black skin, not one Norwegian-German-English-Irish-Scottish-one-eightieth-Shawnee-Indian. According to Bunny. Francine belonged here. Friends continued laughing and connecting. The same waitress passed her table again, but Francine had been shunned by experts, the Didwells. She settled her behind in. She saw the tall bandleader passing her table, and as he stopped to light a cigarette, she tugged his jacket in case he couldn't see her.

"I need to tap dance," she explained.

He looked at her, at the tap heels that stuck out of

either elbow, at her hands, which she held clasped on the table like a church lady. She was strange, but he had seen strange in his day.

Chester Whitmore lowered his eyelids. "Straight time or swing?"

"Swing."

He didn't say she could and he didn't say she couldn't. "Name?" he inquired.

Every real improviser had one. *John Bubbles* was already taken. She thought fast.

"Didwell."

The waitress appeared to ask what she wanted, and she wanted Perrier.

"Lemon?" said the waitress.

She put on her tap shoes to be ready. What if he didn't call her? *When you get nervous, listen to the music*, Al Desio repeated. Eddie Brown looked down from heaven. *THAT ain't right*, he liked to mutter when he lost what he was doing. They played "Don't Mean a Thing If It Ain't Got That Swing."

"Doo-*wa* doo-*wa* doo-*wa* doo-*wa* doo-*wa* doo-*wa* doo-*wa* doo-*waaa*," she whispered. It was thrilling.

"Put your hands together for Ms. Didwell," said Chester Whitmore.

She danced the story of her life with Cyrus, which surprised her. *Don't make it happen, let it happen*, said the great Jimmie DeFore. Out the steps tumbled. She danced how for months she refused to sleep with him, although she had always been a slut with other people. She knew he was dangerous. Her white shoes told about the time they were almost struck by lightning, then jumped to the Saturday they saw the bull moose mounting the cow, that fabulous trumpeting, and then a strong wind blew down a tree ahead of them. She danced the things his skin did to her when she touched it, how they fought until one of them started laughing. There were taps for everything.

"Uh-UH," said a glamorous babe whose enormous size exactly suited her.

Encouraged, Francine's white shoes explained how he loved the dictionary, the persistent blackhead on his forearm, how he still looked at women. They loved Wil Wright's Ice Cream Parlor (now gone), sitting by the fire eating rough chocolate-chip ice cream with a dollop of whipped cream on top. His illness was terrible. She danced how when she saw his childhood pictures, there was his exact same soul looking out of child's eyes. She danced the slow way he moved. A clean fuck was a thing to be longed for, in and out, with a kind of scraping feeling, quiet so you could feel the bump coming. Then the world in flames, and both of you unable to speak, you needed to be flung apart on separate sides of the bed with your arms hanging over. *Don't touch me.* "Sweet Jesus," Cyrus breathed out just before the moment. He wasn't half a bubble off, that old expression that came from a carpenter's level, he had showed her, that insult he liked to fling (unbeknownst to them) at bad drivers. It took rhythm to do anything, rob a bank, write a symphony, be with cats, fuck. She danced how he got ready for the night he died by sitting in the shower, stalwart, shaving while the hot water lasted, how with all that he missed a dime-sized spot of whiskers on his left cheek, the dearest thing he never knew, how she loved it, how she sat there after he threw up, before the hordes descended, just the two of them together as the cells of his brain extinguished one by one, all the lights of the city going out.

The music was drawing down.

For an ending she jumped up in the air and came down with a *shigadeeboom*, thank you Eddie Brown, thank you world, thank you Assembly of God Church. She did a little slide—the floor was slick—and landed near her chair, where she did a prim turn and was seated. She clasped her hands and put her knees together.

The band started "Take the A Train."

She sat and listened through the set and sipped her Perrier, which was the most delicious thing ever invented, the bottle rim cool and smooth. Although the drummer was white, she made no effort to make eye contact with him. When the lights came up, she stood, her tap shoes in her purse, her purse on her shoulder, her feet together, a small, good Pentecostal.

"You was born black," said a voice behind her, and when she turned, it was the long-fingered acoustic bass player.

For a moment they hugged each other.

She was making her escape again when she ran into the glamorous woman. Enormous as a field of grass, she wore a strapless evening dress, and she had defined calves in strutting high heels. Francine had never seen anyone so startlingly beautiful. Jewelry adorned her arms and ears. Her eyelids glittered. She was as big as Story County, Iowa, with long eyelashes in proportion, ditto fingernails. Two huge arms closed around Francine, who collapsed completely. All the bones left her body. Her ear sank into the bosom of bosoms.

"You done good like Mama taught you," said the goddess.

Francine was almost out the door when the white drummer tapped her on the shoulder.

"Bit o' the Irish, eh?" He gave a wink, and gently poked her, with one finger.

13
PARADISO

Mrs. Didwell's accident had happened fast, like Jesus's Sooncoming, in the twinkling of an eye. On Noah's birthday she had stormed out of the house with Muriel, a thing completely unlike her, but what were they thinking? To take the bed? Without her secret powerhouse, her earthly body lying next to Clarence, who was she? On Noah's birthday, she had sat in the car seat in a blind rage, Muriel driving, until Muriel's voice broke in on her hellbent rebellion.

"Mrs. Didwell? Would you like to see the house that I grew up in?"

"Why not?" thought Mrs. Didwell aloud.

It was freeing to be outside of Monrovia. On the freeway they drove even farther east, through Duarte, then West Covina.

The house was clapboard, like houses then, freshly painted green and surrounded by a picket fence broken in places. The lawn needed work (no gardenias, Mrs. Didwell noted). They sat staring for a moment before Muriel turned the engine off. The shady street was full of her memories. Mrs. Didwell waited in the car for help while Muriel slowly removed the key and opened the driver's door and half got out, one leg on the floorboard and one on the ground.

There time stopped.

Something had caught Muriel's attention, perhaps the fence, perhaps the small dilapidated porch—had she been rocked there?—and now she stood with only her lower body showing. The girl needed to lose weight, and Mrs. Didwell thought there might be a kind way to suggest it: fill up on fruits and vegetables. She was pretty. But Mrs. Didwell was going crazy. Was Muriel retarded? Mrs. Didwell sometimes wondered. She didn't want to screech at her, she was a Christian, so in the thrall of today's unusual adventure she took matters into her own hands. Who did her family think they were? How good it felt, to do exactly what she wanted.

She unbuckled her seat belt.

When she opened her own door, there was just room to step out should she need any more adventure. She wasn't dead yet. And with the bed, they had not even asked her! Francine had been the one who took them shopping for their coffins, just before she ran away with Cyrus. The other children couldn't bear to think of it, but from the moment they hit Forest Lawn the three of them went into some silly feeling, as if they were already in heaven, the scenery so beautiful, and so much laughter discussing which casket suited their personalities that the saleswoman had given them her telephone number, hoping they might all sometime have dinner. "It does my heart good to see a family this close," she kept saying. Somewhere in West Covina, Mrs. Didwell waited, reminding God that He had promised: None of her children would be lost. She prayed God would return Jack the dog to the faded place on the front porch. What on *earth* was wrong with Muriel? One fat leg still in the car, one leg out, she didn't move. Until her skeleton had shrunk down, Mrs. Didwell could outwalk anybody, including her one son and three daughters. You could feel air whoosh past you as you walked faster, faster. Mrs. Didwell moved her right leg out, with effort, into West Covina. She had once moved a small stove to the second-floor apartment of the Melrose property, she could feel just how the muscles twisted and gripped, and held, no assistance whatsoever. "There is power in the blood of the Lamb," she hummed to herself. What a helpmeet she had been to Clarence. When they had no money, it had been exciting.

Pushing up with both hands, she wet her lips. She had never defiled them with lipstick.

"Find Jack," she reminded God.

She stood.

God gave man dominion over all the animals. When she lifted her hand to praise Him, she felt the weight of His full glory and then she was on her back looking up, a few birds flying. One second she was strong and upright, and the next second she lay with her head against the curb, something sticky coming out while she looked at open sky, like on the prairie. You could tell that you were still in California from the bright blue color. She thanked God again that He had needed Clarence to preach the gospel in Monrovia. The family was divided down the middle with three Californians, the rest hard-core Midwesterners. Now there were faces peering down at her, with uniforms. The man's neck next to her face looked scrunched, he ought to lift his chin up, up. The uniform was awful polyester.

"Where are we?" said Mrs. Didwell.

So that was how they got to Arcadia Methodist Hospital, her head bleeding. They cleaned her up and sent her home while they consulted. Dr. Love said she ought to have a pin put in her hip at her convenience, although she didn't need to if she didn't want to walk. To live you needed to walk. You needed a bed.

"I'll take it," she told the doctor.

And now here they were two weeks after Bunny's party, in a private room, with chairs for all. Mr. Didwell had good insurance.

"Mother? Are you comfortable?" Noah leaned over her.

She said nothing but sat looking around at private room 1414, very spacious, with a bed and room to walk around. They weren't poor any longer! It was hard to fathom. One whole wall was made of sliding glass through which lost souls in need of Jesus scurried back and forth, and Mrs. Didwell hadn't yet had time to ask if they knew Him. She sat with her hands folded on the little coverlet they brought her, a quite nice cotton blend. Her fingers tested the thread. There must be a way to steal it. Because insurance paid the hospital, and the Didwells paid insurance. She was too tired to think about it. Some doctors (not her Jewish one, Dr. Love, but some unknown types, she trusted no one) were to put a pin in her left hip early tomorrow morning to fix it where the bone was broken. She had had bronchitis but Jesus healed her. But Mrs. Didwell loved to walk! The freedom! The wheelchair made her feel like a stick figure and really not alive, so here they were. The day before, her youngest daughter, Bunny, had taken her on a mad tour of yard sales, and they came back three times for money, three hundred dollars total, but her hubby gave her anything she wanted. In the hospital bed, she wet her lips again. If the yard sale tag said fifty cents she offered ten cents, and almost nothing she bought had been over half the price it said. She had once been kicked out of the Old City of Jerusalem for bargaining too hard with Arab shopkeepers who, it turned out, knew not the first thing about applying and withstanding pressure. The best discovery, yesterday, had been a cuckoo bird that sang *Cuckoo!* while it revolved after you wound it.

"How are you doing?" said Nurse Ratched.

"Do you know Jesus?" said Mrs. Didwell.

The Didwells were lounging around the room waiting to go to heaven, Francine and a tall man in the corner. The family needed to be civil. The Didwells managed to have fun down here below where God had put them and where Satan hid behind every outcropping. But they were holiness. Now Mrs. Didwell peeked at a McCall's pattern, brought with her at the last minute, gotten for a nickel, such a cute dress with a princess waistline, all the days she had sewn for the children. Muriel wandered back and forth waving a dishtowel. The family minus Francine was going on a Didwell Healing Cruise and Bible Study just as soon as Mrs. Didwell recovered from her operation—a pin in the hip—as a kind of test run for Bunny's newfangled scheme to be a famous person. A lost young man came in and took Mrs. Didwell's blood pressure.

She held up her free hand. "And where do you attend church?"

She had been witnessing nonstop, the nurses, the orderlies, the anesthesiologist who came in to lecture her an hour ago, the maintenance crew who came to collect the trash. She was in a small evangelistic fervor, like in the old days. Mrs. Didwell hit her thigh, as if it were a tambourine. Francine had her rhythm. Her unsaved daughter and the tall fellow stood across the room, too obviously not touching. Mrs. Didwell was no fool. She kept her own counsel. She wondered did he have a good spirit? Because when she first met Cyrus before Mr. Didwell lost his mind, she had been crazy about him.

"Muriel?" called Mrs. Didwell sweetly; that one was saved and sanctified and on her way to heaven: a million more to go before the harvest. "Will you take Daddy the Kleenex?"

There is a time when everything falls away except what's important. Francine stood looking at her mother from ten feet away across 1414. She had grown up with signs and wonders, so it was no surprise that the tall man who drove the Peugeot with the SCHLESWIG-HOLSTEIN: LOVE IT OR LEAVE IT bumper sticker was standing here in

Schleswig-Holstein. But the real reason he had come with Francine was that she needed courage.

"Now?" the man whispered to Francine.

"I'm not quite ready."

Mr. Didwell again asked for Kleenex. Muriel said, "I love Jesus." Noah had discovered one Old Testament passage in original Hebrew that until this point in history had been misinterpreted. Francine's eyes widened. Ilene had run off and married a classical acoustic bass player and moved to Alabama. The family deduced that she had met him at the Aztec Bar, where she had sung in secret in green earrings. She was on her way back, but her plane had been delayed on the runway; still, she would be here in a matter of hours only.

"How go the apartments?" said Mr. Didwell without turning, because his whole spine was collapsed and getting worse.

"Now," said Francine to the man with the bumper sticker.

Francine walked toward her mother. She and her mother were just alike, and looked alike (same face) and had the same sense of funny. For a minute, Mrs. Didwell had been crazy about Cyrus, before her husband entered through the gold curtains. When they reached the bed, the daughter waved.

"This is Bill."

"Do you know Jesus as your personal Savior?" said Mrs. Didwell.

"In my tradition we don't have personal salvation." Mrs. Didwell brightened at the prospect of battle. His father, the tall man was explaining, had been Catholic. She sat up, a conqueror for Christ. She sparkled.

"How are you?" said Francine.

"I have to get ready."

Psalm 91 lay open across Mrs. Didwell's stomach. *He*

that dwelleth in the secret place of the Most High shall abide under the shadow of the Almighty, said Scripture. All the Didwell children knew it. Mrs. Didwell kept her head raised; last night, a neighbor had given her a perm because Ilene was coming, and she didn't want to squash it.

"Mom? I saw your bed in a movie. The Italiano! With Kirk Douglas."

"I don't attend the movies." Mrs. Didwell smiled. "I'm going up!"

She pointed at the ceiling. She still had it. All eyes followed.

"Not down."

She pointed down. The eyes descended.

Mrs. Didwell was a busy woman, and the two sinners were making her task harder. Her one job was to make heaven, and to that end she intended to stay up all night and pray and read the Bible. A person on their way to surgery did not need doubters near her bed. *O ye of little faith!* Mrs. Didwell looked through her daughter. Morning was coming. *Faith is the substance of things hoped for, the evidence of things not seen.*

"I need to prepare," said Mrs. Didwell.

Francine reached out to touch her mother's leg—she needed contact—but Mrs. Didwell flinched a hair. Sinners pierced your armor. The stranger Bill bent forward and gave Mrs. Didwell a smackeroo on the cheek. It was a small one, but potent.

"Oh!" said Louella. A pink flush covered her face. Her daughter had good sense. Louella's eyes processed this information.

"Muriel? The Kleenex," Mr. Didwell said for the third or fourth or fifth time.

Francine and the tall man backed out the sliding glass door and Mrs. Didwell returned to her Bible.

* * *

Late at night, Francine and Bill walked down Paradiso and turned south along the ocean. Her mother had died at 10:42 a.m., approximately in the middle of the operation to put a pin in her hip, and it was totally unexpected. *Totally*, said everyone. The last thing she said before they wheeled her out was, "Tell Daddy I love him." As she went under, according to the nurse, Mrs. Didwell had been witnessing to the anesthesiologist. During surgery, she had internal bleeding, and they telephoned the on-call vascular surgeon because they couldn't find the bleed, but then they stopped it and telephoned the surgeon back and told him to go ahead to dinner, but then it started again, and the vascular surgeon was dining in a fancy restaurant so far down the freeway that traffic prevented him from getting back, so then Mrs. Didwell went to heaven.

In Venice, the two stopped outside the Sidewalk Cafe and Small World Books and turned toward the sound of breaking surf, and now she realized who Bill looked like: Uncle Sly. He had quiet wild energy, and his hulk was reassuring. Ilya had given him the thumbs-up, even without the box spring test!

"It does not matter," Ilya concluded. She was lucky to have a guru. "He has spatial reasoning, so he is all right on that front."

Under the streetlights, a homeless woman huddled in her sleeping bag, only her head sticking out, her shoulders just inside the entryway to the bookstore, where she could be safe from the alleys. Had books raised her? The homeless woman kept one eye open to see if there might be danger.

"Look," said Francine.

A duck was walking across the grass, and another duck was following the first one.

After the Great Duck Massacre, it turned out with

testing that not a single Venice duck had ever been infected with anything, but of course the captured ducks were already dead. Outside the Sidewalk Cafe and Small World Books was a little park of flat grass that rose up a small hill to overlook the ocean, and the two confused ducks were running to and fro. All the ducks lived in the canals a few blocks inland, but to a duck a few blocks was like the Sahara. Ducks were too short to see the lay of the land. How on earth had they crossed Pacific Avenue, where cars went fast?

"Those ducks are lost," said Francine.

"I have a packing box in my car," said Bill.

"I have a laundry basket at the house."

They went to their respective destinations, hurrying, and met again.

The ducks walked in ever-widening circles on the grass in front of them, growing more panicked. Their quacking had a desperate note. Two witnesses to the Great Duck Massacre, the two humans refused to be silenced this time.

Quack quack, said the missus.

Quack quack, said the mister.

The humans assumed duck mind as they walked after the duck couple, because it was necessary to communicate. It was necessary to think like one. You could see by simple observation that the ducks were losing all access to reason as they hurried to and fro looking for their home. Where were the little flowers that lined the canals? What was this dry place? How could a duck float when the grass ended in more grass?

Bill lunged at one but missed by a feather. He slowed down to a saunter in a change of technique. Ducks were quicker than they looked on two short legs, and slow to trust after the Great Duck Massacre.

Quack! Quack! Quack! The ducks became more frantic.

First the one duck got away from them and then

the other. Bill and Francine followed, one holding an upside-down box and one a laundry basket, entirely committed, doing whatever the ducks did, but nothing worked. While each duck appeared to move slowly, each duck stayed just out of reach by microns. The humans didn't talk. They tried standing still. They tried speeding up. They were sweating.

The ducks waddled forward.

At this moment, the humans were on the right side of history. They would work all night, if necessary, to save the Ducks, Mr. and Mrs. At 1:30 a.m. they fell back against the Sidewalk Cafe's waist-high wall that tourists looked out over; and they did this not to rest but to trick the ducks into thinking they had left, because the ducks were slow to think of them as saviors. They wiped their foreheads. They were getting tired, but they stood up, as if on cue, and picked up their cardboard box and laundry basket.

"Those ducks come here every weekend," said the homeless woman in the sleeping bag. Her face stuck out from the nose up. Now her hand materialized. She managed to light a cigarette and proceeded to ignore them.

"Pardon me?" said Bill.

"Those two come out from the canals to eat the scraps the tourists leave on weekends." She wasn't gloating. She was tired and wanted to go to sleep. She didn't like the residents, but despite her feelings of superiority she couldn't help but be kind to these two doofuses. The housed knew nothing. They saw nothing. "They glut themselves and then they waddle back to the canals before the sun comes up. They'll be here next Saturday."

Bill laughed, a roar to make the woman jump, but she didn't scold them. In truth, the grass was littered with delicious pizza.

"They cross Pacific?" said Francine.

The woman ignored her.

"You took a fright," the woman said, or Francine thought she said, because she mumbled. Her head disappeared into the sleeping bag, their signal to leave, but they had had one good, connected moment, and they felt it. At the last table in the Sidewalk Cafe—the walls were open—a man was sitting hunched over his plate.

"I'll catch up to you," Francine told Bill, and he went ahead, because Venice has interruptions.

It was Cyrus sitting there, and when he said *I need to get this potato airborne,* she stepped toward him. He didn't look up. When he lifted the hot item with a fork and knife, she quickly pulled off the tinfoil, no burny fingers, and kept walking, but she did an eye roll. The man was difficult. He would show up when he damn well pleased. The man drove her crazy.

She took a little skip and caught up with Bill just opposite the tattoo parlor, and they stood looking out at the ocean. The usual suspects were there, because Venice Beach was never empty: drug dealers, the pretty woman who practiced harp, the insomniac fortune teller, people with their dogs. How Venetians loved them.

"I have an idea," she said suddenly. It came out of nowhere, like things do when you're tired and your mother cannot answer the telephone. Bill listened but didn't babble. "To make money."

Bill waited.

"Balloons."

She went on to explain. It was a fabulous idea in the entrepreneurial spirit, the kind that no one thinks of until someone does. Then it seems obvious. Then everyone says "I could have thought of that!" but the first person gets the money.

"For tidal waves," she continued.

The ocean remained flat. But life could change in a second.

They resumed walking.

"Okay." The slower Bill walked, the more he outpaced her. His legs were longer.

When the ocean came, each person on the walk streets would have, inside his or her front door—this could be legislated, like insurance for a mortgage—a helium balloon attached by cute ropes to a basket just big enough to stand in and hold your cat and dog. No children lived in this neighborhood. Before stepping in, the Venetian must guide his or her balloon out the door to a place free of obstacles: a tree, a light post. With disaster rushing toward you in the form of a wall of water, up up up you floated while the ocean crashed under you.

Now balloons filled the sky of Venice. In this scenario the sun was out. While houses and cars were inundated, the free Venetians floated above all disaster. In real time, at that moment, standing on Venice Beach, Francine knew she looked pretty. Her face could be neutral, but in happiness something happened, and you had to wait to see it.

Bill's hulk loomed in the atmosphere beside her.

Pretty, she described how in the blue sky neighbors yelled the usual ordinary greetings. *How's it going? Did you get your car fixed?* Dogs barked from baskets. The whole sky was a party, with each balloon a different color.

When the water went out, the Venetians landed.

Francine got rich.

It was that simple.

"Your balloons would have to be awfully big." Bill's spatial sense was actually annoying, but also, he was ballast. She leaned against him.

"I haven't worked out the details yet."

"How do you come down?"

She looked at him. Men were crazy. "Push a button."

When Hank had started barking the first night Bill stayed over, Bill (who had long arms) reached down and lifted him off his short legs onto the mattress. Hank settled in the farthest corner at the bottom, *I'm not even here*. Every night thereafter he crept up about six inches, and tonight, the three of them asleep, he had almost reached the middle of the pillows. His goal was world domination.

Francine sat up.

Waking no one, she rose and tiptoed to the top drawer of her dresser. Inside were the fourteen white collars her mother had foisted on her over the years to brighten her face: mostly snap-ons. Some were cotton lace, some linen, many antiques, all beautiful. They were from another time in history, the 1950s. Francine lifted her favorite, which had belonged to Great-Aunt Amelia, a sturdy cotton with loops at the edges.

Downstairs she put the collar on. It snapped in back.

In her bare feet she tiptoed to the answering machine. It said One Message. Her mother had left it on the terrible night after Spires Restaurant, but Francine had refused to listen. Angry, she had turned it off the minute she heard Mrs. Didwell's voice. The hairs on her arms stood up.

She stepped closer.

She did nothing. She adjusted Aunt Amelia's collar. She pressed Play.

Francine? said the recording.

The living room filled with the awful sound of Mrs. Didwell's grief. Love was terrible. An inhuman noise was coming out of Mrs. Didwell's throat, indecent, like a death rattle. Kitty raced to listen. Francine endured the sound as long as she could, and then kept enduring it. Mr. Didwell stood between them. Francine held still while the sound stopped, and Mrs. Didwell tried and failed to speak. She tried again.

Something terrible must have happened to you, said her mother.

MESSAGES FINISHED, said the recording.

Outside the air was fresh. Although at night you couldn't see the ocean, you could hear it.

Mr. Venice was wheeling his bike up the red line, tonight dressed in the white bougainvillea, very beautiful, some with pink centers. Francine stepped back against the fence, and as he passed he looked directly at her, and she nodded in observance of his three PhDs.

"These flowers feel so good on my head," said Mr. Venice.

At the bottom of the street, a gate had opened, and out came a casket borne by six men in suits. In Venice, these things happen.

Where she stood in Aunt Amelia's collar, Francine squashed back to give the procession room. Several bougainvillea thorns poked her.

The casket floated toward her. It moved in the direction of the hearse that waited on Pacific Avenue. The casket itself was plain but had good lines, a burnished metal sheen with some decoration. How she was sure the occupant was a woman, she didn't know, but when the casket reached her, she saluted and held the salute. The woman had lived a long life here. The woman was making room for Francine on Paradiso.

Francine turned with the casket. On deserted Pacific Avenue, a street with cars, a man in gloves opened the hearse's back end. The casket slid in, and this window on eternity closed.

Francine went in the house, and hit ERASE on the machine. She could feel Louella.

"We are surrounded by a great crowd of witnesses," Mr. Didwell had said earlier that night, when he left his wife's body alone and came home one person and sat at the kitchen table.

We are surrounded by a great crowd of tap dancers,

Francine wrote in her Imaginary Tap Dance Handbook. She said good night to all the people on the street, and got a drink of the good water, and went up to the others.

ACKNOWLEDGMENTS

Two excerpts from this novel were published in *Santa Monica Review*: "Rima," spring 2012, and "Thief," fall 2014.

I am grateful to Michelle Latiolais for her rare insight and friendship over many years, and to Ron Carlson for his fine mind and lively encouragement. I could not have gone the distance without Susan Segal, Bruce McKay, and Jayne Lewis. The generosity they bring to the page opens a path forward. Andrew Tonkovich offered invaluable support, as did The Community of Writers. I was cheered by artist Peggy Reavey's humor and deep imagination. Carol Munday Lawrence guided me in the tap world, and Dorothy Fielding believed in me at crucial moments. Thanks to Chester Whitmore for his love of rhythm, and to Al Young for his excellent spoon-playing, and to Hama's dance class. I am grateful to the Programs in Writing at the University of California, Irvine, and for my teachers, Oakley Hall and Donald Heiney. It has been my great good luck to work with Delphinium editor Joseph Olshan and publisher Lori Milken. They demanded more, that great gift, and they each bring vision and heart. At last my thanks to Bill McDonald for reading, and for being there, and for being an optimist.

ABOUT THE AUTHOR

Rhoda Huffey is a tap dancer and a writer. She lives in Venice Beach, California with her husband and a houseful of rescue animals. She received an MFA from the University of California at Irvine. She has published a novel, *The Hallelujah Side*, and short stories in numerous magazines including *Ploughshares*, *Green Mountains Review*, and *Santa Monica Review*. The daughter of two Pentecostal preachers, Huffey writes with sympathy and feeling about a world she knows well.